Wilson Flagg

Mount Auburn

its scenes, its beauties, and its lessons - Vol. 1

Wilson Flagg

Mount Auburn
its scenes, its beauties, and its lessons - Vol. 1

ISBN/EAN: 9783337288365

Printed in Europe, USA, Canada, Australia, Japan

Cover: Foto ©Andreas Hilbeck / pixelio.de

More available books at **www.hansebooks.com**

MOUNT AUBURN:

ITS SCENES, ITS BEAUTIES,

AND

ITS LESSONS.

By WILSON FLAGG,

AUTHOR OF

"STUDIES IN THE FIELD AND FOREST."

"And we will sleep a pleasant sleep,
And not a care shall here intrude,
To break the marble solitude,
So peaceful and so deep."
HENRY KIRKE WHITE.

BOSTON AND CAMBRIDGE:
JAMES MUNROE AND COMPANY.
1861.

CAMBRIDGE:
THURSTON & MILES,
PRINTERS.

TO

JACOB BIGELOW, M. D.,

TO WHOM THE PUBLIC IS INDEBTED FOR THE

FIRST IDEA OF RURAL BURIAL FOR THOSE WHO

DIE IN THE CITY, AND THE ORIGINAL

PROJECTOR AND PATRON OF

MOUNT AUBURN CEMETERY,

THIS VOLUME

IS RESPECTFULLY INSCRIBED BY

THE EDITOR.

PREFACE.

It was the intention of the Editor to prepare a work that should contain a particular description of the objects in Mount Auburn. He was afterwards persuaded that this could not be so interesting as certain themes suggested by these objects, and having a general application to burial customs. The details which have been omitted were more suitable to a work intended as a guide-book to Mount Auburn. Similar matters, compiled in a judicious and interesting manner, are published weekly in "*The Mount Auburn Memorial*," — a journal conducted with excellent taste and judgment by Mr. Safford. As announced in our Prospectus, it was also a secondary object of this work to offer incidental remarks on the general principles of taste, that should govern the artist and proprietor in the construction of monuments and fences, in the planting of trees, shrubs, and flowers, and in the general disposition of all these objects. We have endeavored to avoid all uninteresting details ; for it is designed that the work shall not possess entirely a local or temporary interest, but shall be instructive to many, and afford themes of consolatory reflection to all.

CONTENTS.

X   CONTENTS.

LIST OF PLATES.

MOUNT AUBURN:

ITS SCENES, ITS BEAUTIES, AND ITS LESSONS.

ANCIENT AND MODERN TOMBS.

WHEN comparing the funereal structures of ancient and modern times, I have been struck with one remarkable difference between them. Those of the ancients seem more generally to have been built for the purpose of exciting the sentiment of admiration, while those of the moderns appeal rather to our ideas of fitness and propriety. Men displayed their patriotism in the early ages, by consenting to give their labor for the construction of some vast work that should proclaim their national greatness to the rest of the world. It was no matter whether this great building was devoted to the living or to the dead, to the purposes of religion or of war, if it was only of sufficient magnitude to excite the astonishment of mankind. The works of the ancients are distinguished, therefore, by their cost and magnificence. Their temples, their palaces, and their tombs, far surpassed the same class of structures erected in modern times; and the more remote the date of these ancient works, the more stupendous and costly do they appear to be made. The inference to be drawn from these facts

1

is, that the sentiment of admiration is fully developed in the savage and the barbarian, and that it precedes the development of those finer sentiments that distinguish the civilized man.

But though man in a barbarous state can deeply admire certain works and objects, his admiration must be excited by something massive, stupendous, and indicative of great physical power. To arouse this feeling, sculpture must be colossal, architecture must vie with the mountains and emulate the skies, or sink deeply into the recesses of the earth. Intellect he cannot appreciate, except as it is manifested by its control over large masses of material objects. Hence the monarchs of ancient nations sought the reverence of their subjects, not only by the display of magnificent trophies of war, and costly and splendid temples and palaces, but also by the vastness and magnificence of their tombs. The sepulchres of Thebes and the pyramids of Egypt could not be built in the present age. The intelligence of modern times would revolt at any such sacrifice of the labor of men for the erection of works, which could serve no better purpose than to excite the awe and wonder of an ignorant populace. Men are not more utilitarian in their intellectual habits than in former times; but the public will not tolerate the follies of ancient despotisms; and the masses, being more intelligent, will not submit to being employed in labor for which they receive no just recompense. The privileged classes know, that if they could afford to build such works, they would become a theme of ridicule and not of admiration.

Hence, as the world has advanced in intelligence, the magnificence of all such structures has proportionally diminished. The period that preceded the invention of writing, or the age of hieroglyphics, was the epoch of vast temples, palaces, and tombs, and of colossal statuary. During this era were built the temples of Tentyra, the pyramids of Egypt, the sepulchres of Thebes, and other vast works which cause us to wonder no more at the genius and perfection of art manifested in them, and at the immense labor and cost that must have attended their construction, than at the stupidity of the people who could thus slavishly do the will of the projectors of these works.

The next epoch was that which succeeded the invention of letters, before the art of printing was discovered. The tombs of this period were less magnificent, though the priests and monarchs still sustained their sway over the minds of the people, by appealing to their sentiment of admiration in the greatness of their temples and the trophies and statues which were deposited in them. The ruling classes were intelligent and enlightened by science, as in Greece and Rome, though the masses had not risen above the level of the barbarous nations. In this age the relics of the dead were burned, and their ashes deposited in urns. Tombs were, therefore, less revolting, and the burial places of friends were held more sacred than by the barbarous nations, who buried their dead in sepulchres and pyramids.

The third epoch was that of Christianity, when knowledge and cultivation were spread among the common people, through the equalizing influence of this religion. Mankind began to think less of the particular mode of sepulture and more of the state of the soul after death, and felt, in a limited degree, the influence of those tender sentiments connected with the dead, which are most observable in a highly civilized people. Barbarous nations, it is true, venerate the tombs of their ancestors, but they manifest little of that feeling of posthumous friendship and romantic veneration for the memory of the departed which are peculiar to modern Christian nations. It is a sentiment too spiritualized and poetic for any of the ancients, except the Greeks and Romans. It seems to have come up at the same time with the sentiment which we call a love of nature, and is perhaps one of the legitimate fruits of Christianity. The dead were buried in the churchyard, from the belief that, by such a mode of burial, they secured the salvation of the soul when placed under the protection of the cross ; and they were laid in a grave, that they might sleep in the bosom of nature, and under the sacred light of heaven.

But Christianity has been very slow in performing its work. In the middle and feudal ages great expense was still lavished upon the tombs and monuments of kings, princes, and nobles. Hence the fourth epoch, or that of rural cemeteries, is of recent date, and affords an example probably of the most expedient and benign method of disposing of the remains of the dead. In the United States this mode of burial has been carried to the nearest perfection ; and though there is a proneness among our people to copy some of the senseless follies of the Parisians, in manifesting their respect for the dead, and some of the useless ambition of the English, in the erection of costly marble monuments, — notwithstanding these circumstances, rural burial is probably destined to be carried to perfection in beautiful simplicity, by some future examples in this country.

When we read of the tombs of the ancients, and consider their grandeur and their magnitude, we are prone to feel humiliated, because the monuments of those early times so far surpass our own in cost and magnificence, and even in the genius that must have been required to plan and design them. But we should cease to humble ourselves by any such reflections, if we did but consider that, at a remoter period, extending far back into the ages of barbarism, they were still more costly and magnificent than in the middle ages ; and if we could look with a prophetic eye beyond the present, into that period of the future, when the human race shall have attained the perfection of civilization, we should probably witness a simplicity unsurpassed by anything the world has ever seen, in connection with the finer works of art.

The Bunker Hill Monument, which is a mere toy, in comparison with similar works of ancient times, was yet too vast for the superior intelligence of our people. Had it been delayed fifty years longer, it could not have been erected. The people of New England are free, and colossal architecture is the united work of despotism and slavery. As men advance in intelligence and freedom, they make art contribute to their comfort, their convenience, and their pleasures ; and the works of architecture and sculpture will be constantly growing less and less stupendous, the palaces of the wealthy and noble will be less costly, and the dwellings of the common people more comfortable and commodious, as the light of a more rational system of Christianity is shed abroad among men. Tombs can never again be so magnificent as in the early ages, unless mankind should relapse into barbarism. Men will think more of nature and less of art, when providing memorials and a resting place for the dead.

The ancients built stupendous tombs, in which the dead were piled up without regard to any feeling, except perhaps, that of rescuing them from the dust, as if by embalming and preserving their bodies, they obtained for them the boon of immortality. Now we place the body in the grave ; we consign dust to dust ; we restore the remains of our friends to the bosom of the earth, and we make their mortal part a humble offering to nature, while we commend the immortal spirit to the God who gave it.

The ancients had less distinct ideas of the soul's immortality, and cherished an inferior amount of tender sentiment in connection with the dead. They had no love of nature ; since the love of art, for the display of art, precedes in the human breast, this more fervent and poetic feeling. Hence their tombs, — many specimens of which exist on a small scale in every burial ground at the present time, — were mostly revolting objects. It is now customary to bury the dead in graves, covered with the green turf and the wild flowers of the field. Men will gradually learn to set less value upon art in this connection, and will think more of nature. They will learn that the only service we ought to render the dead is to secure their remains from desecration in the grave, and to provide a simple and durable monument, for the record of their virtues, and to serve as the means of identifying their place of burial.

On the left is seen the marble sarcophagus erected in memory of BARTHOLOMEW CHEEVER, one of the Pilgrim Fathers, who came to America from Canterbury, England, in 1637. On the monument also are inscribed the names of some of his descendants and their families.

On the right is a view of the monuments of S. QUINCY, J. SHAW, A. RICE, and T. HAVILAND.

wishes. Even the enjoyment of the present is greater, because we know that our possessions may slip away from us ; and we are prompted by this insecurity to continual action and watchfulness. From this activity and suspense, this hope and uncertainty proceed all the zest of life. We are not permitted to know the truth of all we believe. Imagination presents us glimpses of divine truths, which reason will not allow us to believe with the full assurance of a positive faith. Imagination affords us these gleams of light to cheer and encourage the ardor of hope ; but reason suggests doubts, lest in the full certainty of celestial happiness, we should renounce the grosser cares of this world, and surrender ourselves entirely to the future. The benevolence of the Deity does not wholly conceal, nor does it fully unfold the most delightful realities of the heavenly world.

Hence the different forms and aspects of nature are allowed by the Deity, to be the material representations of the blessings of another existence. Every object that is charming to our senses derives half its charm from its moral, religious, and emblematical signification. From these suggestions of divine things proceed all the poetry, the beauty, and the romance of the material world ; and the reason why many persons have no passionate love of nature is, that they have never learned to interpret these emblems that appear on the face of the earth and the heavens. The pleasures we derive from the verdure of the fields, the pyramidal forms of the trees, the blooming, the fading, and the resurrection of flowers, are the pleasures of a religious and a poetical mind ; and there is not a beautiful object in nature that does not borrow its light and its loveliness from heaven.

How would the gorgeous and varied tints and forms of the clouds fade upon the imagination, if it perceived in them no similitude to the conceptions we have formed of celestial glory and beauty, or if these objects never suggested a thought beyond this mundane world. The mind is enabled to extend its thoughts further into infinity by the sight of these radiant hues of sunset, and to feel a rapture which is capable of being inspired by no other natural scenes. All this proceeds from our habit of associating them with our ideas of the soul's immortality, with the infinite attributes of the Divine Being, and with our hopes of another and a brighter life.

If an unbeliever derives a similar pleasure from the same objects, he too is religious in the midst of his unbelief. Though his reason does not acknowledge a system of theology, he cherishes these fond ideas in his mind as pleasing illusions to which he yields a sort of poetic faith. The very uncertainty of religious truths renders them more dear to our souls, as we cling with greater affection to a friend who is absent, and whose fate is involved in mystery. The doubtfulness of these points is necessary for our contentment with the unsatisfying realities of life —a contentment which is needful to the enjoyment of our existence.

Through nature, in her myriad forms of beauty and sublimity, has the Deity benevolently given us intimations of these truths; and the more we study their forms and aspects, the more vivid will be these intimations, and the more devoted our faith in the dim but pleasing assurances which they bring to our minds of the reality of what cannot be known, until mortals have become immortal. It is while animated by these feelings that we delight to surround the tombs of our departed friends, with all the beautiful objects of nature; in the fields where the sods that cover their graves are full of significant forms — the symbols of life, death and immortality:

beneath the blue sky, which is the emblem as well as the
real image of infinity; and beneath the clouds, which,
under their ethereal banners, seem to open the gates of
heaven to those who are leaving this world.

One day in the summer of 1850, as I was taking a
solitary stroll in one of our rural villages, I saw a young
woman, neatly but plainly attired, sitting upon a knoll,
under a large tupelo tree, that spread its branches over
the widening of a small stream in the valley. She had
evidently been weeping, and had dried her tears on seeing
me approach. I made an apology for interrupting her,
and then remarked that the little valley in which we had
met was remarkably beautiful and almost enchanting.
" Yes," she replied, " and it is particularly so to me, for
here my sister, who died three years ago, used to come
with me often, on pleasant afternoons; and here we sat,
sometimes with a book and sometimes with our needle-
work; and here we gathered a great number and variety
of wild flowers, which she pressed with her own hand
between papers, and gave them a name. Some of the
names were of her own invention; but I always call the
flower by the name she gave it."

I inquired if her sister was buried here. " She is not,"
she replied, " but here I know, if her spirit dwells near,
she would delight to have been buried; and I have transplanted many of these flowers upon her grave and around
it, taking them up on a trowel with the sods, while they
are in bloom, and they have seldom failed to come into
blossom there the following seasons. I have often wished
she was buried here, but in that case, I should not enjoy
the pleasure of transplanting these flowers on her grave,
which is in a burial place not far distant." Do you think
your sister is conscious of these offerings to her memory.
" I think so; and this belief is the source of all my

present happiness. It is this only that saves me from despair. I feel when looking over her preserved flowers, and when I am watching the budding and blossoming of the flowers upon her grave, that I am in her presence; and it is this reflection that solaces my grief. These flowers, and all the objects in this beautiful valley, are emblems to my mind of my sister's life in heaven; and I think more of the flowers that spring up from her grave, than I should of the proudest monument that was ever carved out of marble."

Thus memory, as well as poetry and religious sentiment, endears and hallows these natural scenes as the proper places for the repose of the dead. Our remembrance of the incidents of their life is intimately associated with the grove, the hillside, the path by the river, and with other rural walks. In their company have we become familiar and delighted with these scenes and objects. The trees have a sacredness which is due to their alliance with the memory of our departed friends; the flowers are the reflection of the smiles of those whom we loved. And when we come abroad under the open sky, surrounded by these memorials of our friends, in the midst of these material forms of loveliness and beauty, and these emblems of our religious faith and our trust in heaven, we do not turn away gloomy and desponding; but sit down with full assurances of meeting them again, when the evidence of divine truth, which is only emblemized in nature, beams upon us in the full blaze of celestial glory.

2

STANZAS.

By Rev. C. Wolfe.

If I had thought thou could'st have died,
I might not weep for thee,
But I forgot, when by thy side,
That thou could'st mortal be ;
It never through my mind had past,
The time would e'er be o'er,
And I on thee should look my last,
And thou should'st smile no more !

And still upon that face I look,
And think 't will smile again ;
And still the thought I will not brook,
That I must look in vain !
But when I speak thou dost not say,
What thou ne'er left'st unsaid ;
And now I feel, as well I may,
Sweet Mary, thou art dead !

If thou would'st stay, e'en as thou art, —
All cold and all serene, —
I still might press thy silent heart,
And where thy smiles have been !
While e'en thy chill pale corse I have,
Thou seemest still mine own ;
But then I lay thee in thy grave, —
And I am all alone.

I do not think, where'er thou art,
Thou hast forgotten me ;
And I, perhaps, may soothe this breast,
In thinking, too, of thee :
Yet there was round thee such a dawn
Of light ne'er seen before,
As fancy never could have drawn,
And never can restore !

THE GATEWAY.

ONE of the first objects that would attract the stranger's attention, on approaching Mount Auburn, is the Egyptian gateway at the principal entrance. It is built of granite, and is a very imposing and appropriate structure. The cornice with which it is surrounded is a single stone, twenty-four feet in height by twelve in breadth. It bears the device of a winged globe, which is emblematical of divine protection. Underneath is this inscription in raised letters : —

"THEN SHALL THE DUST RETURN TO THE EARTH
AS IT WAS, AND THE SPIRIT SHALL RETURN
TO THE GOD THAT GAVE IT."
MOUNT AUBURN ;
CONSECRATED SEPTEMBER 24TH, 1831.

The two lateral buildings contain rooms which are used as the offices of the Porter and the Superintendent.

THE CHAPEL.

The Chapel was erected for the performance of burial services in those cases in which the state of the weather, or other circumstances connected with the funeral of the deceased, might render it necessary or convenient. It was designed also to afford a depository for statues and other works of sculpture which require protection from the weather. This building is also of granite, and is situated on a conspicuous elevation, at the right of Central Avenue. It is sixty feet by forty in its dimensions, and its decorations are in the pointed style of architecture.

The windows are of colored glass, and in the head of the large nave window is an emblematical device, consisting of a winged female figure reposing in sleep upon the clouds, and holding two sleeping infants in her arms. It is designed to symbolize the tranquillity of death.

The rose window in front contains a painted emblem of immortality, represented by two cherubs with an upward and prayerful look of devotion.

THOMAS DOWSE.   BENJ. FRANKLIN.

THE DOWSE MONUMENT.

THIS monument is on Gentian Path, and consists of a simple obelisk of granite. The graves of the different members of Mr. Dowse's family are marked by headstones in the same lot. The monument erected to Franklin, by Mr. Dowse, is also a granite obelisk, of larger dimensions. It bears the following inscription :

To the memory of Benjamin Franklin, the Printer, the Philosopher, the Statesman, the Patriot, who, by his wisdom, blessed his country and his age, and bequeathed to the world an illustrious example of industry, integrity, and self-culture. Born in Boston, M DCC VI. Died in Philadelphia, M DCC XC.

2*

HISTORY OF MOUNT AUBURN.

IT appears that the earliest meeting assembled to consider the project of a Rural Cemetery in the vicinity of Boston, was held in November, 1825, at the house and by the request of Dr. Jacob Bigelow. The individuals who were present on this occasion, besides Dr. Bigelow, were John Lowell, George Bond, William Sturgis, Thomas W. Ward, Samuel P. Gardiner, John Tappan, and Nathan Hale. The project met with unanimous approval, and Messrs. Bond and Tappan were appointed a Committee to make inquiries, and report a suitable spot of ground for the purpose. The Committee were unsuccessful in their inquiries; they made no report of their proceedings, nor was the subject actively revived by the above named persons.

The next movement was made in 1830, when Dr. Bigelow, — who seems to have remained firm in his original purpose, — having obtained from George W. Brimmer the offer of the grounds known as *Sweet Auburn*, for a public Cemetery, at the price of six thousand dollars, communicated the fact to the other officers of the Massachusetts Horticultural Society, — of which institution he was at that time Corresponding Secretary, — and engaged their co-operation in an earnest effort to accomplish the object of his wishes. A meeting of the members of that Society was held on the twenty-third of November, by invitation of Dr. Bigelow and John C. Gray, to discuss the project of a Cemetery, to be connected with an *Experimental Garden* of the Society. A Committee of the Society was appointed, consisting of H. A. S. Dearborn, Jacob Bigelow, Edward Everett, George·Bond, John C. Gray, Abbott Lawrence, and George W. Brimmer.

These gentlemen called a more general meeting on the eighth of June, 1831, to consider the same subject. Joseph Story took the Chair, and Edward Everett acted as Secretary. Great interest and entire unanimity were expressed in regard to the design of the meeting. It was also voted to purchase " Sweet Auburn," provided one hundred subscribers could be obtained, at sixty dollars each. A Committee of twenty was appointed to report on a general plan of proceedings proper to be adopted for effecting the objects of the meeting. The following are the names of the Committee : — Joseph Story, Daniel Webster, H. A. S. Dearborn, Charles Lowell, Samuel Appleton, Jacob Bigelow, Edward Everett, George W. Brimmer, George Bond, A. H. Everett, Abbott Lawrence, James T. Austin, Franklin Dexter, Joseph P. Bradlee, Charles Tappan, Charles P. Curtis, Zebedee Cook, Jr., John Pierpont, Lucius M. Sargent, and George W. Pratt.

An eloquent Report on the general objects of the meeting was presented by the Chairman of the previously appointed Committee,· H. A. S. Dearborn.

Another meeting was held on the eleventh of June, 1830, and heard the following Report of the Committee of twenty : —

1. That it is expedient to purchase, for a Garden and Cemetery, a tract of land, commonly known by the name of Sweet Auburn, near the road leading from Cambridge to Watertown, containing about seventy-two acres, for the sum of six thousand dollars : provided this sum can be raised in the manner proposed in the second article of this Report.

2. That a subscription be opened for lots of ground in the said tract, containing not less than two hundred square feet each, at the price of sixty dollars for each lot, the subscription not to be binding until one hundred lots are subscribed for.

3. That when a hundred or more lots are taken, the right of choice shall be disposed of at an auction, of which seasonable notice shall be given to the subscribers.

4. That those subscribers, who do not offer a premium for the right of choosing, shall have their lots assigned to them by lot.

5. That the fee of the land shall be vested in the Massachusetts Horticultural Society, but that the use of the lots, agreeably to an Act of the Legislature, respecting the same, shall be secured to the subscribers, their heirs and assigns, forever.

6. That the land devoted to the purpose of a Cemetery shall contain not less than forty acres.

7. That every subscriber, upon paying for his lot, shall become a member, for life, of the Massachusetts Horticultural Society, without being subject to assessments.

8. That a Garden and Cemetery Committee of nine persons shall be chosen annually, first by the subscribers, and afterwards by the Horticultural Society, whose duty it shall be to cause the necessary surveys and allotments to be made, to assign a suitable tract of land for the Garden of the Society, and to direct all matters appertaining to the regulation of the Garden and Cemetery; five at least of this Committee shall be persons having rights in the Cemetery.

9. That the establishment, including the Garden and Cemetery, be called by a definite name, to be supplied by the Committee.

The Society, on this occasion, accepted the Report, and authorized the same Committee to proceed in the establishment of a Garden and Cemetery, in conformity to their Report.

In June, 1831, the following Act of Incorporation was obtained from the Legislature : —

COMMONWEALTH OF MASSACHUSETTS.

In the year of our Lord one thousand eight hundred and thirty-one.

AN ACT, in addition to an Act entitled, " An Act to incorporate the MASSACHUSETTS HORTICULTURAL SO-CIETY."

SECTION I. *Be it enacted by the Senate and House of Representatives in General Court assembled, and by the authority of the same,* That the Massachusetts Horticultural Society be, and hereby are, authorized, in addition to the powers already conferred on them, to dedicate and appropriate any part of the real estate now owned or hereafter to be purchased by them, as and for a Rural Cemetery or Burying Ground, and for the erection of Tombs, Cenotaphs, or other Monuments, for, or in memory of the dead ; and for this purpose, to lay out the same in suitable lots or other subdivisions, for family, and other burying places ; and to plant and embellish the same with shrubbery, flowers, trees, walks, and other rural ornaments, and to enclose and divide the same with proper walls and enclosures, and to make and annex thereto other suitable appendages and conveniences as the Society shall, from time to time, deem expedient. And whenever the said Society shall so lay out and appro-priate any of their real estate for a Cemetery or Burying Ground, as aforesaid, the same shall be deemed a per-petual dedication thereof for the purposes aforesaid ; and

the real estate so dedicated shall be forever held by the
said Society in trust for such purposes, and for none
other. And the said Society shall have authority to
grant and convey to any person or persons the sole and
exclusive right of burial, and of erecting Tombs, Cenotaphs, and other Monuments, in any such designated lots
and subdivisions, upon such terms and conditions, and
subject to such regulations as the said Society shall, by
their By-Laws and Regulations, prescribe. And every
right so granted and conveyed shall be held for the purposes aforesaid, and for none other, as real estate, by the
proprietor or proprietors thereof, and shall not be subject
to attachment or execution.

SECTION II. *Be it further enacted,* That for the purposes of this Act, the said Society shall be, and hereby
are authorized to purchase and hold any real estate not
exceeding ten thousand dollars in value, in addition to
the real estate which they are now, by law, authorized
to purchase and hold. And to enable the said Society
more effectually to carry the plan aforesaid into effect,
and to provide funds for the same, the said Society shall
be, and hereby are authorized to open subscription books,
upon such terms, conditions, and regulations as the said
Society shall prescribe, which shall be deemed fundamental and perpetual articles between the said Society
and the subscribers. And every person, who shall become a subscriber in conformity thereto, shall be deemed
a member for life of the said Society without the payment
of any other assessment whatsoever, and shall moreover
be entitled, in fee simple, to the sole and exclusive right
of using, as a place of burial, and of erecting Tombs,
Cenotaphs, and other Monuments in such lot or sub-
division of such Cemetery or Burying Ground, as shall
in conformity to such fundamental articles be assigned
to him.

SECTION III. *Be it further enacted*, That the President of the said Society shall have authority to call any special meeting or meetings of the said Society at such time and place as he shall direct, for the purpose of carrying into effect any or all the purposes of this Act, or any other purposes within the purview of the original Act to which this Act is in addition.

At a meeting of the subscribers held August 3d, 1831, it appeared that the subscription had become obligatory, according to the program above stated, by the taking of a hundred lots. The paper was filled up to a greater extent than was either required or expected, — a result which was mainly attributable to the zealous efforts of the late Joseph P. Bradlee, efficiently aided by others. The following are the names of the " Garden and Cemetery Committee " chosen at this meeting : — Joseph Story, H. A. S. Dearborn, Jacob Bigelow, E. Everett, G. W. Brimmer, George Bond, Charles Wells, Benjamin A. Gould, and George W. Pratt. Arrangements at the same time were made for a public religious consecration, to be held on the Society's grounds. The topographical survey of Mount Auburn was performed by Alexander Wadsworth, Civil Engineer.

The consecration of the Cemetery took place on Saturday, September 24th, 1831. A temporary amphitheatre was constructed, with seats, in one of the deep valleys of the wood, and a platform for the speakers was erected at the bottom. An audience of nearly two thousand persons were seated under the trees on this occasion. The order of performances was as follows : —

1. INSTRUMENTAL MUSIC, by the Boston Band.

2. INTRODUCTORY PRAYER, by the Rev. Dr. WARE.

3. HYMN,

WRITTEN BY THE REV. MR. PIERPONT.

To thee, O God, in humble trust,
    Our hearts their cheerful incense burn,
For this thy word, " Thou art of dust,
    And unto dust shalt thou return."

For, what were life, life's work all done,
    The hopes, joys, loves, that cling to clay,
All, all departed, one by one,
    And yet life's load borne on for aye !

Decay ! Decay ! 'tis stamped on all !
    All bloom, in flower and flesh, shall fade ;
Ye whispering trees, when we shall fall,
    Be our long sleep beneath your shade !

Here to thy bosom, mother Earth,
    Take back in peace, what thou hast given ;
And all that is of heavenly birth,
    O God, in peace, recall to Heaven !

4. ADDRESS,

BY THE HON. JOSEPH STORY.

5. CONCLUDING PRAYER, by the Rev. Mr. PIERPONT.

6. MUSIC BY THE BAND.

A cloudless sun and an atmosphere purified by showers, combined to make the day one of the most delightful
we ever experience at this season of the year. It is
unnecessary to say that the address by Judge Story was

pertinent to the occasion, for if the name of the orator were not sufficient, the perfect silence of the multitude, enabling him to be heard with distinctness at the most distant part of the beautiful amphitheatre in which the services were performed, would be sufficient testimony as to its worth and beauty. Nor is it in the pen's power to furnish any adequate description of the effect produced by the music of the thousand voices which joined in the hymn, as it swelled in chastened melody from the bottom of the glen, and, like the spirit of devotion, found an echo in every heart, and pervaded the whole scene.

Some account of Mount Auburn itself, as it existed at this stage of its history, may with propriety be here introduced. The tract of land which bears this name is situated on the southerly side of the main road leading from Cambridge to Watertown, partly within the limits of both those towns, and distant about four miles from Boston. Formerly it was known by the name of Stone's Woods, the title to most of the land having remained in the family of Stones from an early period after the settlement of the country. Mr. Brimmer made purchase of the hill and part of the woodlands within a few years, chiefly with the view of preventing the destruction of the trees, and to his disinterested love of the beautiful in nature, may be attributed the preservation of this lovely spot. The first purchase of the Society included between seventy and eighty acres, extending from the road nearly to the banks of Charles River. The Experimental Garden commenced by the Association was to have been upon that portion of the ground next to the road, and separated from the Cemetery by a long water-course, running between this tract and the interior wood-land. The latter is covered, throughout most of its extent,

3

with a vigorous growth of forest trees, many of them of large size, and comprising an unusual variety of kinds. This tract is beautifully undulating in its surface, containing a number of bold eminences, steep acclivities, and deep shadowy valleys. A remarkable natural ridge with a level surface runs through the ground from south-east to north-west, and has for many years been known as a secluded and favorite walk. The principal eminence, called Mount Auburn in the plan, is one hundred and twenty-five feet above the level of Charles River, and commands from its summit one of the finest prospects which can be obtained in the environs of Boston. On one side is the city in full view, connected at its extremities with Charlestown and Roxbury. The serpentine course of Charles River, with the cultivated hills and fields rising beyond it, and having the Blue Hills of Milton in the distance, occupies another portion of the landscape. The village of Cambridge, with the venerable edifices of Harvard University, are situated about a mile to the eastward. On the north, at a very small distance, Fresh Pond appears, — a handsome sheet of water, finely diversified by its woody and irregular shores. Country seats and cottages, seen in various directions, and those on the elevated land at Watertown, especially, add much to the picturesque effect of the scene.

The grounds of the Cemetery were laid out with intersecting avenues, so as to render every part of the wood accessible. These avenues are curved and variously winding in their course, so as to be adapted to the natural inequalities of the surface. By this arrangement the greatest economy of the land is produced, combining at the same time the picturesque effect of landscape gardening. Over the more level portions, the avenues are made twenty feet wide, and are suitable for carriage roads. The more broken and precipitous parts are approached by foot-paths, which are six feet in width. These passage-ways are smoothly gravelled, and planted on both sides with flowers and ornamental shrubs. Lots of ground (containing each three hundred square feet) are set off as family burial-places, at suitable distances on the sides of the avenues and paths.

The nature of the privileges now granted to the purchasers of these lots, by the proprietors, may be learned by reference to the form of conveyance employed. We have inserted also the names of the hills, foot-paths and avenues, which it was found convenient to adopt. These were laid out by a Committee, of which Gen. Dearborn was Chairman. The Egyptian gateway, which forms the chief entrance to the grounds, was designed by Dr. Bigelow.

The first choice of lots was offered for sale, by auction, Nov. 28th, 1831; the first two hundred being then made purchasable to subscribers on the following conditions:

1. Each lot contains three hundred square feet, exclusive of ground necessary to fence the same, for which sixty dollars are to be paid.

In addition to said sum of sixty dollars, the sum bid for the right of selection is to be paid, and the bidder is to decide on the lot he will take at the moment of sale.

3. If any subscriber be not satisfied with the lot sold or assigned to him, he may at any time within six months exchange the same for any other among the lots already laid out, if any such remain unappropriated.

4. If any subscriber shall wish to enlarge his lot, the Garden and Cemetery Committee may, if they see no objection, set off to him land for that purpose, on his

paying for the same at the rate of twenty cents per square foot.

5. A receiving tomb is provided in the City, and one will be constructed at Mount Auburn, in which, if desired, bodies may be deposited for a term not exceeding six months.

At this sale, the one hundred and fifty-seven lots previously subscribed for, were assigned, at sixty dollars each. The amount bid for the right of selection at the same time, (from twelve dollars to one hundred dollars, each lot,) was $957.50.

Mount Auburn, it is generally well known, is now the property of a separate and distinct Corporation, having no connection with the Horticultural Society. This transfer was effected in 1835.

THE PLEASURE OF TOMBS.
By the Abbe de St. Pierre.

THERE are no monuments so interesting as the tombs of men, and especially those of our ancestors. It is remarkable that every nation, in a state of nature, and even the greater part of those which are civilized, have made the tombs of their forefathers the centre of their devotion, and an essential part of their religion. From these, however, must be excepted the people, whose fathers rendered themselves odious to their children by a gloomy and severe education. I mean the Southern and Western nations of Europe. This religious melancholy is diffused throughout every other part of the world. The tombs of progenitors, all over China, are among the principal embellishments of the suburbs of their cities, and of the hills in the country. They form the most powerful bonds of patriotic affection among savage nations. When the Europeans have sometimes proposed an exchange of territory to these people, the reply was: — " Shall we say to the bones of our fathers, arise and accompany us to a foreign land?" They always considered this objection as insurmountable.

Tombs have furnished to the poetical talents of Young and Gessner, the most enchanting imagery. Our voluptuaries, who sometimes recur to the sentiments of nature, have cenotaphs erected in their gardens. These are not, it must be confessed, the tombs of their parents. But whence could they have derived this sentiment of funereal melancholy in the very midst of pleasure? Must it not have been from the persuasion, that something still subsists after we are gone? If a tomb suggested to their imagination the idea only of what it is designed to contain, the thought would shock rather than delight them. How terrified most of them are at the thoughts of death! To this physical idea, then, some moral sentiment must undoubtedly be attached. The voluptuous melancholy resulting from it, arises, like every other attractive sensation, form the harmony of the two opposite principles; from the sentiment of our fleeting existence, and that of our immortality, which unite on beholding the last habitation of mankind. *A tomb is a monument erected on the confines of two worlds.*

It first presents to us the end of the vain disquietudes of life, and the image of everlasting repose; it afterwards awakens in us the confused sentiment of a blessed immortality, the probabilities of which grow stronger and stronger, in proportion as the person, whose memory is recalled, was a virtuous character. It is then that our veneration becomes fixed. And this is so unquestionably

3*

true, that though there be no difference between the dust of Nero and that of Socrates, no one would grant a place in his grove to the remains of the Roman Emperor, though they were deposited in a silver urn ; whereas, every one would exhibit those of the philosopher, in the most honorable apartment of his house, though contained only in a vase of clay.

It is from this intellectual instinct, therefore, in favor of virtue, that the tombs of great men inspire us with a veneration so affecting. From the same sentiment too, it is, that those which contain objects which have been lovely, excite so much pleasing regret ; for as we shall presently show, the attractions of love arise entirely out of the appearances of virtue. Hence it is that we are moved by the sight of a little hillock, which covers the ashes of an amiable infant, by the recollection of its innocence ; hence, again, that we are melted into tenderness, on contemplating the tomb in which is laid to repose a young female, the delight and hope of her family, by reason of her virtues. In order to render such monuments interesting, there is no need of bronze, marble, and gilding. The more simple they are, the more energy do they communicate to the sentiment of melancholy. They produce a more powerful effect when poor rather than rich, antique rather than modern, with details of misfortune rather than with titles of honor, with the attributes of virtue rather than those of power. It is in the country, principally, that their impression makes itself felt in a very lively manner. There a simple unadorned grave causes more tears to flow than the gaudy splendor of a cathedral interment. There it is that grief assumes sublimity ; it ascends with the aged yews in the churchyard ; it extends with the surrounding hills and plains ; it allies itself with the effects of nature, with the dawn of the morning, the murmuring of the winds, the setting of the sun, and the darkness of the night. The most oppressive labor and the most degrading humiliation, are incapable of extinguishing the impression of this sentiment in the breasts of the most miserable of mankind.

"During the space of two years," says Father Du Tertre, "our negro Dominick, after the death of his wife, never failed, for a single day, as soon as he returned from the place of his employment, to take his little boy and girl, and conduct them to the grave of their mother, over which he sobbed and wept before them, for more than half an hour together, while the poor children frequently caught the infection of his sorrow." What a funeral oration for a wife and a mother! This man, however, was nothing but a wretched slave.

Our artists place statues of marble weeping round the tombs of the great. It is very proper to make statues weep when men shed no tears. I have been often present at the funeral obsequies of the rich; but rarely have I seen any one shedding a tear on such occasions, unless it were now and then an aged domestic, who was, perhaps, left destitute. Some time ago, happening to pass through the unfrequented streets of the Fauxbourg Saint Marceau, I perceived a coffin at the door of a house which had but a mean look. Close by the coffin was a woman on her knees, in earnest prayer to God, and who had all the appearance of being absorbed in grief. This poor woman having discovered, at the further end of the street, the priests and their attendants coming to carry away the body, got upon her feet and hurried away, putting her hands to her eyes and crying bitterly. The neighbors endeavored to stop her, and administer some consolation, but to no purpose. As she passed close by me, I took the liberty to ask, if it was the loss of a

mother, or of a daughter, that she lamented so piteously.
"Alas! sir," said she to me, the tears gushing down her
cheeks, "I am mourning the loss of a good lady, who
procured me the means of earning my poor livelihood;
she kept me employed from day to day." I informed
myself in the neighborhood respecting the condition of
this benevolent lady, who was the wife of a petty joiner.
Ye people of wealth, what use do you make of your
riches during your lifetime, if no tears are shed over
your graves?

PILGRIMS.

BY MARY HOWITT.

MID hopes and fears, — from youth to age
Man goeth on a pilgrimage ;
Or rich or poor, unlearned or wise,
Before each one his journey lies ;
'Tis to a land afar, unknown,
Yet where the great of old are gone,
Poet and patriot, sage and seer ;
All whom we worship or revere,
This awful pilgrimage have made, —
Have passed to the dim land of shade.
Youth with his radiant locks, is there ;
And old men with their silver hair ;
And children sportive in their glee ; —
A strange and countless company.
Ne'er on that land gazed human eyes ;
Man's science hath not traced its skies,
Nor mortal traveller e'er brought back
Chart of that journey's fearful track.

———

Thou art a pilgrim to that shore, —
Like them thou can'st return no more !
Oh, gird thee, for thou needest strength,
For the way's peril as its length !
Oh, faint not by the way nor heed
Dangers, nor lures, nor check thy speed ;
So God be with thee, Pilgrim blest,
Thou journeyest to the land of Rest.

THE MORAL INFLUENCE OF GRAVES.

The melancholy pleasure which we derive from visiting a place of burial is common to those who possess an ordinary amount of cultivation. There are few persons so frivolous as not to be made thoughtful, and few so heartless as not to feel some emotions of humanity, after an hour's meditation among the tombs. The cause of the pleasure derived from this source, it would be difficult to explain, except on the supposition that melancholy, when gently excited, is an agreeable sentiment. The grief we suffer from the death of a friend, is for many days extremely painful, and it is only our veneration for the dead that prevents our making a resolute effort to banish the subject of it from the mind. This painful grief is not very lasting, except in extraordinary cases, or in minds predisposed to insanity. As time wears away, it subsides into a quiet state of the mind, which is the melancholy of the poets, and a very different sentiment from that to which the same term is applied by medical writers. At this later period, the remembrance of the virtues of our departed friend, and of the many happy hours we have passed together, forms an agreeable retrospect, which is hallowed and made affecting by our subdued sorrow.

Men in general are not prone to seek those objects that forcibly suggest the idea of death ; but the contemplation of the graves of our fellow beings, produces a pensive state of the mind that overcomes our natural horror of death, especially when associated with certain fanciful images emblematical of peace and immortality. We are more agreeably affected in grounds of a simple and rustic appearance than in a highly ornamented scene, where the artificial objects that are placed over the dead remind us only of the wealth or the vanity of the living. People are attracted in multitudes to a burial place that is covered with gewgaws and expensive follies; but they go there to gratify their curiosity, not to yield up their hearts to meditation. The emblems of grief and of the relations of time and eternity are picturesque and affecting; those of vanity are simply diverting; and when the works of vanity are conspicuous among the tombs, the visitor, while examining the several objects which are before him, forgets the character of the place, and feels only that idle interest that leads one passively along among the objects of a museum. A cemetery is the last place in the world that ought to be made a scene of any such idle diversion.

Neither ought these grounds to be made a place for general recreation. The idea of connecting them with a public garden was unwise, and were proved inexpedient. If our citizens feel the want of a place for rural recreation, where they can employ themselves in cheerful festivities, and enjoy the beauties of nature, they should purchase a pleasant and extensive tract of pasture and woodland, and devote it to these purposes. But a place of burial should be consecrated to sorrow and meditation, and to that religion which offers consolation to those who are laden with grief. No merry-making or idle and thoughtless amusement should ever desecrate this spot, which has been made holy by the sad and solemn purpose to which it is devoted; and the flowers and the landscape should be made to smile and look beautiful around it, not to render it a scene of pleasure, but that it may seem more closely allied to heaven.

To these consecrated grounds we would resort as we attend service in the house of God, to indulge in serious meditation, and to ponder on those themes which are

neglected by the multitude, during the hurry of business
or in the idle whirl of pleasure.   We come here not to be
saddened, but to be sobered; to think more earnestly of
the higher purposes of life, of its transient duration, and
of the importance of neglecting no duty of religion, charity, or benevolence, which would be profitable to ourselves, or render us more useful to our fellow creatures.
We need not be the disciples of a theological faith to feel
the truth of these remarks, or to understand the benefit
we derive from scenes that tend to conquer an excess of
frivolity, or to moderate that entire devotion to mammon
which, like intemperance and vice, has ruined many a
noble heart.   Many a mind is destitute of philosophy because it has not been trained in a school of wisdom; and
many a soul is destitute of virtue, because the multiplied
cares of fortune and ambition crowd out every thought of
other things.   Hence the chastening influence of the loss
of friends.   Grief is often the fountain head of virtue and
of poetic enthusiasm; and he who is unacquainted with
it, is too apt to lead a life that is entirely selfish and pro-
saic.   Yet if one has suffered no such bereavement, an
occasional visit to the graves of those whom he has once
known, must affect him with a deeper sentiment of religion and virtue.

To a mourner who has never been inspired with a love
of nature, the rural cemetery may present a new gospel
of consolation.   If he be a religious man, his observations
in this place may confirm his trust in the beneficence of
the Deity, and his faith in the soul's immortality.   There
is something associated with the grave of a fellow being
that must impress the most unreflecting mind with
thoughts that do not occur to him in the common circumstances of life.   There comes up from these green
mounds, and from the sad and beautiful things around

them, an impression of subdued melancholy, allied with the sentiment of a new existence, which is the consolation and a part of the happiness of those who have buried their friends, which prepares the selfish for a full exercise of benevolence, and leads the thoughtless to meditation. A rural cemetery is a school both of religion and philosophy.

It is in great measure our love of virtue, and our proneness to remember exclusively the good deeds of departed friends whom we loved, that prompt us to visit a place of burial. When we are strolling among its scenes, the virtues of the dead form the principal subject of our thoughts and of our discourse, and we carefully banish the remembrance of those failings which would tend to diminish our reverence for the dead. This habit, often indulged, acts reciprocally upon the mind, in fostering a greater love of virtue and an ambition to be worthy, after our death, of the same veneration which we feel for the good who are in their graves. A respect for the dead cannot exist apart from our respect for virtue. We wish, as it were, to deify the spirits of the departed; and we can approximate to this idea only by attributing to them the possession of extraordinary goodness. If the virtuous and redeeming traits of their character be not sufficient to hide by their lustre the faults or vices that belonged to them, we soon cease to cherish them in our remembrance.

Thus as time passes away, those who had but few virtues are gradually forgotten, and sink into oblivion, while the remembrance of those who were known for their benevolent and amiable qualities is always growing brighter. Hence the cemetery becomes, at length, the seeming depository of the remains only of the good. As we cannot by sumptuous marble confer immortality upon

4

one who has performed no deeds of greatness; neither can those be long remembered even by their own friends, who in their lifetime rendered no service to their fellow men. The names only of the good and the just awaken in our souls any emotion of reverence ; but these seem to be in alliance with beings of a divine nature, and every thought we bestow upon them plants a seed of virtue in our breasts, that gradually ripens into some moral excellence in our own character.

It is the duty of all persons, therefore, in order to render the cemetery more entirely a school of virtue, to be true to justice and morality, in the honors which they bestow upon the dead. Let no one who has lived a depraved or a selfish life, how conspicuous soever the position he may have occupied, be exalted by honors that should be paid only to the good, or by a tribute of false praise recorded upon his tomb. Neither let private and humble virtue be paraded before the world with an ostentation that would turn every spectator into a skeptic of its reality. Humble virtue is always dishonored by an ostentatious monument.

LIFE AND DEATH.

By Florence.

WHENCE are ye, fearful ones? Speak forth! Reply!
'Twas thus my spirit's deep and earnest cry
Went up.   The midnight's burning fever wrought
Its fiery shadows with each swelling thought;
And proud and high amid the darkened night,
My voiceless cry went forth, for light — for light!

I asked — of life, whence came the peerless gift
That gives to senseless clay a power to lift
Itself in burning dreams unto the skies?
How genius looked from wildly beaming eyes,
Upon the still, and dark, and dreamless earth,
On which we live, and move, and have our birth?

I bade the winds, the stars, the earth reply,
If that which thinks and wills can ever die?
And to what bourne the gift returned, which here
But shone, a transient ray, to disappear?
And winds, and stars, and earth, gave answer back
But this — " Thou canst not know its hidden track!"

I spoke to death and to eternity,
As to a spirit conjured up for me,
By that prevailing cry, and bade them say
If that which lives and loves, can know decay?
Or if this feverish thirst, this strong wild strife
For that we seek, but seek in vain, is life?

Love, sorrowing love, bereaved and lone,
Love from which kindred love had flown,
Looked sadly up, and asked if all was o'er ; —
If they who meet on earth, shall meet no more ; —
If but this brief companionship in woe,
Was all that life or love on earth might know ?

I importuned the grave, as with a friend,
Beseeching it but once its veil to rend, —
To tell me why, with such o'erwhelming strife,
It even trod upon the steps of life ?
And death, eternity, the grave, replied,
" We have no voice for doubt, thou child of pride."

My baffled spirit bowed in anguish low, —
The victim of a doom it could not know :
Above, beneath, without a mark or bound,
Was space, illimitable, dark, profound : —
And in the agony of struggling powers,
It asked why such a mockery was ours ?

Then came a low, sweet voice, like music sent
Upon the dark abyss, where storms had spent
Their wrath, — 'Twas thine, meek Faith, and thus it
        spoke,
Stilling the deep whose waves so wildly broke ; —
" Trust thou in Heavenly Love : the power which
        gave
Thee life, can lift from doubt, and from the grave."

ALVIN ADAMS.

THE ADAMS MONUMENT.

THIS is an elegant monument of pure white marble, situated on Spruce Avenue, and erected by Alvin Adams.

4*

SEPULCHRAL MONUMENTS OF THE MIDDLE AGES.

(Compiled.)

The earliest tombs found in Great Britain, which can be considered as at all of an architectural character, are the stone coffins of the eleventh and twelfth centuries. The covers of these were at first simply coped; afterwards frequently ornamented with crosses of various kinds, and other devices, and sometimes with inscriptions. Subsequently, they were sculptured with recumbent figures in high relief; but still generally diminishing in width from the head to the feet, to fit the coffins, of which they formed the lids. Many of the figures of this period represent knights in armor, with their legs crossed. These are supposed to have been either Templars, or such as had joined, or vowed to join, in a crusade to the Holy Land. These figures usually had canopies, which were often richly carved over the heads, supported on small shafts, which ran along each side of the effigy, the whole worked in the same block of stone. This kind of tomb was sometimes placed beneath low arches or recesses, formed within the substance of the church wall, usually about seven feet in length, and not more than three high above the coffin, even in the centre; these arches were at first semicircular or segmental at the top, afterwards obtusely pointed. They often remain when the figure, or brass, and perhaps the coffin itself, has long disappeared and been forgotten. On many tombs of the thirteenth century, there are plain pediment-shaped canopies over the heads of the recumbent effigies, the earliest of which contain a pointed, trefoliated arched recess. Towards the end of the century, these canopies became gradually enriched with crockets, finials, and other architectural ornaments.

The most of the monuments of the middle ages were erected soon after the death of the persons whom they commemorate; but in some instances, the parties buried in them, prepared them during their lifetime. These were frequently the wealthy ecclesiastics. There are but few existing monuments which are earlier than the twelfth century. In the reign of Edward I., the tombs of persons of rank began to be ornamented on the sides with armorial bearings, and small sculptured statues, within pedimental canopied recesses; and from these we may progressively trace the peculiar minutiæ and enrichments of every style of ecclesiastical architecture, up to the Reformation.

Altar, or table tombs, called by Leland "high tombs," with recumbent effigies, were common during the whole of the fourteenth century. These sometimes appear beneath splendid pyramidal canopies, and sometimes beneath flat testoons. In the early part of the same century, the custom prevailed of inlaying flat stones with brasses, and monumental inscriptions frequently occur. The sides of these tombs are sometimes relieved with niches, surmounted with decorated pediments, each containing a small sculptured figure; sometimes with arched panels filled with tracery. Other tombs, about the same period, but more frequently in the fifteenth century, were decorated along the sides with large, square, panelled compartments, richly foliated or quatrefoiled, and containing shields.

Many of the tombs of the fifteenth and sixteenth centuries appear beneath arched recesses, fixed in, or projecting from the wall, and inclosing the tomb on three sides; these were constructed so as to form canopies, which are often of the most elaborate and costly workmanship. These canopies were sometimes of elaborately carved wood, and sometimes the altar tomb of an earlier date was at a later period inclosed within a screen of open work, with a groined stone canopy, and an upper story of wood, forming a mortuary chapel or chantry.

In the early part of the sixteenth century, the monuments were generally of a similar character to those of the preceding age; but alabaster slabs, with figures on them, cut in outline, were frequently used. The altar tombs, with figures in niches, carved in bold relief, were also frequently of alabaster, which was extensively quarried in Derbyshire. The Italian syle of funereal architecture soon came into general use, and was often mixed with the old style. In the two following centuries every sort of barbarism was introduced on funereal monuments; but the ancient style lingered longer in some places than in others.

The fashion of representing on tombs the effigy of the deceased graven on a plate of brass, which was imbedded in melted pitch, and firmly fastened down by rivets leaded into a slab of Purbeck marble, appears to have been adopted about the middle of the thirteenth century. These memorials, where circumstances permitted, were often elevated upon altar tombs; but more commonly they are found on slabs which form part of the pavement of churches; and it is not improbable that this kind of memorial was generally adopted for convenience, that the area of the church, and especially the choir, might not be encumbered, as was the case when effigies in relief were introduced.

The sepulchral brass, in its original and perfect state, was a work rich and beautiful in decoration. It is by careful examination sufficiently evident that the incised lines were filled up with some black resinous substance; the armorial decorations, and in elaborate specimens, the whole field or background, which was cut out by the chisel or scorper, were filled up with mastic or coarse enamel of various colors, so as to set off the elegant tracery of tabernacle work which forms the principal feature of ornament.

In England it was usual, with few exceptions, to inlay on the face of the slab, the figure and the different ornaments, arms, and inscriptions, graven on detached plates in distinct cavities, which seem to have been termed casements; so that the polished slab was left as the field or background. On the continent, possibly, in consequence of the brass plate being more readily obtained, the fashion was different. One large, unbroken surface of metal was obtained, formed of a number of plates, soldered together, and upon this surface all parts that were not occupied by the figure, or the shrine work around it, were enriched by elaborate diapering, usually armorial, the design being sometimes arranged lozenge-wise. Brasses of this more costly kind exist in England, but all hitherto observed are of Flemish workmanship. It may be remarked that the barbarous custom of using old gravestones, when they happened to be convenient, is to be found in early times as well as late; and monumental brasses do not appear to have been exempt from the same fate, as older inscriptions may frequently be found on the back of them. The author of Piers Plowman's Creed taxes the friars with this practice, that they might make room for other tombs, and get more fees. The fashion of sepulchral brasses continued for more than four centuries. A remarkable specimen of the latest works of this description is the full-sized effigy of Samuel Harswult, Archbishop of York, at Chigwell, Essex. He died in 1631. On the continent the engraving of sepulchral brasses has, in later times, been resumed; a noble brass

of full size having been engraved in 1837, at Cologne, as
the memorial of the late Archbishop. In England, likewise, a revival of the art has recently taken place, and
several brasses of good character have been executed.

It is to the continent that we must turn to seek the
origin of sepulchral brasses, and it may be traced with
little hesitation to the early enamelled works in France,
chiefly produced at Limoges. This art was introduced,
most probably, by Oriental or Byzantine artists, and as
early as the twelfth century, the "opus de Limogia"
was celebrated in southern Europe. Of the larger works
of this kind scarcely any specimens have escaped. The
costly tombs, with effigies of metal enamelled, which,
prior to the revolution, were seen in many cathedrals
in France, were all converted into cannon and copper
coin.

"Most of the earlier brasses are lost, and it is lamenta-
ble to reflect upon the causes of their destruction, having
been produced either by puritanical affectation or by theft.
The value of the metal was a temptation to sacrilegious
robbery; the brasses were with little difficulty torn up,
and in times of disturbance these were removed, the
places they occupied being now alone remaining to us,
and giving simply the outline of their figure:

> "' ——— dark fanaticism rent
> Altar, and screen, and ornament.'

"How short-sighted is man! The means adopted by
him to secure posthumous reputation, by the employment
of the valuable metals, in the construction of tombs and
sepulchral memorials, have only served to stimulate the
cupidity of others, and occasion their removal. Thus
have the names of many highly, and perhaps deservedly
celebrated in their day, passed into oblivion!"

THE GRAVE AND THE TOMB.

By John Pierpont.

The tomb is not so interesting as the grave. It savors of pride in those who can now be proud no longer; of distinction, where all are equal; of a feeling of eminence even under the hand of the great leveller of all our dust. And how useless to us are all the ensigns of magnificence that can be piled up above our bed! What though a sepulchral lamp throw its light up to the princely vaults under which my remains repose! They would rest as quietly were there no lamp there. The sleeping dust fears nothing. No dreams disturb it. It would not mark the neglect, should the sepulchral lamp be suffered to expire. It will not complain of the neglect, should it never be lighted again.

And why should my cold clay be imprisoned with so much care? Why thus immured, to keep it, as it would seem, from mingling with its kindred clay? When " that which warmed it once " animates it no more, what is there in my dust, that it should be thus jealously guarded? Is it lovely now in the eyes of those who may have once loved me? Will my children, or the children of my children, visit my vaulted chamber? They may, indeed, summon the courage to descend into my still abode, and gaze by torch-light upon the black and mouldering visage, which, not their memory, but my escutcheon, not their love, but their pride, may tell them is the face of their father; and this may eloquently remind them how soon the builder of the house of death must take up his abode in it; how soon the dust that we have, must mingle with the dust that we are; but still there is a feeling of horror in the atmosphere of the tomb, which chills all that is affectionate and tender in the emotions that lead them into it, and is anything but favorable to the moral uses to which the living may convert the dwellings of the dead; uses that will be secured by every daughter of affliction, of whom it may be said, as it was said of the sorrowing Mary, "She goeth unto the *grave* to weep there." Yes; though all whom I have loved or venerated sleep within its walls, I retreat from the tomb, the moment that I can do it without impiety, or even with decency. But I am differently affected when, with the rising sun, or by the light of the melancholy moon, I go alone to my mother's grave. There I love to linger; and, while there, I hear the wind sigh over one who often sighed for me. I breathe an air refreshed by the grass that draws its strength from the bosom from which I drew mine; and, in the drops of dew that tremble upon it, I see the tears that so often bedewed her eyes as she breathed forth a prayer that her children might cherish her memory, and escape from the pollutions of the world.

Yes; to the lover of nature, in its simplicity, the grave is more interesting and more instructive than the tomb. It speaks in a voice as full of truth, and more full of tenderness, to those who visit it to indulge their griefs, or to hold spiritual converse with the sainted spirits that are gone. And if the spirit that, while on earth, was loved by us, does not, when it leaves the earth, lose all interest in its crumbling tenement, would *it* not rather see the child of earth clasped again to the sweet bosom of its mother, to be again incorporated with her substance, to assume again a form attractive and lovely, to become again the recipient of light, an object of admiration, and a conscious medium of enjoyment, than that it should lie and moulder away in darkness and silence — a cause of offence to strangers, and a source of terror to those whom it still loves ?   Rather than see our own clay thus dwelling in coldness and solitude, neither receiving enjoyment nor imparting it, would not our spirits, purged from all vanity and pride, be pleased to know that it was starting forth again into life and loveliness ; that it was moving again in the fair light of heaven, and bathed in its showers ; that it was giving forth the perfume of the rose, or blushing with its great beauty ; or, that, having clothed the oak with its robe of summer, it was throwing a broad shade over the home of our children ; or that, having once more felt the frost of death, it was falling withered upon their graves.

The grave, when visited thoughtfully and alone, cannot but exert a favorable moral influence. It has already been remarked that it speaks in a voice full of tenderness and of truth.   Its instructions reach not the ear, indeed, but they do reach the heart.   By it, the departed friend is recalled in all but a visible presence, and by it, " he, being dead, yet speaketh."   At such a time, how faithfully will the grave of your friend remind you of the pleasant moments when you were conversing with him in the living tones of affection and truth ! when you were opening your hearts to each other, and becoming partakers, each of the other's hopes and purposes and cares ; when with a generous confidence those secret things were shown to one another, which were locked up in the heart from all the world beside ! Will the grave of your friend allow you to forget his single-heartedness in serving you ; his unsullied honor ; his plighted faith ; his readiness to expose himself to danger that he might save you from it ; and the calmness with which, when he perceived that his hold on life was breaking away, he gave up life's hopes, and, turning his eyes for the last time to the light, and looking up, for the last time, to the faces of those who loved him, he bade farewell to all, and gave up his spirit to the disposal of his God ?   Is all this forgotten, when you stand by his grave ?   Does not his very grave speak to you ?   Does it not bear its testimony to the value of youthful purity and truth, and of the power of an humble confidence in the Most High, to give dignity to the character of the young, and to disarm Death of the most dreadful of his weapons, even when he comes for his most dreadful work — to cut off life in the beauty of its morning ?   Does there not come up from his grave a voice, like that which comes down from the skies — a voice not meant for the ear, but addressed to the heart, and felt by the heart as the kindest and most serious tones of the living friend were never felt ?

And the children of sorrow — they whose hands have prepared a resting place for their parents in the " Garden of Graves," shall go to that garden and find that their hearts are made better by offering there the sacrifice of filial piety, or by listening there to the rebuke which a guilty ear will hear coming forth from the dust.   The leaf that rustles on his father's grave shall tell the un-dutiful son of disquiet sleep beneath it.   The gray hairs of his father went down to the grave, not in sorrow alone, but in shame.   The follies of his son made them thus go down.   Son of disobedience, that tall grass, sighing over thy father's dust, whispers a rebuke to thee.   It speaks of thy waywardness when a child ; of thy want of filial reverence in maturer years ; of thy contempt for a pa-rent's counsels ; and of thy disregard of his feelings, his infirmities, and his prayers.   It will be well for thee if the grave, by its rebuke, shall so chasten thee for thine iniquity, that thine own soul, when called away, may meet thy father and thy God in peace.

How different is the language of thy father's grave to thee, my brother. Does it not recall the many hours to thy remembrance, which were given to his service? Were not his thin locks decently composed, in death, by thine own hand? Did not his dim eye turn to thee in "the inevitable hour" as to the pleasant light of the sun? Did he not, with his last grasp, take hold of thy hand, and did not his pressure of thy hand tell thee, when his tongue could not, that it was *that* which had upheld and comforted him in his decaying strength; and was it not his last prayer that thou mightest be blest in thy own children as he had been blest in his? He has gone to his rest and his reward. But his sepulchre is green, and at thy coming, though it gives him not to thy embrace, it restores him to thy grateful remembrance. His counsels are again addressed to thine ear. His upright life is still before thine eye. His devotion to thine own highest interests sinks down, with new weight, into the depths of thy heart. Thou catchest again the religious tones of his morning and evening prayer. They speak of peace to the venerated dead. They are full of hope and consolation to the living. They tell how "blessed are the dead that die in the Lord," how sweetly "they rest from their labors," and how happy it is for them that "their works do follow them."

And thou, my sister, why dost thou go forth alone to visit thy mother's grave? Will she recognize thy footfall at the door of her narrow house? Will she give thee a mother's welcome, and a mother's blessing? Her blessing shall indeed meet thee there, though not her welcome; for *there* shall gather round thee the sacred remembrances of her care and her love for thee; the remembrance of her gentle admonitions, her patience and faithfulness; of her spirit of forbearance and meekness under provocation, and of that ever wakeful principle of industry, neatness and order, which always made her home so pleasant to those whom she loved ; and *there* shall visit thee, like one of the spirits of the blest, the thought of her own blessed spirit, as it rose in fervent prayers for the welfare and salvation of those who were given to her charge. She will speak to thee there, again, as she often spoke in life, of the hour that is coming, when thou, who didst once sleep upon her bosom, shalt sleep by her side, being gathered to the great congregation of the dead. She will speak to thee, from her grave, of the worth of innocence, of the importance of chastening the extravagance of thy young hopes, and of looking thoughtfully and seriously upon the world as a scene of trying duties and severe temptations, of the countless evils that join hand in hand and follow on in the train of a single folly, and of the momentous bearing of thy present course upon thy peace in this life, and upon thy condition when thy dust shall be mingling with hers. Then,

" Let Vanity adorn the marble tomb
    With trophies, rhymes, and scutcheons of renown,
  In the deep dungeon of some gothic dome,
    Where night and desolation ever frown.
Mine be the breezy hill that skirts the down,
    Where a green grassy turf is all I crave,
With here and there a violet bestrown,
    Fast by a brook, or fountain's murmuring wave ;
And many an evening sun shine sweetly on my grave."

THE BINNEY MONUMENT.

This monument is situated on Yarrow Path, and the figure upon it is an accurate likeness of the child it is intended to represent. It was executed by Henry Dexter, being taken as the child was lying on her pallet, after death. The hands are crossed upon the breast, and the feet bare, and likewise crossed. The marble upon which this infant figure reposes, is surrounded by four small columns, supporting a slab, on which is an urn. This monument contains the first marble statue executed in Boston, and stands in the lot of C. J. F. Binney, of Boston. The sculptured figure has been lately surrounded by a glass case.

5*

FLOWERS AROUND GRAVES.

FLOWERS have been regarded in all ages as the most appropriate ornaments of a burial place, and have always been strewed upon the bier and grave of a friend, as the most significant offerings of affection. So many tender recollections of flowers are linked with the memory of a beloved friend who has departed from us, that when we see them springing up from a new-made grave, the image of the dead is brought vividly before the mind, and while our sorrows are revived, they are soothed and tranquillized. Flowers are particularly suggestive of the interesting events in the life of a little child. So often has a cluster of wild flowers been the occasion of some of its happiest moments, that the smiles of the living child, and their forms and colors are closely allied ; and when we see them adorning the grave of the little slumberer, we feel that its spirit must be more blessed in heaven. The mother who has lost a child is prompted by this sentiment to strew flowers on the grave of the buried one, that its young spirit may see the evidence of the mother's love and the mother's grief, and derive from them the same pleasure which they afforded in its lifetime. But when a flower comes up spontaneously on the little grassy mound, it seems to the disconsolate mother like a tribute of affection from the dead to the living.

It is so common to eulogize flowers as the accompaniments of graves — emblematical as they are of our immortality, and of those virtues which prepare us for the company of higher beings — that we are prone to believe that too many of them cannot be introduced into a rural cemetery. In accordance with this idea, we see them planted not only around graves, but reared so profusely in borders and parterres, that visitors sometimes forget to observe anything but these dazzling horticultural exhibitions. In admitting this profusion, not all persons are aware that they destroy the poetic expression of the flowers. A single violet appearing on the rising mound of a grave, in a country churchyard, never fails to impress the beholder with a pleasing sentiment. It is a talisman that awakens a crowd of delightful images. But it is doubtful whether any such effect would be produced by a glittering row of petunias, pinks, and calceolarias in a spaded border near the grave. Their charm is lost in their profusion. Such a display is worse than a blank, because it destroys the effect of the little azure tufts of violets, that have come up spontaneously on the green mound.

A friend, who was far from being a sentimentalist, once showed me, with melancholy delight, a little flower of the white-weed, that had blossomed upon the new-made grave of an infant son. He said but few words on the occasion, but I could perceive that he set a high value upon the flower that seemed to him, undoubtedly, like a free offering of nature, who, with unseen hand, had reared it upon the grave, to memorialize the innocence of the child, who had been thus prematurely seized by death. I have no doubt that he derived more pleasure from this single flower than he would from a greater number. Its solitary character caused it to be more readily identified with the lost infant. When rambling in a wood, we stop to admire a solitary geranium, under the shadow of a broad-leaved fern, while we take no notice of the gaudy millions of flowers that grow in the open field.

After the burial of a friend, were a little wood-sparrow to perch daily on a bush by the side of his grave, and sing there his morning and evening lays, we should be delighted with this spontaneous tribute to the memory of the dead. Should any one, taking a hint from this romantic incident, carry out a canary bird, and hang its cage on the branch of a tree that extended over the grave of a friend, that it might, like the wild bird, sing the requiem of the departed, the effect would be more ludicrous than poetical. Affection, that loves to see the dead surrounded with images borrowed from nature and the skies, cannot be thus cheated by its own artifices.

There is a very simple and practicable method by which flowers might be made to grow upon a new-made grave, without resorting to cultivation. This is to procure the turfs that are to be placed upon the surface of the mound, from some wild pasture that is sprinkled with violets, anemones, columbines, and other flowers, which are not too rank in their growth to injure the smooth appearance of the turf. The little wildings of the wood and the pasture are the evidence that we are in the presence of nature. We feel, while we behold them unmixed with the artificial flowers of the florist, that we are treading upon nature's own ground, and we are led to pleasing meditations, which the scenes of a voluptuous flower garden could never inspire. There is an emotion of cheerful solitude felt in the midst of a field of wild flowers, that causes it to seem to a religious mind, the intermediate ground between the busy world of man and the world of spirits ; and I am persuaded that the charm of some of our old graveyards is intimately connected with this sentiment.

In a garden we look for beauty ; and we are satisfied if our eyes are affected with the voluptuous sensations that spring from brilliant forms and colors. In a grave-yard, on the contrary, we wish to give ourselves up to tender sentiments and emotions, which are more sensibly awakened by the simple wild flowers. The blue violet and the little golden-eyed cinquefoil carry back the memory to times of companionship with the dear friends whom we have buried, and carry forward our hopes to a probable re-union with them in a happier land. The showy flowers, that are cultivated in the borders of some of our cemeteries, do not harmonize with the solemnity of the grave, nor offer any solace to a wounded heart. Did we look upon a cemetery as a mere flower garden, we should pause with delight to contemplate the brilliant forms and colors that greet the sight. But amid the scenes of a graveyard, we are affected by these displays as we should be affected by gaudy pictures of butterflies on a magnificent Doric pillar of marble.

These remarks are not designed to condemn flowers as the ornaments of the grave, but to discourage their pro-fusion, and to recommend the spontaneous wildings of nature, rather than the careful products of art and culti-vation. Wild flowers are more poetical than those of the florist, which always suggest the idea of art, and of something that is to be bought and sold. Thus a wild rose would be more pleasing than a garden rose, as an ornament of a grave, because the former is a literal pro-duction of nature, while the latter is associated with the wreaths and bouquets of a confectionary store. Let the cultivators of the grounds, therefore, be advised care-fully to preserve all the simple and beautiful wild flowers, and those conditions of the soil which are promotive of their growth, that nature may not be thwarted in her spontaneous efforts to cover the grave with beauty, as she covers the pasture and the solitary haunts of the birds.

This principle in our nature that causes the effect which is produced by a single object to be lost when a multitude of similar objects are presented to the mind, is illustrated in the works of the painters as well as in the works of nature. In the delineations of life there must be a confinement of the design to one or two individuals. Crowd together in the picture of a cottage a large number of poor people who are so interesting in a single group, and the scene is not affecting. We can easily identify ourselves with a single family, and easily go along with them in their pleasures, their wants, and their sorrows. But we cannot sympathize with a crowd; we cannot follow a multitude in their journey of life; and if we try to do so, we soon turn away with a sense of confusion. The same may be said of historic details. When we read an account of the massacre of St. Bartholomews, when thousands were murdered at once, we are struck with a confused and awful sensation of horror; but our sympathies by this description are not powerfully excited. Indeed, I doubt if a general history of all the sufferings of the Polish exiles in Siberia would awaken our sympathy so powerfully, as the simple narrative of Prascovia, the daughter of the exiled Loupuloff.

This principle, which is so carefully regarded by the painter and by the writer of romance, should not be overlooked, when we are designing the objects of a cemetery. The delightful, though melancholy sentiments, which are associated with a few simple flowers, from the garden or the field, blooming upon the grave of a friend, could never be produced by a dazzling array of them in crowded profusion. The same remarks will apply to monumental sculpture. A plain headstone, with a single affecting device, may draw tears from hundreds, who would be entirely unaffected by the same device if it was accompanied by several other interesting objects, and might look upon the whole assemblage with indifference. Let not the poetic influence which has always been justly attributed to flowers, or which is attributable to a single sculptured image or device, be destroyed by their excessive multiplication. If we cultivate the cemetery as a gorgeous parterre, or as a puppet show, it must fail to cherish them delightful sentiments which are so needful to the comfort of the mourner, and so grateful to all who come to the grave to meditate.

BURIAL AT MOUNT AUBURN OF A CHILD OF THE REV. MR. WATERSTON.

By Mrs. Sigourney.

Rest in Mount Auburn's sacred arms,
   Oh ! early called to lay
The blossom of this mortal life
   Down in unconscious clay.

Sleep 'mid its flowers, thou cherished form,
   For Summer's hand hath shed
Her glowing charms profusely forth
   To deck the dreamless bed.

And what so fitting for thy couch,
   Which Love had ever drest,
As yon unfolding buds that hide
   The dew-drops in their breast.

But for the spirit, pure and sweet,
  Earth yields no symbol fair,
The fulness of that bliss to show
  Which it hath risen to share.

And ye, who night and day deplore
  With keen, paternal pang,
The silence of that home that erst
  With infant gladness rang;

Press to your wounds, like healing balm,
  The faith that conquers pain, —
Sees the child-angel in the skies,
  And feels how great its gain.

Nº 2325
T.J. LELAND.

THE LELAND TOMB.

This is situated opposite the Gate, and below the eminence on which
the Chapel stands. It has a granite front, surmounted with an urn.
The whole is simple, durable, sensible, and without ostentation.

6

ANCIENT INTERMENTS IN GREAT BRITAIN.

FROM PENNANT'S TOUR IN WALES.

SEPULCHRAL tumuli are very frequent in the village of Llanarmon. I was present at the opening of one, composed of loose stones and earth, covered with a layer of soil about two feet thick; and over that a coat of verdant turf. In the course of our search were discovered, towards the middle of the tumulus, several urns made of sun-burnt clay, of a reddish color on the outside, black within, being stained with the ashes they contained. Each was placed with the mouth downwards, on a flat stone; above each was another, to preserve them from being broken by the weight above. Mixed with the loose stones were numerous fragments of bones. These had escaped the effects of the fire of the funeral pile, and were deposited about the urns, which contained the residuum of the corps, that had been reduced to pure ashes. This custom appears to have been of very high antiquity; it was in use with the most polished nations, — with the Greeks and the Romans, as well as with the most barbarous. The ancient Germans practised· this rite, as appears from Tacitus. The Druids observed the same, with the wild addition of whatsoever was in use in this life, under the notion that they would be wanted by the deceased in the world below; and in confirmation of this, arms and many singular things of unknown use, are to this day discovered beneath the place of ancient sepulture. The remote Sarmatae, and all the Scandinavian nations, agreed in burning the dead; and the Danes distinguished by this, and the different ceremonies, three several epochs: —

The first, which was the same with that in question, was called Roisold and Brendetiide, or the age of burning.

The second was styled Hoigald, and Hoielse-tiide, or the age of tumuli, or hillocks. The corpse at this time was placed entire, with all the ornaments which graced it during life. The bracelets, and arms, and even the horse of the departed hero, were placed beneath the heap. Money, and all the rich property of the deceased used to be buried with him, from the persuasion that the soul was immortal, and would stand in need of these things in the other life. Such was the notion both of the Gauls and of the northern nations. Among the last, when piracy was esteemed honorable, these illustrious robbers directed that all their rich plunder should be deposited with their remains, in order to stimulate their offspring to support themselves, and the glory of their name by deeds of arms. Hence it is that we hear of the vast riches discovered in sepulchres, and of the frequent violations of the remains of the dead, in expectation of treasures, even for centuries after the custom had ceased.

The third age was called Christendons-old, when the introduction of Christianity put a stop to the former customs; for " Christians," as the learned physician of Norwich observes, " abhorred this species of obsequies; and though they stickt not to give their bodies to be burned when alive, detested that mode after death; affecting rather depositure than absumption, and properly submitted to the sentence of God, to return not unto ashes, but unto dust again."

From the remarks of these able writers we may learn the time of the abolition of the custom of burning among the several nations; for it ceased with Paganism. It therefore fell first into disuse with the Britons; for it was for some time retained by the Saxons, after their conquest of this kingdom; but was left off on their receiving the light of the Gospel. The Danes retained the custom of urn-burial the last of any; for of all the northern nations who had any footing in these kingdoms, they were the latest who embraced the doctrines of Christianity.

I cannot establish a criterion by which a judgment may be made of the people to whom the different species of urns and tumuli belonged, — whether they are British, Roman, Saxon, or Danish.

Some of the tumuli consist of heaps of naked stones, such as those in the Isle of Arran, in many parts of Scotland, and in some parts of Cornwall. Others are composed, like this of Llanarmon, with stones and earth, richly covered with earth and sod. Of these, the last is, in certain places, level with the ground; in others, surrounded with a trench; they were sometimes found of earth only. Others were of a conoid form, and some oblong; of which there is an example in the neighborhood of Bryn y pys, called the Giant's Grave. Finally, other places of ancient sepulture consisted only of a flat area, encompassed, like the Druidical circles, with upright stones; and such were those of Ulbo, and of King Harold, in Sweden.

The urns are also found placed in different manners; with the mouth resting downwards on a flat stone, secured by another above; or with the mouth upwards, guarded in a like manner.

Very frequently the urns are discovered lodged in a square cell composed of flags. Sometimes more than one of these cells are found beneath a cairn or tumulus. I have met with, near Dapplin, in Perthshire, not fewer than seventeen, disposed in a circular form. When numbers are found together, the tumulus was either a family cemetery, or might have contained a number of heroes who perished with glory in the same cause; for such honors were paid only to the great and good.

The urns found in these cells are usually surrounded with the fragments of bones that had resisted the fire; for the friends of the deceased were particularly careful to collect every particle, which they place, with the remains of the charcoal, about the urns, thinking the neglect the utmost impiety. We have no certainty of the ceremonies used by the ancient Britons on these mournful occasions; but from many circumstances which we continually discover in our tumuli, there appear many analagous to those used in ancient Greece and Rome.

The Greeks first quenched the funeral pile with wine, and the companions or relations of the departed performed the rest. Such was the ceremony at the funeral of Patroclus.

> Where yet the embers glow,
> Wide o'er the pile the sable wine they throw,
> And deep subsides the ashy heap below.
> Next the white bones his sad companions place,
> With tears collected, in the golden vase;
> The sacred relics to the tent they bore;
> The urn a veil of linen covered o'er; —
> That done, they bid the sepulchre aspire,
> And cast the deep foundations round the pyre;
> High in the midst they heap the swelling bed,
> Of rising earth, memorial of the dead. — POPE.

The duty of collecting the bones and ashes fell to the next of kin. Thus Tibullus pathetically entreats death to spare him in a foreign land, lest he should want the tenderest offices of his nearest relations: —

6*

Here, languishing beneath a foreign sky,
An unknown victim to disease, I lie ;
In pity, then, suspend thy lifted dart,
Thou tyrant, Death, nor pierce my throbbing heart ;
No mother near me her last debt to pay, —
Collect my bones, my ashes bear away ;
No sister o'er my funeral pile shall mourn,
Nor mix Assyrian incense in my urn ;
Nor Delia, thou, O thou, my soul's first care !
Shall, with thy dear, dishevelled locks, be there.

— R. W.

I beg leave to add the account given by Virgil of the funeral rites of Pallas. We find in it many ceremonies that were used by the northern nations. Animals of different species were burned or deposited with the body. The spoils of war, and weapons of various kinds, were placed on the pile ; the bones and ashes were placed together ; and a heap of earth or a tumulus flung over them. Some of each of these circumstances are continually discovered in our barrows. Horns, and other relics of quadrupeds, weapons of brass and of stone, — all placed under the very same sort of tombs as are described by Virgil and Homer. Perhaps the other ceremonies were not omitted ; but we have no record that will warrant us to assert that they were in all respects similar.

The Tuscan chief and Trojan prince command
To raise the funeral structures on the strand ;
Then to the piles, as ancient rites ordain,
Their friends convey the relics of the slain.
From the black flames the sullen vapors rise,
And smoke in curling volumes to the skies.

The foot thrice compass the high, blazing pyres ;
Thrice move the horse in circles round the fires.
Their tears, as loud they howl at every round,
Dim their bright arms, and trickle to the ground.
A peal of groans succeeds ; and heaven rebounds
To the mixed cries, and trumpets martial sounds.
Some in the flames the wheels and bridles throw,
The swords and helmets of the vanquished foe ;
Some the known shields their brethren bore in vain,
And unsuccessful javelins of the slain.
Now round the piles, the bellowing oxen bled,
And bristly swine ; in honor of the dead,
The fields they drove, the fleecy flocks they slew,
And on the greedy flames the victims threw.

PITT.

Since I am engaged in this funebrial subject, it will
be fit to observe, that a discovery of an entire skeleton,
placed between flags of a proportionable size, was made
near this place. This, as well as others similar in different parts of our islands, evinces that the ancient inhabitants did not always commit their bodies to the fire ;
for, besides this instance, a skeleton thus enclosed was
found in one of the Orkneys, and others in the shire of
Murray ; and with one of the last was found an urn with
ashes, and several pieces of charcoal; which shows that
each practice was in use in the same age.

CURIOUS RITES OF DIFFERENT NATIONS.

Muscovian Funerals. — In Muscovy, when a man dies, his friends and relations immediately assemble, and seat themselves in a circle around the corpse, and ask the dead the following questions : — "Why have you died? Is it because your commercial affairs went badly? Or was it because you could not obtain the accomplishment of your desires? Was your wife deficient in youth and beauty? Or has she been faithless to her obligations?" They then rise and quit the house. When they carry the body to be buried, it is covered, and conveyed on a bier to the brink of the intended grave; the covering is then withdrawn, the priest reads some prayers, the company kiss the dead, and retire. These ceremonies finished, the priest places between the fingers of the dead man a piece of paper, signed by the patriarch confessor, purporting his having been a good Christian. This, they suppose, serves as a passport to the other world ; and from its certifying the goodness of the deceased, St. Peter, when he sees it, will open to him the gates of eternal life. The letter given, the corpse is removed, and placed in the grave, with the face towards the east.

Interesting Custom. — A custom that was once prevalent in Spain is deserving of notice. When any one dies, the relations, friends, and neighbors, carry to the survivors, at meal times, for three days, one or more plates of food, under the idea that the grief they feel will not allow them to think on nutriment. Some persons also accompany these dishes, in order to offer consolation to the family.

"In Louisiana, there is a custom," says an anonymous female writer, "which I believe is peculiar to the place — that of bearing a young bride to the grave in her wedding attire; and there is something in such a rite which must deeply affect the most heartless. Some months since I stood by the bier of a young bride. She had been lovely in life, and there was a sculpture-like beauty in the marble face before me, — a solemn loveliness in the rigid countenance, — which spoke more forcibly to my heart, than it could have done when animated by the changing expressions of life, for it told of a far, far land. I had expected to see her arrayed in the simple robe with which we dress the dead, and to feel alone in the presence of the mighty conqueror who sways his sceptre over all.

"I was ushered into a large gloomy room; long wax candles shed a flickering light through the apartment, and the deep and smothered sobs of the mourners were all that broke its silence. I went with others to look upon the dead, and I shall never forget my surprise, or the strange and singular emotions which that view excited. Stretched upon her bier lay the young bride, who a little while before had been animated with life and joy. The rich and costly robe which she had worn upon her wedding day, enveloped her figure, and her pale hands, with their glittering jewels, were clasped upon her breast; while the orange blossoms shone among her dark locks, and the veil, with its gaudy folds, fell beside her. It was a lovely, yet a mournful sight, to see her arrayed in the habiliments of joy, and lying in her still, calm beauty, in the embrace of death — the bride of the grave. The gloom and silence of the room, the rigid features of the dead, the low solemn chant of the priest, and the noiseless ceremonies of the Catholic burial ser-

vice, when contrasted with the severe simplicity of the
Protestant service, produced an effect which it is impossible to forget.

"A young child is always carried to the grave in the
robe in which it was christened; and fresh white flowers
are strewn upon its coffin. What can be more appropriate or more beautiful? It lies down in its innocence
and beauty, like a young flower broken by some rude
wind; and our grief for its loss is tempered by the
thought that it has escaped the snares and toils to which
humanity is subject; that its young spirit has flown back,
unsullied by sin, to the Being from whom it emanated.
It is to the French part of the population that these customs belong; and in these and many others, they remain
distinct from the Americans."

VIEW FROM CONSECRATION DELL.

VIEW FROM CONSECRATION DELL.

In front is a view of the Pond, and of a marble sarcophagus, inscribed, MARTHA COFFIN DERBY. 1832.

In the middle and on the left we see four marble tombstones, the first a sarcophagus over the remains of

ABEL KENDALL,

In the other group is the monument erected to the memory of FRANCIS STANTON, by his friends and associates.

ON THE PRINCIPLES OF ART AS APPLIED TO RURAL CEMETERIES.

It is not many years since our modern rural cemeteries were established. An innate sense of the superior influence of the burial place of the dead, when allied with the beauty of nature and art, first suggested the plan of such grounds. There was also a necessity for burying the dead of our cities in the suburbs. This latter part of their original purpose has been fully accomplished. But there are some imperfections in the manner of carrying out the original design of our rural cemeteries, which are fair subjects of criticism and satire. In many important respects, relating to their moral and religious objects, they are failures. They exhibit too many sad attempts to carry the arbitary distinctions of social life down to the grave, where all the slumbering inhabitants should be united in one common brotherhood, remembered only for the virtues of their life.

These imperfections exist chiefly in the character of particular objects, rather than in the general style of laying out the grounds. It is doubtful whether the latter could be greatly improved. The general disposition of the paths and sites would produce an admirable effect, were the objects contained within the grounds designed with equal taste. The cause of this imperfection in the details, and of the superiority of the general plan, may be apparent, when we consider that the former are the works of different individuals, many of whom must be very defective in judgment, while the latter has been almost uniformly the work of one or two persons of taste and refined education.

It is a task, requiring, perhaps, one of the highest efforts of genius, to combine the works of nature and art, wherever there is a multiplicity of objects, in such a manner as to produce in the combination a harmonious and beautiful unity. There is no place where this exercise of judgment, on the part of the artist, is so necessary, as in a cemetery. Sculpture might be carried to perfection in these grounds, and be made to enhance the desired effect, if the artists would always govern themselves by certain general principles. An obelisk rising up in the centre of a grove of trees, is an object which no rules of taste would condemn. Build a highly ornamented fence around it, and you introduce a trifling formality, that injures the unity of expression, in the same manner as if you were to plant a border of box, or a circular hedgerow, about each of the trees. The most venerable ruins have always sprung from the finest styles of architecture. A chaste style of sculpture is necessary on the same principle, to produce that union of simplicity and grandeur, without which a rural cemetery becomes like a mere magnificent toy-shop.

In laying out a rural cemetery, two points deserve consideration : — first, the general design of the whole ; second, the particular design of individual objects. The general design is to impress the visitor with a profound religious sentiment, and a feeling of devout contemplation. This can only be promoted by causing the grounds to wear an expression of *solemnity* and *grandeur ;* and these may be said to constitute the two general effects which are to be studied.

The particular design of individual objects is to perpetuate the memory of the dead ; and this is promoted by constructing the monuments and their appurtenances in a beautiful, simple, and appropriate style. *Beauty, simplicity,* and *propriety* are, therefore, some of the particular effects which ought to be studied by the artist. In this essay we shall confine our attention chiefly to the general design.

Solemnity is a sentiment allied to that of sublimity, and is calculated to prepare the mind to receive impressions of a religious and moral nature. The architects of the magnificent cathedrals in the cities of Europe have exhibited this art to perfection, in the style of their edifices, especially of their interior, where every object serves to impress the mind of the visitor with a deep, religious solemnity. The necessity of inducing such a state of the mind, in order to increase its susceptibility to the influence of the divine services, must be evident to all. The eloquence of the preacher, unless his performance be so low as to displease by contrast, is thereby greatly heightened ; and the picturesque character of the interior of these churches, has undoubtedly preserved in many a mind its original attachment to the services of religion, after it had become skeptical in regard to its divine origin.

Even at the theatre this expression of solemnity is not overlooked in the management of the scenery, whenever it is desirable to prepare the minds of the audience to be deeply moved. But we may learn this lesson also from nature, who teaches it in her own wilds. The notes of birds attract comparatively but little attention, when they are singing amidst a multiplicity of sights and sounds, on the trees in our gardens and enclosures, in town. But when we are walking in a dark and majestic pine grove, where there is nothing to interrupt the silence except the murmurs of the wind among the branches, the notes of the solitary birds, that occasionally break the general stillness, possess a charm that is indescribable.

If we would heighten the religious influence of the objects in a cemetery, we must lay out the grounds and build the monuments and their appurtenances in such a style as to solemnize the feelings of the spectator on his immediate entrance. This solemnity of character pervading the place, prepares the mind to feel the emotion of sublimity, which is one of the most exalted of our religious sentiments. It is produced by the contemplation of eternity, and of the immensity of the universe. It is increased by all that is mysterious in the doctrines of religion, in the future condition of the soul, and the infinite attributes of the Deity. It is not the religious alone who are susceptible of such emotions, or who can appreciate the benign influence of such contemplations; for this susceptibility is an innate faculty of the human mind. Were all the accompaniments of a cemetery so designed as to harmonize with these feelings, every one must be aware of the superior impressiveness of its scenery, compared with its present influence. Neither would these circumstances serve to diminish any other effect we might wish to attain. Indeed, when the mind is thus elevated by solemn enthusiasm, it is peculiarly susceptible of all tender and virtuous sentiments; and while the soul is thus exalted to heaven, it feels a deeper and more tender interest in the state of the dead, and the welfare of the living.

Grandeur, which is the second general effect to be studied, is not identical with solemnity; but the latter is greatly promoted by the former, and the same objects are often equally productive of each of these sentiments. A grand style of architecture in the interior of a church adds greatly to its solemnity, and heightens the intensity of all our intellectual emotions. It cannot be denied that the feeling of cheerfulness is exalted almost to a degree of transport by an expression of grandeur and brilliancy, in a hall where a party is assembled, on a joyful or festive occasion The merry music of the dance, and the solemn harmony of the Christian service are equally enhanced by the majestic appearance of the hall in which they are performed. Anything that exalts the mind prepares it to feel more intensely any emotion which the scenes or performances may be designed to produce. There is no feeling or sentiment which it is desirable to cherish, that would not be heightened by a general expression of grandeur amid the scenes and objects of a rural cemetery.

The question next arises, by what means these two general effects may be promoted. They come equally from the style of laying out the grounds, and from that of the objects included within them. It is evident that the desired expression cannot be produced by tombs that are covered or surrounded by ridiculous or meretricious embellishments. But there are, unquestionably, certain decorations which serve the particular purpose of beautifying the monuments, without injuring the unity of the whole scene. Such are all those emblematic designs that are characterized by simplicity, which is not the same as barrenness, or monotony. Simple ornaments are such as do not counteract the effect intended to be produced by the principal object, either by exciting opposite sentiments, or creating confusion in the mind. An illustration of this principle may be drawn from music.

The accompaniments of a simple air are necessary to add force to its expression. If these are of such a character as to give the air a still greater prominence in the hearer's attention, they are compatible with simplicity. But if, while they produce no matter what pleasing effect, they drown the air, either by not harmoniznig with the theme, or by exciting in the mind a different emotion from that which should be awakened by the air, the accompaniments are in bad taste, and the opposite of simplicity. The ornaments around a grave should be emblematical or suggestive of some pleasing moral or religious truth ; but like true wit, they should be obvious and intelligible, and, like a correct style of architecture, free from those trifles that serve to divert the mind from the principal design.

Nothing so greatly interferes with an expression of grandeur as a multitude of small parts. It is on this account that a grove of trees has more majesty when divested of its undergrowth, than when thickly interwoven with shrubbery. In a cemetery, this multiplicity of small parts cannot be entirely avoided ; but it may be remedied, in a measure, by the exclusion of fences, flower beds, all excess of monumental stones, useless ornaments, and a superfluous amount of shrubbery. By avoiding this defect, we should promote both that unity and harmony which are so necessary to produce a deep influence on the mind. In order to secure all these important objects, the grounds ought to be under the supervision of a board of trustees, who should exclude everything that would derange the harmony of the grounds, by the introduction of a false ornament, like an accidental bathos, in a passage of pathetic or sublime eloquence.

7*

MOUNT AUBURN.

BY D. RICKETSON.

HERE I will rest, upon this hillside fair,
And muse upon the scenes within these grounds,
Where towering oaks keep out the mid-day glare,
From whose broad tops come forth sweet mellow sounds,
Like funeral chants o'er these sepulchral mounds.
I am alone, and I would wish it so ;
For with high interest the spot abounds,
And while my thoughts with solemn fervor glow,
I would a lesson learn, ere to the world I go.

It is the hush of Autumn's solemn tide ;
Far in the west the Sun his course hath spent ;
Across the heavens the wild clouds swiftly ride,
While scarce a ray to light my path is lent :
'T is true I come no lost friend to lament,
Yet I 've a tear to give to those who mourn ;
And even now my rising sighs are spent,
As towards yon grave with musing steps I turn,
Where virtue lies enshrined beneath the voiceless urn.

I love the spot, for bright in memory's page,
Comes up the day, when bidding books farewell,
With buoyant steps I came to hear the sage
Whose silver voice arose from yonder dell, *
While crowds sat breathless as his accents fell.

* Consecration Dell.

It was a lovely day, the morning sun
Walked in rich splendor up the ambient sky,
And when his western goal was nearly won,
Each haunt of this fair wood glowed with his brilliancy.

But ah, how changed ! this lovely spot then seemed
Like opening paradise to my young heart ;
And nature here in rich luxuriance teemed,
Where monuments now rise of vying art :
O ! why should pride in this still spot have part !
Rather let nature in her wildness live,
And o'er all scenes her living hues impart,
From whence the soul heaven's blessing may derive,
And feel its lagging powers again in life revive.

The evening shades are fast assembling round,
And to his airy seat each songster hies,
While all is hushed throughout this hallowed ground,
Save where from yonder mart low sounds arise,
That lull the ear like gentle melodies.
And now I bid these scenes a sad farewell,
Where many a noble breast in quiet lies :
Ere I again shall come, ah ! who can tell
How many a breathing form may seek its narrow cell.

THE MOUNTFORT TOMB.

This is a tomb in Willow Avenue, in which are deposited the remains of Col. John Mountfort and his parents, who were, in 1855, transferred from the ancient family tomb in Copps Hill Cemetery.

MOUNTFORE
Drury

RELIGION AND SCULPTURE.

FROM CHRONICLES OF THE TOMBS. — BY T. J. PETTIGREW.

IT cannot fail to have been observed, that a correct taste is generally found to be the accompaniment of true feelings of religious reverence. This is strongly exemplified in the earlier monumental records, in which the expressions of pious feelings are seen to unite most closely with the examples on the tombs of the most refined execution. The secret sympathy by which such an union is cemented it is easier to conceive than to express. If, however, we need illustration of this truth, survey our ancient cathedrals, the ecclesiastical edifices erected when the deepest religious feelings were entertained, and they will satisfy us on this. There is an architecture which we all feel to be peculiarly appropriate to purposes of a devotional character, and whenever this is departed from, a violence is done to the feelings, which all must be ready to admit, they have at one time or other experienced. A deviation from that which most men establish in their own minds as a standard in such matters, is felt at once to be either of a theatrical nature, or an entire departure from the solemn purpose to which the building has been erected.

There is a philosophy in this matter, and it is the philosophy of the heart. Similar feelings apply to the monuments themselves as to the buildings in which they are placed, and classical and heathen personifications and devices are felt at once to be occupying a position to which they are in no manner whatever entitled. The god of war or the deity of the waters are appropriately enough introduced into the monuments erected in honor of our military or naval heroes; but they are fitted for a

National Gallery, a Guildhall, or a Senate House, rather than the House of God. Nothing has ever struck me as exhibiting greater impropriety, or as being more incongruous, than the admission of the representation of heathen gods and goddesses into our funereal monumental shrines; it is utterly indefensible, it is destructive of all devotional feeling, and a defilement of the sanctuary.

There is much truth in the observations Dr. Wiseman makes on this subject in connection with the monuments contained in St. Paul's Cathedral. Alluding to the visitor of this sacred edifice, he says : — " There he sees emblems indeed in sufficient numbers, — not the cross, or the dove, or the olive branch,.as on the ancient tombs; but the drum and the trumpet, the boarding-pike and the cannon. Who are they whose attitudes and whose actions are deemed the fit ornaments for this religious temple? Men rushing forward with sword in hand, to animate their followers to the breach, or falling down, while boarding the enemy's deck : heroes if you please, benefactors to their country; but surely not the illustrators of religion." Again : " sea and river gods, with their oozy crowns and outpouring vases; the Ganges, with his fish and calabash; the Thames, with the genii of his confluent streams; and the Nile, with his idol, the Sphinx; Victory, winged and girt up as of old, placing earthly laurel on the brows of the falling; Fame, with his ancient trumpet, blasting forth their worldly merits; Clio, the offspring of Apollo, recording their history, and besides these, new creations of gods and goddesses, rebellion and fraud, valor and sensibility; Britannia, the very copy of his own unworshipped Rome, and some of those, too, with an unseemly lack of drapery, more becoming an ancient than a modern temple."

Repose must assuredly form the essential quality of all

strictly monumental sculpture. The solemnity of feeling and reverential awe, excited by viewing the depository of the dead, are disturbed by the association of figures implying action or the exercise of strong powers. The able writer before referred to, pertinently remarks, that " though so much money has of late years been lavished, especially on public monuments, no commensurate effect has been produced ; a devotional one was not intended, but none of any kind has been made ; we are not 'really interested by the gigantic memorials at St. Paul's ; they are large and grand, and many of them finely executed, but they do not affect us ; we *behold* them without *feeling* them ; as *monuments* they fail, even allowing that as works of art they succeed ; groups likewise cannot satisfy ; they will be looked at, just as the lions of Van Amburgh would be, were they grouped in marble ; but the inward eye will not follow, and to *it* the best shaped deities are but as shapeless sculpture." * There is great justice in these remarks, and they ought to operate in the guidance of the erection of funereal or monumental memorials.

Foremost among those who form exceptions to this incorrect and vitiated taste, should be mentioned that most excellent and accomplished artist, the late John Flaxman, R. A. His genius as a monumental sculptor, was first displayed in the monument erected in 1794, in Westminster Abbey, to the memory of the Earl of Mansfield ; it principally consists of two figures, those of wisdom and justice, whilst a youth is placed behind a pedestal, holding an inverted torch as personification of death. No other sculptor presents us equally correct ideas with regard to the true character of funereal monuments. No heathen gods and goddesses are exhibited upon any of his

---

* British Critic and Quaterly Theological Review, Vol. XXV. p. 140.

sepulchral works. Figures representing love, or pity, or affectionate sorrow, weeping over a sarcophagus — a figure rising from the grave, angels beckoning, &c., all in excellent keeping, harmonizing completely with the nature and design of the monument, and with the solemnity and purposes of the places in which it appears. Flaxman's works of this description are numerous, and an inspection of them never fails to excite feelings of awe and devotion.

All who have gazed upon the plain coped stone coffin, or those ornamented by a cross, sometimes of the most simple form, at others forming a species of ornamentation, but yet of a truly simple character, have felt much more touched than by the sight of a glaring monument, crowded with figures of various descriptions, and executed with accompanying details altogether in the most elaborate manner.

By the laws of Solon, no one was permitted to raise a sepulchral monument which should occupy ten men more than three days in its construction. The Council of Rouen, in 1581, issued a canon against too costly sepulchral monuments; and Philip II. of Spain, in 1565, directed that monuments should not be erected in churches; the memorials were to be confined to tombs, with a mourning cloth over them.

THE TWILIGHT BURIAL.

BY FLORENCE.

THERE are but few circumstances under which, to me, at least, the Catholic burial ceremonies and services can be deeply imposing. They are too numerous and com-plicated, and involuntarily attract the attention from the simple and stern realities of the scene, to themselves. Society alone makes us creatures of art and of habit, and it is only that which is natural and simple, which renders us again what heaven intended us to be, and awakens the feelings that are implanted in every heart, but which the world has so chilled that we almost learn to doubt their existence. Yet some great and important event that strikes upon the common mind, and calls into exercise general feeling, makes us deeply feel how far we have wandered from the path which nature intended we should tread, and awakens a momentary disgust for the world whose magic has so deceived us, which we deem at the time can never be dispelled.

The burial to which I allude, was one of those which to me offered an exception to the general rule; for there was something in the circumstances more than usually affecting. It was that of a lady whom I had seen but a week or two before, resplendent in youth and beauty; possessed of all the charms which wealth and a very enviable station in life could confer. She was hardly seventeen, yet the idol of many hearts, — a wife and a mother, who was devoted to the fulfilment of the duties of her station. It was now the loveliest, yet the most dangerous season of the year, the very last of September; and I could hardly believe that on the soft and balmy gale that swept by me, was borne the wing of death. But day after day, I had witnessed the slow and solemn processions, which bore the dead to the grave, and in the affecting language of Scripture, had " seen the mourners go about the streets." There was no prevailing epidemic, and the startling news that such and such a one was gone, came upon me with an effect which I could not overcome. Men do not always deceive others; they be-

guile themselves ; and self-deceit is the most dangerous
of all errors, for we can only be awakened from it by
some event which must overwhelm us in sorrow. It is so
natural for us to believe that, because an event which we
have long dreaded has never occurred, it is impossible,
that we learn to feel ourselves secure. It was so in this
case.

We see the aged die with sorrow, it is true, because we
cannot look upon the dissolution of humanity without
emotion, but with grief that is robbed of its bitterness.
They have looked upon changes and revolutions, — for
life, in its earliest, smoothest paths, is diversified with
many a shade ; and if even the young may weary of its
pursuits, may look forward with joy to the hour of release, — will not rest be sweet to those who have long
known the lingering agony of disappointment and of
grief? Great sorrows are not necessary to make us
tired of the world ; there are minds so constituted that
perpetual contrast must meet them in the society which
they learn most naturally to avoid ; and it is only those who
shun reflection that dread the grave ; for though we may
fear the uncertain path, which unassisted reason alone reveals to us, the hopes of revelation enable us to look
calmly upon the mysterious future before us. But we
cannot always contemplate with all these feelings the
death of the young and the happy. If we mourn not for
them, we sorrow for those whom their loss will render
desolate ; we grieve for those who will listen in vain for
the tones once so dear to them, who will sit in loneliness
by their vacant places, full of the memories of the past,
and the imagined bitterness of the future.

It was not usual for a burial to be deferred to so late
an hour as this ; but the service for the dead had just been
read in the only church in Natchitoches, for another, and

as soon as its ceremonies were finished, the young Emeline
was borne to its altar. I have witnessed the poetry of
action, which has seemed to me peculiar to this climate,
when contrasted with the rigidity and stiffness of ours.
It is a natural, spontaneous expression of feelings, which
are, I think, too often repressed by those who learn to
think all kinds of enthusiasm ridiculous. Had I known
nothing of the history of her who was so early lost, I
could have read it in the arrangement of all about me.
A large table, upon which the coffin was laid, was in the
middle of the room I entered ; it was covered with white
linen ; the windows, the walls, the tables, were hung with
the same drapery, tied with bows of white crape ; and the
bridal attire, with its long flowing veil, enveloped the
figure of the dead. To us who had known her in her
youthful loveliness, the scene was most thrilling ; to those
whom her loss had bereaved, how much more so must it
have been.

There is no hour so dreadful as that which removes
the dead from our homes. Before that, even though
they answer not our wild exclamations of grief ; though
they look not upon us with their eyes of love, — they are
with us : we seem to possess one tie which binds us together, and when that is severed we know the full bitterness of the cup we have tasted. We speak, but they do
not answer us, — we may not even look upon them, and
a consciousness of the impossible, the irreparable, comes
over us, and makes us long to rest beside them.

Oh, there is that in our grief for the dead which has no
similitude on earth. Joy and sorrow alike awaken it
afresh. Time may melt away its bitterness, but there
will always be hours when it will sweep over the heart
with a power which we cannot resist. If happiness is
ours, how natural to think of those who would have par-

ticipated it with us; — if grief overwhelm us, of those whose sympathy would have softened its woe. The death of those we love throws, even in the buoyancy of child-hood, a cloud over our lives, which never departs, it takes from the picture before us a sunny hue which it never regains.

Long after we had joined the procession which bore the loved and lost to the altar of death, did the wild ex-clamations of the bereaved husband reach our ears, and pity for the anguish which nothing on earth could ever dispel, melted us to tears. The sun had gone down, and the lingering rays of the twilight, which in this climate is so beautiful, yet evanescent, were losing their bright-ness in the deepening shadows of the evening, when we entered the church. A blaze of light from the numerous candles burning upon the altar, lighted up its recesses with their flickering beams, and the pale rays which emanated from the large silver cross borne by the priests before them, with the solemn musical chant they uttered, produced upon me, who had never witnessed anything of the kind, an effect which it is impossible to describe. It was a mixture of awe, of curiosity, and of the sublimity which is always awakened, when in the neighborhood of death. The services, like all those of the Catholic church, were in Latin, and incomprehensible to me ; but they were long, and gave ample time for those reflections which are always excited by such a scene. Every spectator is pre-sented with a long wax candle, lit from the altar, which they bear to the grave.

The pale stars were gleaming from the sky when we left the church for the burial place. It was a long walk, through a wild and uncultivated place ; and two and two, with the gloomy hearse before us, and the long mantles of black crape waving in the balmy air, we wound along through the tangled woods. The light of innumerable candles, reflected from the green leaves, upon the faces of those who bore them, shed a light that seemed almost unearthly ; and the echo of the measured tones of the priests, which came from the woods, woke in the heart new and most singular emotions. We entered slowly through the gate which was opened for us, and followed the bearers to the grave which was to receive the corpse ; caught now and then in the wild vines that grew upon some old tomb, or stumbling over some leaning stone or new-made grave.

The place was at last reached — the coffin was covered —the prayer was said, and those who surrounded the grave threw upon it a handful of earth. What a sound ! I shall never forget it. Heavily it fell, hiding the loved and the beautiful from our sight ; and we turned and left her, whose heart had so recently throbbed with the full and unchecked emotions of life, to the loneliness and quiet of the grave. The evening, whose balmy breath floated around her, was not more lovely or more gentle than she. And thus they go from among us — they whom we learn to love. Ah ! how sad a thing is life, when we but form ties to have them broken ; weave bright visions but to fade ; love but to grieve. Yet at such an hour one would like to die, that the twilight dews, and the stars whose glory we have loved so well, might be first to shed their beams upon us.

How strange that that which is most beautiful should awaken us to sadness. The charm of music, the enthusiasm of poetic fancy, all that most elevates and ennobles our natures, strike a chord whose tones are too tremulous and indistinct to be defined, but which calls into existence feelings too deep for expression. It is like the glimmering and half faded remembrance of some dream which we

strive in vain to grasp. Such are the feelings awakened
in this delicious climate. The balmy breath of evening
floats around you ; the richest, purest azure bends over
you, and the odors of flowers, the songs of birds, are
borne on every zephyr. All is gaiety and pleasure ; yet
this is a place to wrap the soul in its dreams of futurity
as in a mantle, — to " weave passionate visions of love
and of death," — to make its home among its own wild
fancies and dreamy speculations. The perfect beauty of
nature elevates the heart ; and whatever elevates, whatever awakens the immortal nature which the world de-
bases, carries us into the illimitable future before us, —
lights again a spark of that fire which Heaven created
within us.

I have read somewhere a beautiful theory, which my
fancy, though not my reason, impels me to adopt. It is,
that the spirits of men are those of the angels who fell,
placed upon earth to expiate their offences, and win
their way back again to heaven, — that every infant who
finds here an existence is some seraph embodied. It is
a beautiful theory — who knows but it may be a correct
one? Then were these dreams which haunt us not the
creations of fancy, but half remembered visions of that
better land, to which our aspirations rise.

The " cypress and the myrtle " are the fit emblems of
this climate. They strip death here of many of the terrors
with which it is usually invested. Every plantation has
its burying-ground, and it is a custom to bury its owners
upon their own land. Thus their groves, their gardens
become their homes when they are dead ; and those who
remain show their reverence for them, by twining sweet
vines around their tombs, — by strewing their graves with
the glory of the summer flowers. There are many reasons
why this is a commendable custom. The most important

is that it engenders an attachment to home, to the place where they were born and educated, which nothing else can excite in so great a degree. The deepest, holiest feelings of humanity become involved in its possession, and it is sacred as the grave of their fathers, as well as the home of their infancy.

Upon the high road leading to a town not far from Natchitoches, may be seen a large and ancient oak, from whose trunk the bark has been stripped, and this simple inscription placed upon it : —

" HERE LIES THE REV. WILLIAM GAY, OF PHILADELPHIA."

It has been there for many years, and invests the place with a mournful interest which nothing can dispel. I knew nothing, and could learn nothing of the history of him who has so long slumbered there. Yet, stranger as I am, I could almost have wept upon his grave. Why he was buried thus, in the depths of these Southern forests, I know not. Perhaps he died, homeless and houseless, afar from the eyes that watched for him, and the hearts that loved him. His title proclaims his profession and his object, and it may be that he laid down his life, a willing and joyful sacrifice to the principles which sustained him. There is something more touching and simple, whoever he may be, in this natural monument to his memory, than the richest marble could excite, and many an eye will be moistened with emotion as it rests upon it.

The ancient Romans made the tombs of their illustrious dead even by their daily paths, that their glorious example might incite the living to virtuous designs. The Egyptians ever blended death with life. At their feasts, their bridals, the rigid features of the dead, crowned and girded with life's fading flowers, were beside them, and its fleeting joys became more precious from their contrast with

the silence of the tomb.   If they who worshipped before
the mystic veil of Isis, or hung with awe upon the shadowy
words of the priestess of the tripod and the dove ; if they
made death the companion of their daily paths, — should
not we, to whom the hopes of revelation are given, accus-
tom ourselves to this inevitable decree.   We are taught
from our early childhood to look with too shuddering a
sense of dread upon the grave, and in our efforts to shake
off its memory, we lose the healthful reflections that
should spring from its contemplation.   It is better even
to lose ourselves in vain speculations of what may be,
than to live in a constant forgetfulness of what is sure to
befall us.

THE LOWELL MONUMENT.

This monument is built of granite, and stands in Willow Avenue. The name of "Lowell" is carved in raised letters upon its front, and the monument was erected by the executors of the late John Lowell, Jr., to the memory of his wife, who died a few years after their marriage, and of his two daughters, his only children, who did not long survive their mother.

The Monument bears this inscription :—

ERECTED

BY ORDER OF

JOHN LOWELL, JR.,

IN MEMORY OF

HIS WIFE AND CHILDREN

AS A

TESTIMONIAL OF THEIR VIRTUES

AND OF

HIS AFFECTIONATE REMEMBRANCE.

MONUMENTAL SCULPTURE.

WHEN we are walking in a rural cemetery, it would be instructive to note the different emotions with which we contemplate the various objects that greet our sight. We view this monument without any feeling at all; the next may prompt us to say to ourselves "How much money has been lavished here! The builder must have been either a very rich or a very foolish man." We pass on to another, in which we behold an indescribable quality, that affects us with a sensation of the ludicrous, or with, perhaps, a feeling of indignation. There is something that savors of vanity in the style of it, something that suggests an idea of the sinister character of the proprietor for whom the artist designed it. We may be unable to point out the particular defects of the monument, or the decorations that produce our dislike; as in an ugly face we cannot always determine what are the features that render it disagreeable. The same emotions are probably felt by almost every intelligent person who views the monument. Yet this same monument may be greatly admired and celebrated, because it may be very costly, as a foolish book is sometimes admired because the author has made a fortune by the sale of it. There is only now and then an eccentric individual who would venture to utter his real opinion concerning the book or the monument. Others are either diffident of their own judgment, or are afraid to differ from what they suppose to be public opinion. All despise it, and all pretend to admire it. Thus is the whole community often governed by a delusion, and a bad taste appears to prevail, because no man dares to deviate from a certain standard which falsely represents public sentiment.

We next arrive at a monument that suddenly awakes all our sympathies, that causes us to feel an interest both in the history of the one who lies below, and in the mourner who erected the stone. We do not think of its artistical merits, nor of the wealth, nor the taste, nor of the character of the owner. We think only of the dead as a subject of regret, and of the mourners as objects of sympathy; or something in its appearance awakens a tender sentiment of melancholy, or fills the mind with a deep religious solemnity. All this is the effect of the style of the monument. It produces the effect which ought always to be studied, but one which is very difficult to be produced. Genius is required for such a design; that looks to the moral influence of the work upon the mind, and not to mere display of art.

Splendor neutralizes the influence of every scene that is intended to produce the sentiment of melancholy. Artificial decorations, even when consisting only of flowers, if not arranged with extraordinary skill, mar that simple beauty which is the most interesting in a grave, and rob it of its sacred influence. Yet there are serious and delightful emotions which are often excited by an appropriate and expressive monument. The stone that marks the resting-place of one who was beloved and innocent in life, becomes a symbol of all that is divine in our natures. From the same source comes the pleasure we feel from the perusal of an epitaph, ennumerating the virtues of some humble friend of humanity.

Our ancestors marked the places where their dead reposed by two slabs of dark colored slate, or of red sandstone, whose sombre hues they believed to be in harmony with the solemn character of the grounds. Some of their inscriptions were ludicrous attempts to be pathetic, and the emblems engraved upon their headstones, are often grotesque and revolting. The inscriptions on modern tomb-stones are generally more acceptable to present taste; but the slate and the sandstone used by our predecessors, seem to be better adapted to their purpose than the white marble used at the present day. The glitter of the white marble greatly injures the impressiveness of the scenes in a graveyard. Light colors are cheerful, and dark colors are gloomy. The two extremes should be avoided. Neither black nor white are appropriate, the former being too nearly associated with gloom, and the latter with gaiety. The intermediate shades between white and black — those neutral tints with which nature embellishes her own ruins — these are the most proper for a sepurchal monument.

When we enter a cemetery we desire to be impressed with cheerful but solemn thoughts. This is a feeling common to all, whatever may be their peculiar views of religion. The objects and decorations introduced into such a place, ought therefore to harmonize with the sentiments we are disposed to cherish. If the monuments are black, as the slate stones were formerly painted, and disfigured with frightful emblems of death and of our state hereafter, the mind is filled with aversion, and we turn from the scene, as we would turn from the mouldering relics that are resting beneath them. If, on the other hand, the monuments are all of white marble, and the grounds are decorated as we would decorate a scene of fashionable amusement, the place loses its solemnity, and we visit it with indifference.

The principles of taste are the same in all the arts and in all their applications, and they require that all ornaments should correspond with the purpose of the place for which they are intended. The cemetery should not therefore be decorated like a palace. The monuments should be simple, emblematical, and suggestive of our religious hopes; they should be expressive, not expensive; or, if expensive, their costliness should not be conspicuous. All ostentation of wealth is offensive, especially in a cemetery, where of all situations in the world it seems to be the most out of place. Even in a dwelling in the city, the beauty of art produces a better effect, if its costliness is concealed. There are many who think otherwise, and who labor to make their cheap houses wear the appearance of great cost. A little reasoning on the sources of our agreeable and disagreeable sensations would convince them of their error. The most delightful works of art are those which combine the highest degree of beauty with the greatest possible simplicity.

In designing the objects for a rural cemetery, it should be the aim of the artist to minister to those feelings which are in unison with the character of the grounds. A coxcombical preacher may gratify his own vanity in a higher degree, by exhibiting the elegance of his person and gesture; but he would serve the purposes of a rational ambition more effectually by studying to produce that effect on the minds of his hearers, which would increase their love of virtue and their reverence for the precepts of religion. If we were desirous merely to attract public attention to a monument, without regard to the sentiments, with which spectators would view it, an exhibition of costliness might serve our purpose. But it would not be regarded as a proof of our liberality, since it is notorious that the most selfish men are often the most extravagant in the sums they expend on a piece of ostentatious folly.

If the citizens of a certain place erect a monument over the grave of one who was a public benefactor, this simple fact produces more effect on the mind of the spectator than any thing else connected with it. We feel a reverence for the dead to whom it was erected, because we here see the evidence of his goodness and of his services to his fellow men. It is the record of this fact, and this testimony of his virtues, that produce the principal effect. It is not the style of the monument erected over his remains, that excites our reverence for his memory; yet the style of the monument may harmonize, or it may clash with this feeling. To produce the one effect and to avoid the other, should be the object of the designer, who ought to bear in mind that it is the evidence of the worth and of the virtues of the deceased, more than any other circumstance, that yields a charm to the spot and its accompaniments. If the monument exhibits a great lavishment of expense — the question arises whether the individual commemorated was so much greater than those who slumber around him? The effect of such extravagance is to lessen our respect for the dead by exciting invidious emotions. If the monument is mean and inelegant, the mind is diverted by thinking of the niggardliness of those who, while they joined to honor the deceased, should grudge the expense necessary to render it decent and appropriate. The style of it ought to be that of simple grandeur, betraying no desire to excite our admiration of the splendor of the edifice, but conveying the most affecting memorial of the deceased.

For a monument erected over the grave of a private person, designed merely as a tribute of affection, a different style is required. Some beautiful emblem should express our affection for the dead, and be the memorial of their life. A simple urn, with an appropriate inscription, would awaken more interest in the mind of the spectator than the proudest pile of marble. Nothing that is truly poetical would excite contempt, though it be the least expensive object in the grounds. A certain costliness in a monument erected to a public benefactor, which is very appropriate, would seem ridiculous and ostentatious in one erected by his own friends over the grave of a private citizen. This principle is too apt to be overlooked by designers. But as a cemetery is occupied chiefly by private tombs, the style of private monuments is the most important consideration.

The figures in most general use in monumental sculpture are the cross, the pedestal, the obelisk, the scroll, the urn, the broken column, the slab, the altar, and the tablet. A very common design is a pedestal with an urn placed upon it. The epitaph is usually engraved upon the sides of the pedestal, and not upon the urn. This is what we commonly see in those family pictures which are used as memorials of the dead. A weeping-willow hangs its branches over the monument, and the figure of a woman in the attitude of grief, is leaning on the opposite side.

In Pennant's Town in Wales, there is an account of a monument, erected in a Chapel in which " the figure of Hope reclines on an urn, and is attended with her usual emblem of an anchor. A serpent, with its tail in its mouth, expressive of eternity, includes the inscription on one side of the pedestal." The objectional part of this design is the serpent, with its tail in its mouth, an emblem which is rather ludicrous than impressive.

" The Churchyards in Switzerland (says Simond), are adorned in odd taste, with fantastic crosses on each grave, tricked out with small puppet figures of saints or angels, dangling loose in the wind, the wood curiously carved with devices, and the whole gaudily painted and gilded. Two leagues from Berne, we stopped to see a tomb of another sort — the celebrated monument of Maria Langhans. The lid of the tomb is represented as breaking asunder, at the sound of the trumpet of the day of judgment; and

a young and beautiful woman, pushing away the fragments with one hand, rises out with an infant on her
arm. There is a great deal of sweetness in her face, mixed
with a certain expression of surprise and yet of faith.
But the action is hardly simple enough for the chisel."

Every one must perceive the want of simplicity of this
design, in its representation of an allegory, which is an
extended emblem, or rather something emblematical of
incidents and events. Over a tomb we want a simple
emblem, for a device, not an allegory; a sentiment, for
an epitaph, not a sermon. The figure of the mother and
her child alone might be sufficiently simple; the broken
tomb encumbers the device with too much detail. The
idea would be suitable for a painting, but it is too com-
plicated for sculpture. Such representations do not suit
the taste of the more intelligent of the present age. The
more cultivated the people, the more do they study general effects in their designs, and the less do they admire
such conceits as those above described. The old world
is full of them. It remains for America to set the example of a new and a better taste, instead of blindly imita-
ting absurd designs, which ought to have become obsolete
with the superstitions and fallacies of the age that invented
them.

I believe it is usual among artists in Europe to make
a distinction between those stones which are designed to
memorialize persons of different trades and professions,
and of different sexes and ages. A stone erected over
the grave of a young girl should be made in a style that
should suggest the character of the deceased. It might
be, for example, a simple tablet, rather slender in its
proportions, containing an appropriate device. A matron
should be distinguished by a different stone. An obelisk
is thought to be most suitable for the grave of one who
was engaged in public affairs, and might be used to sig-

nify that the person who lies beneath was a statesman. A clergyman might be d'stinguished by a tablet surmounted with a scroll or a cross. A small pedestal is very appropriate for the grave of a young man who died under circumstances that caused his friends to erect a monument to his memory. The pedestal has an emblematic significance of the foundation of future greatness and usefulness which death has caused to be unfinished. But if one dies in the decline of life, a pillar should be added to the pedestal to signify that his days were finished.

I WENT TO GATHER FLOWERS.

Written for the illustration of a picture representing a young girl, with a basket of flowers at her side, seated near a grave and weeping.

I.

I went to gather flowers, a wreath to bind,
For my young sister's birth-day gift designed;
The birds were singing sweetly o'er my head,
And every knoll was some bright flow'ret's bed.
Lured by the scenes, I wandered far away,
And paused not till the first decline of day;
When, as I looked around to mark my pace,
I found myself within the burial-place;
But knew not thither that my steps were bent,
And stood like one on heavenly errand sent.

II.

I laid aside my flowers to muse awhile,
By sculptured rock and monumental pile.
Ere this, I had been often told of death,
The tears, the farewell, and the parting breath,

Yet knew but little of our last, long home,
Our transient life-time, or the world to come.
The tombs, the gravestones, and the frequent mounds, —
All scenes were strange within these lonely grounds;
They spoke of things I was too young to know,
Of living grief, and senseless sleep below.

III.

I had, as I was told, in infant years,
Another sister, and my earliest tears
Were poured when her young spirit fled away;
I knew not then she must forever stay;
But as I strolled to ponder and to read
The words inscribed by living hearts that bleed, —
I read my sister's name upon the tomb,
And felt at once the nature of her doom!
Here, since that hour, hath my dear sister slept! —
And then I sank upon her grave, and wept!

IV.

And is it here departed friends are laid ? — ·
Is this the final dwelling of the dead ?—
And does, indeed, my sister slumber here, —
That dim-remembered one to all so dear ?
Is this the home of those whom we deplore,—
The friends who leave us, and are seen no more ? —
Until these sacred objects met my eye,
Alas! I knew not what it is to die!
Yet here, indeed, my missing friends have slept! —
And with the bitter thought again I wept.

V.

My sister's death I still remembered well:
Yet why she ne'er returned I could not tell.

But here I learn the cause ; for there she lies,
And sees not these fair flowers, nor hears my sighs!
I'd wreathe her grave, but plants of beauty rare,
With seeming kindness, fondly cluster there.
Then, as I wiped away my blinding tears,
Upon her tomb a sculptured verse appears, —
Addressed, perhaps, to her who now repines :
Beneath my sister's name I read these lines : —

VI.

EPITAPH.

All ye that in these holy precincts tread,
And gather flowers that bloom above my head,
Pause ere you bear the living gems away,
And read the sacred lesson they convey.
Like you, these flowers with youth and beauty glow,
But perish soon, like her who lies below :
Thus all mankind are doomed alike to die,
And buried thus will for a season lie ;
But, as the flowers in spring awake and bloom,
We too shall rise immortal from the tomb !

VII.

I gathered up my flowers ; I roamed no more :
But learned a truth I scarcely knew before.
I learned the state of those we call the dead ;
And on my sister's tomb their hopes had read ;
Yet still sometimes I cannot cease to weep,
To think how drear the places where they sleep !
I dried my tears ; I could no longer roam ;
And to my sister bore the garland home :
But ne'er shall I forget those early hours,
When first I went abroad to gather flowers.

GARDNER BREWER'S MONUMENT.

This monument is situated opposite the south side of the Chapel, and is one of the most beautiful productions of art in Mount Auburn. It is in pointed style, and of fine white marble.

This monument bears the following inscription : -

GARDNER,

ONLY SON OF

GARDNER AND MARY BREWER,

DIED AUGUST 19, 1857. AGED 15 YEARS 8 MONTHS.

GARDNER BREWER.

ANCIENT FUNEREAL PRACTICES.

Selected and Compiled.

Notwithstanding the melancholy gloom which the ancients cast over all their ideas of death and the grave, both in their moral and poetical writings, they appear in reality to have endeavored as much as possible to lighten those impressions, and place at a distance those dark phantoms of the imagination. Accordingly, the deep and solemn sadness attending our burials; the black shades of yews and cypresses; the dreary charnel house and vaulted sepulchres; the terrific appendages of mouldering bones and winding sheets;

> "The knell, the shroud, the mattock, and the grave,
> The deep, damp vault, the darkness, and the worm,"

which, from custom, form so great a part of the horror we feel at the thoughts of death, were to them unknown. The corpse consumed by funereal fires, and the ashes enclosed in urns, and deposited in the earth, presented no offensive object or idea. Besides, to dissipate the sorrow of the living, or, perhaps, with a desire to gratify the spirit of the dead, wines were poured and flowers scattered over the grave. These offices were the grateful tributes of love and veneration. The manes of the deceased, still wandering about the place of interment, might, perhaps, partake of the libation and enjoy the odor; at least his memory would be honored, and his spirit delighted.

Whatever may have been the original purpose of these ceremonies, we find repeated allusions to them in the poets. Anacreon mentions the rose as being particularly grateful. The tomb of Achilles was adorned with the

amaranth, the flower of immortality. Electra complains
that her father's grave had never been decked with
myrtle boughs. Anacreon again beautifully alludes to
the same custom : —

> Why do we precious ointment shower?
> Nobler wines why do we pour?
> Beauteous flowers why do we shed
> Upon the monuments of the dead?
> Nothing they but dust can show,
> Or bones that hasten to be so.
> Crown me with roses while I live;
> Now your wines and ointments give.
> After death I nothing crave,
> Let me alive my pleasures have ; —
> All are stoics in the grave. — COWLEY.

We have an epigram by Leonidas, exactly to the same
purpose : —

> Seek not to glad these senseless stones,
>   With fragrant ointments, rosy wreaths;
> No warmth can reach my mouldering bones
>   From lustral fire, that vainly breathes.
> Now let me revel while I may, —
>   The wine that o'er my tomb is shed,
> Mixes with earth and turns to clay; —
>   No honors can delight the dead.

Hence we may infer that offerings of this nature were
made with a view of gratifying the deceased; and it
seems to have been a very prevailing notion among many
nations besides the Greeks, that men after death retain
the same passions and appetites that distinguished them
when living. In Lycophron, a mountain is placed be-

tween the tombs of two enemies, lest their manes may
be offended, at seeing the funeral honors paid to each
other.

We will offer the reader a few examples of the monumental inscriptions of the Greeks, among which may be
found some of the best and most affecting epigrams that
have come down to us. The following beautiful epigram
is by the poetess Erinne : —

I mark the spot where Delia's ashes lie ;
Whoe'er thou art that passes silent by
This simple column, graced by many a tear,
Call the fierce monarch of the shades severe.
These mystic ornaments too plainly show
The cruel fate of her who lies below.
With the same torch that Hymen gladly led
The timid virgin to her nuptial bed,
Her weeping husband lit the funeral pyre,
And saw the dreary flames of death aspire.
Thou, too, Oh, Hymen ! bad'st the jocund lay,
That hailed thy festive season, die away,
Changed for the sighs of love, and groans of deep dismay.

It is worth while to observe the allusion in this epigram
to another custom of the Greeks, who frequently adorned
the tomb with some symbols indicative of the peculiar
circumstances attending the death of the deceased.

The affecting incident of an unfortunate woman dying
in a foreign land, surrounded by strangers, is preserved
in the following lines of Tymæus, who has accompanied
it with the excellent consolation of philosophy. Philæria
was a native of Egypt, and died in Crete : —

Grieve not, Philæria, though condemned to die,
Far from thy parent land and native sky ;

Though strangers' hands must raise thy funeral pile,
Or lay thy ashes in a foreign isle, —
To all on death's last dreary journey bound,
The road is equal and alike the ground.

The following contains one of the most cheering grounds of consolation which religion allows us to indulge upon the death of friends : —

When those whom love and blood endear,
Lie cold upon the funeral bier,
How fruitless are our tears of woe, —
How vain the grief that bids them flow !
Those friends lamented are not dead,
But gone the path we all must tread ;
They only to that distant shore,
Where all must go — have sailed before ;
Shine but to-morrow's sun, and we —
Compelled by equal destiny —
To the same inn shall come, where they,
To welcome our arrival, stay.

The next epigram, which, in the original, is addressed to one Sabinus (author unknown), is affecting and beautiful : —

How often, Lycid, will I bathe with tears,
This little stone which our true love endears ;
But you, remembering what to me you owe,
Drink not of Lethe in the shades below.

This epigram is interesting in another light, as having probably suggested to Dr. Jortin an idea contained in one of the most beautiful Latin poems of this description, to be found in modern poetry, of which the following is a translation : —

O might the cruel death which ravished thee,
In youth's soft prime, my Pæta, call on me,
That I may leave this earth, this hated light,
To dwell with thee amidst the realms of night, —
I'll follow thee; Love, through obscurest hell,
Shall guide, and with his torch the shades dispel;
But oh, beware the touch of Lethe's wave, —
Remember him who hastens to thy grave.

The truth is, that in their thoughts and reflections on death, mankind have ever had in view some idea of a consciousness that remains and lingers round the " pleasing, anxious " solicitudes and scenes of life. They have ever imagined to themselves a spirit after death, that busied itself in protecting the fame and character of their lives, that was yet sensible to slights or honors paid to the grosser and earthy parts.

THE SEPULCHRES AT THEBES.

BUCKINGHAM.

THE sepulchres of Memphis were placed in splendid pyramids, wholly above ground, and built upon a rock; but at Thebes they are subterranean entirely. They are situated in a spot about a mile from the walls of the city, which is, from this appropriation, called the " Valley of Death." Passing up a narrow ravine, barren and desolate, in which not a blade of verdure is to be seen, the visitor beholds on the left hand the apertures that lead to the tombs. When I was there, there were twenty-four of them open; but since then, Belzoni has discovered twenty more. There may very probably be one hundred more yet to be developed by the researches of future travellers. Such of them as are accessible, resemble each other so closely in all respects, that a description of one may serve for the whole.

The excavations are carried through the solid rock, deep into the bowels of the mountain. Some of these rocks are of limestone, others a species of sandstone. The entrance of the sepulchre is an aperture of twenty by twelve or fifteen feet. This leads to a perforation or tunnel, the walls of which are made to incline inward for the sake of greater strength, and which extends in none of them less than one, and in some as much as two miles. At the termination of this tunnel we come to the Hall of Death. It is wider than the passage leading to it, and contains an altar and a sarcophagus. In some this latter is made of sienite granite ; in others of basalt ; in others of a species of green basalt; and in others again, the sarcophagus is of alabaster. Belzoni brought one of these away, and carried it to London.

These extensive perforations through solid rock must have cost an amazing amount of labor. Each of them is equal in size to the far-famed tunnel under the Thames, the cost of which was nearly three millions of dollars. Admitting that the multitudes employed in these excavations were slaves, and wrought without wages, still they must have been clothed and fed, so that the cost must have been very great. But the mere hewing and removal of the stone was but half the task. As the rock left a rough surface, the whole had to be covered over with stucco, an inch and a half or two inches in depth, like the composition called *chunam*, employed for artificial hearths or floors. On this substance were sculptured battles, triumphs, sacrifices, and all those representations, which form the usual subjects of the Egyptian chisel ; and when the carving was finished, the whole surface was painted, —so profuse of labor, time and cost, were those who executed these astonishing works !

The colors used for this purpose, after the lapse of twenty-five centuries, remain to this day as fresh and bright as if laid on but yesterday. This is a phenomenon which forcibly excites the wonder of all beholders. It is probably to be attributed to some singularity of the coloring matter employed. It was the opinion of Sir Humphrey Davy, that the colors must all have been vitrified, so as to give them the durability of glass or enamel; but he could not conceive what medium had been employed to unite and blend them.

While the walls are thus covered with painted sculpture, the ceiling is painted of a deep azure, and adorned with numerous representations of stars, these having their forms sunk somewhat below the surface of the ceiling around them, and covered with silver leaf. Thus as the astonished visitor is examining these chambers by torch light, he beholds above his head an artificial heaven, while on every side he is surrounded by tens of thousands of figures and devices of various forms, until he feels bewildered and overcome by the strangely impressive scene, and the thrill of mingled awe and wonder seizes every fibre, both of the body and mind. To get some idea of the multitudes of figures on the walls, I took the trouble to count those which occupied a space two feet wide and twenty feet in height, extending from the floor to the ceiling, and I found them to be two hundred and fifty-four. They all seemed to have a meaning; and no doubt many parts of them could have been read and interpreted by one who had the requisite skill ; so that probably the contents of ten thousand volumes may still

remain visibly recorded on the walls of these ancient
tombs, there to be preserved for the instruction of ages
and generations yet unborn.   There are fifty such chambers accessible at present, and the number increases as
investigation proceeds.   Who may conjecture the flood of
historical light which may yet be poured on the latter age
of the world, should the key to these mysterious representations ever be discovered?

CENTRAL SQUARE.

The ground called "Central Square" was originally reserved as a situation for some future public monument. Near this square stands the monument erected to the memory of Miss Hannah Adams, who was the first adult person buried in Mount Auburn. It was raised by her friends, and bears the following inscription:—

TO

Hannah Adams,

Historian of the Jews

AND

Reviewer of the Christian Sects,

THIS MONUMENT IS ERECTED

BY

HER FEMALE FRIENDS.

First Tenant

OF

Mount Auburn:

She died December 15, 1831.

AGED 76.

10 *

OLD GRAVEYARDS.

THERE are few places which we visit with more interest than those old burial grounds, so frequent in our early settlements, and in which the dust of our ancestors is laid. We observe in their appearance a charming simplicity, that attracts the attention of all visitors, enlists their sympathies with the dead, and excites a tender veneration for their memory. No exhibition of pride awakens envious feelings, or causes emotions which are not in harmony with the sacredness of the grounds. The mosses of age have softened the glitter of sculptured art, and given the sober tint of antiquity to the monuments, some of which have lost their upright position, and bend like humble penitents before the divine altar. Many of the works of the chisel, that might originally have emblemized the pride of the builder, have been chastened and subdued by the agency of time, and wear the look of the most humble designs. When we wander among these venerable scenes, we are impressed with all those tender and religious emotions, to which the burial place ought always to minister. We stroll among the most interesting of ruins, and while we look upon the old headstones, with their quaint emblems and devices, our reverence for the dead is exalted to a quiet enthusiasm, and all our thoughts are raised to heaven.

There is some danger that the custom of building showy monuments in our modern cemeteries may prevent our posterity from visiting them with the same feelings which we experience when contemplating those of our predecessors. The simplicity that pervades these old grounds is absent from the new, which are filled with exhibitions of living pride. Time, it is true, will cast a veil over the glitter of all this ambition, and cause the most showy objects to wear a more humble appearance. But the original and unaffected simplicity of our old graveyards must ever be wanting in those, in which the vanity of the living has sought gratification over the resting places of the dead.

Our ancestors entertained certain gloomy views of religion and of our state hereafter, which a more enlightened generation has set aside. Some of the emblems and inscriptions that appear on the headstones in their places of burial, are indicative of their peculiar faith, and do not accord with modern ideas of religion. But intermingled with these are others that point to a happy immortality; and the most of them afford evidence of such an entire resignation of all worldly views to their religious faith, that while we see nothing to admire in the monument or the inscription, we feel a profound respect for their piety and their devotion. The spirits of the dead are there represented, not merely as departing this life, but as embarking for another and a higher world. The angels, in emblematic devices, stand ready to receive their spirits, as of sisters and brothers, who are to be released from bondage and sorrow. Deeply moved by these objects, we never enter an old graveyard, without feeling a portion of the same enthusiasm that breathes from these affecting scenes.

There lie the venerable dead, in one common ground, not separated from one another by family boundaries, nor by the ostentatious marks of wealth and pride. They are united in one great family, whose most eminent members were content to lie down in the grave, without a marble demonstration of their worldly greatness, undistinguished except by the letters on the stone that marks the spot where their remains are buried. The verse that

follows their name and age commends them to their
Saviour, in whose faith they lived and died, and the engraving represents the flight of the immortal spirit to the
God who gave it. No superfluous ornaments bewilder
the mind of him who goes there to meditate, or to read
the brief history of their life and death. The wealth and
the poverty of the dead are not published over their
graves, where we behold a simple record of their virtues,
and a testimony of their faith and trust in the promises
of their religion. In all we see the works of a true
republican simplicity, of that singleness of purpose that
distinguished their lives, and of that humility in which
they resigned their souls to heaven.

The flowers, embosomed in the mosses which for many
years have been accumulating upon the soil, spring up
with a singular charm around these old graves. The
spade has not profaned their venerable mounds since the
earth was first thrown up to receive the mortal remains
that rest beneath them. But many a pious mourner has
bedewed them with tears, and watched with sad pleasure
the first violet of spring that appeared on the recent sods,
and the latest evening primrose that lingered upon them
in the melancholy days of autumn. And after the sorrowing had ceased, and the mourners likewise were
gathered unto the dust, the flowers still performed their
sacred office around the old forgotten graves, as if some
unseen spirit still watched over them and cherished the
neglected sod.

In proportion to the age of these grounds, and as time
has spread a velvet surface of mosses upon them, is their
apparent alliance with nature. The trees that bend over
the tombs have extended their roots into the dilapidated
mounds, and almost obliterated them ; and the old headstones, that lean from their original erect position, are

decorated with lichens of various colors, causing them to resemble the rocks in the solitary pastures. A profusion of wild shrubbery has diffused itself in irregular masses among the graves, and in some places, while the wild roses blossom upon the turf, the vine of the ·American ivy has wreathed itself luxuriantly about the monuments. The most humble shrubs are commonly the most interesting ornaments of these inclosures, because, like humble graves and humble cottages, they are more closely allied with poetry. When I witness these scenes, I am not affected with sadness. Though the living no longer mourn over the dead who lie there, Nature has received them into her own bosom, and with maternal fondness has wreathed the loveliest garlands of beauty around their graves.

In an ancient burial ground, it is pleasing to mark this providence of Nature; to note the tender care with which she clothes the baldness of the crumbling hillock with herbage and flowers, and the old monuments with plants that do not perish like the flowers, but live on, year after year, and symbolize, in their ever durable tints, that immortality which has become the portion of those who have left their mortal remains to the faithful trust of nature and of the tomb. The most reverential efforts of human hands could not have wreathed about their tombs so many objects that endear the spot to our affections. Vainly would the gardener's art attempt to rear in their places groups of more interesting plants, or hallow their graves by more affecting remembrancers.

There are no persons of ordinary education and refinement, who do not linger with rational delight in an old graveyard; and I have observed that they do so, not from a mere desire to read the quaint inscriptions upon the monuments, but evidently from a proneness to indulge

those feelings of reverence for their ancestors which the
scenes inspire. Men who have but little reflection or
sensibility, are by these objects converted for a time into
poets and philosophers. The skeptic cannot enter here,
without a temporary revival of those charming religious
influences that filled and inspired his youthful mind.
Above all, do persons of religious feeling and poetic imagination love to ponder among these scenes. Nature and
art and religion have united to form here a combination
of objects tending to humanize those who have forgotten
their love for their fellow-beings, and to raise the thoughts
of the virtuous still farther above the world.

Notwithstanding the venerable and interesting character of these old cemeteries, there is a disposition among
those who would sweep away everything with the besom
of "improvement," to remove them, to make room for
land speculations. Every old graveyard, though right
in the midst of a village, should be preserved, not to be
used for new graves, but set apart as hallowed ground.
The trees that stand there have formed a grove, which
ought to be as sacred as any that were in ancient days
consecrated to philosophy. Let them never be disturbed,
that the ground may be used for ordinary purposes. Let
them be cherished as memorials of the simple habits of
our ancestors, who, though often condemned for their
disregard for the ideal and the beautiful, never wandered
in search of the vanities that characterize the present
times. It is hardly probable that we shall escape the
satire of posterity, as our predecessors have escaped our
own. Though no living mourners are seen to weep in
these grounds, which have long ceased to be a place of
sorrow ; yet they who go there, while pondering among
the graves of their ancestors, may be persuaded to imitate
their unostentatious virtues, and learn that wisdom which
may be read in their humble biography.

The old headstone that marks the grave of an ancient patriot, has no less value in our sight than if it was a costly marble obelisk.　It is a venerable ruin as dear to a patriotic breast, as the proudest monument of our military glory.　Underneath that stone lies the dust of one whose intellect assisted in modelling our republic, and whose courage, undaunted by the threats of tyrants and the marshalling of inimical hosts, wrought our freedom and established our independence.　The name of many a hero, and patriot, and martyr, is recorded upon these leaning monuments.　Let us preserve them with religious care ; let nature overshadow them with trees, and let the wild-flowers of all seasons attract the young and the old thither for meditation, that, while lingering there, they may learn that wisdom which too many have forgotten, — the wisdom of a humble life, which is the only safeguard of virtue, and the only bulwark of liberty.

THE OLD BURYING-GROUND.

FROM "THE ATLANTIC MONTHLY."

Our vales are sweet with fern and rose,
　Our hills are maple crowned ;
But not from them our fathers chose
　The village burying-ground.

The dreariest spot in all the land
　To Death they set apart ;
With scanty grace from Nature's hand,
　And none from that of Art.

A winding wall of mossy stone,
    Frost-flung and broken, lines
A lonesome acre, thinly grown
    With grass and wandering vines.

Without the wall a birch-tree shows
    Its drooped and tasselled head ;
Within, a stag-horned sumach grows,
    Fern-leafed with spikes of red.

There sheep that graze the neighboring plain,
    Like white ghosts come and go ;
The farm-horse drags his fetlock chain, —
    The cow-bell tinkles slow.

Low moans the river from its bed,
    The distant pines reply ;
Like mourners shrinking from the dead,
    They stand apart and sigh.

Unshaded smites the summer sun,
    Unchecked the winter blast ;
The school-girl learns the place to shun,
    With glances backward cast.

For thus our fathers testified —
    That he might read who ran —
The emptiness of human pride,
    The nothingness of man.

They dared not plant the grave with flowers,
    Nor dress the funeral sod,
Where with a love as deep as ours,
    They left their dead with God.

The hard and thorny path they kept,
  From beauty turned aside;
Nor missed they over those who slept
  The grace to life denied;

Yet still the wilding flowers would blow,
  The golden leaves would fall, —
The seasons come, the seasons go,
  And God be good to all.

Above the graves the blackberry hung
  In bloom and green its wreath,
And hare-bells swung as if they rung
  The chimes of peace beneath.

The beauty Nature loves to share,
  The gifts she hath for all,
The common light, the common air,
  O'ercrept the graveyard's wall.

It knew the glow of eventide,
  The sunrise and the noon,
And glorified and sanctified,
  It slept beneath the moon.

With flowers or snowflakes for its sod,
  Around the seasons ran,
And evermore the love of God
  Rebuked the fear of man.

We dwell with fears on either hand,
  Within a daily strife,
And spectral problems waiting stand,
  Before the gates of life.

The doubts we vainly seek to solve,
　The truths we know are one;
The known and nameless stars revolve
　Around the Central Sun.

And if we reap as we have sown,
　And take the dole we deal,
The law of pain is love alone,
　The wounding is to heal.

Unharmed from change to change we glide,
　We fall as in our dreams;
The far-off terror at our side,
　A smiling angel seems.

Secure on God's all tender heart,
　Alike rest great and small;
Why fear to lose our little part,
　When he is pledged for all?

O fearful heart and troubled brain!
　Take hope and strength from this, —
That Nature never hints in vain,
　Nor prophesies amiss.

Her wild birds sing the same sweet stave,
　Her lights and airs are given,
Alike to play-ground and the grave, —
　And over both is Heaven.

TIMOTHY FULLER
FULLER
ELIZABETH
L. Prang & Co. Lith. Boston.

FULLER LOT.

The following and other Inscriptions are on the Monuments in the Fuller Lot, in Pyrola Path : —

IN MEMORY OF MARGARET FULLER OSSOLI, BORN IN CAMBRIDGE, MASSACHUSETTS, MAY 23, 1810.

" By birth a child of New England, by adoption a citizen of Rome, by genius belonging to the world. In youth an insatiate student, seeking the highest culture. In riper years Teacher, Writer, Critic of Literature and Art. In maturer age, companion and helper of many earnest reformers in America and Europe.

" And of her husband, Giovanni Angelo, Marquis Ossoli ; he gave up rank, station, and home, for the Roman Republic, and for his wife and child.

" And of that child, Angelo Phillip Ossoli, born in Rieti, Italy, Sept. 5th, 1848, whose dust reposes at the foot of this stone. They passed from this life together by shipwreck, July 19, 1850. United in life by mutual love, labors and trials, the Merciful Father took them together, ' and in death they were not divided.' "

ENGLISH CEMETERIES.

ABRIDGED FROM "GOD'S ACRE." BY MRS. STONE.

> "EARTH to earth and dust to dust!"
>   Here the evil and the just,
>   Here the youthful and the old,
>   Here the fearful and the bold,
>   Here the matron and the maid,
>   In one silent bed are laid:
>   Here the vassal and the king,
>   Side by side, lie withering;
>   Here the sword and sceptre rust —
> "Earth to earth and dust to dust."

It may be a fancy, but surely it is akin both to nature and reason, that the environs of the places solemnly dedicated ages ago to God's worship, hallowed by the prayers of succeeding generations for centuries past, where the air is redolent with the breath of prayer offered up by pious Christians now sleeping the sleep of the righteous below; where, perchance, we ourselves were admitted into the Holy Communion of Christ's flock, and where we have seen probably some of those nearest and dearest to us laid in their last narrow house; where, it may be, their spirits are still hovering around; surely, it is most natural, most reasonable, most pious, that there we should wish to repose too.

For it is difficult to understand the feelings of indifference with which some, sincerely good people too, declaim on the worthlessness of the body, and their carelessness of what becomes of it. "What matters," say they, "this old vile garment, these rags?" Oh, much, very much. For are we not told it shall rise again? This contempt- uous indifference is very far removed from a Christian repudiation of pomp and finery. Persons who are indifferent as to the usage of their mortal remains, contemptuous as to its present destination, or callous as to its surgical dismemberment, must quite forget St. Paul's sublime exposition of the doctrine of the resur- rection of the body. Such indifference is at least more philosophical than natural or religious.

For they are not dead. No, oh, no. We are sure of that. The calm, silent, lifeless frame on which we look, shall surely rise again, " clothed and in his right mind." Clothed with immortality, robed in inexpres- sible beauty, fraught with an angel's mind. Yes, this body, — waiting, sleeping, changed, — this human chry- salis shall waken, and soar on radiant wing to that empyreum, whence its immortal spirit first emanated.

Far more consonant with the best feelings of our nature is the impulse which causes parents to lay their lost children in one grave; or children to implore to be interred with their departed parents; or the unfor- getting widow to pray that she may be carried to the grave of her husband, buried fifty years before, and far away from the spot where destiny had fixed her in later life. The observation of Edmund Burke, on his first visit to Westminster Abbey, has been recorded: —

" I would rather sleep in the southern corner of a country churchyard, than in the tomb of the Capulets. I should like, however, that my dust should mingle with kindred dust; the good old expression 'family burying- ground' has something pleasing in it, at least to me."

When, in early times, it was forbidden to inter two bodies in one grave, exception was always made in the

11*

case of husband and wife, — the most touching and reverent acknowledgment of the sanctity of the marriage tie that it is possible to conceive.

We have Scripture testimony to show that this solicitude about a burying place is not only natural, but pious and holy. On the death of the patriarch Jacob, his most dearly loved son Joseph thus spoke to Pharaoh: —

"My father made me swear, saying, — Lo, I die. In my grave, which I have digged for me in the land of Canaan, there shalt thou bury me. Now, therefore, let me go up, I pray thee, and bury my father, and I will come again.

"And Pharaoh said, — Go up, and bury thy father, according as he made thee swear.

"And Joseph went up to bury his father, and with him went all the servants of Pharaoh, the elders of his house, and all the elders of the land of Egypt."

The foregoing remarks were in part suggested by a visit which I made to one of the most favorite and fashionable of English cemeteries. I was not previously acquainted with the neighborhood; but I soon ascertained my near approach to the spot, by the number of stone-mason's yards which I passed, decked with urns, tablets, and other funereal sculptures.

I entered the cemetery: a more beautiful and luxurious garden it is impossible to conceive. The season was autumn, and every path was radiant with dahlias, fuschias, verbenas, heliotropes, salvias, lobelias, geraniums, monthly roses, and a multitude of other flowers, in the richest bloom. Such fine African and French marigolds I never saw, *though I thought them in very bad taste there*. In some country churchyards, where the custom of planting flowers is most rife, no kinds are thought of that are not *sweet-scented*. Merely beautiful looking flowers are never admitted, though it is said these are sometimes planted by stealth, as a sort of satire, on the grave of an unpopular person!

But on the graves of beloved ones, the homely, sweet-scented rosemary, emblem of remembrance, the aconite, the snowdrop, the violet, and lily of the valley; and the rose — ever the rose — type always of purity, affection, goodness; these are suitable to churchyard or cemetery.

These, and the humble, unshowy, fragrant mignionette, had been in far better taste than the flaunting flowers to which I have referred. The beautiful laurustinus, flowering as it does (in England) the winter through, and the arbutus, with its gorgeous fruit, gleamed at frequent intervals, forming a beautiful relief to the gloomy cypress and dismal yew. It is no unusual mistake in churchyards, as well as in modern cemeteries, to plant these latter shrubs so thickly — at the head and foot, for instance, of graves placed closely together — that they cannot possibly have room to grow; and the effect of regular regimental rows of evergreens, dwarfed and crippled like stunted shrubs, is rather ludicrous, than solemn or touching.

I had not proceeded far ere I came to a placard within the grounds, noting that —

"——— the Company undertake to turf and plant graves, and to maintain and keep them in order, on the following terms: —

Per annum, . . . £———

In perpetuity, . . . £———."

It is a pity all the "proprietors of graves" are not acquainted with, or are not inclined to avail themselves of this notification. Some of the graves are in a sad and disreputable state of disorder. The clematis, planted by friends under the first impulse of grief, is trailing disorderly, far and wide beyond its proper bounds, and the branches of cypress unnurtured, unpruned, forgotten, are sere, brown, and unsightly; and rank weeds and trailing, neglected shrubs, deface the very memorials graven on the tombs.

In a plain churchyard, however neglected, decay does not strike such a feeling of desolation to the heart. The long, rank grass, uncared for and unpruned, is unsightly enough; but it does not convey to the mind the idea of the *forgetfulness* of the living which is raised by the sight of a grave, once trim, and surrounded with costly exotic flowers, now carelessly suffered to dwindle and decay.

In many parts of France, but more especially in the southern counties, specific monuments have been built, in order to preserve that remembrance of the dead, which is one of the highest and purest attributes of our humanity. These are the LANTERNES DES MORTS; erections, the chief purpose of which is to throw light on the cemeteries during the hours of night and darkness.

In the twelfth and thirteenth centuries, sepulchral chapels, or else hollow columns, were often erected in the middle of cemeteries, bearing on the summits lamps or lanterns, which, by night, cast their rays on all surrounding tombs. The chapels vary much in size and style, — some being highly elaborate and very ornamental, and having bases, with open pillars around, in which the deceased might be exposed to view, laid in state, or cared for as necessity might require before his interment; or here might be celebrated the office for the dead, and other usages, of which the memory is lost. They had, for the most part, the circular form, which was that of the Holy Sepulchre at Jerusalem.

The *Colonnes Creuses*, which, much less costly, elaborate, and ornamental, still served the same purpose of throwing light on the tombs around, were merely hollow columns, sometimes ascended by a spiral inner staircase, and having a lantern at the top — a sort of homage rendered to the memory of the dead — a signal reminding the passers-by of their presence, and inviting to prayer.

They are more especially met with in the cemeteries touching on much frequented roads, being erected to preserve the living from the fear of ghosts and the spirits of darkness, with whom the imagination of our ancestors peopled the places of burial during the night, and who were suffered always to be scared away by light ; and they were especially to remind the living to pray for the dead.

My pilgrimage to the cemetery I have above referred to had an especial object. I wanted a particular tomb, the grave of one whose memory I honored. Unable myself to find it, I was compelled to apply to one of the persons employed on the ground, and he conducted me to it at once. How pleased was I to find a plain tombstone, perfectly clean and neat, in a remote, secluded corner, with no flaunting exotics or emblazoned trophies to attract the eye of the careless lounger, but environed only by the verdant, green turf, which Nature herself cherishes.

It was on the occasion of the interment at this grave that the touching incident really occurred, which a poet's fancy had created long ago. Southey, in his " Joan of Arc," writes many a long year ago : —

> I remember as the bier
> Went to the grave, a lark sprung up aloft,

> And soared amid the sunshine, carolling,
> So full of joy, that to the mourner's ear,
> More mournfully than dirge or passing bell,
> His joyful carol came ; —

but, at the funeral to which I allude, this incident did occur, and was thus recorded by the friend and clergyman, by whom the solemn service was read, —

> Over that solemn pageant, mute and dark
>   Where in the grave we laid to rest,
>   Heaven's latest, not least welcome guest,
> What didst thou on the wing, thou jocund lark,
>   Hovering in unrebuked glee,
> And carolling above that mournful company ?
>
> Oh thou light-living and melodious bird !
>   At every sad and solemn fall
>   Of mine own voice, each interval
> In thy soul-elevating prayer, I heard
>   Thy quivering descant, full and clear —
> Discord not inharmonious to the ear !
>
> We laid her there, the minstrel's darling child ;
>   Seemed it then meet, that borne away
>   From the close city's dubious day,
> Her dirge should be thy native wood-note. wild ;
>   Nursed upon nature's lap, her sleep
> Should be where birds may sing and dewy flowrets
>   weep.

On a vast many tombs were hung wreaths, or rather circlets of the yellow flower, the French *immortelles*, of which the common English country name is " everlasting."

I passed through the sepulchral chambers, and expressed a wish to descend into the vaults, which I was enabled to do for the fee of one shilling. These show vaults have certainly nothing dark, damp, lugubrious, or unsightly about them — no token of decay as yet; and so well planned are they, and so thoroughly ventilated, that no such natural result seems to be apprehended. They are just as much show-places as the gardens above, only not so much frequented, because some don't like to descend the steps, and some don't like the look of a coffin, and some don't like to part with a shilling. The guide takes you up one corridor and down another, closely planted on each side with niches filled with coffins, several of them plastered up, but the greater proportion left partly open, to display the ornaments on the head of the coffin, which, ever and anon, when very handsome, are pointed out to you by the conductor. Miserable foppery!

Where are the feelings of solemnity and awe with which the mind ought to be imbued in such a scene as this, when, at every turn, you are called upon to admire those clustered gilt nails — that rich ormolu ornament — that golden handle — that elaborate inscription!

But once my guide stopped at a niche closed — yes, it was quite and entirely closed. No inquisitive eye could pry into its recesses.

"Ay," he said, and he tapped on the wall with his keys; "ay, but here's a young lady here, as is a deal more thought of than them folks with the fine, grand coffins."

" A young lady?"

" Ay, quite young. I remember the time, — it's just about three years ago, — and a sight of folks came after her yet."

"Came after her! What for?"

"Oh, just to cry. They *will* always come down into the vault at once. There was some on 'em here only the day afore yesterday, and how they did cry, to be sure! Poor, young thing! They were very fond of her, I reckon."

The man's tone and manner expressed so much feeling, that my heart softened towards him, and I inwardly vowed to bestow another sixpence upon him. At that moment, my eye was caught by a coffin of huge dimensions, black, without ornament, but dusty looking, and quite uncanopied; giving one the idea of a lumber chest put on a shelf out of the way.

"Whose coffin is that?"

"That! Oh, that holds the biggest rogue in Christendom;" and the man sneered somewhat, and entered upon the history of the rogue with such evident gusto, that, on parting with him, I neglected my intended guerdon of an extra·sixpence.

Mine be a grave — not in a fashionable cemetery, where all indifferent visitors may scan the decorations of your coffin for the "low price of one shilling;" nor would I wish to be buried even in the open ground of one of these modern depositories, where city wives bring their children for a "country excursion," on a summer holiday, and ply them with cakes and oranges all the way; or where the *point-device* fops and simpering misses lisp their puerile nonsense — not lovers, only idlers! A lover's tryst — be the rank and manners of the party what they may — if there be true faith, pure affection, earnest love, a lover's tryst is a holy thing.

Neither would I wish to be buried in the dark, cold vaults of a church; as much too dark and noisome as those of a modern cemetery are too airy and light.

But may I lie in a churchyard, with at least the pure, fresh air blowing over me. Let the dust be resolved to dust, the ashes to ashes, as soon as may be, in hope of a joyful resurrection. Let the free air of heaven blow over my grave, the green, fresh grass wave over it also; the trees blossom near, and young lovers meet under their shade. May such be the grave in which I shall hereafter rest!

Whilst transcribing these notes, the following applicable lines from Beattie's *Minstrel* were placed before me : —

Let vanity adorn the marble tomb
　With trophies, rhymes, and scutcheons of renown,
In the deep dungeons of some Gothic dome,
　Where night and desolation ever frown :
Mine be the breezy hill that skirts the down,
　Where a green, grassy turf is all I crave,
With here and there a violet bestrown,
　Fast by a brook or fountain's murmuring wave,
And many an evening sun shine sweetly on my grave!

We have the similar testimony of another poet. Allan Cunningham was offered by Chantrey a place in his own new elaborate mausoleum. The reply was, —

"No, no. I'll not be built over when I am dead; I'll lie where the wind shall blow, and the daisy grow upon my grave."

12

HARVARD HILL.

THE spot that contains the grave of President Kirkland, has been named "Harvard Hill." It was purchased by the Corporation of the University of Cambridge for a burial place for the officers of the institution, and some of its students. The Kirkland monument is an ornate sarcophagus, having on its top an outspread scroll, upon which rests a book. On one side of the monument are these words : —

JOHANNES THORNTON KIRKLAND,

V. D. M., S. T. D.

DECESSIT APRILIS DIE XXVI.,

ANNO DO INI M.D.CCCXL.

AÆTATIS SUÆ LXIX.

On the opposite side is this inscription : —

JOHANNI THORNTON KIRKLAND, &c.

GRAVES OF CHILDREN.

THERE is nothing of a melancholy description more interesting or picturesque than the little grassy mound that marks the grave of an infant. It takes hold of the feelings more sensibly than other graves, and impresses upon the mind the reflection that the little occupant had not lived the allotted period of human life, but was cut down prematurely like a budding flower, before it had opened its eyes to the rays of the morning. On beholding it, we feel a tender sympathy, as for one who has been deprived of joys that were prepared for his fruition. It calls to mind the innocence of the child, its playfulness, its hopefulness, and its occasional sorrows ; and the little mound becomes expressive of many affecting images of hope and disappointment, of maternal love, and its early bereavement. We think of the stern disease that deprived the young child of its life, of sufferings which it could not speak, of maternal tears shed over its cradle, and of the despair that accompanied its burial, so that a perfect poem could hardly be more suggestive than this little mound.

No other graves by their dimensions indicate the age of the occupant, and its diminutiveness becomes, therefore, a part of its interesting character. If one has ever lost an infant child, or an infant brother or sister, how vividly is the remembrance of its life awakened by the sight of one of these hillocks! It is a beautiful emblematic picture, in which the history of the child is related by the turfs, the flowers, and the headstone, each bringing to light some interesting event in its life, or some pleasing trait in its budding affections. No feelings but those of love and of sorrow, — no hate, nor envy, nor jealousy, can be associated with such a grave ; and if

angels ever come from heaven to linger about the scenes
of earth, and to administer consolation to disinterested
grief, they must delight to watch over these little graves,
to receive the sighs that are breathed over them, and to
pour the balm of heaven into the hearts of the mourners.

When children die, the grief we feel is that of affliction
alone, unalloyed with any selfishness or pride ; the fountain of that sorrow is as pure as the dews of morning that
glitter upon mossy turf. If we have no connection with
the departed, we feel a deep sympathy with those who
are afflicted, as sincere and unaffected mourners. But
the mother who has lost a child in its tender. years, as
some one * has poetically remarked, is never without an
infant. The other members of the young group attain
the fulness of their adult years, and they are no longer
children ; and the remembrance of them, as such, has
been obliterated by her intercourse with them in later
life. She seldom thinks of them as children : but the
little one that departed, in its infancy or childhood, remains always bright in the memory of its parent. She
never forgets its countenance, its motions, its smiles, or
any of the interesting features of its character. All the
incidents of its short life are embalmed in her memory,
and remain there with an ever-enduring affection and
veneration.

After the death of a beloved child, it may be truly
said, that there is always an angel in the house, identified with all the scenes and incidents of the past, and
hallowing those few years, during which it tarried on
earth, as a period peculiarly sacred to memory. The
bereaved mother feels ever afterwards that there is a
sanctity about her dwelling, which she perceives in no
other place except the house of God, and the room in

* Rev. Charles K. True.

which she witnessed its dying sighs, is always from that moment consecrated to affection and to sorrow. When the poignancy of recent grief has been softened into a melancholy and quiet remembrance, there is a perpetual fountain of happiness in the recollection of the lost one, whose sacred image is associated with every scene and object with which it was familiar. Everything that was prized by the departed, has become sacred in the eyes of the parent; and the places it frequented are illumined with the light of the affection she bore it, and of the smiles which were returned.

A similar but more melancholy light beams from the grave of the little slumberer: the light that surrounded its death-bed, and which was irradiated from heaven. It carries us back to the time when the dead was living; and while it revives the sorrow that attended its death and burial, it awakens a crowd of cherished memories which are essential to the happiness of a true mourner. It is like the light of the glowing sunset, which awakens a sad thought of the pleasures of the past day that can never return, while its radiant and melancholy beams glow prophetically with the assurance of another morn, which will be ushered by the same celestial hues. Then do we feel that the purest joys of the soul are not those which are experienced in the bright sunshine of our day; but that the melancholy that accompanies our reflections, when we think of past joys and departed friends, purifies and exalts our happiness, and is blended with something that seems born of heaven.

The sight of the grave of an infant is affecting, even to a stranger, who seldom beholds one without the revival of a host of affecting remembrances. He thinks of bereaved affection, of innocence suffering on the bed of sickness, of a soul that is lost to the world, and of pa-

rental grief that must endure forever.   It is on the bosom
of such a grave, that a little wild flower meekly rising
from the green turf, has a charm beyond all the devices
of art, and a significance that leads the mind to a closer
communion with nature and the Deity.   If the spirit of
the departed could communicate with the living, how
delightful would be the messages conveyed by this little
flower, with its meek-eyed representation of innocence,
and its emblematical expression of immortality.

When we look upon the graves of children, and reflect
upon their unseasonable death, we cannot avoid the belief that there must be some bright reversion of their fate
in reserve for their spirits, and that they who were permitted to live but a few brief years or days, and then
returned to dust, must receive a blessed recompense in
heaven.   It may be that they are earlier in their commencement of a new and happier life ; and thus the
cruelty of death, which deprived them of the joys of the
world, may be in reality but the kindness of Providence,
in opening to them prematurely the gates of immortality.

It is a common belief of Christians that some good
arises out of every affliction.   This is not merely a religious, but a philosophic sentiment.   If I had not lost an
infant brother in my youth, nor met with any similar
affliction, I am confident that I should have remained,
during all that period of life, a stranger to some of the
purest affections that flowed from this fountain of sorrow.
With that infant brother, though his death was followed
by the most profound grief, are associated some deep
thoughts that would perhaps have remained latent through
life, until called forth by the sorrows of after years.
They might never have taken root in the mind.   I
could not, at so early an age, have experienced those
rapturous visions that flow from our ponderings on whence

the departed spirit had flown. All that imagined world of bliss that lies far off in the future, which we call heaven, and believe to be allied with the beauties and sublimities of an etherial landscape, is made more vivid to the mind by the death of a near friend, during the religious and imaginative period of youth, especially if the lost one be an infant, who is the image of perfect innocence, and the fit inhabitant of a world of peace.

Hence one can never behold the closed eyes, the pallid form, and the serene countenance of a dead child, without being keenly reminded of all his most pleasing dreams of heaven. We think of a pure spirit released at an early period from the struggling life of this world, to join the company of angels in some more blissful sphere ; and we feel that death, which alone can confer immortal powers upon the soul of a mortal being, is all the change required to transform an infant into a winged cherub. The same thoughts are awakened by the sight of an infant's grave. The flowers that cluster round this diminutive hillock, always seem brighter and holier than those we find in the open field, or by the roadside.

I shall never cease to regret, therefore, the present custom of levelling the ground above the graves, and of leaving no rising mounds in our modern cemeteries, to denote the spot where the mortal remains are entombed. There is a picturesque charm about these funereal mounds, which no design in marble can supply in the place of them. Even the sculptured figure of the child reposing in a niche in the monument, would not be more expressive, nor awaken more romantic images, nor invest the place with more sacredness, than the little hillock that measures the length of the coffin underneath the sods.

THE SPIRIT'S QUESTIONINGS.

By Mary Howitt.

Where shall I meet thee,
 Thou beautiful one?
Where shall I find thee,
 For aye who art gone?

What is the shape
 To thy dear spirit given?
Where is thy home
 In the infinite heaven?

I see thee, but still
 As thou wert upon earth,
In thy bodied delight,
 In thy wonder and mirth!

But now thou art one
 Of the glorified band,
Who have touched the shore
 Of the far spirit land!

And thy shape is fair,
 And thy locks are bright,
In the living stream
 Of the quenchless light.

And thy spirit's thought
 It is pure and free
From darkness and doubt
 And from mystery!

And thine ears have drunk
  The awful tone
Of the First and Last,
  Of the Ancient One!

And the dwellers old
  Thy steps have met,
Where the lost is found
  And the past is yet.

Where shall I find thee,
  For aye who art gone?
Where shall I meet thee,
  Thou beautiful one?

KNIGHT MONUMENT.

This monument is a somewhat curious pointed design, surmounted by a cross. It was erected to the memory of a wife, as shown by the inscription given below. It is exquisitely executed in granite, so finely wrought as to rival the workmanship of the marble slab in front. The front panel bears the following inscription:—

" KNIGHT.

A TRIBUTE OF AFFECTION, SACRED TO THE MEMORY OF ELIZABETH
S. KNIGHT. 1852."

Upon a marble tablet in front, is a device of two joined hands, with a cross over them, bearing the inscription, "One Lord, one Faith, one Baptism." Everything about this monument, — the fence, the steps in front, — bears evidence of a seriousness of purpose which cannot but impress the beholder that it is a most sincere " tribute of affection."

ANCIENT BURIAL.

BY MRS. STONE.

THE care and tendance usually bestowed on this mortal part, when laid to rest and to wait in hope, is a subject which more or less occupies the attention of all thoughtful people. After reading of the barbarous usages of savage nations, or the elaborate rites of cultivated ones, of the vagaries of fanaticism, or the strange fancies into which poor untaught human nature has been beguiled, — we turn with thankful reverence to the serene, simple, and hopeful observances which Christianity teaches, when "man goeth to his long home, and the mourners go about the streets."

Volume upon volume would hardly suffice to exemplify fully such usages, but these few notices, culled in no irreverent spirit, and with no careless hand, from memorials which have met my view, may, I venture to hope, be found acceptable and interesting.

Brief indeed must be our general references; and here, even on the very threshold of inquiry, we are stopped; for when that " reaper whose name is Death," gathered the first-fruits of his human harvest, we have no record, no trace, no intimation of the proceedings of the then wretched first couple, in regard to the remains of their murdered son. Probably he was laid in the earth; for there is a tradition, rife to this day, that his bereaved parent Adam was buried on Mount Calvary; on the very place — that the tradition may lose no point — on which the Redeemer's cross was afterwards elevated; and we are told by a recent traveller, that Golgotha, the place of a skull, was so named, because Adam's was found there, he having desired to be buried, where he knew, prophetically, the blood of the Saviour should, in due time, be shed.

Such a tradition as this is indeed more curious than important, more interesting than trustworthy; but it refers to a requisition of humanity, which never was, never can be regarded with indifference.

"Give me possession of a burying place, that I may bury my dead out of my sight," said the great patriarch to the sons of Heth: a stern necessity — a peremptory duty throughout the whole earth, from the death of the first man to the babe of to-day, — from the beginning of time even until its end; one, too, which touches all the higher and nobler sympathies of our nature, one regarded by the wisest with pious reverence, and by the most ignorant with superstitious awe, and which by all is marked with ceremonial observances, as varied almost as the diverse nations who people the globe.

The Egyptians exhausted all their skill and science in a futile attempt to preserve the perishable body — futile, for though, as recent experiment has proved,

> " The wheat three thousand years interred
>   Will still its harvest bear,"

it is not so with man's mortal frame. The revolting and discolored heap, which is the most successful result of all their vain exertion, crumbles to dust instantly on exposure to the air.

This custom of embalming originated, perhaps, in the opinion which we are told they held, that so long as a body remained uncorrupted, so long the soul continued within it; and this idea accounts also for their frequent custom — so terrible to us — of keeping the dead in their own habitation. Certainly, it was their opinion that of the many thousand years, the soul re-inhabits the body, if it be preserved entire.

The Greeks very often, though not universally, buried their dead, and interred the ashes in urns of more or less expense, surrounded with trophies more or less costly, mingled with coin and jewels more or less valuable, as circumstances might warrant; and the cinerary urns of the Romans, their imitators, are become almost common to our sight; though the earlier practice of this people was probably to bury, not burn. It is said that the latter mode was adopted, when it was found that in protracted wars, the dead remained disinterred. In the fourth century after Christ, cremation was entirely superseded by burial.

The richly and elaborately adorned sepulchral chambers of Etruria, wherein the domestic household was imitated and all the usual circumstances of life portrayed, and the highly decorated mummy tombs of Egypt, all attest the same anxiety, reverence and most earnest care for the dead, in nations of the highest learning and cultivation, which strike us even through the strange and barbarous rites and customs of savage hordes. Strange, indeed, and most barbarous, are many of these. We can only briefly refer to a few of them.

The people near the Ganges lay their dead along the banks at high water mark, for the tide to carry them away, having first filled their mouths with sacred earth. This river is considered very holy, and pious Hindoos implore to be carried there in their dying agonies, believing that their sins are washed away by the sacred waters.

Throughout parts of Hindostan, when all hopes of recovery are over, the dying person is laid on the earth, that he may expire on the element from which he was originally formed. The male relatives attend the corpse to the funeral-pile, and the ashes are sprinkled with milk and consecrated water brought from the Ganges or some other holy stream.

Universally, almost, even among savage hordes, deep reverence is attached to places of burial. In the Tonga islands, the deadliest enemies chancing to meet there, mutually refrain from hostility. The burial places of people of note in New Zealand are universally sacred.

Among the Jews sepulchres appear to have been caves hollowed out, or those natural ones which abound in the rocks of Palestine. These were kept whitewashed, at least such as were appropriated to public burial. Family ones were often contiguous to the residence; Abraham's was at the end of his field; that belonging to Joseph of Arimathea, where our Saviour was laid, was in his garden. The tombs of the kings of Judah were in Jerusalem, and in the royal gardens; those of the kings of Israel, in Samaria. All were regarded with great reverence; for that a man should not come to the tomb of his fathers is a denunciation of Holy Writ.

" He shall be buried with the burial of an ass," was the curse of the greatest horror uttered against the chosen people of God; and that this horror is inherent in our nature, is evident from the prevalence of it in all ages and climes. One of the most celebrated writers of anti- quity has bequeathed us a fine illustration of this feeling in his beautiful tragedy of *Antigone*, when Polynices is refused the rites of sepulture, and his sister, at the risk of a fearful doom, — which indeed she undergoes, — rev- erently buries his corpse. Indeed, it was considered the height of impiety, to leave even a stranger corpse un- buried, though met only by chance. This general ob- ligation of one of the first of moral laws, was heightened in Antigone, by every feeling of relationship, affection, pity, horror, and dismay.

There was a law of Athens compelling the burial of a dead body found by accident, and pronouncing the refusal impious. It was reckoned infamous to disturb a grave; the punishment of death was awarded to slaves and the lower classes for disturbing a corpse; persons of rank incurred the forfeiture of half their property thereby.

" When I inter a dead body," says Seneca, " though I never saw or knew the party when he was alive, I deserve nothing for my so doing, since I do but discharge an obligation which I owe to human nature."

In Holy Writ we read — " Wheresoever thou findest the dead, take them and bury them, and I will give thee the first place in my resurrection."

Human sacrifices in honor of the dead, prevail in Egypt, Assyria, Etruria, &c. In Greece and Rome, gladiatorial combats were supposed to add dignity to the ceremony. Those customs, which in olden time originated in the mistaken idea of the necessities of the traveller bound to the other world, gradually became merely a vehicle for show and ostentation; and at length a man's rank and wealth were estimated by the number and value of the sacrificial offerings at his tomb.

At a Scythian king's funeral, the mourners disfigured themselves, cut off a piece of their ears, shaved their heads, and gashed their arms and faces. It was some such type of mourning, I suppose, borrowed probably from the Heathen nations, which Moses condemned in the children of Israel.

The remains of the royal Scythian were graced at the moment of interment, by the sacrifice of one of his wives, his cup-bearer, his cook, his groom, his valet, and his messenger, who were all strangled and interred with him ; and a few months afterwards, fifty native Scythian slaves and fifty fine horses were strangled, and placed as trophies, or ornament arounds his barrow.

Barrows, or immense mounds of earth, are supposed to be the most ancient and the most general sepulchral monuments in the world. They are found in almost every part of the habitable globe, having been preserved, doubtless, in many instances, by the custom almost universal, of each passer by throwing a stone on the mass. There are a great many barrows in England, where the relics of animals are mingled with those of human kind ; but, indeed, the contents of these tumuli are as varied as are the habits of the different people who occupy the world.

Dr. Clarke, speaking of the barrows in Russia, says : — " Throughout the whole of this country are seen, dispersed over immense plains, mounds of earth covered with fine turf, the sepulchres of the ancient world, common to almost every habitable country. If there exist anything of former times which may afford monuments of antediluvian manners, it is this mode of burial."

In the New World barrows are the inseparable appendages to great settlements. They are of various forms, proportions and sizes. They are called Indian graves ; and one in Virginia was opened which contained the bones of nearly one hundred persons.

This mode of burial was gradually discontinued in every country, as civilization increased and refinement advanced. The barrows raised over the remains of Patroclus, Hector, Achilles, and other Homeric heroes of wide-world renown, have been described and quoted by writers innumerable. But in later days, while the tomb of the accomplished Greek was adorned with all the pride of exquisite sculpture, and celebrated with all the pathos of elegiac strain ; and whilst the magnificent Roman was raising cenotaphs over the remains of friends inurned with all the pomp and circumstance of woe, the Briton continued the rude usages of the Celts and the Belgæ. Many of the large isolated barrows in waste lands, opened in Great Britain, contain urns and burnt bones ; others, bones in their natural state, the body having been buried without burning. The former are guessed to be Belgic Gauls ; the latter the Celtic Britons, a more primitive people, who adopted the most early rites of burial.

Not wanting in solemn pomp, in gorgeous ceremonial, in mystic and awful incantation, but yet reeking with human sacrifice and unhallowed rite, was the religion of our ancestors in Britain, before the "tidings of great joy" had reached our shores — ere "the beautiful feet" of the MESSENGER had alighted on the blood-stained mountains.

The learning and wisdom of the Druids have been largely descanted on ; and there was certainly much to lay hold of the imagination in a cultivated mind, much to impress with awe and terror an ignorant one, in their religious solemnities. The deep, vast and solemn groves, in which these mysteries were celebrated ; the circle of huge altar stones, near each of which stood the attendant priest, ready to ignite the blue flame which at one and the same instant gleamed on all; the Arch Druid, majestic in his gait, venerable in his appearance, waving the asphodel aloft, near the mystical rocking stone, or stabbing to the heart the noble milk-white bull, as a propitiatory sacrifice to an " unknown God," whilst circling around were priestly bands, sweeping with solemn harps,

"Amid the hush of ages which are dead ;"

13 *

looking triumphant strains which rang out gloriously to the skies, or chanting mournful dirges which stole tremulously along the forest glades, mingling with the pure and gentle breath of evening in " a dying, dying fall " — all this is certainly beautiful as a picture ; but it is only an attractive portal to the temple of a religion, ruthless and cruel as bigotry and untamed nature could devise. Not amongst these beguiling accessories were maxims of peace, of dignity, of brotherly kindness taught to the loving; nor a future hope breathed in the stricken ear of the mourner ; or a message of pardon and peace whispered to soothe the agony of the dying.

The poor man, without future hope, or death-bed prayer, —

" Unshriven, unanointed, unaneled, " —

was buried with scant ceremony in a shroud of woolen fastened with a wooden pin, in a hole dug by the side of a hill, or on a waste flat ; while a little mound of soil or turf was heaped upon the spot, or perhaps some common stones — the commonest and smallest of barrows.

When a person of more consequence died, his·horse and favorite domestic animals, and perhaps too his servants, were burned around his funeral pyre. The remains were buried in a stone chest or *kistrean*, which was composed of five large flat stones, the fifth forming the lid. Sometimes this was placed upon a hill or barrow ; very frequently a hill or barrow was built over it, made of earth, with large stones set round about.

Kings and nobles were distinguished by a barrow of greater height and larger dimensions, often surmounted by a monument of one enormous flat stone, raised on three or four upright ones. Hubba, the Dane, was buried under a very large barrow in Devonshire. We are told of another Dane who employed his whole army, and a

number of oxen, to place an immense stone on the tumulus of his mother.

There are large numbers of barrows scattered over
England, and especially clustered in Wiltshire. A great
many have been opened; some containing unburnt skeletons; others, such as have evidently undergone the
action of fire. Besides human remains, there have been
found animals of all sorts, from the skeleton of a horse to
that of a fowl; all imaginable warlike instruments, domestic utensils, or ornamental trifles, from a battle-spear
or a pole-axe, to a bit of amber or a row of glass beads —
from an iron torques, or a silver or gold bracelet, to an
ivory hook or crystal ball.

But happy are we to turn from these slight though
painful memorials of heathenism, to that long predicted
period when the Day-star from on high beamed over the
earth, and the mild rays of Christian hope penetrated
the darkness and gloom, which had hitherto shrouded the
borders of the grave.

CHRISTIAN BURIAL.

BY MRS. STONE.

IT cannot excite our surprise that under the early
impetus, the first impulse of the certainty to resurrection
and the hope of a happy eternity, the consignment to the
tomb was denuded of many of the dismal and dis-
heartening circumstances which attached to the formula
of paganism. The earliest Christians were, probably, because of the bitter persecution to which they were subjected in the performance of their rites, obliged to bury

in secrecy and in darkness, under cover of the night;
but only for that reason was night-time chosen — for in
principle —

> " With tapers in the face of day,
>   These rites their faithful hope display ;
>   In long procession slow,
>   With hymns that fortify the heart,
>   And prayers that soften woe."

In Pagan rites by night, torches were necessarily
borne, but the early Christians used them in full day-
light, as emblems of joyful hope. To these we shall
refer more fully.

Instead of hired mourners' shrilly, keening, dismal
strains, they carried the corpse to the grave, the face
bare, chanting psalms and hymns, not of the lugubrious
strain now so usual, the " dirges due" alike real and
poetical, but of hope, of joy, of holy anticipation ; referring rather to the glory hereafter, than to the bereavement now. Their rites, though performed with humility,
and chastened it may be, by tears, did yet assume somewhat of triumphant aspect, which relieved those most
closely connected, most severely bereaved, from some of
the bitterest feelings of separation.

And these solemn offerings of prayer and praise were
invariably accompanied by alms-giving; the poor and
needy were always remembered. This was the origin
of those " Funeral Doles " which afterwards became a
component part of a respectable person's funeral.

From the time that Constantine ascended the throne,
the Christians had free privilege to inter their dead, and
they performed these rites in the open day. Before this
time, it was a refinement in cruelty with their persecu-
tors, to interfere with the sacred duty of burial.

In reverence to Him, who assumed the body of man for our salvation, who sitteth at the right hand of his Father on high, and who shall come again in the body to judge the quick and the dead for their deeds done in the flesh, — in reverence to this, and to the close connection between the body lowered into the grave, and the one that shall arise from it — the early Christians were always anxious, if possible, to lay the whole body, unmutilated, in the earth ; especially considering, what is too often lost sight of, that the dead, the holy dead, are in the communion of the saints still and forever.

If we remember that even among Pagan nations, this " corporeal act of mercy," the burial of the dead, was not only considered a peremptory duty by the thoughtful, but was enforced by legal enactments on the observance of the most careless ; it will not excite surprise, that, under the elevating influence of the Christian doctrine of the resurrection of the body, it should receive a reverence unknown and unnecessary, when it was considered merely as a piece of corruption, a decaying carcase. Now this outer covering was reverenced as the temple of the Holy Spirit, as the germ whence should spring a scion ripe for immortality. Therefore was the body watched and tended with solemn, unremitting, reverent care ; therefore was it never left from the death-hour, to that of its commitment to the grave ; therefore was it borne thither with all the amenities of honorable tendance ; and therefore, finally, was it committed to the dust with psalms and hymns of faith, of reverence, of hope, of anticipated re-union.

That the early Christians very commonly used the process of embalmment, was probably owing to the necessity which compelled them in those fearful times, to deposit the remains of the dead in the places, close and subterranean, where they were accustomed to meet periodically for worship.

And yet not this only. Though embalmment was a usual custom with the Jews, the Christian practice had, perhaps, a hallowed reference to our Saviour, whose sacred body they " wound in linen clothes with the spices, as the manner of the Jews is to bury " — " a mixture of myrrh and aloes, about an hundred pounds weight."

Their places of burial were called by a general name, *cœmeteria*, " dormitories," or sleeping places, because they looked on death as sleep, merely, and the departed only, as it were, laid to rest until the resurrection should awaken them.*

Among the classical nations, it was considered shameful to neglect a corpse, but the early Christians carried this charity to a much higher pitch; and during times of persecution, they not only incurred enormous expense, but braved great personal risk, in order to obtain for burial the bodies of their brethren. When neither money nor solicitation would avail, they frequently stole them in the night. Entychianus, Bishop of Rome, is celebrated in the Martyrology, for having buried three hundred and forty-two martyrs in several places with his own hands.

Though luxury, cost, and magnificence ("splendid in ashes, pompous in the grave,") of course gained ground despite the invectives of the early fathers against it, the usual funeral attire was new white linen. They clothed the dead in new garments, to signify or prefigure the putting on the " new clothing of incorruption."

By degrees, however, this primitive custom of pro-

---

* Requietorium was a term also used : — The bodies are not only despoiled of all funereal ornaments, but dug up out of their requietories.

priety and purity, became habitually, as it had been occasionally used even from the first. The habits of splendor, dignity, and ceremony to which persons were habituated in their life-time, were borne even into the tomb. Thus emperors and kings were interred in their imperial and royal robes ; knights in their military garments ; bishops were laid in the grave in their episcopal habits ; priests in their sacerdotal vestments ; and monks in the dress of the particular order to which they belonged. An ancient ritual of the monastery of Silos in Spain, expressly orders that the deceased be habited suitably to their rank in life.

Various customs obtained indeed, from time to time, which had been better honored in the neglect than the observance, such, for instance, as that in the old time of burying the priors of Durham in their boots. A decent uniformity of attire has now superseded these unbecoming customs.

Lights were carried before the dead as symbols of the glory to which they aspired; to signify also that they were champions or conquerors, and as such conducted in triumph to their graves. We have a record of a mother carrying a torch in her hand before the body of her son ; the bishops themselves carried torches around the bier of the Lady Paula ; the mangled body of St. Cyprian was buried with great pomp, many torches being borne around. St. Gregory of Nanzianzen, says, that at the funeral of his sister Macrina, a great number of deacons and clergy walked on each side the coffin carrying torches ; and when the body of St. Chrysostom was removed from Comana to Constantinople, " there was such a multitude of people met him in ships in his passage over the Bosphorus, that the sea was covered with lamps."

The corpse was usually carried to burial on the

shoulders of friends ; and the highest order of clergy thought it no reproach to their dignity to carry the bier. At the funeral of Lady Paula, bishops were what we now call under-bearers. There were strict regulations regarding the practice. Deacons were to carry deacons, and priests to be the bearers of priests. Women were never allowed to act as under-bearers.

When a bishop died, it was usual to carry his corpse into several churches, before it was borne to its last resting place. The body was usually laid on a bed of ivy, or laurel, or other evergreen. Gregory of Tours, says, that the bishop of St. Valerian, was laid in his tomb on a bed of laurel leaves.

The poor were buried in coffins of plain wood, at the common charge of the church ; but this duty was not left to indiscriminate care. Early in the fourth century, two classes were instituted, whose specific vocation was to solace the sick, and pay due and requisite attention to the dead. The one were called *parabolani*, from the venturing their lives among the sick in contagious disorders ; the other, *copiatæ, laborantes, lecticarii, fossarii,* and *decani,* whose office was to dig graves for the poor, carry the coffins, deposit them in the ground, &c., as most of the names signify. ·

These officers, kept then under the rigid discipline and surveillance of the church, are the progenitors of the fruitful progeny of undertakers, sextons, &c., who in these days cause many a heart-broken person to count with despair, the few coins in a purse, which, perhaps, has been impoverished by the hand of God himself, in heavy, long, lingering sickness.

The body of the departed Christian was, as we have observed, always reverently watched by prayerful friends, from the hour of death to that of interment ; sometimes

in the house, more often in the church. The corpse of
St. Ambrose was carried to the church and watched
there; that of Monica was tended night and day in her
own house. Gregory Nyssen writes, that over the remains of his sister Macrina, "they watched and sung
psalms all night, as they were used to do on the vigils or
pernoctations preceding the festivals of the martyrs."

When the period for interment came, the corpse was
carried to the grave with psalmody, torches being borne
around.

Funerals were not merely denuded of gloom and sadness, but were invested with somewhat of jubilant *eclat*.
Sorrow there must have been, but it was grief without
bitterness. In the wonderful light which newly beamed
from Calvary, the Christians, " the first-born of a young
faith," in their unlooked-for and exceeding joy, thought
more practically than we, that death was but the dark
passage, which carried their lost relative from their view,
to the presence of his Saviour, to the society of their
friends and brethren, to the companionship of the just
and good of eternal ages. He was, in that hour, they
felt, — he was but " gone before."

Such versicles as these they chanted on their way to
the grave : —

" Return to thy rest, O my soul, for the Lord hath
rewarded thee."

" The memory of the just shall be blessed."

" The souls of the righteous are in the hands of God."

" I will fear no evil, because thou art with me."

" Precious in the sight of the Lord is the death of his
saints."

" Hallelujah ! Thou art the resurrection, Thou, O
Christ."

14

None was denied this privilege of psalmody at the
funeral, except suicides, or criminals who were publicly
executed, or those who died in the wilful neglect of holy
baptism.

If the life of the departed, or his character, had been
marked by any circumstances available as example to
others, some few words were spoken as a just memorial
of his merit, and with reference to him as a pattern to
those around. Several of those funeral orations, made
in the early ages of Christianity, are still extant.

If the interment were in the forenoon, the whole service of the church was gone through, and the Holy
Eucharist was administered ; if it were in the afternoon,
the psalmody and prayers only, accompanied by the more
especial funeral service.

This service consisted of hymns of thanksgiving for the
deceased, with prayer for one entering into that eternal
rest. The bishop gave solemn . thanks to God, for his
(the departed's) perseverance in the knowledge of God,
and in his Christian warfare even unto death ; and the
deacon read such portions of Scripture as contained the
promises of the resurrection. A hymn to the same purpose was sung.

During the celebration of the Holy Communion in
those days, a solemn commemoration was made of the
dead in general, and prayers were offered to the Almighty for them. And this was one especial reason for
the adoption of this service at burials, because prayers
were constantly made therein for all holy men and holy
women departed, among whom was especially named
him about to be committed to the grave.

The kiss of peace is spoken of, and the anointing with
holy oil, as the last rites of all ; but these seem not to
have been always observed. It was very usual to strew

flowers on the grave ; and no old writer, how rigid soever, has reprobated this innocent, beautiful, and most suggestive custom.

And so fulfilled with the grace and benediction of Him whom they had learned to know of their Father in Heaven, as their Redeemer to all eternity, in faith and hope, in the exercise of prayer and almsgiving, the early Christians were enabled to give hearty thanks to God, that he had been pleased to " deliver their brethren out of the miseries of this sinful world."

THE APPLETON MONUMENT.

This monument stands in Woodbine Path, and was erected by Mr. Samuel Appleton, of Boston. It is a miniature Grecian Temple, of fine Italian marble, surmounted by funereal lamps, with appropriate devices on its façade. It is the work of Italian artists.

EPITAPHS AND INSCRIPTIONS.

EVERY person of intelligence and sensibility is alive to the beauties of a brief, simple, and appropriate epitaph which excites a reverence for the dead, and awakens an interest in the events of his life. When we encounter a headstone without an epitaph, it seems like a book with a mere title page, while the leaves that follow are blank. It is an indispensable appendage to a monument, and we turn from one that is without it as from a work of sculpture that is unfinished. The propriety of this tribute to the dead is universally admitted ; and it is not, therefore, a useless task to endeavor to define the principles by which the composition of it should be governed ; for if one that is appropriate and well written, is pleasing to the most indifferent reader, one that is awkward, high-sounding or exaggerated, is ludicrous and demeaning to the character of the subject.

There are some epitaphs that relate particularly to the dead, and are commonly panegyrical ; others that make no direct allusion to the dead, but aim merely to convey a pleasing sentiment or an instructive moral. The former are the most difficult work for the writer ; because it requires great discrimination, in elegiac composition, to avoid the extreme of panegyric, or to present, in a few words, the most appropriate thoughts and images, and to select those points which would produce the most vivid effect upon the mind of the reader. If one is extravagant in his praises of the dead, the reader is sceptical of the truth of those praises ; if the epitaph be long, it will not be read ; and though it were brief, the points selected may not be those which would produce the most favorable impression.

14*

It has been the custom among writers of epitaphs to aim at antithesis; to express pointed thoughts in apposite words and phrases. This is the surest method of clothing a commonplace thought, or a trite image, with the appearance of originality; but this style of writing is too artificial to seem to flow from the heart. When the composition is evidently studied, it loses its charm for the reader; though he may know at the same time, that the most pleasing simplicity is often the result of great art and elaboration. When one reflects that the living friend could write nothing of the deceased except a pointed epigram, he is prone to imagine that, as there was nothing in his character to be praised, he was commemorated only by a witticism. Sincere praise is often exaggerated, but never pointed and rhetorical.

"The difficulty," says Dr. Johnson, "in writing epitaphs, is to give a particular and appropriate praise. This, however, is not always to be performed; for the greater part of mankind have little that distinguishes them from others equally good or bad; and, therefore, nothing can be said of them, which may not, with equal propriety, be applied to a thousand more. It is, indeed, no great panegyric, that there is inclosed in this tomb, one who was born in one year, and who died in another; yet many useful and amiable lives have been spent, which leave little materials for any other memorial. These, however, are not the proper subjects of poetry; and whenever friendship or any other motive obliges a poet to write on such a subject, he must be forgiven if he sometimes wanders in generalities, and utters the same praises over different tombs.

The scantiness of human praises can scarcely be made more apparent, than by remarking how often Pope has, in the few epitaphs which he composed, found it necessary to borrow from himself. The fourteen epitaphs which he has written, comprise about one hundred and forty lines, in which there are 'more repetitions than will easily be found in all the rest of his works."

But the evil arising from the repetition of a thought, which has been frequently expressed in other compositions of the same kind, has been greatly exaggerated; and there are many ideas that would be very appropriate, which are not contained in the compositions of Pope, who fell into the error of aiming to be pointed and antithetical, and to end his pieces in a climax. Hence, there are many natural and appropriate thoughts which he was obliged to reject, because they could not be woven into the pointed style of his compositions. Among the inscriptions to be found in our country graveyards, are many that are preferable to any epigrammatic verses, which are sadly wanting in simplicity and pathos. Any man's life may afford a lesson to others; and if that life was a virtuous 'one, a few words announcing this fact, expressed neither in rhyme nor metaphor, may produce a deep impression upon the mind of the reader.

" He lived in peace, because he was just ; "
" He died in hope, because he was a Christian."

These lines convey no fulsome panegyric, and yet no higher praise could be bestowed upon one in so few words. They contain a two-fold moral, showing the advantage of justice to secure a life of peace, and of a belief in Christianity, to die with a hope of Heaven.

A part of the difficulty, attending the composition of epitaphs, arises from the effort of the writer, to express ideas and images which are not obvious, without considering that this effort, if it be apparent, spoils all their effect. It is not the highest praise that is most exaggerated, for high praise expressed in plain and simple terms, if it produces conviction in the mind of the reader, gives rise to no invidious feelings. A smaller amount of eulogy conveyed in high-sounding language, betrays the wish of the writer to raise his subject to an undue importance, and fails in producing conviction, because it excites our incredulity. An epitaph should always contain more eulogy than is apparent, like a strong and even light that illuminates a room without dazzling the eyes.

It has been customary, at certain times, to omit any inscription upon the tomb, except the name and age of the deceased, and perhaps some other indispensable records. This neglect probably originated in a consciousness of the abuse which has been made of epitaphs; their extravagance in some instances, and their triteness or absurdity in others. These evils were thought to be avoided by omitting the epitaph entirely. But if one objects to the panegyrical epitaph, he might use the other form, in which a sentiment or a moral is merely recorded upon the tomb, without particular mention of the character or history of the subject. Such is that common, but most appropriate and delightful sentiment, which has lost nothing by repetition, and is often inscribed upon the tombstone of a little child : —

"Not lost, but gone before."

There is still another form of epitaph in which the person commemorated is represented as speaking. These different forms of inscription seem to give variety to the expression of the same ideas; and as one form is not absolutely preferable to another, the writer should be governed in his choice by his own taste. Of the last description is the common Latin epitaph — "*Sum quod eris, fui quod sis.*" "I am what thou shalt be, I was what thou art." This verse communicates only a trite and common piece of information. It is neither pleasing nor poetical, but it is somewhat impressive, from the hint it conveys to be prepared for death. Poetry and religion are so nearly allied, that an epitaph, if it be religious, can hardly be otherwise than poetical, unless it conveys a gloomy impression of our future state. If it contains neither a religious nor a moral sentiment, it is no better than a mere blank.

Whether the reader be a believer or an unbeliever, he is pleased with a verse that suggests an idea of the soul's immortality. He loves to indulge this sentiment as a poetical illusion, if he cannot make it a point of his faith, or the true foundation of his hopes. The idea of " death and eternal sleep," though it be a part of some men's belief, could not fail to affect the same persons with horror, as an inscription on a tombstone. It was only during the anti-religious excitement of the French Revolution, that the most philosophic atheist could endure such a sentiment, when blazoned upon a sepulchral monument. In the unexcited moments of such a man's life, he would prefer the religious epitaph based on the idea of the soul's release from mortal bondage, into the celestial enjoyment of a new life, though he recognized it only as a flattering image of poetry.

The themes which, by general consent, are regarded as the proper subjects for an epitaph, are the virtues and good actions of the deceased; the lessons which his life and death may impart to the living; the hopes he entertained of happiness beyond the grave; rest from the toils and cares of this world; the soul's immortality and entrance into a new life. These are the appropriate subjects of discourse in monumental inscriptions; and there seems to be no good reason for rejecting them, on account of the difficulty of avoiding the repetition of ideas which have been recorded many times before. The same objection might be made to the erection of a headstone over the grave of a friend, because a new pattern could not be invented. We must not expect the works of art to exceed the variety of nature. The forms of trees are but the repetitions of resemblances; but the landscape is not rendered tiresome by their similarity. Neither is a cemetery necessarily tiresome on account of the frequent recurrence of similar monumental stones.

The visitor is not expected to read the inscriptions upon all the gravestones. He may read many before he meets with a literal repetition of a previous one. If the words, " Not lost, but gone before " were inscribed on fifty stones in Mount Auburn, a stranger who should linger an hour in these grounds might not see them but once. As we cannot invent anything new, we must be satisfied with presenting an oft-repeated thought in a new phase, or by making a new application of it. It would be as unwise to leave the stone without an epitaph, on account of the difficulty of saying a new thing, as to refuse this tribute to a friend, because his virtues were not brilliant, but of the humble sort, that do not seem to elicit eulogy. These are, indeed, the virtues which are the most appropriate themes for monumental inscription.

It is better to dwell on those general traits of humanity which are common to all good men, than to confine the epitaph to certain extraordinary qualities. We do not come to the grave to study and analyze each person's peculiarities of character. We are better pleased with a few words, expressing in general terms his virtuous and peaceful life, and its happy and hopeful termination, than with an epigram or a dissertation. A sentiment conveyed in language simple enough to be intelligible to all, banishes the suspicion that the writer is endeavoring unjustly to exalt the dead above his real merits. The epitaph should be simple, that all may understand it; obvious, that it may require no study; brief, that all may read it; moderate, that it may be credited; poetical, that it may lay hold of the imagination; cheerful, that it may reconcile us to our inevitable fate; religious, that it may inspire the hope of a new life.

An epitaph is of no value, if it does not obtain the faith and the sympathy of the general reader. For this end it should give proof of the writer's own deep feeling and sincerity. He must address the reader, therefore, as a humble friend of the departed, and not as a sermonist or a censor. He must be serious and solemn, but not gloomy; believing and hopeful, but not extravagantly elated. His lamentations must be heartfelt, but not too painfully wrought; for the reader, though he loves to sympathize, does not wish to be afflicted. We sympathize more easily with sorrow that is sincere without despondency; for we wish to see a probability that the mourner will obtain relief and a renewal of happiness, as we are delighted with the promise of morning that gleams through the darkness of night. An epitaph should make no parade of one's lamentations, any more than of the virtues of the subject. As a silent tear flowing down the cheek of an unquestionable mourner, excites more sympathy than boisterous wailing, so does one line of tender anguish affect the sensibility of the reader more deeply than a long paragraph of earnest complaint.

A sepulchral monument is no place for wit or for satire. We may be excited to mirth by a humorous epitaph upon a gravestone; but it interrupts the flow of

tender melancholy which one is disposed to cherish in his
meditations among the tombs. It disqualifies the mind
to receive congenial impressions, and does not avert
gloomy reflections with the same power as the hopeful
utterance of religious faith. Satire, which is always
more or less malignant, ought to find no place here.
Anything like malice or contempt towards our fellow
beings, should never be exhibited in these sacred inclosures. The sight of the graves of our fellow men brings
forcibly to mind the reflection that we are all travelling
the same road ; and here we should unite in mutual
trust and forbearance ; and if we have lessons to impart
to the living in the lines which we carve upon the monuments of the dead, let them be conveyed in the simple
language of love. Let the graveyard be a school of religion and virtue, not a place for the wit of the epigram-
matist or the sneers of the misanthrope.

Death must be mentioned as our inevitable fate, and as
the occasion of sorrow ; but not as the cause of despondency, or the destroyer of hope. The tomb should be
invested with those circumstances that will shed light on
the gloom of the grave ; and nothing serves more effectually to diffuse this cheerfulness around it, than a
poetical and hopeful inscription that points to a world
beyond this mortal sphere.

The individual commemorated is to be presented to the
reader as one who has not lived in vain, nor died without hope ; and the claims upon the reader's interest and
sympathy should be based on his ordinary, not extraordinary deserts. The first idea commands our sympathy,
the second excites our incredulity. If the subject has
performed certain noble and heroic acts, it is better to
name the acts, and let them praise him, than to follow
them with extravagant laudation. To say that one died in

his efforts to save others from perishing, is stating a fact that exalts him to a hero, and no eulogy could elevate the reader's idea of his heroism.

We should cast a veil of charity over the faults of one whom we wish to commemorate, and a veil of modest claims over the lustre of his virtues, that we may not wrong his memory by harsh judgment, nor excite envy by praising him with exaggeration. An epitaph is not to be a daguerreotype of the character of the dead; but it should resemble an illuminated shadow in which we may see a pleasing resemblance to him, that shall excite our veneration the more, because of the indistinctness of its delineations. The more general the praise the better, provided its meaning is significant; for as soon as we descend to particular points in our eulogy, we may possibly be opposed by the opinion of those who knew the subject of it.

But it is not the virtuous alone who may be made the subjects of an affecting epitaph. If the dead has been unfortunate on account of his vices, the writer might carefully allude to them in some cases, not to hold him up to execration, but to mourn over his fate, to hint at the virtues which he might have cultivated, and to offer a kindly warning to those who are tempted to go astray in like manner. All this should be done as we eulogize the virtues of a good man, with care and moderation; and so kindly, that the reader may even suppose that a brother or sister might have written it, while overwhelmed with the kindest as well as the saddest recollections.

THE BURIAL GROUND AT SIDON.

By Mary Howitt.

The burial ground, with the old ruin, supposed to be
the castle of Louis IX, is without the town ; and the tall
trees cast their shadows on the sepulchres, some fallen
and ruined, others newly whited and gilt, covered with
sentences in the Turkish character, the headstones usually presenting a turban on a pedestal. Several women
had come to mourn over the graves of their relatives, in
white cloaks and veils that enveloped them from head to
foot ; they mostly mourned in silence, and knelt on the
steps of the tomb, or among the wild flowers which grew
rank on the soil. The morning light fell partially on the
sepulchres, and on the broken towers of the ancient castle ; but the greater part of the thickly-peopled cemetery
was still in gloom — the gloom which the Orientals love.
They do not like to come to the tombs in the glare of
day ; early morn and even are the favorite seasons, especially the latter.   This burial ground of Sidon is one
of the most picturesque on the coast of Syria. The ruin
of Louis, tells, like the sepulchres, that this life's hope and
pride is as a tale that is told.   When the moon is on its
towers, on the trees and tombs beneath, and on the white
figures that slowly move to and fro, the scene is solemn,
and cannot be forgotten.

The dead are everywhere !
    The mountain-side, the plain, the woods profound ;
All the wide earth, — the fertile and the fair,
    Is one vast burial ground !

Within the populous street;
  In stately homes; in places high ;
In pleasure domes where pomp and luxury meet,
  Men bow themselves to die.

The old man at his door;
  The unweaned child murmuring its wordless song ;
The bondman and the free ; the rich, the poor ;
  All, all, to death belong !

The sunlight gilds the walls
  Of kingly sepulchres enwrought with brass ;
And the long shadow of the cypress falls
  Athwart the common grass.

The living of gone time
  Builded their glorious cities by the sea ;
And awful in their greatness sat sublime,
  As if no change could be.

There was the eloquent tongue ;
  The poet's heart ; the sage's soul was there ;
And loving women with their children young,
  The faithful and the fair !

They were, but they are not ;
  Suns rose and set, and earth put on her bloom,
Whilst man, submitting to the common lot,
  Went down into the tomb.

And still amid the wrecks
  Of mighty generations passed away,
Earth's boonest growth, the fragrant wild-flower decks
  The tombs of yesterday.

And in the twilight deep,
    Go veiled women forth, like those who went,
Sisters of Lazarus, to the grave to weep,
    To breathe the low lament.

The dead are everywhere !
    Where'er is love, or tenderness, or faith ;
Where power, form, pleasure, pride ; where'er
    Life is, or was, is death !

1855
2951
C. G. EDWARDS
No. 2964
JOHN S. WRIGHT
L.Prang & Co. Lith. Boston.

HAZEL DELL.

Two Tombs in Hazel Dell, belonging to C. G. Edwards and John S. Wright, constructed of fine granite, with a chaste Grecian front in plain style, and calculated for endurance.

15*

ON INSCRIPTIVE WRITING.

By Dr. Drake.

To commemorate a deceased or absent friend, to express the sensations and moral effect arising from the contemplation of beautiful scenery, to perpetuate the remembrance of some remarkable event, or to inscribe the temple or the statue with appropriate address, appear to be the chief purposes of the Inscription. It is evident that no species of composition, when well written, can better answer the wishes of the friends of virtue than this; and almost every polished nation, therefore, has made use of it to impress the feeling mind and incite it to emulation. Among the Greeks it was cultivated with success, and the Anthology abounds in pieces of this kind, written with the most elegant simplicity. Several of the English poets, likewise, have excelled in inscriptive writing.

It will not be an employment altogether void of interest, perhaps, to trace and give a few specimens of these elegant compositions which are calculated to awake the purest affections, to call forth the tear of friendship or of love, to nurse the patient feelings, and to soften and ameliorate the heart, by giving a moral charm to the features of cultivated nature. Nothing, however, requires more taste, more discrimination of character, circumstance, and place, than the attempt to decorate in this manner. Should the inscription be ill-chosen, or the scene ill-adapted to the impression meant to be conveyed, contempt or disgust will inevitably follow, and the disappointed contriver, become an object of ridicule. The most delicate and correct feelings, therefore, and a taste for picturesque beauty, must ever guide the experiment.

The ostentatious display of sorrow is always offensive; in the scene, therefore, sacred to departed genius or friendship, the utmost simplicity should reign; sequestered and free from interruption, nothing should appear to attract the steps of the stranger. The following little piece by Leonidas — a mother deploring the loss of her son — is the best style of the Greek epigram. It is inscribed on an urn containing the ashes of the beloved youth.

Ah! dear helpless boy, art thou gone?
  Sole support of my languishing years!
Hast thou left thy fond mother alone,
  To wear out life's evening in tears?

To forsake me thus old and forlorn,
  Ere thy youth had attained its gay bloom!
Thy sun was scarce risen at morn,
  When it set in the night of the tomb!

Alas! the fresh beam of the day
  Happy mortals with thankfulness see;
But I sicken, O sun! at thy ray,
  It brings sadness and wailing to me!

Oh! might the dear child but return,
  From despair his lost mother to save,
Or might I but share in his urn,
  Might I flee in his arms to the grave!

WAKEFIELD.

It is evident, that in the moral inference to be drawn
from surrounding scenery, the hand of a master is required, and that the poet should not attempt to say everything that the view suggests, but rather lead the mind of
the spectator to a train of associations, which at the
time appears to be the offspring of his own intellect; yet
what would not have been conceived without the original
hint arising from the inscription. The following is a
model of this species of inscriptive writing; in delinea-
tion, beautiful; in moral, exquisite: —

FOR A TABLET ON THE BANKS OF A STREAM.

Stranger! awhile upon this mossy bank,
Recline thee.   If the sun ride high, the breeze,
That loves to ripple o'er the rivulet,
Will play around thy brow, and the cool sound
Of running waters soothe thee.   Mark how clear
It sparkles o'er the shallows, and behold
Where o'er its surface wheels with restless speed
Yon glossy insect, on the sand below,
How swift the shadow flies.   The stream is pure
In solitude, and many a healthful herb
Bends o'er its course, and drinks the vital wave;
But passing on amid the haunts of men,
It finds pollution there, and rolls from thence
A tainted tide.   Seek'st thou for Happiness?
Go, stranger, sojourn in the woodland cot
Of innocence, and thou shalt find her there.
SOUTHEY.

Many national advantages might be derived from the
custom of erecting inscriptions, to perpetuate the memory
of any remarkable event or deed.   Were the efforts of

the patriot thus cherished; the exertions of tyranny,
cruelty and oppression, thus held up to detestation and
infamy; were the spot on which any memorable struggle
for the welfare or liberty of mankind had occurred, thus
gratefully consecrated; fresh motives to excel in all that
is laudable would be acquired, and the national character,
perhaps, ameliorated, through the medium of emulation.
From Southey's Letters on Spain and Portugal, we have
selected an inscription for the birth-place of Pizarro,
which is an excellent specimen of what, among other
moral purposes, pieces of this class should effect — the
reprehension of cruelty and inordinate ambition.

INSCRIPTION FOR A COLUMN AT TRUXILLO.

Pizarro here was born; a greater name
The list of glory boasts not.   Toil, and want,
And danger, never from his course deterred
This daring soldier; many a fight he won;   ·
He slaughtered thousands; he subdued a rich
And ample realm; such were Pizarro's deeds;
And wealth, and power, and fame, were his rewards
Among mankind.   There is another world.
O reader! if you earn your daily bread
By daily labor, if your lot be low —
Be hard and wretched, thank the gracious God
Who made you, that you are not such as he.

To him who secedes exhausted from the busy world,
from the tumultuous cares and anxiety of public life, his
retirement charms in proportion to the force of contrast; and the rustic shed, and the pastoral hermitage,
have for a season irresistible attractions. The rocky glen
or deep secluded valley, clothed with wood and watered

by the rill, there soothe to peace the wearied spirit, dis-
perse each angry and injurious thought, and melt the
heart to all the tender offices of humanity. In situations
such as these, the lover of sequestered nature has delighted to imagine the pious anchorite had formerly
dwelt, and cherishing a thought which opens new sources
of reflection, and throws a more awful tint upon the
scene, he builds the rude dwelling of his fancied hermit,
and gives almost the features of reality. Many such
scenes, the offspring of a romantic imagination improving
on the wild sketches of nature, are scattered over the
land, and heightened by inscriptions more or less adapted
to the occasion. One of these, valuable for its sweetness of style, but still more for its moral imagery, may
be adduced here as an example, —

INSCRIPTION FOR A HERMITAGE BELONGING TO SIR ROBERT BURDETT.

O thou, who to this wild retreat
Shall lead by choice thy pilgrim feet,
To trace the dark wood waving o'er
This rocky cell and sainted floor ;
If here thou bring a gentle mind,
That shuns by fits, yet loves mankind;
That leaves the schools and in this wood,
Learns the best science — to be good ;
Then soft as on the deeps below
Yon oaks their silent umbrage throw,
Peace to thy prayers by virtue brought,
Pilgrim, shall bless thy hallowed thought.

BAGSHAW STEEVENS.

Anxious to preserve the memory of departed friendships or genius, affection and gratitude have endeavored

to effectuate their wishes through the medium of sculpture, and the bust, the medallion, or the statue, claim our notice, and give an interesting character to the scenery in which they are placed. Some of the mythological figures of Greece and Rome have also been adopted, but require much judgment in the choice of scene, and much attention to classical details to produce their due effect. Beneath sepulture of this kind, inscriptions are common, though seldom attaining the end proposed. A curious felicity of expression, terse and pointed brevity and orignality of conception, should be united, requisites not easily obtained, though assiduously sought for.

FLOWERS FOR THE DEAD.

By Mrs. Stone.

Sought for in every pageant of life, from the cradle to the tomb, flowers seem particularly adapted to, and have been almost universally used in the ceremonies of the latter. Among the classical nations, the tokens of death being in a house were branches of pine and cypress suspended near the threshold; and Lycurgus ordered laurel leaves as part of the funeral habit of persons of merit, and garlands of flowers were cast on the body as it passed to interment. Tombs were strewed with flowers, especially roses, which both by Romans and Greeks were used in profusion; roses, lilies, hyacinths, parsley, and myrtle, were customary; and by the Greeks, the Amaranth was much esteemed, being considered, as its name imports, unfading, immortal —

> " A flower which once
> In Paradise, fast by the tree of life,
> Began to bloom."

Homer describes the Thessalians as wearing crowns of Amaranths at the funeral of Achilles. The asphodel was a sacred flower devoted to the deity who presided over life, death, and sepulchral rites. Milton has made beautiful use of the superstitions attaching to it, in causing the nymph Sabrina, when she threw herself into the Severn, to be bathed

> " In nectared leaves, strewed with asphodel,
> .   .   .   till she revived,
> And underwent a quick immortal change. "

It is said that the absolute repudiation of everything appertaining to paganism, which marked the first days of Christianity, induced the early Christians to discontinue the use even of flowers. But this was only for a short time. Very soon were they used abundantly, and the practice has never since been *entirely* laid aside in any Christian country. It has, indeed, in some country places fallen into desuetude; so much so, that on a marked occasion, the use of them was deprecated, because " the people about would think it was papistical."

The most superficial reader of Holy Scripture must remember how the offering in their Temple, of fruits of the earth and flowers, was made incumbent on the Jews by the fiat of God. We have the authority of Sacred Writ too, for considering the olive the type of abundance, the lily of purity. Our blessed Saviour gave us in the vine a type of his church, in the fig-tree of his coming; and he bade us " mark the flowers of the field, how they grow."

Considering this divine sanction, we cannot be surprised that flowers should have been used as *emblems* to a considerable extent. We do not refer to mere secular types, adopted from the imaginative people of the east, indicating passion by a tulip, love by a rose, where the myrtle, and cypress, and poppy are enwreathed to denote despair, the bergamotte and jasmin to betoken the sweets of friendship, or the acacia of chaste love.

But it was no unholy feeling which referred the eternal quiver of the aspen leaf, to the then supposed fact of our Saviour's cross having been made of that tree, and, therefore, that from that moment the leaves have trembled — can never rest. There is a pretty superstition, that the dark spots on the leaf of the *arum* (dragon-flower), were·caused by a few drops of the Saviour's blood falling on the plant; there is a prettier, which attaches to the same cause the color of the robin's breast, it having chanced to nestle at the foot of the cross.

The hawthorn, called *aubepine*, or morning of the year, called also the noble thorn, as supposing it to have been the thorny crown of Christ, is traditioned from that circumstance, doubtless, to have the power of counteracting poison, while he who bears a branch shall be unscathed in thunder ; as, also, that no malevolent spirit can enter the place where it may be.

That would surely be a right and truthful sentiment which would cause the " wise of heart " watching the snow-drop — so fragile and so pure — noiselessly, patiently, but surely, making its way through a bed of snow in the inclemency of winter, to point to it, and to use it as an emblem of consolation. It was dedicated from its purity to the blessed Virgin. Even that holiest of all created women was not dishonored by the ascription. Many a young child has been taught quickly by

16

the passion-flower that history of his Saviour, which could
not otherwise have been impressed without many lessons.
From the scarlet pimpernel, the " cheerful pimpernel,"
" the poor man's weather-glass," as it is commonly called,
how well was he taught precaution and foresight; from
the sunflower and all its numerous class, which

> " Turn to their God, when he sets,
>   The same look which they turned when he rose,"

faithful gratitude to the bestower of life and warmth.
From the day's eye, or common daisy, and myriad other
flowers which open cheerily in a morning, and in the
evening fold their leaves and droop " as if in prayer,"
was taught the duty of morning thanksgiving, the necessity of evening supplication. Nature herself, not the
church, taught the infant, who, having been accustomed
to watch an acacia tree, would not go to bed. He said
" it was not bed-time, for the acacia tree had not begun
its prayers."

Is it any marvel that the Christian church, the only
one to recognize fully Him,

> " Whose sunshine and whose showers
>   Turn all the patient ground to flowers,"

should have habitually resorted to these mute but eloquent remembrancers at that solemn service when the
dust returned to earth as it was, and the spirit returned
to God who gave it?

Nor was the superstition unpleasing, however ill-
founded, which taught that the surest way to prevent
evil spirits from haunting the graves of those we loved,
was to keep them freshly planted, or strewn with flowers,

which by their purity are supposed to prevent the approach of any earthly evil.

As under the Promise the first plat of ground was a sepulchre, so under its fulfilment the first sepulchre was in a garden; "in a garden Christ was placed in the earth, that the malediction on Adam might be eradicated."

The bay has been more especially appropriated to funeral solemnities, because it has been said that this tree, when apparently dead to the very root, will revive, and its withered branches reassume their wonted verdure; and its decay is said to be predicative of some accident. The ancients believed it to be a protection from lightning, and it has often been planted in England as a security therefrom. It used to be supposed also that the aromatic emissions of these trees cleared the air and resisted contagion.

The primitive Christians decorated young women with flowers when they were buried; a custom which always obtained in England, where it has also been common until lately, and perhaps is still so in places, to hang a garland of white roses over the grave of a person dying young. These are the " virgin crants," the " maiden strewments," alluded to by Shakspeare, as being granted to Ophelia instead of the " shards, flints, and pebbles," which (she having committed suicide) should be thrown on her; and so when Fidele is supposed to be dead, Arviragus bursts out thus : —

> " With fairest flowers
> While summer lasts, and I live here, Fidele,
> I'll sweeten thy sad grave ; thou shalt not lack
> The flower that's like thy face, pale primrose, nor
> The azured bell, like thy veins ; no, nor
> The leaf of Eglantine."

Some of Herrick's prettiest lines run thus : —

" Follow me weeping to my turf, and there
　Let fall a primrose, and with it a tear ;
　Then, lastly, let some weekly strewings be
　Devoted to the memory of me ;
　Then shall my ghost not walk about, but keep
　Still in the cool and silent shades of sleep."

Rosemary, so commonly used at weddings, is in great request at funerals, in several parts of England, even to this day. In former times it was considered indispensable. Friar Lawrence, when the Capulets are weeping over Juliet, directs thus : —

" Stick your rosemary
　On this fair corse ; and as the custom is,
　In all her best array, bear her to church."

And Gay writes : —

" Upon her grave the rosemary they threw,
　The daisy, buttered-flower, and endive blue. "

Herrick's couplet shows its constant adaptation to marriage and death : —

" Grow for two ends, it matters not at all,
　Be it for my bridal or my burial."

A French writer describing an English funeral in the time of William III., says that every one takes a sprig of rosemary to put in the grave ; and an engraving of a funeral in Hogarth, represents each mourner as carrying a sprig.

Doubtless, from its greenness and fragrance, having "seeming and savor all the winter long," it was a token of remembrance. So poor Ophelia to her brother — "There's rosemary, that's for remembrance ; pray you, Love, remember."

Aubrey, in his Miscellanies, records the custom at Oakley, in Surrey, of planting rose-trees on the graves of lovers by the survivors ; and in Wales, to this day, not only are roses planted round graves, but it is usual to keep the graves freshly strewn over for twelve months with green herbs and flowers.

16*

CHANNING'S MONUMENT.

The Monument to William Ellery Channing is situated in Yarrow Path. It is wrought in fine Italian marble, from a design by Washington Allston.

On one side of the sarcophagus is this inscription : —

Here rest the remains of

WILLIAM ELLERY CHANNING,

Born 7th April, 1780,

At Newport, R. I.

Ordained June 1st, 1803,

As a Minister of Jesus Christ, to the Society worshipping God

In Federal street, Boston :

Died 2d October, 1842,

While on a journey at Bennington, Vermont.

On the other side are these words —

In Memory of

WILLIAM ELLERY CHANNING,

Honored throughout Christendom

For his eloquence and courage in maintaining and advocating

The great cause of

Truth, Religion, and Human Freedom,

This Monument

Is gratefully and reverently erected

By the Christian Society of which, during nearly forty years,

He was Pastor.

FUNEREAL EMBLEMS AND DEVICES.

THERE are many truths not explained by philosophy, nor demonstrable by reason, which may be illustrated in a pleasing manner by emblems. Science does not teach us all we wish to know, and imagination often suggests a truth which is too deeply involved in mystery, to be clearly comprehended or fully believed. Religion is half buried in obscurity, and reveals doctrines which are inexplicable, as heaven itself is invisible and the spiritual world incapable of being located. Many ideas, connected with the state of our existence hereafter, belong to the same mysterious circle of truths. These ideas are pleasingly illustrated by emblems, which contain intimations, not demonstrations of truth, and afford glimpses of light which has never yet fully irradiated the human mind. It is for these reasons that emblems are so generally employed to convey to the mind an image of the soul's condition in the future world, and to impress it with a belief of things which are only dimly seen by the eye of faith.

An emblem may be defined a visible image, or a picture that suggests to the mind the idea of some abstract truth. It is indeed a pictured allegory or parable. In the East, emblems are still freely used in profane as well as in sacred things. Among the Persians fire is the emblem of their Deity, expressing by the same image his power and his beneficence — heat being the source of all life, and having power to destroy all created forms of matter. The serpent with its tail in its mouth is an Egyptian emblem of eternity; but modern taste revolts at its puerility, and it really affords no idea of infinity, such as might be represented by a light whose rays extend illimitably in all directions from the centre. There is a savor of the burlesque in this emblem of the serpent; and it is surprising that any person will admit it among the devices of monumental sculpture.

In India there are still in existence statues of immense size which are emblematical of virtue. They are furnished with several arms, to indicate the necessity of so many forces to enable one to contend successfully against vice. Xenophanes, an ancient poet, remarks in certain verses, that every animal suggests images that assist the human mind in forming conceptions of the Deity. The wings of birds are associated with the idea of progress upward and through space, without contact with the earth. Hence they are found in all mythological pictures of supernatural beings, and are not confined to the Jewish and Christian theology. Many of the Pagan Deities are furnished with wings which, in the sacred books, are confined to angels. The image of the true God needs no such aid, as he is everywhere present at the same moment. By the Hebrew Prophets he is represented as seated on the clouds, from which he issues his commands to the inhabitants of the earth. There is no material image that affords so exalted an idea of the power of the Deity as this. Plato, and after him Pascal, in his "Pensees," adopted the beautiful emblem of Timæus of Locris, who describes the Deity by the image of "a circle whose centre is everywhere, and whose circumference nowhere."

One of the most delightful of our sacred emblems is that which represents Hope as the image of a female leaning upon an anchor, the symbolical representation of steadfastness and confidence, without which hope cannot exist. This is a very appropriate emblem for a cemetery, where our only consolations are derived from our confidence in a future life, and our faith in the assurances of religious hope. The emblem of the Dove has been employed by poets and artists of all ages and nations. The chariot of Venus is drawn by turtle doves; and the dove and the lamb, so remarkable for their gentleness and innocence, have always been used as symbols of Christian virtues, and engraved on funereal monuments, the one as the emblem of innocence, and the other of constant affection on the part of the mourner. The dove bearing an olive-branch, has been regarded as an emblem of peace, because it bore the olive-branch to the ark, as proof that the deluge had ceased, and that the Deity was reconciled to man.

The study of emblems is closely connected with that of monumental sculpture, inasmuch as they are the foundation of all those devices which are used to decorate a tombstone. A pleasing device is to the artist what a pleasing metaphor is to a poet. Indeed, a sculptor has no other way of expressing his ideas upon marble, than by means of emblems, unless he gives the real image of a thing. The head with wings, that appears so often on the upper part of the head stones, in our old graveyards, is an interesting device which was probably derived from that of the winged globe. The head is intended to represent the soul, and the wings the image of its flight. These and other devices, which were so generally employed by the Puritans, are vastly more poetical than those which are seen on the monuments of noble and royal families in Great Britain. On the latter are represented the armorial bearings of the family and various symbols of heraldry. The effigy of the Earl of Pembroke, who died in 1324, reposes in Westminster Abbey, on the summit of the tomb, with the feet and hands bare, and the latter elevated and joined as in prayer. The rest of the figure is clad in the prevailing armor of that period, and equipped as the Earl was when he was living. At the head, which rests on a double cushion, are two small figures in flowing drapery, kneeling on one knee and supporting a third, intended to represent angels supporting the soul in its ascent to heaven. At the feet of the Earl is a lion couchant. The only religious emblem on this monument consists of the angels which are really made secondary in importance to the lion. In almost all the monuments of that day, a lion is introduced crouching at the feet of the effigy; and among these ancient sculptured figures we find but few religious emblems, though the effigies, for the most part, are clasping their hands as in prayer.

The emblem of the cross is historical, referring to the manner of the death of Jesus Christ, and is intended to signify the Christian faith of the dead, and the dedication of his remains to the founder of that faith. In our cemeteries it is usually confined to the graves of members ot the Catholic Church, though it should be strictly emblematical of the Christian religion. The drooping figure of sorrow, in the attitude of weeping, is interesting and appropriate, and is rendered still more picturesque by the bending branches of the willow that extend over it. A figure of a rose and a rose-bud signifies the repose of the mother and child in the same grave, and the image of a lamb alone is emblematical of an infant. A butterfly just emerged from a chrysalis is intended to represent the mortal putting on immortality.

Nearly all the monuments in our cemeteries are, themselves, emblems, no less than the devices upon them. Such are the altar, the cross, the broken column, signifying life cut short in its prime, and the funereal urn which refers to the custom of urn-burial. The burning taper upon the altar is a pleasing device connected with a Catholic ceremony. A Phœnix rising out of its ashes is a very happy emblem of resurrection. A sleeping child is rather a picture than an emblem, because it presents to the mind a literal fact rather than a fanciful image. Many interesting emblems are derived from plants. The white star of Bethlehem is an emblem of purity, and would be an appropriate device on the tomb of a virtuous young girl, and a wreath of amaranth suspended over it would symbolize the immortality upon which she has entered. The snow drop is a beautiful symbol of hope, because it blooms before the snows of winter are gone, and brings to us the promise of spring. The passion flower would be an appropriate device on the tomb-stone of a Christian, as it represents the crown of thorns, the cross, the nails of the cross, and the five wounds of Christ. The asphodel might be used as a device to signify grief or regret, as it was planted near tombs among the ancients, with the same signification. Many other pleasing devices might be derived from the vegetable world, but they must be apparent; if far-fetched and difficult of interpretation they lose their effect.

On the portal of Mount Auburn is a winged globe, which is intended to signify or emblemize the care of Divine Providence, the earth being sustained on wings, as the children of the earth are sustained by the invisible arm of the Deity. This is an Egyptian device, and was taken from the façades of the Egyptian temples. The figure of a mountain which was employed by the Egyptians as a symbol of death, was probably connected with the pyramids; though it is not unlikely that the idea of the pyramids might have been derived from the mountain, which was excavated by that people for the construction of tombs.

THE FUNERAL. — An Eclogue.

By Robert Southey.

STRANGER.

Whom are they ushering from the world, with all
This pageantry, and long parade of death?

TOWNSMAN.

A long parade, indeed, sir; and yet here
You see but half; round yonder bend it reaches
A furlong farther, carriage behind carriage.

STRANGER.

'Tis but a mournful sight, and yet the pomp
Tempts me to stand a gazer.

TOWNSMAN.

         Yonder school-boy,
Who plays the truant, says the proclamation
Of peace was nothing to the show, and even
The chairing of the members at election
Would not have been a finer sight than this,
Only that red and green are prettier colors
Than all this mourning. There, sir, you behold
One of the red-gowned worthies of the city,
The envy and the boast of our exchange,
Ay, what was worth, last week, a good half million,
Screwed down in yonder hearse.

STRANGER.

         Then he was born
Under a lucky planet, who to-day
Puts mourning on for his inheritance.

TOWNSMAN.

When first I heard his death, that very wish
Leaped to my lips; but now the closing scene
Of the comedy hath wakened wiser thoughts;
And I bless God, that when I go to the grave,
There will not be the weight of wealth, like his,
To sink me down.

STRANGER.

　　　　The camel and the needle, —
Is that then in your mind?

TOWNSMAN.

　　　　Even so.　The text
Is gospel wisdom.　I would ride the camel, —
Yea, leap him flying through the needle's eye,
As easily as such a pampered soul
Could pass the narrow gate.

STRANGER.

　　　　Your pardon, sir;
But sure, this lack of Christian charity
Looks not like Christian truth.

TOWNSMAN.

　　　　Your pardon, too, sir;
If, with this text before me, I should feel
In preaching mood!　But for these barren fig-trees,
With all their flourish and their leafiness,
We have been told their destiny and use,
When the axe is laid unto the root, and they
Cumber the earth no longer.

17

STRANGER.

Was his wealth
Stored fraudfully, the spoil of orphans wronged,
And widows who had none to plead their right?

TOWNSMAN.

All honest, open, honorable gains;
Fair legal interest, bonds and mortgages,
Ships to the east and west.

STRANGER.

Why judge you then
So hardly of the dead?

TOWNSMAN.

For what he left
Undone: — for sins, not one of which is mentioned
In the Ten Commandments.   He, I warrant him,
Believed no other gods than those of the creed:
Bowed to no idols, — but his money bags;
Swore no false oaths, save at a custom-house;
Kept the Sabbath idle; built a monument
To honor his dead father; did no murder;
And prudently observed the seventh command,
Never picked pockets; never bore false witness;
And never with that all commanding wealth,
Coveted his neighbor's house, nor ox, nor ass.

STRANGER.

You knew him then, it seems?

TOWNSMAN.

As all men know
The virtues of your hundred thousanders:
They never hide their lights beneath a bushel.

STRANGER.

Nay, nay, uncharitable, sir ! for often
Doth bounty, like a streamlet, flow unseen
Freshening and giving life along its course.

TOWNSMAN.

We track the streamlet by the brighter green
And livelier growth it gives : — but as for this —
This was a pool that stagnated and stunk :
The rains of heaven engendered nothing in it,
But slime and foul corruption.

STRANGER.

          Yet even these
Are reservoirs, whence public charity
Still keeps her channels full.

TOWNSMAN.

          Now, sir, you touch
Upon the point. This man of half a million
Had all these public virtues which you praise : —
But the poor man rung never at his door ;
And the old beggar at the public gate,
Who, all the summer long, stands hat in hand,
He knew how vain it was to lift an eye
To that hard face. Yet he was always found
Among your ten and twenty pound subscribers,
Your benefactors in the newspapers.
His alms were money put to interest
In the other world, — donations to keep open
A running charity account with heaven :
Retaining fees against the last assizes,
When for the trusted talents, strict account

Shall be required from all, and the old arch lawyer
Plead his own cause as plaintiff.

STRANGER.

                        I must needs
Believe you, sir : — these are your witnesses,
These mourners here, who from their carriages
Gape at the gaping crowd.   A good March wind
Were to be prayed for now, to lend their eyes
Some decent rheum.   The very hireling mute
Bears not a face blanker of all emotion,
Than the old servant of the family !
How can this man have lived, that thus his death
Costs not the soiling one white handkerchief ?

TOWNSMAN.

Who should lament for him, sir, in whose heart
Love had no place, no natural charity ?
The parlor spaniel, when she heard his step,
Rose slowly from the hearth, and stole aside
With creeping pace ; she never raised her eyes
To woo kind words from him, nor laid her head
Upraised upon his knee, with fondling whine.
How could it be but thus !   Arithmetic
Was the sole science he was ever taught.
The multiplication table was his creed,
His pater-noster and his decalogue.
When yet he was a boy, and should have breathed
The open air and sunshine of the fields,
To give his blood its natural spring and play,
He, in a close and dusky counting-house,
Smoke-dried, and seared, and shrivelled up his heart.
So from the way in which he was trained up,

His feet departed not ; he toiled and moiled,
Poor muck-worm ! through his threescore years and
    ten,
And when the earth shall now be shovelled on him,
If that which served him for a soul were still
Within its husk, 't would still be dirt to dirt.

STRANGER.

Yet your next newspapers will blazon him,
For industry and honorable wealth,
A bright example.

TOWNSMAN.

Even half a million
Gets him no other praise.   But come this way,
Some twelve months hence, and you will find his
    virtues
Trimly set forth in lapidary lines,
Faith, with her torch beside, and little cupids
Dropping upon his urn their marble tears.

17*

THE BOWDITCH STATUE.

The Bronze Statue of Dr. Bowditch stands upon a granite foundation, facing the main entrance to Mount Auburn, and is the work of Ball Hughes, an English artist, formerly a resident in the United States. It is said to be a very correct likeness of the great Mathematician.

MOURNING CUSTOMS.

By Mrs. Stone.

HARDLY more diversified are the nations who people the earth, than are the customs and observances used by them to signalize the arrival of the commonest of all visitors, though most awful of all guests, the " black veiled king of the dead." The Jews of old rent their garments and sprinkled dust on their heads, a practice followed to this day in Abyssinia. The practice of tearing the garments is, we are told, commuted by the Jews of these economical days into carefully cutting away a small, and probably a perfectly insignificant portion thereof. They bottled their tears also, a custom referred to in the 56th Psalm; and that this practice was customary with the Greeks and Romans, the number of lachrymatories, or tear bottles, found among their sepulchral remains, sufficiently testifies.

. A late writer has pointed out the analogy between a mourning custom of the Australian savages of to-day, and of the ancient Hebrews, viz., the cutting or scratching the face with the nails, tearing the flesh between the eyes, and otherwise maiming the person, as is the custom of the female aborigines of Australia on the death of a relative. Hence the warning in Holy Writ — " Ye shall not make any cuttings in your flesh for the dead, nor print any marks upon you." Lev. xix. 28.

The " cup of consolation " referred to in Scripture, and the " bread of mourning," sometimes called also the " bread of bitterness," were the refreshments always among the Jews, supplied by friends to the bereaved person on his return from the funeral — in its origin a most kind and hospitable relief to the bereaved family.

The Jews cherished their grief in every way; they invited it; they pampered it; they took all pains to recall the poignancy of their affliction. They ate their food seated on the ground and without shoes. For three days they strove not to repress their tears. For seven days people came morning and evening to weep with them. At the end of seven days the mourner might attend the synagogue; but thirty days must elapse ere he was allowed to bathe, or to dress his beard.

In many countries the term of mourning was fixed by law. The Jews, as we have seen, mourned thirty days; the Lacedæmonians but eleven; the Egyptians from forty to seventy days. Romulus fixed a widow's mourning at ten months, the length of his year. The Imperial Code not only ordained a year's mourning, but declared the widow infamous if she married within that period. The time of mourning is fixed by law in China, three years being the period required for a parent.

The Jewish fashion of throwing ashes on the head, beating the breast and tearing the flesh with the nails, was, on occasions of peculiar concernment, adopted by the Greeks. But in addition to the funeral feasts, which among Greeks and Romans soon ceased to wear an entirely lugubrious aspect, they enlivened their melancholy with games and funeral processions. These entertainments among the Greeks consisted chiefly of horse-races, where garlands of parsley were awarded to the victors. The Roman games were processions, and the very characteristic entertainment of the mortal strife of gladiators and the funeral pile. These funeral games were abolished by the Emperor Claudius.

A custom prevailed among some of the ancient nations of cutting off the hair and casting it on the body or into the tomb. So did the Roman women on Virginia; so did the Ephesian matron on her husband — all unluckily for her second nuptials; so did Orestes on his father's tomb; Hecuba on her sons; and so did the pure, and gentle, and pious Antigone on her brother's. The shaving of the head, or at least the cutting off the hair, seems in all ages to have been considered an emblem of mourning, and a token of violent affliction. The Jews made their heads bald, and clipped their beards.

The classical nations also cut off their hair; indeed, it seems it was their opinion that a lock of hair from the head of the dying person must be offered to Proserpine, before the soul of the sufferer could be released. Hence, perhaps, the custom of mourners to shave their hair as in Alcestes : —

> " Nor vase of fountain water do I see
>   Before the doors, as custom claims, to bathe
> · The corse ; and none hath on the portal placed
>   His locks, in solemn mourning for the dead,
>   Usually shorn."

They were afterwards cast on the funeral pile.

The Persian soldiers cut off their hair on the death of Alexander. This custom continued to be the expression of general mourning. The Empress Irene cut off her hair when the Emperor Alexius died; and we are told that the modern Greek women retain the usage. Even so late as the middle of the sixteenth century, a writer, describing the cemetery of a Servian town, says — " Large bunches of hair also hung from many of the tombs, which had been deposited there by the women as a sign of mourning."

It seems to have been ever usual to utter noisy demonstrations of sorrow for deceased friends, and also to hire assistance that the noise might be great enough. Such assistants were the Præficæ, the old women hired by the Romans to shed tears and sing the praises of deceased persons, and who usually followed after the trumpeter or other musician in the funeral procession. The Jews used to hire minstrels and others to mourn and lament for the dead.

"And when Jesus came into the ruler's house, and saw *the minstrels and the people making a great noise,*

"He said unto them, Give place : for the maid is not dead, but sleepeth." Matt. ix. 23, 24.

The poorest man in Israel, when his wife died, never had less than two pipes, and one mourning woman. Thus *mourning became an art*, which devolved on women of shrill voices, copious of tears, and skilful in lamenting and praising the dead in mournful songs and eulogies. On a signal from the chief mourner, these mourning women took the chief part, and the real mourners remained comparatively silent. So in ancient times.

In modern days the most sedate of all people, the Chinese, on the occasion of a funeral, burst out into loud shrieks and lamentations. All along the Levant also the practice of *keening* is in full vogue. Buckhardt, in his travels, tells us that a particular class of women is called in on the occasion of a death, whose sole profession is that of howling, in the most heart-rending accents, for a small sum paid to them by the house, Medina being the only town where this custom did not prevail. At Yembo, where the plague was raging, he heard when he retired to rest, innumerable voices breaking out on all sides into heart-breaking and dreadful cries, which kept him awake the whole night.

This practice seems, indeed, universal in the East. The funerals of most people in decent circumstances are attended by singers and howlers. The Roman Mulieres Præficæ correspond precisely, it is said, with the women who lead the keen in Ireland, where the outcry is too outrageous to be taken as an effusion of real sorrow. The custom is said to be of ancient, even of supernatural origin, having been first sung by invisible spirits in the air, over the grave of one of the early kings of Ireland. So we are told in Mrs Hall's Ireland, from which the following description of the Irish Keen is taken : —

" The keen commences. The women of the household range themselves on either side of the bed, rise with one accord, and moving their bodies with a slow motion to and fro, their arms apart, they continue to keep up a heart-rending cry. This cry is interrupted for awhile, to give the leading keener an opportunity of commencing.

" The rapidity and ease with which both the blessings and curses of the keen are uttered, and the epigrammatic force of each concluding stanza, generally bring tears into the eyes of the most indifferent spectator, or produce a state of terrible excitement. The dramatic effect of the scene is very powerful : the darkness of the death chamber, illumined only by candles that glare upon the corpse — the manner of repetition, or acknowledgment that runs round when the keener gives a sentence — the deep, yet suppressed sobs of the nearer relatives, and the stormy, uncontrollable cry of the widow or bereaved husband, when allusion is made to the domestic virtues of the deceased, all heighten the effect of the keen.

" The keener having finished a stanza of the keen, sets up the wail (indicated in the music, by the *semibreve* at the conclusion), in which all the mourners join. Then a momentary silence ensues, when the keener commences again, and so on, each stanza ending in the wail.

" The lamentation is not always confined to the keener. Any one present who has the gift of poetry may put in his or her verse, and this sometimes occurs. Thus the night wears away in alternations of lamentation and silence; the arrival of each new friend or relative being, as already observed, the signal for renewing the keen."

From the old classical epithet of " black veiled king of the dead," one would suppose that black had been universally, as with ourselves, the mourning color. Not so, however. Plutarch writes that in their mourning, women laid aside their purple, gold and jewelry, and clothed themselves in white, " like as then the dead body was wrapped in white clothes. This color was thought the fittest, because it is clear, pure, and sincere, and least defiled."

So in our own country (England) some white, an emblem of purity, is always displayed on the hearse and pall of a child or unmarried person. In the northern parts of England, indeed, a white linen scarf or hat-band is an indispensable part of mourning for the dead at any age.

Coarse red hempen cloth is the only dress allowed in China for the first and deepest mourning. In time this is changed to white; and silk may be worn in half-mourning, but blue or white sleeves are indispensable. White being chosen as expressive of the belief that the dead are in heaven, the place of purity. So more practically in Egypt yellow is chosen, because it represents natural decay as exhibited in fruits and flowers; whilst in Turkey blue is often adopted to denote the sky as the place of departed spirits. All this, however, whether in good or bad taste, is moveable mourning; but we are told that the first duty of the women of Medina, on assuming mourning, is *to dye the hands* with indigo.

In France and England, however, black is the universal mourning color, and in the former country, at any rate, the formalities of grief were of a very peculiar nature; for any royal mourner was compelled to lie in or on bed. The higher the rank of the person, the longer was this prostration of grief expected to continue.

On the death of any royal or noble person, or indeed of one of gentle blood, the nearest of kin always went to bed, and there remained, or was supposed to remain, a certain number of weeks or days. And if the mourner were of the blood-royal, the degree of affliction to be exhibited was prescribed by authority. In the fifteenth century a Queen of France was required to confine herself in bed, *or appear to do so*, for one year, from the time of her royal husband's death.

Affliction being proportionately softened as lofty rank graduated to a lower level. Peeresses were required to lie in bed only nine days ; but for the remainder of the six weeks, so passed by royalty, these mitigated mourners were to sit in front of their beds " upon a piece of black cloth."

That there is to the most earnest mourner a feeling somewhat consolatory, or at least soothing in a mourning robe, there is no question ; but it is the black, the mourning, the change from gay attire and jewelry, to something completely opposite — something whose dim hue assimilates with the shadow on the heart, that is sought. One truly sorrowing cares little about tucks " graduated " to a shade in crape, or silk, just as much *glacé* as modern fashion allows to mingle with that lugubrious ornament.

It is right that those who can afford the pomp and circumstance of woe, and who are comforted thereby, should have that solace to its utmost extent ; whether the pomp be displayed in Chinese red cotton, or in English crape-

robed mutes and weepers. It is *wrong* that this pomp
and circumstance should be so engrafted on our national
habits, that the desolate widow, the penniless orphan, or
unportioned sister, *must* cruelly embarrass themselves to
obtain the precious vestments which custom dictates, or
be supposed to fail in respect to the husband, the father,
the brother, whom they loved in their heart of hearts, and
to a re-union with whom they look as their chiefest hope
and comfort.

The mourning which Christ hath hallowed — for *he
wept for Lazarus* — has no communion with crape bands
and weepers. There is no teacher like Death. In his
dread presence the great mystery of life opens on the
sorrowing heart, the awakened mind. He teaches that
faith and hope by which the bruised seed is bound, the
broken heart healed ; and as fragrance, which in its per-
fectness was unknown, emanates from an herb when it is
crushed, so does sorrow develope virtues and consolations
undreamt of in gay and happy hours.

Thus does the faithful mourner learn that sorrow and
pain and suffering — those " many waters," which threatened but did not overwhelm — passed, the purified and
renewed spirit will emerge on that happier shore, where
sin and sorrow are unknown, where tears are wiped from
every eye, and where the toil-worn, grief-worn, stricken,
but contrite denizen of the earth, shall stand blessed, pure
and happy as a little child, in the presence of his Creator.

And so chastened and subdued, and passing " cheerly
on through prayer unto the tomb," the true mourner
looks beyond that solemn vestibule, to re-union with those
deeply and enduringly loved on earth, who are — not
lost — but gone before.

ANCIENT GREEK EPITAPHS.

A PECULIAR pathos characterizes the Greek Epitaphs, and though they are generally wanting in those expressions of hope in an existence after death that distinguish the epitaphs of Christian nations, they are still read with interest by all persons of cultivated mind. The Romans were more accustomed to weaving a moral lesson in their epitaphs, but those of the Greeks surpass them in tenderness of sentiment and felicity of expression. The following examples are selected from Pettigrew's collection.

Of general application, and in relation to the universality of death, and the moral lesson to be derived from it, we have, —

By Archilochus : —

Jove sits in highest Heaven, and opes the springs,
To man, of awful and forbidden things.
Death seals the fountains of reward and fame :
Man dies, and leaves no guardian of his name.
Applause awaits us only while we live,
While we can honor take and honor give :
Yet were it base for man, of woman born,
To mock the naked ghost with jests or scorn.

By Simonides : —

Human strength is unavailing ;
Boastful tyranny unfailing ;
All in life is care and labor ;
And our unrelenting neighbor,

> Death, for ever hovering round;
> Whose inevitable wound,
> When he comes prepared to strike,
> Good and bad will feel alike.

The Greeks do not appear to have considered the introduction of the name as essential to an inscription; thus on some who were shipwrecked, —

By Archilochus: —

> Loud are our griefs, my friend, and vain is he
> Would steep the sense in mirth and revelry
> O'er those we mourn; the hoarse resounding wave
> Hath closed and whelmed them in their ocean grave.
> Deep sorrow swells each breast. But Heaven bestows
> One healing med'cine for severest woes —
> Resolved endurance — for affliction pours
> To all by turns, — to-day the cup is ours.
> Bear bravely, then, the common trial sent,
> And cast aside effeminate lament.

There is much feeling in the following, —

By Amyte: —

> Drop o'er Antibia's grave a pious tear;
> For virtue, beauty, wit, lie buried here.
> Full many a suitor sought her father's hall,
> To gain the maiden's love; but Death o'er all
> Claimed due precedence: Who shall death withstand?
> Their hopes were blasted by his ruthless hand.

The following contains some hint of future existence,—

By Leonidas of Tarentum : —

BY A MOTHER ON HER SON.

Unhappy child !   Unhappy I, who shed,
A mother's sorrows o'er thy funeral bed !
Thou'rt gone in youth, Amyntas : I in age,
Must wander through a lonely pilgrimage,
And sigh for regions of unchanging night,
And sicken at the day's repeated light.
O guide me hence, sweet Spirit, to the bourn
Where, in thy presence, I shall cease to mourn.

By Simmias of Thebes : —

ON SOPHOCLES.

Wind, gentle evergreen, to form a shade
Around the tomb where Sophocles is laid.
Sweet ivy, wind thy boughs, and intertwine
With blushing roses and the clustering vine.
Thus shall thy lasting leaves, with beauties hung,
Prove grateful emblems of the lays he sung.

By Speusippus : —

ON PLATO.

Plato's dead form this earthly shroud invests ;
His soul among the godlike heroes rests.

By Callimachus : —

Beside the tomb where Bathus' son is laid,
Thy heedless feet, O passenger ! have strayed.
18 *

Well skilled in all the minstrel's lore was he;
Yet had his hour for sport and jollity.

By the same: —

EPITAPH ON HIS FATHER.

Know thou, this tomb who passest by,
At once both sire and son am I,
To a name most dear to us,
Cyrenean Callimachus.
One of his country was the shield,
In many a glorious battle-field:
The other sang so sweet a strain,
That Envy listened with disdain,
And strove to vanquish him in vain.
For him on whom the Muses smiled,
Even at his birth — their favorite child —
In age they never will forsake,
But his gray hairs their temple make.

By Meleager: —

ON HELIODORA.

Tears o'er my Heliodora's grave I shed,
Affection's fondest tribute to the dead.
O flow, my bitter sorrows, o'er her shrine,
Pledge of the love that bound her soul to mine!
Break, break, my heart, o'er-charged with bursting
    woe,
An empty offering to the shades below!
Ah! plant regretted! Death's remorseless power
With dust unfruitful choked thy full blown flower.
Take, Earth, the gentle inmate to thy breast,
And soft entombed, bid Heliodora rest!

The next, by an anonymous author, places some hopes upon another and better land ;

ON PROTE.

Thou art not dead, my Prote ! though no more
A sojourner on earth's tempestuous shore ;
Fled to the peaceful islands of the blest,
Where youth and love, forever beaming rest ;
Or joyful wandering on Elysian ground,
Among sweet flowers where not a thorn is found.
No winter freezes there, no summer fires,
No sickness weakens and no labor tires ; ·
No longer poverty, nor thirst oppress,
Nor envy of man's boasted happiness ;
But spring forever glows serenely bright,
And bliss immortal hails the heavenly light!

The Epigrammatic style of many of the Greek epitaphs is well illustrated in that ascribed to Anacreon, on the tomb of Timocritus : —

Timocritus adorns this humble grave ;
Man spares the coward, and destroys the brave.

It was common among the Greeks to inscribe epitaphs to those who had distinguished themselves in war, and had fallen in battle. The commemoration of those who were distinguished for their wealth alone, was not so common as with us.

By Simonides : —

ON THOSE WHO FELL AT THERMOPYLÆ.

In dark Thermopylæ they lie ;
O death of glory, there to die !

Their tomb an altar is, their name
A mighty heritage of fame :
Their dirge is triumph — cumbering rust,
And Time that turneth all to dust —
That tomb shall never waste nor hide, —
The tomb of warriors true and tried.
The full voiced praise of Greece around
Lies buried in that sacred mound ;
Where Sparta's King Leonidas,
In death eternal glory has.

By the same : —

ON THE SAME.

These for their native land, through death's dark shade,
    Who freely passed, now deathless glory wear.
They die not ; but by Virtue's sovereign aid,
    Are borne from Hades to the upper air.

By the same : —

ON THOSE WHO FELL AT THE EURYMEDON.

These by the streams of famed Eurymedon
Their envied youth's short-brilliant race have run :
In swift-winged ships, and on th' embattled field,
Alike they forced the Median bows to yield,
Breaking their foremost ranks.   Now here they lie,
Their names inscribed on rolls of victory.

CONSECRATION DELL.

This is the name given to the valley which was the spot chosen for the service of consecration. The engraving represents the appearance of the dell on one side, the monument in the foreground being placed near the point where the orator stood, and the opposite slope being occupied by the crowd of persons who assembled to hear the address. At present this is a very imposing hollow, containing Forest Pond in the centre, and surrounded by paths and grounds laid out in the most pleasing and appropriate style of art. The monuments erected in the surrounding lots are seen to better advantage than any others perhaps in the Cemetery. There are many noble trees of the primitive grounds in this basin, among which are some tall beech trees, a species which is not very common in the vicinity.

GRAVES WITHOUT A STONE.

Not every good, nor every great man, has had a monument erected over his grave. Many a hero and many a philanthropist lies in a grave that is unmarked by a stone, while the craven and the unworthy, who have occupied places of honor during life, have been glorified by a monument to conceal their infamy after death, as the glitter of state concealed it while living. There would be some wisdom in endeavoring to win a monument, if it were always the reward only of real merit and of virtuous actions. So pleasing is the idea of being honored by succeeding generations, that one who is striving through persecution, neglect, poverty, and disgrace, to accomplish some great good for his fellow men, might feel compensated by the reflection that after death his actions would be recorded with praise upon a conspicuous marble edifice. But those who lie under sumptuous monuments after their death, are the same that dwelt in mansions and palaces while they were living. These marble piles have too often been erected from the same motives that prompt the courtier to flatter those who are exalted by their position; and society has learned that the inscriptions upon them, like the flattery of the living, are often without truth.

The simple headstone is seldom intended for anything more than an object by which the friends might identify the spot where the remains of the dead repose. It is commonly a mere tribute of friendship, designed not to exaggerate the worth of the dead, but to pay a tender respect to his memory. It tells that the buried one had friends who wished to keep him in remembrance, and to bear an affectionate testimony to his virtues. When, therefore, we look upon a simple headstone, we feel sensible of no attempt to exalt the dead by factitious honors: we feel that every good citizen is worthy of this humble tribute; and the record of his name and age, of the time of his death, and some few important circumstances of his history, may interest not only the living friends, but likewise the posterity of the departed, when the present generation has passed away.

But when we see a grave without a stone, we know that the person buried there was either friendless, or that his friends were too indigent to pay this last respect to his obsequies. To a person of susceptible feelings and lively imagination, a mere suggestion is often better than a full account of the circumstances of an event. When we examine a grave that is marked by a stone, the inscription commonly satisfies our curiosity in relation to the dead. The name, the age, the birth-place, and perhaps the character of the occupant are there recorded. We turn away satisfied, and read the next epitaph. As we proceed we arrive at a green hillock that stands alone and is unmarked by a stone. The rising of the ground denotes the character of the spot. It makes known that the remains of a human being are there deposited, and the imagination is left to conjecture the cause of the neglect that has attended him in his sepulture.

It may be the tomb of a stranger; of one who was lost from his family and friends, who have never heard of his death, who are still seeking for him, and waiting his return. He may have been the only son of a widowed mother, who lives in a foreign land, and who still daily offers prayers to heaven for his safety and his restoration. She wonders at his long absence, and dreams not that he lies here in a stranger's grave, which can never be known as his resting place, and where no human being can identify his remains. How many tears have been wasted that should have been poured as a sacred offering upon this green turf! How many conjectures have alternately raised the hopes and depressed the spirits of this bereaved mother, which might have been tranquillized, had she but followed the remains of this unknown slumberer to his final rest!

Many are the dead who lie in these nameless graves, and many who died with a pang of deep sorrow in their hearts, when they thought that they were far from those who knew them, and that their place of burial could never be recognized. Some perhaps would be dishonored by their own history: but how many are they whose lives would awaken in our hearts the most tender emotions, the liveliest interest in their affecting adventures, and the deepest sympathy in their misfortunes. The obscurity in which these unknown tenants of the grave is involved, affixes a romantic interest to their biography. No envy is excited by a view of their lonely resting place, as when a sumptuous marble crowns the sepulchre of one whom we knew and who was undeserving of honor. It was with a view to this escape from the envy of the world, that the youthful poet wrote these lines : —

> " Thus unlamented, let me die,
>   Steal from the world, and not a stone,
>   Tell where I lie."

Even those who during their life-time are desirous of fame and position, feel that a monumental pile, be it ever so unpretending, is calculated to excite the envy of the world, and that after all their struggles for distinction, a humble life, and an unambitious grave, are perhaps the most sincerely honored.

There is a moral in these facts which is worthy of deep study and reflection; that teaches a lesson of humility to the ambitious, and accords with the saying of Jesus, that " he that humbleth himself shall be exalted."   It proves that we do not elevate the dead by piling up costly honors on their graves, and that we may indeed exalt the truly great by the simplicity with which we mark the place of their sepulture.   When one is laid in the ground, an unpretending stone with simply his name and age recorded upon it, and a few lines referring modestly to his character and his virtues, without any ostentatious brevity, and without direct or implied eulogy, attracts the attention and wins the approbation of all.   If he attained great distinction in life, some may think that he deserved more honor after his death; but if he were truly great and worthy, his reputation is safer in the memory and affections of his countrymen, than upon the glittering marble that towers above his grave.

The most interesting graves, indeed, are those which are without a stone.   What is more picturesque than a little hillock rising up among the herbage, that marks the grave of an infant!   And how easily might this charm be destroyed by a few of those accompaniments which vanity or bad taste might have caused the surviving friends to heap up around it!   At the sight of this diminutive grave we say, how often has this green turf been sprinkled by the tears of some indigent mother, who wept the more because her tears were all the gift she had to bestow upon the grave of her beloved and lost.   A monument may be the cold offering of duty, when there were no affection and no sorrow; but the tear-drops of a sincere mourner sanctify the spot, and make it blessed forever!

To be interesting in the highest degree, a grave should be alone, or where but few others rest. Our sympathies are lost in a crowd, and a single object that is calculated to touch the heart, always most powerfully excites the imagination. Sometimes by the way-side, or on the edge of a solitary pasture, have we encountered one of these neglected graves. The poor mortal whose remains lie there, must have been friendless, or he died, perhaps, of some disease that caused him in his last moments to be forsaken. How many sad tales of affliction might be related by the spirits of those who are thus at their death set apart from the rest of the dead ! What a bitter satire on the inhumanity of man might be drawn from their history : of their virtues unnoticed and unrewarded in their humble poverty ; of their offences unjustly revenged ; their humble wants unsupplied ; their modest ambition treated with scorn ; their last sickness unvisited by friends, and their death followed by an obscure and solitary burial !

But the faith of the Christian informs him that the dead will not be judged by the honors which a mistaken world may have heaped upon them, or by the neglect to which it may have left them. The crown of righteousness may glow with heavenly lustre from the brows of many whose mortal remains lie obscure, degraded and forgotten, in these nameless graves.

THE UNKNOWN GRAVE.

By Adelaide Anne Proctor.

No name to bid us know
  Who rests below,
No word of death or birth ;
  Only the grasses wave
Over a mound of earth,
  Over a nameless grave.

Did this poor wandering heart
  In pain depart ? —
Longing, but all too late,
  For the calm home again,
Where patient watchers wait
  And still will wait in vain ?

Did mourners come in scorn,
  And thus forlorn,
Leave him with grief and shame
  To silence and decay,
And hide the tarnished name
  Of the unconscious clay ?

It may be from his side
  His loved ones died,
And last of some bright band,
  (Together now once more,)
He sought his home, the land
  Where they were gone before.

No matter — limes have made
    As cool a shade,
And lingering breezes pass
    As tenderly and slow,
As if beneath the grass,
    A monarch slept below.

No grief, though loud and deep
    Could stir that sleep ;
And earth and heaven tell
    Of rest that shall not cease,
When the cold world's farewell
    Fades into endless peace.

J. FOSS.

THE FOSS MONUMENT.

This monument is situated on Snowdrop Path. It is a noble granite block, and tastefully enclosed. Various emblematic designs of the Masonic order are cut upon it. In front of the monument is a marble table. Upon it rests the figure of a lamb, cut on a marble block. Beneath the table, on a slab, is an encased boquet of flowers. The following are the inscriptions upon the front of the monument : —

> Make us eternal truths receive,
> And practice all that we believe.

J. FOSS.

> For modes of faith let graceless zealots fight;
> His can't be wrong, whose life is in the right.

On the right hand side is also placed the following : —

"God is Love."

SACRED

TO THE MEMORY OF

MEHITABLE H.,

WIFE OF JACOB FOSS,

WHO DEPARTED THIS

LIFE, APRIL 10, 1846;

AGED 54 YEARS.

> Go, live! for the heaven's eternal year is thine,
> Go, and exalt thy mortal to divine.

19 *

THE CATACOMBS OF ROME.

EPITOMIZED FROM THE ATLANTIC MONTHLY.

THE Roman Catacombs consist, for the most part, of a subterranean labyrinth of passages, cut through the soft volcanic rock of the Campagna, so narrow as rarely to admit of two persons walking abreast easily, but here and there, on either side, opening into chambers of varying size and form. The walls of the passages, through their whole extent, are lined with narrow excavations, one above another, large enough to admit of a body being placed in each; and when they remain in their original condition, these excavations are closed in front by tiles, or by a slab of marble cemented to the rock, and in most cases bearing an inscription. Frequently there are several stories connected with each other by sloping ways.

There is no single circumstance, in relation to the catacombs, of more striking character than their vast extent. About twenty different catacombs are now known, and are more or less open, — and a year is now hardly likely to pass without the discovery of a new one; for the original number of underground cemeteries, as ascertained from the early authorities, was nearly, if not quite, three times this number. It is but a very few years since the entrance to the famous catacomb of St. Callixtus, one of the most interesting of all, was found by the Cavaliere de Rossi; and it was only in the Spring of 1855, that the buried church and catacomb of St. Alexander, on the Nomentan Way, were brought to light. Earthquakes, floods, and neglect, have obliterated the openings of many of their ancient cemeteries — and the hollow soil of the Campagna is full "of hidden graves, which men walk over without knowing where they are."

Each of the twelve great highways which ran from the gates of Rome was bordered on either side, at a short distance from the city wall, by the hidden Christian cemeteries. The only one of the catacombs, of which even a partial survey has been made, is that of St. Agnes, of a portion of which the Padre Marchi published a map in 1845. " It is calculated to contain about an eighth part of that cemetery. The greatest length of the portion thus measured is not more than seven hundred feet, and its greatest width about five hundred and fifty ; nevertheless, if we measure all the streets that it contains, their united length scarcely falls short of two English miles. This would give fifteen or sixteen miles for all the streets in the cemetery of St. Agnes." Mr. Northcote, from whose work the preceding paragraph is taken, estimates the total length of the catacombs at nine hundred miles.

Taking the above account as a fair average of the size of the catacombs, for some are larger and some smaller, we must assign to the streets of graves already known a total length of about three hundred miles, with a probability that the unknown ones are at least of equal length. This conclusion appears startling when one thinks of the close arrangement of the lines of graves along the walls of these passages. The height of the passages varies greatly, and with it the number of graves one above another; but the Padre Marchi, who is competent authority, estimates the average number at ten ; that is, five on each side, for every seven feet, — which would give a population of the dead, for the three hundred miles, of not less than two millions and a quarter. No one who has visited the catacombs can believe, surprising as this

number may seem, that the Padre Marchi's calculation
is an extravagant one as to the number of graves in a
given space. The writer of this has counted eleven
graves, one over another, on each side of the passage,
and there is no space lost between the head of one grave
and the foot of another. Everywhere there is economy
of space, — the economy of men working on a hard material, difficult to be removed, and laboring in a confined
space, with the need of haste.

The question of the number of the dead in the catacombs opens the way to many other curious questions.
The length of time that the catacombs were used as
burial places ; the probability of others, beside Christians
being buried in them ; the number of Christians at Rome
during the first two centuries, in comparison with the
total number of the inhabitants of the city ; and how far
the public profession of Christianity was attended with
peril in ordinary times at Rome, previously to the conversion of Constantine, so as to require secret and hasty
burial of the dead ; — these are points demanding solution ;
but at present those only will be taken up that relate immediately to the catacombs.

There can be no certainty with regard to the period
when the first Christian catacomb was begun at Rome,
but it was probably within a few years after the first
preaching of the Gospel there. The Christians would
naturally desire to separate themselves in burial from the
heathen, and to avoid everything having the semblance
of Pagan rites. And what mode of sepulture so natural
for them to adopt in the new and affecting circumstances
of their lives, as that which was already familiar to them,
in the account of the burial of their Lord ? They knew
that he had been " wrapped in linen, and laid in a sepulchre which was hewn out of a rock, and a stone had

been rolled unto the door of the sepulchre." They would be buried as he was. Moreover, there was a general and ardent expectation among them of the second coming of the Saviour; they believed it to be near at hand; and they believed also that then the dead would be called from their graves, clothed once more in their bodies, and that as Lazarus rose from the tomb, at the voice of his Master, so in that awful day when judgment should be passed upon the earth, their dead would rise at the call of the same beloved voice.

But there were, in all probability, other more direct, though not more powerful reasons, which led them to the choice of this mode of burial. We read that the Saviour was buried, " as the manner of the Jews is to bury." The first converts in Rome, as St. Paul's Epistle shows, were in great part among the Jews. The Gentile and Jewish Christians made one community, and the Gentiles adopted the manners of the Jews in placing their dead, " wrapped in linen cloth, in new tombs hewn out of the rock."

Believing, then, the catacombs to have been begun within a few years after the first preaching of Christianity in Rome, there is abundant evidence to prove that their construction was continued during the time when the Church was persecuted, or simply tolerated, and that they were extended during a considerable time after Christianity became the established creed of the Empire. Indeed several catacombs, now known, were not begun until some time after Constantine's conversion. They continued to be used as burial places certainly as late as the sixth century. This use seems to have been given up at the time of the frequent desolation of the land around the walls of Rome by the incursions of barbarians, and the custom, gradually discontinued, was never resumed. The catacombs then fell into neglect, were lost sight of, and their very existence was almost forgotten. But during the first five hundred years of our era, they were the burial places of a smaller or greater portion of the citizens of Rome, — and as not a single church of that time remains, they are, and contain in themselves, the most important monuments that exist of the Christian history of Rome for all that long period. — *Atlantic Monthly*, Vol. I. p. 513.

HEART BURIAL.

From "Chronicles of the Tombs."

The custom of burying the heart separately from the rest of the body prevailed in the sixteenth century, in the case of death at a distance from home. The body was deposited in a grave in the place where the person died, and the heart was sent home to the friends of the deceased. Thus, in 1569, Sir Robert Peckham, dying at Rome, his body was buried at St. Gregory in that city, and his heart at Durham Church in England.

Mr. Steele, an early writer, relates the following incident in connection with the burial. " As I came accidentally into the church, Sept. 25, 1711, a vault at the east end of the north isle being opened, into which I went, and found a small box of lead fashioned like a heart, but flat, being scarce two inches in thickness, with the lead sawdered, but the under part corroded ; the heart of Sir Robert Peckham discovered itself, wrapped within several cloths, and still smelling strong of the embalmment." On the lid was his inscription.

At Wedmore is a monument " Sacred to the memory of Captain Thomas Hodges, of the County of Somerset,

Esq., who, at the siege of Antwerp, about 1583, with un-
conquered courage, won two ensigns from the enemy,
where receiving his last wound, he gave three legacies;
his soul to his Lord Jesus, his body to be lodged in Flemish earth, his heart to be sent to his dear wife in England.

> Here lies his wounded heart, for whom
> One kingdom was too small a room,
> Two kingdoms, therefore, have thought good to part
> So stout a body and so brave a heart."

In 1859, Henry III. of France, was slain by a Jacobin
Friar.   Camden says his heart was enclosed in a small
tomb, with an inscription in Latin, of which the following is a translation : —

> " Whether thy choice or chance thee thither brings,
> Stay, passenger, and wail the hap of kings.
> This little stone a great King's heart doth hold,
> That ruled the fickle French and Polacks bold,
> Whom, with a mighty warlike host attended,
> With traitorous knife, a cowled monster ended.
> So frail are even the highest earthly things.
> Go, passenger, and wail the fate of kings."

Lord Edward Bruce fell in a duel in Holland, with
Sir Edward Sackville, in 1613.   His body was buried in
the great Church of Ber-genop-Zoom, the place where
the duel was fought, and where a monument was erected
to his memory.   His heart was found in 1808, in the old
Abbey Church of Culcross, in Perthshire, in a silver box
shaped like a heart, with name and arms inscribed and
delineated on it.

Mr. Faulkner states in his History and Antiquities of
Hammersmith Church, that it was the custom to take

out the heart from the urn in which it was deposited, and on the aniversary of its entombment, *to refresh it with a glass of wine.* This practice was continued for upwards of a century and a half, with the heart of Sir Nicholas Crispe.

The heart of Sir William Temple was, in 1699, buried in a silver box, at Moore Park, under the Sundial in the garden. His body was placed in Westminster Abbey.

The heart of James II., in 1701, was buried at St. Mary of Chaillot, near Paris: his brain in the Scotch college, and here also the heart of his Queen. The disposal of the body and its members of this monarch is very singular. Rev. Longueville Jones states, that the king left his brains to the Scotch College at Paris, and some other parts to the Irish and English Colleges in the same city. His heart was bequeathed to the Dames de St. Marie, at Chaillot; but the body was interred in the Monastery of English Benedictine Monks, in the Rue du Faubourg St. Jacques, close to the Val de Grace.

The distribution of the several parts of the body did not, in the earlier instances, take place without opposition. The practice was even forbidden by Pope Boniface VIII., and disobedience to his order on the subject was threatened with excommunication. His successor, however, Pope Benedict, permitted Philip de Bel to employ it in relation to the Princes and Princesses of his royal house, in cases where it might be difficult to transport the entire body to the place of their sepulchre. The authorities of St. Denis also protested strongly against the practice, and claimed a right to the bodies entire; but the Frères Préchems and Condelier prevailed over the Benedictines, and obtained for their churches portions of the bodies. — *Compiled.*

WHERE DWELL THE DEAD.

SELECTED.

WHERE do they dwell?   'Neath grassy mounds, by
    daisies,
Lilies, and yellow-cups of fairest gold :
Near grey-grown walls, where in wild, tortuous mazes,
Old clustering ivy wreathes in many a fold :
       Where in red summer noons
       Fresh leaves are rustling,
       Where 'neath full autumn moons
       Young birds are nestling —
        Do they dwell there ?

Where do they dwell ?   In sullen waters, lying
On beds of purple sea-flowers newly sprung ;
Where the mad whirlpool's wild and ceaseless sighing,
Frets sloping banks by dark green reeds o'erhung ;
       Where by the torrent's swell,
       Crystal stones glitter,
       While sounds the heavy bell
       Over the river —
        Do they dwell there ?

No : for in these they slumber to decay,
And their remembrance with their life departs ;
They have a home, — nor dark, nor far away —
Their proper home, — within our faithful hearts.
       There happy spirits wed,
       Loving forever ;
       There dwell with us the dead,
       Parting — ah, never —
        There do they dwell !

REPUBLICAN BURIAL.

It is not every American who reflects, when he is designing a monument, for his own use, or for a friend's memorial, that we are members of a republic, and that the costly and highly decorated monuments and sculpture, which may be seen in some of the cemeteries of the Old World, are not fit subjects for our imitation. However capable we may be of equalling, or even excelling the models produced by foreign artists, and however abundant our wealth — a simple stone, to stand as the memorial of our life, and the index of our place of repose, with a few obituary lines, and some pleasing devices upon the stone, is the most befitting a citizen of a country where all are politically equal. An honest private citizen of a republic is as worthy as a monarch or a nobleman, who is possessed of the same virtues, of a monument to hand down his name and his deeds to posterity. But kings and noblemen are few, and private citizens are many. The former might for centuries indulge their taste in monumental sculpture, and when they died, be represented in marble effigy ; and ages might elapse before their monuments would become inconveniently numerous. But were all the wealthy citizens of a republic to indulge themselves in the same luxury, it would require but a few years to cover all our land with monuments, until those objects, which are intended to awaken a reverence for the dead, would become a mere inane and ludicrous exhibition of pride.

The names of our ancestors are perpetuated on their humble headstones ; and it is delightful to wander in old graveyards and read the brief history of these members

of a past generation, among whom many of us recognize
the names of our own ancestors. We are disappointed
when we cannot find the stone that should mark the
grave of some person who is well remembered in history.
If our ancestors had made it a general practice to erect
a monument to the head of every family, no great evil
would have attended their multiplication, because the
people of that early period, in our own nation, were few.
Let the same be done by every family at the present day,
and not a half a century would be required to whiten all
the land with monumental marble, and to deaden all its
pleasing effect by its increase. Expediency, therefore,
requires us to be modest in indulging ourselves in this
kind of luxury, or in fostering this kind of pride. Fifty
years hence, our people will feel more interest in our
revolutionary history, than in the history of the present
period, and the ordinary men of our revolution will stand
out in greater prominence than the greatest among our
contemporaries. Posterity will search among the tombs
for the original monuments over the graves of men who
were famous in our revolutionary era. They would look
for them in vain : but in the place of them they would
find sumptuous marbles piled on the graves of men whose
names are entirely unknown to them, and which are
buried in utter oblivion. Would it be unnatural, if, in
consequence of this disappointment, they should feel contempt for an art that was used to commemorate those
who must necessarily be forgotten, and which had neglected to commemorate those who were conspicuous in
their country's annals ?

It is the part of wisdom to see that we do not deviate
from a rigid rule of simplicity, either in the number or
the extravagance of our monuments. A simple obelisk
or monumental pillar, is very properly used in frequent

instances, to memorialize the different individuals of the same family, the name of each member after his death being inscribed successively upon it. In some cases there is an ambition manifested to assign a separate monument to every individual who is paramount in the affections of one who is able to command the pecuniary means of building it. People do not always consider that they cannot force immortality upon one who lived a private life, or who was conspicuous only in a circle of fashion, who remembers her votaries only while they shine, and forgets them if they become old or indigent before their death. To aim at immortalizing oneself or a friend, without any claims, by a pile of imperishable stone, though it surpass all that was ever built, is like endeavoring to acquire literary immortality by publishing one's name in the title page of a splendid gilded quarto, containing only blank pages. The monument may immortalize the sculptor, and publish the obscurity of him who lies under it.

In the history and pedigree of the heads of noble families, however unworthy they may have been of the honor their position commanded, a large part of the nation feels an interest, because it is connected with the history of their country. If marble is used to perpetuate the memory of such men, we do not consider it an offering to virtue, but to history. In erecting a sumptuous monument to a private citizen of exhalted merit, we make an offering to virtue. If he were not remarkable for his virtues, the marble is simply an offering of affection. Were every person who leaves a friend to mourn for him, to be glorified with one of these sumptuous tributes, their frequency must at last render them entirely vin and insignificant. The public sight would be wearied with their universal glitter and their unavailing pretensions.

The true principle of republican burial is to be content that all the dead should remain as obscure as they
were in their lifetime. It is absurd to endeavor to exalt
a person, who has lived all his life in obscurity, whose
very name was only known to his neighbors and to those
with whom he had commercial dealings, by the art of the
sculptor. It is nothing to the purpose that he was in
truth a greater and more virtuous man than the occupant
of the next grave, who is honored by a tower of granite
or a marble effigy, on account of his distinguished position
as a hero or a statesman. The last belongs to history,
and however mean his virtues or his talents, the nation
will always be interested in his biography. It is no anti-
republican principle, therefore, which admits the propriety
of erecting a costly monument to a man of ordinary worth
and talents, who has been a President of the United
States, and which does not admit the expediency of building such a tribute to an obscure citizen of the highest
virtue, who performed no public acts. Let the stone that
marks his grave give humble testimony of his virtues,
and in proportion to its humility will the reader who
stoops to read his epitaph, believe it to be true.

To posterity a monument containing the name of one
whose name or deeds cannot be traced in the literary,
civil, or ecclesiastical history of his time, must be regarded in the same light as one containing a fictitious
name. There could exist no motive to preserve such a
monument, unless on account of the extreme scarcity of
such works, it might be valued as a curiosity and a relic
of antiquity. In the eighteenth century, in this country,
almost every private name was connected with the public
events of the time. We have, therefore, a strong motive
to preserve every monument of their dead, both on account of their historical importance, and their value as

antiquities. Such circumstances no longer exist in this country, and can never exist hereafter. Henceforth, those few only, who are the most distinguished among the prominent men of the age, can afford any interest to posterity. The discoverer of a new world, or of a new science, the leader of some great moral or political revolution, — the Father Mathew, or the Wilberforce of his own time, — such names alone amidst the tens of thousands of men who are great by position, who are great in an ordinary way, will be noticed or even remembered by a succeeding generation. The remainder will be like so many names upon a vast and interminable catalogue.

Who is this man, posterity will inquire, with a tower of stone erected over his remains, whose works and deeds are not recorded even in the local history of his own neighborhood? Whosoever he might be, his monument does but record and publish his obscurity and inferiority to a succeeding generation. The philosophy of that sort of reputation which is gained after one's death by marble tower or effigy, if properly studied, would demonstrate that one might as well attempt to scale the heavens by another tower of Babel, as to purchase it of the sculptor.

A wealthy citizen in the town of ———, had lately buried his father, who was a man of rare excellence of character. He erected a plain headstone over his grave, and recorded in a few touching lines a testimony of his worth and of his own veneration for his memory. His neighbors inquired why he had paid so little respect to the memory of his father, whom all the citizens of the place would delight to honor, by the proudest work of sculpture. " My father," replied the son, " lived all his days in obscurity, doing good without ostentation, seeking no honors, but satisfied with the approbation of his own conscience, and with the pleasure it afforded him to think of the happiness he had conferred upon others. Were I to erect a costly monument over his remains, I should perform an act which would be inconsistent with the tenor of his life, and the principles of his conduct. He lived a humble life, and he is honored by this humble grave, and by the filial testimony which is recorded of his virtues. His deeds are embalmed in the memory of hundreds whom he has reformed, blessed, and alleviated; and this plain headstone honors his memory more than the proudest column of marble."

THE PAUPER'S DEATH-BED.

By Collins.

Tread softly — bow the head —
In reverent silence bow —
No passing bell doth toll —
Yet an immortal soul
Is passing now.

Stranger! however great,
Though laurels deck thy brow,
There's one in that poor shed —
One by that paltry bed —
Greater than thou.

Beneath that beggars roof,
Lo! death doth keep his state:
Enter — no crowds attend —
Enter — no guards defend
This palace gate.

That pavement damp and cold
No smiling courtiers tread ;
One silent woman stands
Lifting with meagre hands
A dying head.

No mingling voices sound —
An infant wail alone ;
A sob suppressed — again
That short, deep gasp, and then
The parting groan.

Oh ! change — Oh ! wondrous change ! —
Burst are the prison bars —
This moment there, so low,
So agonized, and now
Beyond the stars !

Oh ! change — stupendous change !
There lies the soulless clod.
The sun eternal breaks —
The new immortal wakes —
Wakes with his God.

N. H. EARLE.

THE EARLE MONUMENT.

Tuis is a beautiful slender marble column, situated on Mistletoe Path. On the top of the monument is a devotional figure of an angel child. The front is tastefully decorated with wreaths of flowers. The following are the inscriptions upon it : — .

My Wife and Child.

———

Oh lovely pair so soft and mild,
In equal beauty dust;
Our Saviour blest the little child,
And such as they are blest.

———

N. H. EARLE.

TREES IN MOUNT AUBURN.

It is not generally understood that there may be too many trees, as well as too many flowers, in a rural cemetery, too many for the beauty as well as for the convenience of the place. When trees are crowded closely together, they lose their lateral branches and all their characteristic beauty. One broad-spreading tree that covers a large space of ground is more serviceable for shade, and more beautiful and attractive in its appearance, than ten or twelve tall, slender trees occupying the same space. This remark is particularly applicable to trees in cemeteries, in which it is desirable to obtain as great a canopy of shade and foliage, with as little encumbrance from the roots and stems of trees, as can be made to subsist together. The trunk of one broad-headed tree occupying the space of one or two feet in diameter, leaves the remainder of the ground that is shaded by it free to be used for a burial spot. A number of smaller trees occupying the same space fill it up so closely with their roots and stems, as to render it useless for the burial of the dead ; and though it will not be denied that there is grandeur in a dense forest of such trees, there is vastly more of this quality in a grove of trees which are broad and perfect in their shape. The first may be compared to a hall with a flat roof sustained by a large number of small pillars ; the last to a roof consisting of a few noble arches resting on massive columns, leaving unoccupied a wide intermediate space.

Mount Auburn would be at present a more beautiful place, and more convenient for the purposes to which it is dedicated, if, at the time of its consecration as a cemetery, it had been entirely free from wood, and afterwards had been judiciously planted with young trees of the prevailing species. Very few well formed trees are to be seen in these grounds, because they are mostly the elongated trees of the forest, which occupy a great deal of space in proportion to the amount of shade afforded by them, and greatly encumber the burial lots.

It may be further remarked, that it is injurious to the monuments to stand under the drip of trees, which ought not, therefore, to grow inside of the burial lots ; the only trees that ought to be planted near the lots are such as do not widely extend either their roots or their branches. Such are the different species of the *arbor vitæ*, and other coniferous trees that acquire a slender pyramidal shape. The advantages of trees in a cemetery cannot be enjoyed without a few attendant evils; but the latter might in some measure be avoided, if the larger kinds of trees were confined to the avenues and to certain tracts which are not to be used for the burial of the dead.

The avenues, to answer this end, should be made of sufficient width to permit a row of large trees to stand and spread their branches freely on each side. The footpaths, on account of their narrow width, should be bordered only with shrubbery and trees of a slender, spiry growth. The elm and the oak, which require great amplitude of space, ought to be extirpated from all narrow and confined situations.

The idea of attaining picturesque effects in a rural cemetery, by the grouping of trees, cannot be carried into practice. The necessary formality that must prevail in the construction of the paths and avenues, and in the geometrical forms of the burial lots, especially when they are enclosed by a fence, prevents any such groupings and combinations. A formal irregularity is

no more picturesque than any other kind of formality.
The wild and rather pleasing disorder apparent in the
natural arrangement of the trees in Mount Auburn, is
every year becoming obliterated, as the proprietors cut
down the trees in the lots and leave those only in the
paths and avenues. As often as a new proprietor lays
out a burial lot, he is obliged to destroy all or nearly all
the trees within its bounds. They must at last, therefore,
be confined almost entirely to the avenues, forming rows
that correspond to their directions, and exhibiting in
their disposition the same irregular formality. But as
the remaining trees will increase in breadth, in proportion as their number is lessened, the grounds will continue to · be as well shaded as they are at the present
time, and will be improved in grandeur and beauty.

It is apparent that in many cases, either some fine
trees must be sacrificed, or the burial lot must be devoted
to the trees instead of the graves. A great deal of judgment must be required to determine when it would be
expedient to reserve the lot in order to save a tree. If
the latter be young, vigorous, and of good proportions, it
ought to be transplanted into a convenient and appropriate location ; if it be too large to be removed, the
value of the tree should decide its fate. The fate which
must, at some not very distant period, come upon the
trees now within the lots, might suggest the expediency
of planting trees near them in the avenues, in anticipation of it. The young trees thus planted would supply
the places of the old growth as it is removed ; and exhibit superior size and beauty. Twenty years hence, the
aspect of Mount Auburn will be less wild ; it will have
less of the peculiar attractions of a forest ; but if nothing
be neglected that ought to be done, it will be a more
beautiful place, independently of its monuments, than it
is at the present time.

If we were preparing a rural cemetery for the use only of those who may be on the stage, after the present generation has passed away, our wisest course would be to select a spot that is entirely destitute of trees, and plant them, after laying out the grounds, in those places only in which they might always conveniently remain. But our predecessors could not have acted more wisely than they did when they selected a wooded tract of land. The present must not be wholly sacrificed to the future; and Mount Auburn, which was perhaps the most beautiful tract of forest in the country, became, immediately after its establishment, admired as a garden of nature, no less than as a place consecrated to the burial of the dead. Since that time, while to a certain extent it has been suffering the loss of its original attractions, of its primitive and characteristic beauty, trees of a nobler growth have been advancing to supply the places of the less beautiful denizens of the forest, and under their shade a highly dressed surface is taking the place of the moss-grown turf of the pasture.

When selecting trees for planting in a cemetery, we should reject all those species which are inclined to throw up suckers from their roots, as this habit is the source of a great deal of trouble to the keeper of the grounds, and the cause of considerable mischief to the burial lots. Of the kinds which are the most addicted to this habit may be mentioned the beech, the locust, the wild cherry, the abele, and all the species of poplar. In the vicinity of any of these trees the grounds will generally be covered with suckers, often overrunning the graves, and choking the turfs and the flower-beds with their intrusive growth. Among exotic shrubs, the common white spiræa of the gardens and the lilac, are of this description. Of the wild shrubs, the barberry and the elder have the same

21

habit, though the viburnums, whose flowers resemble those of the elder, are free from it.

The preceding remarks are intended as mere suggestions of some of the obvious means of improving the arboreous features of Mount Auburn. The beauty and grandeur of fully developed and wide-spreading trees have not been sufficiently appreciated, and the value of a mere forest growth has been comparatively overrated. How would the majestic appearance of the trees on Boston Common be diminished, if the space now shaded by them were occupied by ten times the present number, with only the same amount of branches and foliage? The forest has certain charms which cannot be transferred to a grove of perfect trees ; but the decorations of art and the elegance of dressed grounds cannot be made to harmonize with the former, and in proportion as the works of the sculptor and the operations of the gardener are made manifest, must the park-tree be allowed to take the place of the forest tree. It is important that the proprietors. of lots should consider these points, that all their operations may be consistent, and may serve to bring about one grand and uniform result.

FUNEREAL CHARACTERS OF TREES.

MOUNT AUBURN was originally selected for a cemetery, on account of the beauty and variety of its primitive forest growth, no less than for its pleasing diversity of surface. The greater part of the indigenous species of Massachusetts may be found here. The native shrubs were also numerous in the original grounds; but these have been nearly extirpated, to make room for foreign shrubs. The proprietors of lots have generally preferred the latter; according to the principle that governs them in trade, — namely, that the most valuable article is the one that bears the highest price in the market. Hence the dwarf kalmia, one of the most beautiful of nature's productions, and the different cornels and viburnums, must resign their places to altheas, smoke plants, and Judas trees.

In selecting locations for other rural cemeteries, a similar regard has been paid to trees, which are considered indispensable at the outset; but how well soever the place may be diversified with trees, many will necessarily be removed for convenience, and others will need to be planted to fill vacancies, and to supply the want of certain valuable species. A cemetery without trees would be very blank and unattractive, however well supplied with flowers. But all kinds are not equally well adapted to this situation; some being remarkable for certain funereal characters and associations, while others are fitted for a cemetery from their advantageous manner of growth. Deciduous trees are to be preferred for the greater part of the grounds; but an occasional admixture of evergreens adds to their impressiveness, as well as to their variety. On account of the sombre appearance of this class of trees, a grove made up entirely of them would be very gloomy in the interior; but a good proportion of evergreens is promotive of that seclusion which the deciduous kinds could not afford in the winter, or after the fall of the leaf.

There is no object more solemn and impressive than a venerable wood, full of majestic trees. Poets have always delighted to celebrate their stillness, their seclusion, their grandeur, and their deep and benevolent shade; and we may ultimately secure all these effects by judicious planting and selection. Among the trees which are associated with funereal images, by our familiarity with English literature, the yew is the most important. It is considered by all nations as emblematical of sorrow for the dead; it has been planted from the earliest times by the English in their burial grounds, and many of great age are still to be seen in those places. The general employment of this tree, for funereal purposes, must have originated in the sombre shades of its foliage, and in its adaptedness to the topiary art; and it will probably never cease to be admired as an ornament of the graveyard in those countries of which it is a native.

The weeping willow is another tree which is associated with funereal scenes; and trees of this species are common in American burial grounds. The custom. of planting them in cemeteries probably originated from the suggestion of sorrowful images conveyed by the drooping character of their branches. But, notwithstanding the drooping habit of this tree, there is no expression of melancholy in its general aspect, which, on the contrary, is rendered peculiarly lively by the light hues of its foliage, and its floating, graceful spray. The weeping willow possesses a highly poetical character, on account of the frequent mention made of it in sacred history and prophecy. It is a native of Palestine, and of the banks of the rivers of Babylon, where the Israelites sat down and wept over their exile, and hung their harps upon its branches.

There is reason to believe that the drooping trees acquired the epithet "weeping," which is applied to them, from the resemblance of their attitude to that of a person in tears, who bends down with affliction, as with a material burden. This is the general attitude of sorrow in allegorical representations. This habit of growth is far from giving the drooping trees a melancholy appearance, which is more commonly produced by dark, green foliage; but it is in agreeable consonance with funereal scenes. There is a flowing grace about the drooping trees that is preferable in a cemetery to the stiff and formal shape of many of the evergreens.

Among trees of the evergreen sorts, the different species of arbor vitæ are well fitted for burial grounds, on account of their slender, pyramidal growth, which agrees with the general forms of the monuments. The shape of the arbor vitæ is not unlike that of an obelisk; and its name, "Tree of Life," is suggestive of that immortality to which the grave is the humble, though triumphal entrance. There is a great deal of beauty in its foliage which is always green and never sombre, and hence it is ornamental in winter as well as other seasons. The trees of this species have nothing disagreeable in their habits, and they charm every beholder while gracefully pointing to heaven with their slender, evergreen spire.

Allied to the arbor vitæ is the cypress, called by Shakspeare "the emblem of mourning." This tree was,

by the early Christians, esteemed significant of dying
forever, because, if once cut down, it would never revive
and flourish again ; but it was esteemed by the Romans,
and many other nations, in their funereal observances.
The European cypress is a long-lived evergreen, and is
a favorite tree for burial grounds among the Turks, who
plant it sometimes upon graves as well as around them.
Under its branches the Mussulmans assemble for prayer
and religious meditation, and to honor the memory of
their buried friends. This tree, having never been
naturalized in this country, is not seen in our American
grounds.

The American cypresses are not adapted to cemeteries, as they thrive well only in swamps. The northern
cypress — the white cedar — is a well-known tree, resembling the arbor vitæ in its foliage, which is more
delicate and beautiful ; but it cannot often be successfully
transplanted from its native, aquatic haunts. The southern cypress is a grand and beautiful tree, but its foliage
is deciduous. It sustains the climate of the north
without injury, and would be a valuable ornament of
the low grounds in our rural cemeteries.

In this family of trees we note the ever-varied, the
weird, the romantic and unpretending juniper. This
tree deserves cultivation in our burial grounds, from
which it has been carefully excluded, because it har-
monizes with the rude forms of nature, rather than the
tasteful representations of art. I would cherish it in
these places, were it but for this quality which enhances
the pleasing effect of plain and humble grave-stones, and
because in its emblematic suggestions it affords lessons of
humility. Not so sombre as the yew, it is sufficiently
sober to increase the desired expression of the grounds,
and it is consonant with funereal images. When nature

is dressed in the dreary uniformity of winter, it assumes a browner hue, as if it sympathized with the general sleep of nature. In summer it wears a brighter verdure, but, in its ever-enduring sobriety, it still blends charmingly with the universal brilliant hues that pervade the summer foliage of the woods.

In Europe the pine is associated, in its funereal character, with the yew and the cypress, and it is probably the most common ornament of the cemeteries in New England. Perhaps no tree which has been mentioned exceeds the white pine as a standard in a cemetery, though it is too large to be conveniently planted in the burial lots. This tree possesses qualities which adapt it to almost every situation, where we would seek for seclusion or shade; and the solemnity and grandeur of its appearance render it one of the most appropriate and magnificent accompaniments of the gardens of the dead.

The management of shrubbery is hardly less important than that of trees. The error most frequently committed is the selection of exotics, to the exclusion of many beautiful and appropriate shrubs of indigenous growth. The advantage of the latter is that they require no spading of the earth for their culture; and they also pleasingly remind us of the woods and fields. After they have been planted, they flourish without care, and present a thrifty and spontaneous appearance, which is more agreeable than the trim formality of the exotic shrubs and the spaded earth about their roots. It is a great enhancement of the beauty of the grounds, if all the shrubs and flowers appear to be nature's own free offering, with little about them to remind us of expensive labor or careful cultivation.

There is a large variety of native shrubs which should always find place in our rural cemeteries. Such are the shrubs that grace the stone walls by the sides of old rustic lanes and roads, which are more charming to the sight than the most elegant of artificial hedgerows. The small birds love to nestle in this shrubbery, which is their natural shelter, and supplies them with an abundance of food. And if we would hear their tuneful voices over the graves of our buried friends, we must provide them with their native harborage, in a supply of indige·nous shrubbery, which will crown the place with deep verdure in summer, with splendor in the autumn, and at all seasons afford a shelter and a retreat to the songsters of our woods and fields.

But with all these pleasant gifts of nature, half their charms would be lost, and half their beauty blotted out from the landscape, were it not enhanced by the rose. Mankind have universally agreed in placing this flower above all others of the field; but of the endless varieties which have been obtained by the arts of the florist, none is so beautiful as the simple wild rose of the pastures. Vain are all our attempts to improve the simplicity of nature. Her gifts, as they come unaltered from her hands, possess a grace, and delicacy, and loveliness, that cannot be surpassed; and the wild rose by the side of a stream, and the sweet brier of the pasture, still reign in the hearts of all the true votaries of nature.

FRAIL LOVELINESS.

By Mrs. H. J. Lewis.

Oh, scatter not your leaves
So lavishly upon the thankless earth,
Bright flowers, sweet flowers! My spirit inly grieves
That swift decay so waits upon your birth!

Ye do but look to heaven,
A few bright hours, and your fine fragrance shed
Upon the dewy wings of tranquil even,
And glowing morns succeed, and ye are dead!

For you we hail the showers,
Whose gentle baptism like a blessing falls
Upon your peerless beauty! Summer flowers,
Through you how free the voice of Nature calls.

It bids us leave the room
Darkened by many shadows, some of care,
And some that memory deepens into gloom,
And wander forth where all is calm and fair.

It woos us to the sea,
Whose cooling breath has swept o'er many a wave;
And unto mountain heights, where bird and bee
Never the tempest or the the silence brave.

Through wood-paths fringed by you,
Children of light and warmth! it bids us tread,
And list the song of birds forever new,
'Mid the green branches, like a dome outspread.

Oh ye! whose hour is brief,
Yet all sufficient for your blissful need,
Teach us, with every falling bud and leaf,
To lean henceforth upon the trustful reed !

———

FENCES AND HEDGES.

In our modern cemeteries it is customary to erect an iron fence around the spot which is appropriated to a single family, thereby setting it apart from the remainder of the ground. This appurtenance is plainly no ornament to the place, and the present necessity of it is not very apparent, though after an example is set before the public, it is not difficult to account for the general imitation of it. When Fashion has sanctioned any practice, people will accommodate themselves to it, without regard to its needfulness or convenience. The original purpose of the fence was undoubtedly to protect the monuments from injury. It is manifest that no such protection as they afford is at present required, because brute animals are not allowed to run at liberty in the grounds, and if any injury was designed by men, the fence could not prevent it.

The principal objection to fences is, that they cut up the cemetery into numerous divisions; they destroy the unity and harmony of the grounds, and conceal the monuments and other objects which ought to be exposed to view. It is impossible to construct fences of any sort that will not produce more or less of these effects, and it would be an improvement of the general appearance of Mount Auburn, if there were no fences at all except the one that encloses the cemetery. A fence would be both necessary and appropriate to protect a burial lot or a monument in a field or by the road-side. But in a cemetery it is pleasing to meditate on all who lie there as belonging to one great family; and the sight of numerous little square enclosures, surrounded by a prim iron paling, suggests at once the very opposite of this. It reminds one of exclusiveness, jealousy, aristocratic pride, of anything rather than that brotherly harmony and union, which are the foundation of the Christian religion.

When I look upon these things, I do not believe them to be the result of the sentiments they seem to express. The practice might have originated in some exclusive feeling in the minds of those who first introduced it, and it would afterwards be imitated by others without reflection. None will deny the impropriety of introducing into these sacred enclosures anything expressive of selfishness or pride, or anything that does not comport with the Christian idea of equality. All would agree that the style of the grounds and of the monuments of the dead should not, by their expression, deny the doctrines of that faith, in which they lived and died, who are buried there. But it is not this expression alone that constitutes the objection to fences : it is chiefly their discordancy with the general air of freedom, — openness and grandeur which the grounds would exhibit without them.

After the designer of the grounds has tastefully laid them out, in a style the opposite of formality, in order to give them a pleasing and picturesque appearance, it is certainly very unwise to destroy this effect by surrounding the burial lots with prim iron fences. One or the other was a piece of impertinence. Either the fences ought to be omitted, or the walks ought to be laid out in the same angular and geometrical style, for the preservation of congruity. The same objection would not with equal force apply to the square form of the lots without the fence, as their shape would not be sufficiently conspicuous to produce a harsh dissonance in the general aspect of the place. There are some lots which are unprovided with a fence. When they are also without corner or boundary stones, every one must be struck by their superior air of freedom and beauty, and by the more pleasing effect of the monuments erected upon them.

If the reader be not convinced of the correctness of these remarks, let him construct a miniature model of some part of Mount Auburn, or of any other cemetery, laid out with fenced enclosures, and compare it with another model in which the fences are omitted. The superior beauty of the latter would be apparent at once. The fences not only destroy the grandeur and unity of the grounds by dividing them into a multitude of small parts, but they likewise destroy all that rural appearance which it is so desirable to cultivate. I would mark the lots only by corner stones, the tops of which should be sunk several inches below the turf, to serve merely as legal marks. A shrub might then be planted over each of these corner stones, to mark the boundaries to the eye, which would not be offended by so obscure a formality.

Many people imagine that fences were originally made for ornaments, though it is apparent that they disfigure a landscape, under almost all circumstances. Little can be said in their favor, except that where they are indispensable, they are necessary evils. Let any one take a view of an extensive landscape, that is marked only by a very few fences, and compare it with another of a similar character, that is minutely intersected by them, and subdivided into a multitude of parts, and he will be struck by their injurious effect upon the prospect. It is true that the fences and stone walls that mark the boundaries of our farms in the country are often interesting, on account of their suggestiveness of some pleasing images; but setting these associations aside, it must be admitted that they are only so many disagreeable lines drawn over the surface of a beautiful picture. Fences are not intrinsic ornaments: they may be made ornamental or plain, yet it must be allowed that the most ornamental are not the most pleasing. I have seen many a landscape spoiled by the removal of an old stone wall, covered with wild vines and shrubbery, and the substitution of an elegant fence in the place of it. When we are riding through the country, a road that is not bounded by fences, is generally the most attractive, and of those which are fenced the most pleasing are concealed by vines and shrubbery.

As I have intimated in another place, the effect of a fence around a monument is similar to that of a hedgerow or boxen border around a tree. Imagine a grove of beautiful trees, growing at pleasing distances apart, and extending their beneficent shade over a wide extent of smooth green lawn or pasture. A view of the field underneath the branches of the trees would be grand, cheerful and imposing, and would impress every visitor with emotions of delight. Surround each of these trees with an iron fence or a hedgerow, and we should obtain an idea of the injury done to the scenery of a rural cemetery by the fences around the lots. The beauty of Mount Auburn and of every other cemetery would be greatly improved if every fence were removed from it, except the one that encloses the whole place.

Many who disapprove of iron fences think that hedgerows around the lots would be entirely unobjectionable. But hedges, though more interesting objects of sight, divide the grounds into the same multiplicity of parts. They would be preferable, so far as they are natural and not artificial, and green and leafy shrubs, and not stiff iron rods. But they would hide the monuments from observation still more than the iron fences, and would present in a less degree the same displeasing formality. If I used them at all, I would plant them only on one side of the monuments, to form a sort of back-ground, for which purpose a mass of shrubbery, rather than a clipped hedge, would be preferable.

It seems the most advisable method to mark the boundary of the lots by a very slight elevation above the surface of the path or space between the lots, or by a low and humble hedgerow of miscellaneous shrubbery, which if left to itself would never rise above a foot or two in height. These shrubs ought not, however, to make a formal hedgerow, but rather a series of clumps of shrubbery, separated by irregular distances, and formal only so far as they are placed on the boundary of the lot. Taller shrubs of an evergreen sort might be planted on the back side of the lot, forming a background to the monuments. After this the whole surface should be covered with turfs, consisting of moss intermingled with wild flowers, and divested of vines and stiff luxuriant grasses.

NEATNESS OF THE GROUNDS.

One of the most important points in the management of a rural cemetery, is to preserve throughout the year a neatness of the grounds: not that every path and every lot should look as if the gardener with his spade and shears was constantly at work; but rather that the paths should contain no unsightly weeds, and that the lots should be free from all litter and rubbish. At present this neatness is preserved only by means of a great deal of expensive labor; and this labor being frequently omitted in certain cases, the weeds and decayed stalks of plants accumulate and become offensive to the sight. When we go into the wild pastures we see but little of this tangled and unsightly appearance, which seems, therefore, to be the result of tillage. In the pastures the plants that appear first in the season are not so luxuriant as the later ones, and the decayed stalks of the early plants are therefore covered and concealed by the more exuberant growth of those which succeed them; and not until the hard autumnal frosts arrive, do we see any accumulations of decayed plants. It is not so in grounds which are subjected to tillage, causing early in the season a luxuriant crop of plants, and forming a mass of decayed stalks and foliage at an early period. The cultivated grasses grow with so much luxuriance that they must be frequently cut in order to preserve a neat surface in a garden or a cemetery.

The remedy for this evil and this expense is to pursue a system of embellishment that requires no tillage. At present the greatest effort is made to preserve a smooth shaven lawn, and to cultivate the best lawn grasses.

These require, from the first, a deep and fertile soil: otherwise the native and more vigorous grasses would quickly supersede them, or " run them out." To keep them in good condition, — to preserve anything like an appearance of neatness, — they must be cut six or eight times during the season ; and in a place like Mount Auburn, the scythe cannot be used, and the gardener must perform almost the whole labor with the shears or the pruning hook. If the grasses are allowed to remain uncut until they have flowered, they cover the ground with their stiff stalks, and spoil the verdure and softness of the surface. The aggregate expense of keeping all the grass of the cemetery in proper condition, from May to September, is immense, and the larger the proportion of lawn grasses and other cultivated plants, the greater the amount and expense of the labor required to keep the place in order. The consequence of this difficulty and expense is, that certain portions of the grounds are frequently neglected, and too often present a tangled growth of herbs and grasses from midsummer till the end of the year.

All this trouble might be avoided, if the enclosures were covered with sods taken from the wild upland pastures, in which there is a large proportion of lichens and mosses, that furnish a bed for the wild flowers, and check the luxuriance of the grasses. When these turfs are used, they should be laid upon a thin and natural soil, and all the rank species of wild grass should be eradicated. If they are placed upon a good garden soil, that has been well composted, the herbs of luxuriant growth will " kill out " all the mosses and wild flowers. The latter require a certain amount of shade and protection, but not a deep nor fertile soil. If, instead of an iron fence, the lots were surrounded with a miscellaneous .

growth of wild shrubbery, the ground would receive that sort of shade and protection which nature affords the flowers and mosses in the wild lands, and a constant verdure would be produced by the mosses, and a continued succession of flowers. The grounds in the lots would not require any culture: nothing more would be necessary than to eradicate by the hand such plants as are too luxuriant, and those of a thorny description. No spade, nor scythe, nor shears, would need to be used from the beginning to the end of the season; and the visitor would behold a perpetual series of wild flowers, and flowering shrubbery, without any of the ordinary. expense of tillage.

The principal labor which would be required is to procure and lay down the sods, and in some cases, when the soil was not favorable, to renew the sods, which ought, in all cases, to be taken from upland tracts, because it is presumed that the burial lots, if originally wet, are made artificially dry. The cemetery, if universally treated in this manner, would wear the appearance of nature without its redundances — an appearance which would be delightful to all, and confessedly superior to the present highly dressed and artificial look, combined with a weedy and tangled growth in those places which have been neglected a few days. Some people associate a tangled and weedy appearance with wild lands: but a close observation would prove to them their mistake. This appearance is seen in a neglected garden and other tilled lands, but seldom or never in lands which are in a state of nature.

I would admit into a rural cemetery, no work at all for the scythe or the shears, if it be possible to avoid it. The spade should also finish its work, after having completed the grave, covered it and sodded the surface. I

22*

would have no spaded borders of earth for the cultivation of flowers that require the fostering hand of the gardener. In the place of the crocus, the hyacinth, and the daffodil, the yellow Bethlehem star, the Canadian columbine, the anemone and the violet, should spangle the virgin turf, green with the mosses that gladden the sight of the rambler in the fields. It would be delightful to mourners to see the familiar faces of the field-flowers around the graves of their friends, coming up and unbidden, as if nature had reared them for the commemoration of the dead.

Thorns and briers may be easily exterminated; for though they are the usual, they are not the necessary accompaniments of the wild flowers. Among the shrubbery, or in the wire-work of the fence, the clematis and the glycine would wreathe their vines and their blossoms, like the drapery of mourning, but without its gloom. The violet and the anemone would greet the visitor in the spring of the year, yielding their places in the summer to the graceful neottia, and the sweet-scented consumption flower, until autumn brought up the rear with the purple gerardia, the trichostema, and the pensive and solitary blue fringed gentian. The grave, under these circumstances, would never be without its flowers, coming up to greet the mourner without his care, and surprising him with their constant variety. I can imagine that a native of Great Britain would be pleased to see the daisy and the cowslip upon the grave of a friend, because these would awaken pleasing memories of his native land, and of the scenes of his early days. But to a New Englander, who from his childhood has been familiar with the wildings of the wood and the pasture, no foreign flowers would seem half so charming.

It is not the design of these remarks to recommend an

imitation of natural wildness, but merely a substitution of mossy turfs and wild flowers, in the place of lawn grasses and exotic flowers. The avenues and paths should be covered with a neat spread of gravel, and all weeds, thorns, briers, and other noxious plants, should be eradicated. I would recommend the moss grown sods of the pasture, instead of lawn grasses, wherever the former could be substituted for the latter. This may certainly be done in the burial lots, and perhaps in all parts of the cemetery. The more general this substitution, the less will be the labor and expense of keeping the grounds in order.

The reader should bear in mind that that sort of expensive preparation of the soil which is necessary for the growth of lawn grasses, foreign bulbs and annuals, and indeed for all exotics, whether they are shrubby or herbaceous, is absolutely fatal to the wild flowers. If we would have these, we should dispense with the others. If we would have the crocus, the hyacinth, and the narcissus, we cannot have the wood anemone, the pyrola, the orchis, nor the ground laurel. If we would cultivate any of the former, we must dispense with all of the latter. The exotics are cultivated only in a rich soil, and require the constant attention of a gardener. The wild flowers, in a charming variety, may be made to come up year after year, without any other trouble than the first planting of the sods upon a natural soil, which is an indispensable condition, and occasionally rooting up a plant that was usurping too much space, and by divesting the spot of thorns and briers.

OUR LOST CHILDHOOD

By Miss L. L. A. VERY.

WHITHER has our Childhood fled ?
   We look not out with the same eyes ; —
The morning's rosy blushes spread,
   And Nature paints her bluest skies,
But Heaven lies no more overhead.

The road-side flower looks smiling up,
   But fairies drink the dew no more
The morning sprinkles in its cup ;
   Nor dance upon its leaves' green floor,
And 'neath the moonbeams careless sup.

Time once seemed a rosy boy, —
   And while we frolicked he stood still,
Seemed in our sports to find a joy ;
   But now he drives us at his will, —
We work as slaves in his employ.

Once the earth for us was made ;
   We revelled in its sunshine warm ;
Ours were the flowers that decked the glade,
   Our plaything was the wintry storm.
Now what we own is marked by sexton's spade.

We gaze upon a lock of hair,
   And marvel if its gold were ours ; —
If eyes so faded erst were fair ; —
   If cheeks once blossomed like the flowers,
So pallid now and lined by care !

Earth's childhood comes with every Spring;
   But ours soon spent returns no more;
Earth sees but once its blossoming,
   Time counts but once its treasures o'er;—
But mem'ry still to it will cling.

And Faith points out where yet again
   The Soul its robes of white shall wear
Without a blemish or a stain:
   Blest is the Angel that shall bear
The Soul its childhood to regain.

OXNARD'S MONUMENT.

This is a Gothic monument erected to the memory of HENRY OXNARD, who in his early life was a sea-captain, and afterwards became a merchant in Boston.

MONUMENTAL TREES.

" This is the bower she loved,
And here is the tree she planted."

In some parts of the continent of Europe, parents, in in compliance with an ancient custom, are in the habit of planting a tree at the birth of every child. This tree is ever afterwards identified with the individual for whom it was planted; it is associated with his life, and, when he is dead, it is viewed by his friends and companions as a living monument to his memory. I have often thought that we might derive from this custom a hint, to be turned to an important advantage; that, in in the place of marble, our departed friends might be commemorated by a noble tree, that should, every year when it put forth its leaves, awaken fresh memories of the dead. After the remains of a friend are laid in the grave, a tree should be selected, not in the cemetery, but in our own grounds, and dedicated to his memory. A cenotaph placed in the ground, near the tree, should indicate the dedication of the tree to the memory of the person whose name is recorded upon the stone. On that spot it should ever afterwards be allowed to remain, and no profane hands should venture to disturb it.

How much more noble a monument would such a tree afford than the sculptured marble. There must be some satisfaction in the thought, that, after we are laid in the grave, we are still doing good to our fellow-men. A monumental stone, while it commemorates the dead, encumbers the ground on which it stands. A tree, on the contrary, is constantly performing a useful office, in the economy of nature, for all living creatures. To the earth, and to the creatures that find shelter under it, it is a guardian angel of nature. A century hence, if the land should be decorated with millions of these monumental trees, shading the earth, and holding up their arms to heaven, whence they call down a perpetual store of blessings to the living, how would posterity revere the custom that had saved so many from destruction!

Trees, when thus consecrated, might be regarded as the medium of constant messages from the dead to the living, who might view in one of these trees the emblem of some of the transcendent joys of heaven. See how it is constantly shedding blessings and bounties upon the earth, many of which are unperceived, like those we receive from the hand of Providence. It puts forth its leaves in the spring, affording a beautiful image to look upon, and purifying and renovating the vital atmosphere, and in the autumn it sheds it leaves to serve as a warm covering for the flowers in winter. The birds that sing in its branches do but communicate those pleasing thoughts that cannot be expressed in words, but serve to awaken in our hearts a gleam of those joys which are felt by the blessed in heaven. When we sit under its shade in summer, we feel as if overshadowed by an angel's wings, so musically do the zephyrs, as they play through the leaves and branches, whisper of the world of the past and the heaven of the future. It is pleasing to think, that when our friends are sitting after our death under this canopy of shade, we may be remembered by them, and that the tree that commemorates our life is the source of constant benefits to our fellow-men, who have not yet passed through the gate of mortality.

Were the custom of adopting trees as monuments to commemorate our departed friends to be adopted, the

most enduring species should be selected for this purpose,
such as the elm, the oak, the ash, the lime, and the
maple. The soft-wooded trees are not in general sufficiently durable, and might decay before the friends of
the dead had passed away. After the selection of a tree
for this purpose, a small slab should be set down into the
earth, near the trunk of the tree, and, on the face of it,
these words, or others of similar import, should be inscribed : — " To the memory of C. L., whose remains
are laid in Mount Auburn, this lime-tree, under whose
shade she has often reclined, is affectionately dedicated.
May no profane hands ever destroy it, or disturb the
birds that sing among its branches. Henceforth this
tree, with its winged inhabitants, is sacred to her
memory."

The general prevalence of a custom like this would
lead the public to place a higher value upon trees, and
less upon showy monuments of marble, which have
always been the most sumptuous in the early stages of
civilization. As mankind advance in civilization or in-
intellect, they prize nature more and art less. In a very
exalted stage of general social culture, sumptuous monuments would become extremely rare.

We should not neglect to consider that every tree thus
hallowed and preserved becomes a public benefaction.
The rude purveyor of the lumber market, who measures
the value of a tree only by the surveyor's guage, and
who is never at peace as long as a single old oak or
elm, or other valuable timber tree is standing, which can
be purchased with money, would know that the curse of
the whole community would be upon him, if he allowed
his venal hands to touch one of these monumental trees.
Religion and affection might succeed in preserving what
reason, and taste, and philanthropy, have advocated in

vain for the last century. Men who have no regard for
a tree as one of the noblest works of nature, and one of
the greatest gifts of heaven to mankind, who have not
science enough to understand its value in the economy
of nature, nor taste enough to appreciate its beauty, may
feel some religious respect for an object that has been
selected to commemorate the death of a friend. Posterity,
who may take an invidious satisfaction in destroying the
works of vanity, when they have become inconveniently
and oppressively numerous, would respect these trees as
heir-looms from their ancestors. And how vastly more
noble a monument to any one's memory, a century hence,
must an elm be regarded, which is the pride of every
beholder, than the proudest marble monument and sculptured effigy in Westminster Abbey.

THE PAST OF AMERICA.

By Florence.

Time hath a mighty power, to which we all must bend. He tears away the young, the loved, the beautiful, from our grasp, like flowers which the autumn's breath has withered. But not alone does he hide from us the light of youth and loveliness; he touches with his effacing fingers the tablet of the soul, — he erases the loves, the friendship, the memories, which years of agony, it may be, had imprinted there; he makes the past, almost like the future, a blank. The proudest work of art, beneath his touch, is levelled with the dust, and its memory becomes but a lingering shadow on the magic mirror of the heart. Yet, strange to say, we look upon the wrecks which he has made, with an intensity of interest, which the days of their glory could never have awakened. We reverence the hoary head, for revolutions have passed over it, mysterious and strange. We gaze with deep and unchanging emotions upon the silver hair which his touch has whitened, for it falls over a brow that possesses a greater charm, because it is hidden from our knowledge.

We look upon the magnificent structures of the artist with delight, because they awaken in us that nice perception of the beautiful, which affords us exquisite pleasure. We admire the beauty of the design, and the taste and skill displayed in the execution; but never does the structure in its meridian glory become as dear to us, as when the frosts of time have beautified and adorned it; when it becomes a part of the past, and linked with deeds of high device, and manly daring, with gentle tales of the affections, of bower and hall, of heart and lute. We admire it at first, we love it at last. It comes into the

inner soul, and we pour over it the fitful and changing
effusions of the fancy ; we invest it with a charm, wrought
of imagination and feeling. Earth holds no home so
sweet as that which high romance and poetic enthusiasm
have hallowed. I have gazed upon the grouping of fluted
columns, under high and swelling domes, and have turned
from their newness, their nakedness of feeling, to the
humble cottage by the wayside, with the deepest and
most intense emotion. There was poetry in its moss-
covered walls which could never invest the first. Here
the fire of the household hearth had burned brightly, —
the prattle of childhood had been heard, — life's tenderest, holiest charities, had been displayed. There had
been loves and friendships, and death had strove with
love, to weave a spell which should render it sacred ; had
given it a power to touch " the electric chain wherewith
we are doubly bound," and to call up from the heart's
depths, its best and purest feelings. Why is it that we
turn thus from the future to the past ? There are hours
when we speculate upon what is to come — upon the
destiny of man ; but we cannot rest here ; we turn from
the ideal of what may be, to the certainty of what has
been. There is no abiding place for the wing, when it
becomes wearied of its flight : all before is wide, illimitable space, and we turn back with relief to the record
of events and feelings with which time has combined
events of fancy and reality, to blend the idealism of one
with the harshness of the other. The first resolves itself
into doubt and uncertainty of the most painful nature, if
unassisted reason alone guide us ; the last into the melancholy of remembered pleasure.

It is thus, perhaps, that the veneration with which we
look upon the remains of former ages becomes so universal a sentiment. We feel interested in all that tells us

of a race who have lived, and suffered, and died; who have trod the same path which we are to tread, and have entered upon the long journey which is yet before us. I know of no country which is capable of awakening these emotions in a greater degree than our own. "We call this country new," says Mr. Timothy Flint, "but it is old; age after age has rolled away, and revolution after revolution passed over it." The whole valley of the Mississippi is full of proofs that it was once inhabited by a race of men, civilized and enlightened like ourselves. There are remains of ancient cities and fortifications; there are implements of war and of husbandry; there are proofs of mathematical skill and of science, which could never have been possessed by the rude and uncultured tribes which the encroachments of the white men have displayed. Yet so far back in the vista of time do these carry us, that even tradition tells us nothing about the race that left them for us. Did they exist in one portion of this great valley alone, there might be less to awaken our interest and curiosity; but they are vast and numerous as the territory itself, and furnish the most conclusive proofs, that it was once far more thickly populated than now. Bricks, medals, and vessels of various kinds, have been discovered in a soil which has been undisturbed for ages. Hieroglyphic characters have been found inscribed in various places; implements of war, of singular and difficult construction; wells stoned up; regular walls; everything which could be necessary to prove the existence of a great and enlightened people.

Mr. Flint divides the former inhabitants of this country into three classes, and attributes these remains of more perfect art to the first; the immense mounds of earth which have so long been the objects of our curiosity, to the second — a race less enlightened and civilized

23*

than the first. These are generally found in the neighborhood of large cities and towns, and many of them
have trees growing upon them, which are computed to
be several hundred years old. It is not improbable that
in these very places, where it has become convenient for
us to erect cities, formerly existed others perhaps far more
mighty than they. The question naturally arises, who
were that race, and where are they? For this no reasoning can furnish a definite answer. That they existed and
that they have ceased to exist we know; but when and
how, we know not. From one of these mounds in Ohio,
tons of human bones have been taken. It is as if they
erected these works of art, to astonish those who should
come after, — then built for themselves a grave, — and
passed away! One of them, near Marietta, may be seen
as you go down the river. It is no great distance from
the river, and bears trees of a large size. It is impossible
to describe or forget the feelings with which we gaze
upon it for the first time. They are too various and too
mingled. We pass through the dense forests which
have grown up since these people were lost in oblivion ;
we stand where their homes were once made, and then
come thronging round us imaginings of the past — dreams
of what may have been, upon which reasonable conjecture can throw but little light. We are dizzy, confused
with the rush of thoughts that overwhelm us ; the very
sighing of the forest leaves, and the murmur of the mighty
mass of waters, which the onward course of our vessel
troubles, seem to come to us blended with strange mysterious whisperings of the past. Oh, had but this giant
stream a tongue, what could it not tell us ! There, perhaps, upon its banks, stood large and populous cities ;
gallant barks, freighted with all that art could furnish,
went and returned again. Men lived and loved, and

waned and died. Yet how? Not, we dream, as we die, leaving others to bear our names and fortunes; but swept in judgment from the earth, by the fiat of the Almighty! Many of these relics of the past become so linked with our home feelings, that they become matters almost of personal interest; they awaken emotions different in their kind, yet most thrilling and intense. When building the Louisville canal, bricks were found nineteen feet below the surface of the earth, laid in regular hearths, " with the coals of the last domestic fire upon them."

Where are those who once clustered around these domestic hearths? Here, it may be, ages ago, the mother's heart bounded for joy, as it rested on her loved ones; the song and the dance made gladness around the hearth-fire; here filial and parental affection found its home; flowers bloomed upon the brow of youth and beauty; hopes blossomed and died, and fading as those flowers, evanescent as those hopes, the feast, the bridal, and the burial passed away. Childhood, with its mirthful prattle; youth, with its bright imaginings; age, with dimming light, all sleep together; and all have slept, till time has left but a dim memorial that they once existed.

Yet in the midst of all this, the American turns coldly away to other climes, for the inspiration of high thoughts; he looks upon the dim gray palaces which tell of the shadowy greatness of other days, and finds nothing to admire here, when in the very infancy of what he looks on there, was passing away in his own land — a race, perhaps, far more mighty than they. He stands by Herculaneum, with its buried greatness, he descends into its excavations, and looks upon the relics of former days, with an emotion which he cannot control; he pictures to himself thrilling tales of the affections; he raises around him a magic company, whom he endows with passions, with hopes, with memories, with all that makes life palpable and real ; he basks in the sunshine of beauty and of wit, and he courts the enthusiasm it awakens as the brightest proof that heaven has made the mind, which lives thus in all ages, immortal ; and yet he deems that his own land furnishes no material for such high themes.

Revolution after revolution is destined to pass over us ; and it may be, that in that future time, to which the eye of the spectator is bent, developments will be made of what has been, — of which we do not now dream, — that some future antiquarian will read among these relics of by-gone days, of a race proud and mighty as our own — that while the hero of Thermopylæ won the meed of immortality, or the Goth marched in triumph to imperial Rome, — cities vast and magnificent were mouldering away, beneath the touch of time, in this Western world, — that a nation whose origin these developments will discover to him, had passed through the stages of helpless infancy, of powerful inquiring manhood, of imbecile age, and had at last, mouldered to oblivion. Greece, with its classic lore, Rome, with its faded splendor, Egypt, with its colossal grandeur, cannot furnish more to awaken those high emotions, than our own land. I reverence these things. I could stand upon the narrow pass where Leonidas fell ; I could gaze upon the sarcophagi of Egyptian kings, — upon the mighty pyramids upon which time hath sought in vain to leave his impress, with deep and uncontrollable emotion ; — but here, too, in the depths of the immense forests, which have grown up where their hearth-fires once blazed, I could muse as sagely upon the destiny of man, the weakness of his own futile plans, and the mighty power that rules and overrules all his works.

America is rich in its stores of antique knowledge ; and he who would feel most deeply the vanity of human ambition and human greatness, needs only to dwell here upon the lessons which it teaches. Amid all this, the weakness which is attributed to us, of admiring what is foreign, merely because it is so, becomes equally ridiculous and unreasonable with the absurd prejudice that leads us to denounce everything unallied to us. The vast territory stretching from Maine to Florida, from the Atlantic to the Rocky Mountains, contains in itself wonders of nature and wonders of art which no other country possesses ; and while we learn to admire what is worthy of admiration in other lands, let us also study and venerate the wonders of our own country.

MOUNT AUBURN IN AUTUMN.

By Mrs. Eliza Lee Follen.

I love to mark the falling leaf,
   To watch the waning moon ;
I love to cherish the belief,
   That all will change so soon.

I love to see the beauteous flowers
   In bright succession pass,
As they would deck life's fleeting hours,
   And hide his ebbing glass.

I love the rushing wind to hear,
   Through the dismantled trees,
And shed the sadly soothing tear
   O'er joys that fled like these.

I love to think this glorious earth
   Is but a splendid tomb,
Whence man to an immortal birth
   Shall rise in deathless bloom ; —

That nothing on its bosom dies,
   But all in endless change
Shall in some brighter form arise,
   Some purer region range.

On this fair couch then rest thy head
   In peace, thou child of sorrow ;
For know the God of truth has said,
   Thou shalt be changed to-morrow ;

Changed, as the saints and angels are,
   To glories ever new ;
Corrupt shall incorruption wear,
   And death shall life renew.

GOSSLER'S MONUMENT.

THIS monument was erected to the memory of J. II. GOSSLER, of Ger
many, who had become a citizen of the United States.

INTERIOR BEAUTIES OF MOUNT AUBURN.

In treating of the interior beauties of Mount Auburn,
I shall confine my remarks chiefly to the natural scenery.
Every visitor must notice that the grounds are remarkable for a great and beautiful diversity of surface, as well
as a large variety of trees. Long before any one thought
of it as a cemetery, it was a favorite resort of students
and others who sought it on account of its beautiful and
romantic scenery. There are hundreds still living, who
remember it as the scene of many a delightful ramble,
alone and with company. It was no vulgar place of recreation ; but a spot whither the thoughtful and studious
fled for that needful rest from mental weariness, or for
employing themselves in those studies of nature which
are even better than entire repose from labor.

Many a student has resorted to these grounds for his
first botanical explorations, as they were the nearest in
the vicinity of the Colleges, where there was any remarkable variety of native plants. In these protected dales,
the spring flowers made their earliest appearance ; and
in the same places, under the shelter of the old oak-trees,
lingered the latest flowers of autumn. The name which
was given to the place, is associated with some of the
most interesting poetic images, and served to endear it
still more to the readers and admirers of the most delightful poem in the language. Every spot within the
grounds became at length hallowed in their remembrance.
Every stream had its goddess, and every fountain its
Naiad. Every wooded hill seemed to be the haunt of
the Muse, and some rustic deity presided in every grove.
There are many persons who may regret the changes
which have taken place. When any spot is thus en-

deared by memory, we delight in preserving its original appearance. Everything about it is sacred ; and every alteration that might be highly gratifying to a stranger, is painful and displeasing to those who were familiar with it in their early days.

When we examine the natural beauties of Mount Auburn, we can easily account for all these attachments, and do not wonder that in the eyes of hundreds, it was regarded as hallowed ground, long before it was consecrated to the dead. Some of those who delighted to ramble here are now dead, and their dust is deposited in these grounds and amidst the scenes which they loved in their lifetime. Among the living there are numbers who regard the spot with still more affection, since it has been thus consecrated, and who, when they visit the place, behold the scene of many a pleasant and studious excursion, while they view the graves of the companions with whom they were associated in their adventures. The grounds are, therefore, hallowed in a twofold sense, and their original beauties have received a double charm ; first from the pleasing recollections of youth which they awaken, and second, from having become the depository of the sacred relics of early friends and comrades.

It is at the beginning of summer, and the middle of autumn, that the lover of forest scenery would find the most pleasure in a general view of the natural beauties of Mount Auburn. The trees, as I have remarked in another place, have but little individual beauty ; but in their collective beauty, when viewed from a near eminence, they are unsurpassed. When the leaves are opening, before they have assumed their deepest verdure, and when they are tinged with a paler shade of the tints that mark them just before the fall of the leaf, the woods of the cemetery present to the eye of the spectator a very

interesting variety. The oaks are particularly conspicuous at this time, as their sprouting leaves are seldom
green, but rather of a cinereous hue, intermingled with
shades of red, purple, and lilac. The young leaves of the
ash are generally of a deep purple, becoming green as
they advance towards maturity. The same may be said
of the foliage of other trees which assume any of the
shades of red and purple in the autumn. But all that
remain green or turn yellow in the autumn, may be distinguished in early summer by the purity of their green
tints, differing from their summer tint only by its lighter
shade. Here, then, are to be seen at this time, not
only a charming variety in the different shades of verdure, but another variety proceeding from the mixture of
other colors.

In the later summer these colors and shades have
become blended into one nearly uniform dark shade of
green, which attracts but little attention. About the
third week in September, the ash, the maple, the tupelo
and the sumach, begin to assume their bright autumnal
metamorphosis — the ash varying from a salmon color to
a deep chocolate or maroon, and the others exhibiting all
the shades between an orange and a scarlet. At this
period very few landscapes exceed the glorious display
of colors which may be seen from the tower.

There is not only a pleasing diversity of surface in
Mount Auburn, but there is a remarkable correspond-
ence in the laying out of the paths and avenues, with
this diversity. There is no affected irregularity. The
paths seem to take their course in the line of the inequalities of the ground, and the visitor can always find a
sufficient cause for every turn and bend of the principal
avenues. In riding or walking over them we meet with
constant changes of scene. If there be a similarity in the

general style of the monuments, this sameness is compensated by the varied scenery. The ponds of Mount Auburn, though small, are a pleasing feature of the place. One of the most interesting portions of the ground, is a natural ridge, that passes over considerable space, from north to south. This has been named Indian Ridge. The principal elevation is called Mount Auburn, and is one hundred and twenty-five feet above the level of Charles River, and from the tower which is erected on its summit, is a grand panoramic view of the environs of Boston.

The following descriptions are from the pen of Mr. Safford, Editor of the Mount Auburn Memorial, a journal which is peculiarly adapted to the wants of the visitors and proprietors of that cemetery : —

THE SCOTCH BURIAL GROUND.

"The morning smiled on — but no kirk-bell was ringing,
Nae plaid or blue bonnet came down frae the hill,
The kirk door was shut, but no psalm tune was singing,
And I missed the wee voices, sae sweet and sae shrill." — WILSON.

At the foot of Laurel Hill, the base of Mount Auburn, where Cypress, Walnut, and Fir avenues intersect, in a northwest direction from the Tower, is a large lot, surrounded by a massive iron fence, with the Scotch Thistle and Battle Axe for the ornamental part of the design ; and two figures of Saint Andrew embellish the gates. This lot is appropriated by the Scot's Charitable Society in Boston, as a burial place for its members, the sons and daughters of old Scotia who have died in this country.

A number of pines, with their dark and dense foliage, ever verdant, interspersed with walnut and oaks, shut out the light of the noon-day sun, and protects the fine carpets of greensward which covers the spot, from the too hot breath of summer ; rendering it a pleasant resting

place for visitors to and from the Tower. The place is
rich with pleasant memories, and affords ample material
for thought and reflection. Here sleep natives of Ar-
gyleshire, Falkirk, &c.; the Pattersons, Gordons, Cam-
erons, &c., who have here found their last resting place
thousands of miles from their native shores. There are
besides these a number of nameless graves, the occupants
of which were also sons and daughters of Scotland, the
land of Burns, Scott, and Wilson; and around whose
heathclad hills, extended plains, mountains, dells, glens,
and streams, the warm imagination of those men have
thrown the light of their genius, investing the whole
country with the beautifully colored embellishments of
romance and poetry, making her sons and daughters
models of nobleness, purity, and religious faith.

VIEW FROM THE TOWER.

This imposing structure is built of Quincy granite, on
the highest point of land in the cemetery grounds. The
highest battlement of the tower, is one hundred and
eighty-seven feet above the level of Charles River.
The view from the top of this tower for variety and
beauty of scenery, and for historical association, is probably not surpassed on this continent.

It is now the hour of twilight, and the more rugged
aspects of nature are softened into beauty. Mount Auburn with its hundred acres of graves, its winding avenues
and paths skirted with cenotaphs, monuments, obelisks,
and other memorials of affection which are covered with
garlands of evergreens and bouquets of flowers, spread
before us. Its eminences are crowned by the stately
oak and walnut, its dells and glens bordered with evergreen firs and pines, and enamelled with flowers, the
combined products of nature and art.

As we stand facing the north, on our right is Charles River, winding among its green banks, forming a beautiful semicircle; before us is Cambridge College, with its classic walls made venerable by time. It was from this place that Prescott started with his chosen detachment of a thousand men to fortify Bunker Hill, on the eventful night of the 16th of June, 1775. Under the old elm at the corner of the common, Washington first drew his sword and assumed the command of the American army in the July following. A little to the left, is the house now occupied by Prof. Longfellow, which was the head-quarters of the great chief during the siege of Boston. To the right is Charlestown with its Bunker and Breed's hill and Mystic River. Still farther to the north is Medford, where the Vermont and New Hampshire militia formed under the gallant Stark on the morning of the eventful 17th of June, to fight the battle of Bunker Hill. To the right is Boston with its Fanueil Hall and Dorchester Heights. North-west is Concord and Lexington, where the torch of the revolution was first lighted on the 19th of April, 1775. To the west is Watertown, the chosen seat of the Provincial Congress, from whence Warren started on the morning of the 17th, for battle and death. In this town are the United States Arsenal, and the old Puritan burying-ground, where sleep the stern and austere fathers of New England, contemporary with Cromwell and Milton.

Beyond the circle embraced by the foregoing description, the attention is arrested by the not less attractive beauties of other places, which though possessing, historically, but little interest, are in these modern times well worthy of a brief description. Beyond Charles River, may be seen the towns of Brighton and Newton. The former is one of the most important Cattle Markets in the country, and the latter embraces within its limits no less than six distinct villages, any one of which if situated in Vermont, would compare favorably with those already there in regard to location and surrounding scenery. At the "Center," there is a flourishing Theological Seminary, under the patronage and control of the Baptist Denomination. In contrast to this, directly across, or upon the opposite side of the circle at a distance of some six miles from Newton, the buildings of Tufts College, a Universalist Theological school may be seen. At a short distance northeast from the latter, the blackened walls of the Ursuline Convent testify that New England has not been exempt from lawless explosions of popular violence.

AUBURN LAKE.

> " In the still waters here,
>   Imaged we see,
> Where they are bright and clear,
>   Pictures of thee."

Inscription from Mrs. Osgood's Memorial.

WATER, in its ever varying and shifting forms, is an element of great beauty; and whether seen in the wide ocean, the rapid river, the quiet lake, or falling fountain, its presence wonderfully enhances the beauty of the surrounding scenery. Mount Auburn, until recently, has been nearly destitute of the fine imagery and poetic pictures which the presence of a large body of water produces; but Meadow Pond, which has now been curbed and graded, supplies this deficiency, and has already become the most attractive resort in the cemetery, and the avenue which encloses its shores will soon be regarded as the finest promenade within the grounds.

It is situated in the southeast part of the cemetery;

the space occupied by the water has most of it been obtained by excavating a bog or peat meadow ; its form is quite irregular ; it is enclosed by Indian Ridge and two or three other paths on the east, Willow and Oak Avenues on the west, and Larch Avenue on the south. The northerly portion of this pond extending from the fountain at the head to the bridge or embankment which now separates it from the southern portion, was a large part of it curbed and graded in 1857 ; but the whole of the southern portion, extending from the bridge to the lower or southern embankment, has been done since the opening of the spring of 1858. The outline of the eastern side was quite irregular ; and while building the embankment walls its shifting form gave a fine opportunity to curve it in a graceful manner, and the elegant shapings of the curves add greatly to its beauty. On the west the outline is more regular ; but contrasts well with the east, and gives a pleasing variety to the whole work.

The length of this little lake is somewhat over six hundred feet, and its breadth, in the widest part, less than one hundred. The banks on the sides present a somewhat steep declivity or slope, but are extremely well adapted for the new style of catacomb tombs ; at the north end the slope is gentle towards the pond : while at the south end, or embankment, the surface is nearly level. A narrow width of border above the curb stones has been neatly sodded the whole length of the pond. At each end the banks recede from each other, but at the first embankment they approach, forming a narrow neck that has been bridged by a neat and tasty structure, which makes a fine addition to the landscape. Fountain Path leads from Willow Avenue, and encloses the northerly portion of the pond ; at the bridge it widens into a fine avenue, or carriage-road, which extends into

Larch avenue on each side. A large portion of ornamental ground bordering on the pond, is enclosed by this new avenue. When the arrangements are completed, and this ground is more fully embellished with shrubs, with their dark glossy leaves and showy flowers, and also fringed with weeping willows, it will add much to its present attractions, already presenting some of the finest specimens of scenic beauty to be found in Mount Auburn. It is a deep glade in the forest, with an elegant natural mirror to reflect the beauties of earth and sky. Its banks are shaded with hardy oaks, interspersed with a few evergreens and Norway maples : at the north end there is a number of white willows standing in a commanding position, overhanging the water. In this wide vista of beauty there will be a strange blending of life and death, beauty with grief and sadness ;

" Pleasure's smile and sorrow's tear,"

will be here in close proximity. The finest view of this pond is obtained from Mrs. Loring's ornamental ground at the head ; and the best time for observing it is at sunset, while the dark forest lies softened by twilight shadows, and the reflective qualities of the water are increased by the slightly darkened atmosphere, and act as a faithful mirror to reproduce the beauty of an inverted landscape, reflecting the dark tombstones, the trees with their highly tinted autumnal foliage, the image of the blue sky, and the distant stars. In the midst of this varied beauty, whilst surrounded on all sides by the emblems of death, the scene is highly impressive.

THE NAMELESS GRAVE.

BY MISS L. E. LANDON.

A NAMELESS grave, — there is no stone
  To sanctify the dead :
O'er it the willow droops alone,
  With only wild flowers spread.

" O, there is nought to interest here,
  No record of a name,
A trumpet call upon the ear,
  High on the roll of fame.

" I will not pause beside a tomb
  Where nothing calls to mind
Aught that can brighten mortal gloom,
  Or elevate mankind ; —

" No glorious memory to efface
  The stay of meaner clay ;
No intellect whose heavenly trace
  Redeem'd our earth : — away ! "

Ah, these are thoughts that well may rise
  On youth's ambitious pride ;
But I will sit and moralize
  This lonely stone beside.

Here thousands might have slept whose name
  Had been to thee a spell,
To light thy flashing eyes with flame, —
  To bid thy young heart swell.

LORING'S MONUMENT.

ERECTED to the memory of ELIJAH LORING, an eminent merchant of
Boston.

HUMILITY·IN ARCHITECTURE AND MONUMENTAL SCULPTURE.

THERE must be something particularly pleasing in the virtue of humility, or it would not be so often affected by those who do not possess it. I believe the expression of this quality has never been regarded as one of the beauties of architecture, because this art, from the earliest ages, has been used almost entirely as an instrument of ambition. Still it is an important quality in home architecture and private monumental sculpture, and its merit, if not acknowledged by artists in these departments, is clearly recognized in the works of the painters. As modesty is a virtue in the greatest as well as the least of men ; in like manner humility sets off the graces of every beautiful structure and every beautiful house, from a peasant's cottage to the mansion of a nobleman. The public has committed the error of regarding humility as the opposite of grandeur : whereas the opposite of grandeur is littleness or meanness, and the opposite of humility is ostentation. Two opposites cannot be blended in harmony, but the combination of grandeur and humility produces effects which are beyond comparison greater than either of these qualities alone could produce.

Humility in architecture is obtained by the careful avoidance of every appendage and every quality in the style of a building that seems to indicate an attempt on the part of the owner to render himself conspicuous. We love to see in the style of a dwelling, the evidences, not only of the comforts and conveniences of the house, but also, so far as they can be made to appear, of certain estimable traits of the owner or occupant. " I take care in my solitary rambles," says St. Pierre, " not to ask information respecting the character and quality of the person who owns the seat which I perceive at a distance. The history of the master frequently disfigures the beauty of the landscape." The style of the landscape and of the house may also disfigure the reputation of the master. So congenial to the soul is the evidence of certain virtues, that we are delighted to see them emblemized in the works of nature and of art, and if this evidence be wanting in the artificial objects of a landscape, we feel no desire for the friendship of the people who are associated with them.

Of all sinister qualities pride is the most easily manifested and the most despicable, when exhibited in works of art; for men hate, even while they profess to admire, everything that arbitrarily exalts others above themselves. We dislike, in the dress, manners and conversation of a man, any appearance that plainly intimates his consciousness of superiority. This remark is no disagreeable reflection upon human nature; for it is not actual superiority that we dislike, but the ostentation or counterfeit of it. We are led instinctively to feel assured that the affectation of any quality is an evidence of the want of it. This is notoriously true of the affectation of wealth. Envy, which, after all, is but a hatred of false distinctions, not of real merit,—

> —— " a morbid better sense
> Of justice, that is prone to take offence
> At sight of wrongful inequality,"—

always attaches to false greatness, when its falsity is perceived. He, therefore, who aims at admiration, should carefully avoid all those appearances which are liable to excite the envy of his fellow citizens, who cannot, while under the influence of this feeling, see anything to admire

in the object that has excited in their hearts this painful
indignation.

It might occur to the critical reader of these remarks,
that if the principles they maintain were fully carried
out, all houses would be hovels. With equal justice it
might be said, if objections were made to covering the
person with jewelry, that one was in favor of restoring
the primeval costume of fig-leaves. Thi prevalent
rivalry in dress, in fine houses, and in sumptuous monuments, is a rivalry in the display of wealth, not of personal qualities ; and it is something that will wear away
with a better civilization. When that enlightened era
arrives, both the art of dressing, and the art of building,
will be more of a science and less of a pantomime, than at
the present day. In that era of better civilization, art
will be exercised to increase our own pleasures and comforts, and at the same time to confer an agreeable satisfaction upon others. It is used, at the present day,
chiefly for the purpose of advertising, or rather, of publishing the evidence of wealth. Monumental stones
which should be designed only to commemorate the
dead, are erected now to gratify the pride of the living.
Such a desecration of the art of monumental sculpture
will be ridiculed, like any other folly, when men have
become wiser and less idolatrous. At that period of intellectual progress, humility will be acknowledged as one of
the beauties of a house, or of any other structure that is
designed for private or domestic purposes. This principle is now very generally felt, but not understood.

Humility of expression is aided by anything that
causes a structure to manifest less sumptuousness and
cost than might be discovered by careful examination.
A work that cost an immense sum of money may possess
this desirable quality, while in a very cheap work it may

be entirely wanting. In architecture and sculpture all depends on the manner in which appendages intended for ornament are displayed; and whether the assemblage of parts seems to have been dictated by a love of beauty and propriety, or by emulation and a feeling of rivalry. In the marble of our cemeteries, this rivalry is made apparent by the constantly increasing endeavors, on the part of the builders of new monuments, to outdo the most sumptuous and costly which are already completed.

It is a maxim in the arts to avoid raising agreeable expectations which cannot be gratified. For this reason a perfect orator would avoid high-flown language, and a pompous address. He avoids raising expectations, in order that every charming sentiment, every rational argument, and every happy turn of wit, may strike the hearer with an agreeable surprise, and penetrate more deeply into the mind. Pompous orators and ostentatious artists enjoy more notoriety: they are better " stars " ; but their words and works produce no indelible impression on the mind of the public ; their reputation is ephemeral ; and their works dazzle without enlightening the community.

The shallowness of such pretensions is more readily discovered in daily conversation, when the speaker or actor is frequently before us. All persons are pleased with a plainly dressed man or woman, whose manners and conversation indicate a high degree of benevolence, intellect, and refinement. We note with pleasure the entire absence of any apparent intention to impose upon us by etiquette or by elegance of apparel. On the contrary, when we are led by the elegant and costly dress of a woman, to expect a corresponding superiority of manners, refinement, and education, and perhaps of personal beauty, and find, on introduction to her, a countenance of vulgar expressions, and manners and conversation that afford incontestable proof of ignorance and lowbreeding, we are affected with contempt. There is many a quality that becomes despicable only by position. Bad grammar and bad pronunciation may be associated with some of the most noble virtues of the human character. In a laborer's cottage, they might not diminish our respect for the inmates ; but they become contemptible when playing a part in a splendid mansion and in fashionable costume.

This principle is at the foundation of our dislike of a structure that exhibits promises which, on close inspection, it cannot fulfil ; as in a dwelling-house that appears on general inspection to be built for hospitality, and on closer inspection betrays only meanness and pretence ; or in a monument that seems to be raised for the commemoration of some distinguished benefactor of mankind, — but is found on a near view, to be erected in celebration of the fortunes of a living person who has risen to wealth, without any talents or virtues to distinguish him from others. Our love of truth affects our opinion of the arts as well as of human conduct.

When expectations, but feebly excited, are suddenly rewarded by gratification, our pleasure is greatly magnified by our surprise. This happens, after contemplating the neatness and simplicity of a humble headstone, or tablet, when we read in the inscription, the name of some deceased person whose memory all delight to honor. The dead who slumbers beneath it is not demeaned by this simple tribute to his memory ; and the spot becomes sanctified by those poetical associations that always hover round a tomb so humble and so picturesque. The name even of Washington may be demeaned by the ambition of those who would signalize his virtues by sumptuous marble, which, by its splendor, implies some doubt of the immortality of its subject. The principle here inculcated is one of the lessons of the founder of Christianity, but Christians have neglected it in their practice. I believe no hero was ever exalted by a splendid mausoleum. Men are delighted to visit the spot in which he was interred, and a durable monumental stone must be provided to mark its situation ; but in proportion to the greatness of the subject, is there a charm of sublimity thrown around the scene, by a humble and unpretending monument. Ostentation is vulgar ; and it degrades those who were truly great to the level of the mere votaries of fortune. If the spot where Jesus was buried were known, how would it be desecrated by such a tribute as Dives, if he were living, would erect for his own glorification in Mount Auburn !

It may be objected that this principle of humility would be fatal to progress in the arts ; but this is not to be feared ; it would, on the contrary serve to give them a more rational and pleasing direction. The object of ornamental art is to give pleasure, and it is misdirected when it is used only for mere display. No man comes away with a feeling of genuine pleasure from a gaudy display of the idols of another's ambition ; but he is always filled with delight by looking at objects that vividly awaken in the mind those cheerful and complacent feelings, which arise from our sympathy with goodness and benevolence. Our love of virtue is indeed the well-spring of our taste in the arts, unless this taste has been corrupted by fashion, or by the dogmas of arbitrary criticism. The best rules of art are those which are obtained by careful study of the effects of different works upon our own minds ; they cannot be learned by dictation.   By studiously analyzing his own feelings, almost every man would discover that he is not so well pleased with an object that suggests the idea of ambition, as with one that wears the charming expression of repose and humility.

THEY ARE NOT THERE.

SELECTED.

They are not there! where once their feet
Light answer to the music beat;
Where their young voices sweetly breathed,
And fragrant flowers they lightly wreathed.
Still flows the nightingale's sweet song;
Still trail the vine's green shoots along;
Still are the sunny blossoms fair; —
But they who loved them are not there!

They are not there! by the lone fount,
That once they loved at eve to haunt;
Where, when the day-star brightly set,
Beside the silver waves they met,
Still lightly glides the quiet stream;
Still o'er it falls the soft moonbeam;
But they who used their bliss to share
With loved hearts by it, are not there!

They are not there! by the dear hearth,
That once beheld their harmless mirth;
When through their joy came no vain fear,
And o'er their smiles no darkening tear

It burns not now a beacon star ;
'T is cold and fireless as they are ;
Where is the glow it used to wear ? —
'T is felt no more — they are not there !

Where are they then ? — Oh ! passed away,
Like blossoms withered in a day ;
Or, as the waves go swiftly by,
Or, as the lightnings leave the sky.
But still there is a land of rest :
Still hath it room for many a guest ;
Still is it free from strife and care ; —
And 't is our hope that they are there !

ON THE AFFLICTIONS OF LIFE.

FROM ZIMMERMANN.

WHO has not in the moment of convalescence, in the hour of melancholy, or when separation or death has deprived one of the intercourses of friendship, sought relief in the salutary shades of the country ! Happy is the being who is sensible of the advantages of a religious retirement from the world, of a sacred tranquillity, in which all the benefits to be derived from society impress themselves more deeply in the heart, and every hour is consecrated to the practice of the mild and peaceful virtues ! But these advantages become much more conspicuous, when we compare the modes of thought which employ the mind of a solitary philosopher with those of a worldly sensualist ; the tiresome and tumultuous life of the one with the soft tranquillity of the other ; when we oppose the fear and horror that disturb the death-bed of the worldly-minded man, with the peaceable and easy exit of those pious souls who submit with resignation to the will of heaven. It is at this awful moment that we feel the importance of turning the eye inwardly upon ourselves, if we would bear the sufferings of life with dignity, and the pains of death with resignation.

Retirement affords us the most incontestable advantages, under the greatest adversities of life. The convalescent, the unfortunate, the disappointed, here find equal relief; their tortured souls here find a balm for the deep and painful wounds they have received, and soon regain their pristine health and vigor. Sickness and affliction would fly with horror from retirement, if its friendly shades did not afford them that consolation which they are unable to obtain in the resorts of fashion. The subtle vapor which sensuality and intoxication shed upon the objects that surround a state of health and happiness, entirely disappear; and all those charms which subsist rather in imagination than reality, lose their power. To the happy every object wears the delightful colors of the rose; but to the miserable all is blank and dreadful. The two conditions are equally in the extreme; but they do not, in either case, discover the errors into which they are betrayed, until the curtain drops; when the scene changes, and the illusion is dissipated.

How unhappy should we be, if Divine Providence were to grant us everything we desire! Even under the very afflictions by which man believes his happiness to be destroyed, heaven may propose something extraordinary in his favor. New circumstances excite new exertions. In solitude and tranquillity, if we earnestly endeavor to conquer misfortune, the activity of life, which, until the moment of adversity, had been perhaps suspended, suddenly changes, and the mind regains its energy and vigor, even while it laments the state of inaction, to which it conceives itself to be irretrievably reduced.

If sorrow force us into retirement, patience and perseverance soon restore the soul to its natural tranquillity and happiness. We ought never to inspect the volume of futurity; its pages will only deceive us; on the contrary, we ought forever to repeat this experimental truth, this consolatory maxim, — that the objects which men behold at a distance with fear and trembling, lose, on a nearer approach, not only their disagreeable and menacing aspect, but frequently in the event, produce the most agreeable and unexpected pleasure. He who tries every expedient, who boldly opposes himself to every difficulty, who stands steady and inflexible to every obstacle, who neglects no exertion within his power, and relies with confidence upon divine aid, extracts from affliction both its poison and its sting, and deprives misfortune of its victory.

The opportunity which a valetudinarian enjoys of employing his faculties with facility and success, in a manner conformable to the extent of his designs, is undoubtedly short, and passes rapidly away. Such happiness is the lot only of those who enjoy robust health; they alone can exclaim, "Time is my own." But he who labors under continual sickness and suffering, and whose avocation depends on the public necessity or caprice, can never say that he has one moment to himself. He must watch the fleeting hours as they pass, and seize an interval of leisure when and where he can. Necessity, as well as reason, convinces him, that he must, in spite of his daily sufferings, his wearied body, or his harassed mind, firmly resist his accumulating troubles, and if he would save himself from becoming the victim of dejection, manfully combat the difficulties by which he is attacked. The more we enervate ourselves, the more we become the prey of ill health ; but a determined courage and obstinate resistance frequently renovate our powers ; and he, who in the calm of retirement, vigorously wrestles with misfortune, is certain in the event, of partial conquest.

But under the pains of sickness, we are apt too easily to listen to the voice of indulgence ; we neglect to exercise the powers we possess, and instead of directing the attention to those objects which may divert melancholy and strengthen fortitude, we foster fondly in our bosoms, all the disagreeable circumstances of our situation. The soul sinks from inquietude to inquietude, loses all its powers, abandons its remaining reason, and feels from its increasing agonies and sufferings, no confidence in its own exertions. The valetudinarian should force his mind to forget its troubles : should endeavor to emerge from the heavy atmosphere by which he is enveloped and depressed. By these exertions he will certainly find unexpected relief, and be able to accomplish that which before he conceived to be impossible.

A slight effort to obtain the faintest ray of comfort, and a calm resignation under inevitable misfortunes, will mutually contribute to procure relief. The man whose mind adheres to virtue, will never permit himself to be so far overcome by the sense of misfortune, as not to endeavor to vanquish his feelings, even when, fallen into the unhappy state of despair, he no longer sees any prospect of comfort or consolation. The most dejected bosom may endure sensations deeply afflicting, provided the mind be not inactive ; it will exercise its attention on some other object than itself, and make effort to withdraw the soul from brooding over its torments and its sorrows, by inspiring the mind with ideas of virtuous sentiments, noble actions, and generous inclinations. For this reason it is necessary to cultivate in our minds the love of action, and after a dutiful and entire submission to the dispensations of heaven, force ourselves into employment, until, from the warmth of our exertions, we acquire an habitual alertness. I consider a disposition to be active, amid that disgust and apathy which dry up the fountains of life, as the most sure and efficacious antidote against the poison of a dejected spirit, a soured temper, or a melancholy mind.

The influence of the mind upon the body is one of the most consolatory truths, to those who are the subject of habitual sufferings. Supported by this idea, they never permit their reason to be entirely overcome; religion, under this idea, never loses its powerful empire in the breast; and they learn from experience, that even in the extremity of distress, every object which diverts the attention, softens the evils we endure, and frequently drives them unperceived away.

Many celebrated philosophers have by this means at length been able, not only to preserve a tranquil mind in the midst of the most poignant sufferings, but have even increased the strength of their intellectual faculties, in spite of their misfortunes. Rousseau composed the greater part of his immortal works under the continual pressure of sickness and of grief. Gellert, who, by his mild, agreeable, and instructive writings, became the preceptor of Germany, certainly found in this interesting occupation, the surest remedy against melancholy. At an age already far advanced in life, Mendelsohm, who, though not by nature subject to dejection, was for a long time oppressed by an almost inconceivable derangement of the

nervous system, by submitting with patience and docility
to his sufferings, maintained in old age all the noble and
sublime advantages of his youth.

A firm resolution, a steady adherence towards some
noble and interesting end, will enable us to endure the
most poignant affliction. An heroic courage is natural
in all the dangerous enterprises of ambition, and in the
little crosses of life is much more common than patience ;
but a persevering courage, under evils of long duration,
is a quality rarely seen ; the soul enervated by melancholy, is prone to abandon its own efforts, and looks up
to heaven alone for protection.

DEATH OF THE AGED MAN.

By Mrs. Sigourney.

Who scans the fulness of a powerful mind,
Which more than fourscore years hath held its course
Among the living ?   We, of yesterday,
Tread not its halls, with ancient pictures decked,
Still freshening 'neath the ministry of time,
Nor haunt its secret cabinets of thought,
Where shadowy people of a buried age
Sit in communion.   He who died to-day,
Was rich in imagery of other times.
Ye might have asked him, and he would have told
How step by step, his native place threw off
Its rude colonial features, for the garb
That cities wear ; — and how the cow-path changed
To a thick peopled street, and the cold marsh
To garden beauty.

              Yes, he might have told
Had ye but asked him, how the dark, red brows
Of the poor Indians, glided here and there,
Unpitied strangers, in their own fair land : —
And how yon stately roofs and fair designs
Of public spirit or bland charity,
Sprang from a germ which he had helped to nurse;
And he could tell you stories of a race
Now rooted up and perished.   Many a date,
And legend, slumbers in that marble breast,
Which history coveted.   For memory sat
With her strong pen, and clearly noted down,
On life's broad tablet, till the step of death
Stole suddenly upon her.   Then his voice
Gave glorious witness of the faith that lives
When nature fails, and told the listening friend
That underneath the everlasting arms
Broke the rude shock of pain.

                   And so his breath,
In one unstruggling, gentle sigh went forth,
Relying on the Saviour he had loved,
Mid all the tempting vanities of youth,
Here rocked his cradle, and there yawns his grave.
To him, perchance, it seemed a little space,
As of a bow shot, 'tween his boyhood's sports,
And the thick coming of those silver hairs,
Which were to him a crown of righteousness.
— No more he cheers his household with the smile
Of tender love, or greets the entering youth
With the old warmth of hospitality.
No more we see him leaning on his staff,
Measuring with vigorous step his wonted way ;
Nor mark, amid the mellowness of age,

Those fruits, which through the tears and clouds of life,
Ripened for heaven.

                 'T is mournful thus to see
The fathers of our city, one by one,
Take up their dwelling with the silent worm.
We shrink to fill their places.   Reverend men,
Of such well-balanced and rare energies,
Courteous and dignified, and true of heart,
We dread to find their high example gone ;
We grieve that thus th' insatiate grave should lock
The gold of their experience.   O'er life's tide,
We steer without them, by a broken chart,
Too late lamenting we so lightly prized
The pilotage of wisdom, while it dwelt
With hoary head among us.

                 Grant us grace,
Father of all ! so to revere the words
Of saintly age, and so to keep the path
Of those who pass before us unto Thee,
That, shunning snares and pitfalls, we may come
To the sure mansions of eternal life.

H.S.CHASE.

THE CHASE MONUMENT.

This monument — a solid shaft of marble — is situated on Sorrel Path;
is of elaborate design and finish. On the front is placed the following : —

I GO TO PREPARE A PLACE FOR YOU.

ELIZABETH AUGUSTA,
WIFE OF
H. S. CHASE,
DIED AUGUST 28, 1855,
AGED 39 YEARS.

Calm on the bosom of thy God,
Fair spirit rest thee now!
Even while with us thy footsteps trod,
His seal was on thy brow.

H. S. CHASE.

On the right and left and back of the monument is also inscribed
the following : —

THIS MORTAL SHALL PUT ON IMMORTALITY.

IF A MAN DIES SHALL HE LIVE AGAIN.

I AM THE RESURRECTION AND THE LIFE.

SCHUYLER CHASE,
BORN SEPT. 18, 1843,
DIED SEPT. 20, 1843.

SCHUYLER CHASE,
BORN DEC. 28, 1845,
DIED APRIL 9, 1846.

HALLOWED GROUNDS.

TIME, the great limner of nature, who tints the hills and plains with verdure, and garnishes the rocks with variegated leafage, enhances all the charms of old familiar places. Scenes that in the early period of youth were bleak and cheerless, seem, when time has given them a place among our distant recollections, clothed with a lavish beauty; filled with the light of brighter skies, and vocal with sounds that are sweeter than music. The human soul, capable of a variety of affliction and of solace, finds in each something to alleviate its burden. In the bosom of these scenes, we are transported in imagination back to this romantic stage in the journey of life; the streams renew their ancient babbling, and return sweet responses to our silent invocations; and in the gleaming objects of the landscape, we behold the hazy pictures of memory resolved into bright realities. Every once familiar object opens a separate page in our history; and when we are absent from them, the book is closed, and all our retrospect is dark and mournful.

Man alone is sensible to those enjoyments that spring from contemplating the scenes of past sorrows. Nature has given us this sentiment, which is allied to that of divinity, to raise us above our mere physical being to the contemplation of sublimer themes. Hence there is always some religious faith — though it may be unattended with rational assurance — accompanying the sentiment of pleasure that springs from the remembrance of affliction. The benevolence of the Deity has converted all our sorrows into so many sources of happiness, causing them, after their poignancy is gone, to reflect back upon our souls a beam of divine solace, — as in the mists of the storm that has passed over, are reflected the bright hues of celestial beauty. In the clouds of grief that have passed away, there is also a bow of promise, upon which we look with melancholy delight, and thank heaven for this bright covenant with our sorrows.'

On frequent occasions we cheerfully renounce the pleasures of sense, to experience emotions that are divine. Thus we leave the places of gaiety and feasting, to muse in solitude over the old roads we have travelled. The effect of this sentiment is to bear the soul into the presence of some deity, who inspires us with a cheerful melancholy that surpasses pleasure. What throngs of delightful images sometimes hover about an old guide-post; the same that used to direct our youthful ramblings to some desired resort, or that pointed our homeward way when returning from a weary absence abroad, — one that was always seen on our excursions of pleasure, or daily recurring errands of duty! How many memories are lettered upon it — invisible to strangers — but clear, bright and intelligible to our own minds! Every object that was prominent to our observation, on these errands and these wanderings, however homely its appearance, is beautiful in our sight; because we do not behold its deformity, — for outside of it, like the vinery that covers a dilapidated wall, do we see the clustered assemblages of a thousand blessed visions, made bright and conspicuous by this talisman.

What is beauty to the sophisticated mind of a connoisseur, or to the vulgar mind of one who is captivated by splendor, is not of divine source. Wherever a deity is enshrined, there dwells the highest beauty to those who can see, in its outward expression, the manifestation of this divinity. The more homely the object, indeed, if it be not disagreeable, the more charming is its influence,

because it has no visual attractions, to divert us from the
pleasing suggestions of the imagination. It is for this
reason that so many plain houses, plain tombs, and rude
landscapes, have a charm in our sight which we cannot
behold in others more tasteful and adorned. And
hence almost all the hallowed spots in our remembrance
are simple and unartistic. It is on the rude rock that
overlooks an unadorned prospect, in the old road that
leads through a mass of tangled shrubbery, in the moss-
grown cottage, and the rustic hamlet, where memory .
delights to dwell, and weave for us the weft of her inspiration.

The house in which I was born, and where I lived
during the period of childhood, has lost its original and
endearing simplicity by a few alterations. These are just
sufficient to deprive the place of a great part of the
sacredness, with which I have always regarded it, as the
scene of my earliest recollections. The hollow, situated
a few rods behind it, and which was then filled with a
grove of locust trees, is now cut up into gardens ; and
the gentle slope, so enchanting to the lovers of nature,
has been terraced by the owners, for ornament and the
convenience of tillage. The locust trees are all gone, and
with them the beauty of the place has departed. I sometimes look over the fence, and endeavor to bring back
to my mind the whole scene, as it was when I first looked
abroad upon the earth under these trees. Then I cannot
avoid giving myself up to regrets, and lamenting the
changes that are constantly depriving the scenes of our
early life of their sacredness and their identity.

Other objects about this place are not greatly altered.
The next house, with its old-fashioned garden, still remains in its primitive condition. It has not yet been
ruined by improvements. When a child, I used to listen

to the cawing of crows, as I walked along the footpath on the sidewalk that was bounded by this garden fence. I look forward, with a gloomy anticipation, to the time when this place also will be modernized, and the footpath, that leads through the grassy sidewalk, will be covered with a neat spread of gravel, for the convenience of an increasing population. At present, this whole sidewalk is to me a consecrated spot; and as I sometimes stroll along its path, I listen for the cawing of crows that, strangely enough, are the only sounds which are vivid in my memory in connection with the scene. By a revival of these memories, one is inspired with a sense of that freshness of existence, which gave every object in life a brightness and beauty, that fade and become tarnished at a later period of our years.

In vain do we endeavor to fix our affections upon any new places as we are enamored with those of other days. There cheering voices come sounding up from every once familiar nook and turn; and the enlivening echo of remembered joys falls like music on the ear. Lights that have a quaint, endearing lustre, gleam fondly from the cottage windows; and in the still moonlight, the shadows present their well-remembered forms with a startling fidelity, — as if time here had stayed his progress, and kindly waited to satisfy our lingering affections. As one grows older, these scenes become so many remembrancers, reviving not only the recollections, but the very feelings and hopes that, early in life, relieved every place of its insipidity.

I am guilty of no egotism when I recount such recollections: for these experiences of my life are those of every person of feeling. There is no one who does not cherish some spot in his native village and among the scenes of youthful frequentation, as holy ground. Here do we, as it were, meet again and converse with those who are now dead or absent; whom we seek in vain to call back into our presence in any other situation. Here is a tree, in whose shade we have sat with friends long since dead; and under this tree will memory give us back their features more vividly than even a portrait of their living countenance. The sainted forms of departed friends are always sitting in these familiar arbors; in the garden or orchard, in the nook by the seaside, in the path of the old wood.

Happy are they, whose native and paternal dwelling remains unaltered, with all the objects around it; who, when tired of employment, can turn thither and be charmed with all those trifles that yield it somewhat of the sacredness of antiquity. Many are they, however, whose youth was spent in moving from place to place, and who have fixed upon certain outward scenes as their hallowed grounds; — the inclosures of a schoolhouse, a once familiar walk, and the plain or the eminence whither they resorted for toil or amusement. Even these are often revolutionized; and nothing is left that is sacred in one's memory, save the blank surface, where he vainly endeavors to picture to his mind the absent landmarks, — the greensward then sparkling with flowers, the trees jubilant with birds, and the pleasant nooks enlightened with happy faces that are to be seen no more!

When I was a student, it was my custom, with two of my schoolmates, to walk over the road that led us homeward, at the end of each quarter, and on our return to school. During my three Academical years, between the ages of thirteen and sixteen, I performed many of these pedestrian journeys, which, so often repeated at this early age, have rendered the whole of this route a consecrated ground. Many a time since have I walked the

same road — a distance of eighteen miles — for the pleasure of reviewing the fields, the houses, the lakes, and the
woods, which are now a beautiful chart of the scenes of
this period of simple adventure. I am not a gloomy or
an unhappy man ; but my happiness depends greatly on
these things. My spirits are nurtured by a review of old
accustomed places ; and my hopes are still bright as in
youth, when my mind is lighted by the sunshine of the
same fields in which it received its first lessons of nature
and humanity.

In every part of this old road, I meet the images of my
companions with whom I was associated in these pedestrian journeys. How beautiful is every clump of vinery
that flings its umbrage over fence and pathway, and
every green thicket that is mirrored upon the glassy pool
beneath ! And how like sacrilege seems the labor that
has removed any one of them, for convenience or improvement ! I am greeted here by thoughts that never
come to me in any other place ; forms and visions of
friends and of friendship which no other scene or prospect
can awaken. Here they are enshrined by memory, made
visible among the shadows and the sunshine, and appearing in joyous wakefulness among the trees and flowers —
fond messengers of past happiness which the genius of the
place alone can revoke.

Memory is not wholly the result of a voluntary effort.
The power of recollection depends greatly on suggestions
from outward objects ; and if we would recall the events
and feelings, the ideas and sensations of youth, we must
visit the places where they first impressed our minds.
Many a delightful fancy then rises to cheer the soul with
the freshness of the morning of life, and many a hope we
thought was lost, comes to us, like an old friend, with
glad assurances of the future.

There is a certain kind of melancholy which, unattended with despondency, becomes a source of the purest pleasure which the human soul can feel. Such is the sentiment that is awakened by the sight of those objects upon which both time and memory have stamped their sacred lineaments. The world is entirely uncheerful, when I dwell beyond access to these hallowed grounds ; and I must frequently revisit them to imbibe new contentment and new inspiration, to preserve the light of my soul until another review. It may be the inclosures of a dwelling-house ; a narrow lane that passes through a wood ; a hillside that overlooks the sea or the adjacent villages ; it may be only a footpath by the side of a brook : — but it is something through which I must pass, to arrive at my own paradise.

A perpetual fountain of delight wells up from these scenes of memory ; and when I see them changed by improvements, I mourn as over the grave of a friend. For these are the pages whereon is written the history of our life ; and with every old tree that is cut down, every umbrageous thicket that is removed, and every ancient house that is modernized by the hand of taste, some bright page is torn from this book of life. We hear messages of early friendship that come only from the voices of these streams ; music that accords but with these rustling boughs and foliage ; we behold beauty that revives only with these flowers ; love that wakes and weeps forgotten tears, never save among these dripping fountains and these echoing hills. Hence the wretchedness of a man of feeling who is an exile from his native land, and from the scenes of his early years. He sees many beautiful and pleasant places ; but no familiar deity resides in them ; no memory haunts them. They are mere blanks : like strangers, they do not smile upon him, and e cannot love their features.

All our hopes and our affections, our dreams of love and of ambition, have each their separate locations, and as long as these places remain, we may still go and abide with them, obtain a bright retrospect of the past, and look again with the hopeful feelings of childhood upon our more narrowed future. The forms of the landscape may disclose a little recess, where reposes some pleasant image of the past, enshrined there like the sacred relics of our affection or our worship. The violet that peeps out from the green turf has a beam that penetrates the heart ; and should a little sparrow but open its throat on the pinnacle of one of these rocks — his notes are like the melodies of morning, when it first greeted our waking from the peaceful slumbers of childhood. How can one live apart from these hallowed grounds and still find happiness ! Save me from the oblivion that must follow such an exile ! Let me ever be surrounded by these familiar scenes, where the deities reside who lead along the hours, in whose hands are all the blessings of memory and imagination.

THE TIDE OF TIME.

As streams are ever flowing to the bay,
Borne by mysterious force along their way
To join the sea — we thus are moved along
The tide of time, with all the living throng.
The summer flowers, th' autumnal fruits decay;
All things inhabiting this earth obey
One signal doom. We pass from youth to age,
Through many a pleasant, many a weary stage ;
And as the winds, with pensive murmuring,
Scatter the leaves upon their fluttering wing, —

So all things, as they rise, and blush and bloom,
Are seared, at last, and scattered for the tomb.

New happy hosts, unceasing, pass away ;
For time, their pilot, suffers no delay.
In toil and tumult, full of hope and trust,
They rise and revel and return to dust ;
Some dropping by the wayside in their prime ;
Some lingering, till forgotten in their time.
While Providence still hides our journey's end —
Thus dreaming, hoping, joying, we descend,
Like insects in our path that creep or fly,
Are born and flutter, and grow old and die,
But love and mate, and chaunt their life-long tune,
In but three revolutions of the moon.

We chase our object, leave it, and pursue
A brighter vision opening on our view.
Still other phantoms guide us and allure ;
For these we hope, and battle and endure.
Our preparations are our daily feast ;
The joys of our fruition are the least.
The sounds of heaven, the bird's, the insect's lay,
The gems, the fruits, the flowers that gird our way ; —
By these spell-bound, entranced, in sun and shower,
We laugh and linger, till our last brief hour.
Life, luring, glittering, still is but a chase :
We drop our prizes, to pursue the race.
Then comes the final act : our course is run ;
The pageant disappears, and death is won.

But let us not lament this sad decree—
This fate that stamped us with mortality.
For there are mystic lights in heaven that show
Man's being ends not here in death and woe.

Hope dies not with the visions of our youth;
It glows at all times with immortal truth.
Whene'er we question fate — this signal light
Gleams with prophetic joys upon our sight;
Appearing in the starlight and the skies;
Repeated in the wind's low symphonies;
Pictured in nature and embossed in art;
Beaming in thought, and glowing in the heart;
Pillowed upon the clouds of morn and even;
Enshrined on earth and emblemized in heaven!

This bright, mysterious spark — this fleeting flame —
Restored to the great fountain, whence it came,
Shall not be quenched, but shine with purer light,
When to the deathless sphere, it takes its flight.
And when the dream of youth is only known,
As the sad memory of a joy that's flown;
And hope, that brightly beamed upon us then,
Like the full moon, that shines to bless all men,
Has waned into a crescent, like a line
Of light that dimly gleams, but cannot shine : —
Then as remembrance wakes her pensive theme,
And fancy gilds the vision of her dream;
O'er the dense gloom that melancholy strews,
The angel faith will shed her fairest hues;
And truths and lights, but feebly emblemed now,
Illume the soul with an unfading glow.

27

THE THREE FUNERALS.

BY MISS PARDOE.

I WAS once visiting in town, when in weak health and depressed spirits, and was slowly pacing to and fro on the broad pavement which extends in front of the proud line of lordly dwellings that overlook Hyde Park on its northern boundary, endeavoring to inhale new vigor from the keen air, and in the pale sunshine of a winter's noon, when my attention was attracted to a modest funeral, which advancing up Park Lane, was, with less solemnity than is generally observed in such processions, approaching the burial ground at the termination of St. George's Terrace. The death bell was already tolling, the grave was awaiting its tenant, and I paused for an instant, until the little train of death passed by.

There was a whole history of suffering, penury, and bereavement beneath my eye. The single ill-clad undertaker who led the way, the coffin of unpolished wood, the faded pall that fluttered gloomily in the chill wind ; the bowed and pale-browed man, whose mourning cloak failed to conceal the laboring garb beneath it, as he led by either hand a little girl, to whose shapeless bonnets of rusty straw the charitable care of some kindly-hearted neighbor, perhaps as poor as themselves, had added a bow and a pair of strings of black ; — the one a child of about eight years of age, weeping bitterly ; and the other, still an infant of some three or four, gazing about her in mute but silent wonder, now looking earnestly towards the coffin, and then lifting her large blue eyes to the face of her father, as if to ask the meaning of so unwonted a ceremony. But the man made no reply to those earnest eyes, neither did he weep ; it was easy to see that he

was heart-broken ; easy to understand that he had been
poor before, very poor, but that he had struggled bravely
on, while he had one to help, and to cheer and to support
him ; but that now the corner-stone of his energy and of
his hope had been removed, and the whole foundation of
his moral energy had given way. That there, in that
rude coffin, beneath that squalid pall, lay the wife of his
bosom, the mother of his children ; and that for him and
the two helpless ones whom he led along, there was no
longer a hope of better days in this world.

I felt the tears gush over my heart, as the pauper funeral passed me by ; and it had scarcely done so when
it was overtaken by a second death train, consisting of a
hearse without plumes, and a single mourning coach, so
wretchedly appointed, that the struggle between narrow
means, and the desire to escape the stigma of " a walking
funeral" was closely apparent. Strange, that human
vanity should uprear its paltry crest even upon the
death-path — but so it is ; and I remarked that as this
second funeral passed the one in which I felt so sudden
an interest, the drivers of the two sable vehicles cast a
glance that was almost scornful upon the little band of
mourners, and the coffin which they followed. It is
probable that I alone detected that contemptuous glance ;
for the soul-stricken man, who was about to give up to
the grave all that had been to him the staff and the sunshine of his poor struggling existence, had no perception
beyond that of his own misery, no pride with which to
combat his despair.

The sad dogma of life-in-death, upon which I was
then looking, had not, however, yet reached its close ;
for the body which was dragged to the grave by a pair
of black horses had scarcely left behind it that which was
borne to its resting-place upon the shoulders of two of its

fellow men, when suddenly there appeared, round the corner, turning from the Edgeware Road, a mute, bearing a plateau of white plumes, and followed by a hearse drawn by four horses, all similarly decorated, and a couple of mourning coaches, with the usual attendance of undertaker's hirelings. Vile mockery of Almighty God! to whom we cannot even be content to resign our dust, without flaunting, as if in defiance of his holy precepts, who bade us be meek and humble, if we would gain heaven, — our poor and sordid vanity at the grave-side; rendered in this instance the more revolting from the fact that all the decorations of the funeral were grim with dirt, and tarnished by long use. Nevertheless they produced their intended effect. Every foot passenger paused by the grated entrance of the burial place, to wait the halt of the procession. Children, who had pursued their walk or their sports, heedless of the bereaved husband, or the solitary coach, suddenly paused in astonishment and admiration; sauntering nursery-maids quickened their pace to participate in the spectacle; reckless butcher boys pulled up their coats and almost ceased to whistle, as the imposing mockery moved towards them; and when the varnished coffin was followed to the graveyard by the attendant mourners, the outlay which had been lavished upon the funeral was repaid to the survivors, by the earnest and curious stare of the idle mob that had hastily collected.

I asked the names of the dead, — I might have spared the question. The smile with which the first reply was given — for I began with the widowed pauper — was one of pity, which implied some doubt of my perfect sanity; while on the subject of the unplumed hearse, I was told "to look straight ahead, and I should see that it was not anybody"; and so far my inquiries were unavailing;

but as I glanced towards the bustling officials, who were
rapidly dismantling the more pretending *cortége*, and
flinging plumes, staves and pall-trappings into the lugubrious vehicle so lately tenanted by the early dead, I
believed that I should be more successful. Not so, however; the undertaker and his myrmidons — and with
these I had no desire to be forced into contact — were
alone acquainted with the name of the deceased. The
crowd, satisfied with the amusement of a moment, cared
little to whom they were indebted for its enjoyment.
" Some young person," said a portly man, standing near.
" So I infer from what are meant for white plumes."
" You may well say meant, ma'am," remarked a decent
looking woman, who stood beside me with a child in her
arms. " Lord help us ! here's a waste of money, that
would gladen many a hungry heart. Miss Some-one,
they tell me, a rich shop-keeper's daughter — poor thing !
She's to have a grand tomb, they say, and of course
her name will be on it : but till that's done, nobody but
her own people know who she is."

A grand tomb ! A name graven upon stone ! And
the pauper mother will have neither tomb nor name.
But sleep peacefully in thy long rest, O stricken sister !
The marble that presses upon the breast of the proud,
is only so much more that parts them from their God ;
while thou hast upon thine unlettered grave the rain-drops
for tears from above ; the wind that rocks the heads of
the rank weeds that wave over thy brow breathes thine
ever-recurring requiem ; and the deep blue vault of
heaven is the ETERNAL MONUMENT raised above thee by
thy Maker !

27 *

PRESENT IN THE SPIRIT.

BY MRS. H. J. LEWIS.

NOT o'er that dreary void
That the tomb opens do I look for thee,
But o'er the still and pleasant summer sea,
And o'er the green fields drenched in golden light,
And off beyond the mountain's silent height :
And mounting star by star, till lost in space,
I fain would see the glory of thy face,
    Which death hath not destroyed.

Through forest aisles at eve,
Where the birds' lonely vespers haunt the trees,
By running brooks, where cowslips woo the bees,
Where the sweet violet nestles in the moss,
Where, mid o'erhanging rocks the waters toss
Their foam-wreaths to the sunlight, there thou art,
Unseen, but present to the yearning heart
    Thou didst so early grieve.

Thy name forever more
Hath a soft sound like music, and is blent
With flowers and song and sunshine, and is sent
On every perfumed breeze, and through the night
Whispered to moon and stars that beam more bright
With the fair burden ; so, from day to day,
We walk with thee along life's chequered way
    Sustained as e'er before.

The form thou wearest now,
Hath not, perchance, the old familiar look,
And dazzled mortal vision might not brook

The glory of thy face and vestments, meet
For one made welcome at her Master's feet:
So we will wait God's bidding to behold
Thee as thou art within the Saviour's fold,
His signet on thy brow.

ON THE BURIAL OF THE DEAD.

BY JOHN BRAZER, D. D.

THE appropriate burial of the dead is suggested and enforced by the natural sentiments of the human heart. Philosophize as wisely as we may, on the worthlessness of our mortal frames, when life is extinct, and their component parts have obeyed their mutual affinities, and have gone to mingle with their kindred elements, — the argument is wholly unavailing. Let it be admitted in its full and literal force, it touches not the question at issue. This is one of feeling, sentiment, emotion; and cool ratiocination is out of place. The heart is the fitting advocate here, and its unprompted and untaught suggestions supersede all argument. Even a stranger's grave is not to us as the common earth; and the spot where the ashes of our departed friends repose is ever held in cherished consecration. We are not, and as a general fact, we cannot be, indifferent to the treatment of our own remains, even when they have mingled with the clod of the valley. The well-known Oriental form of salutation, — " May you die among your kindred," — has a deep significance to which the soul responds, not only because we desire that our final trial should be passed in the midst of friendly attention and sympathy, and that our fainting sight should rest last upon those we have loved the best ; but also, because we would commend to their willing and pious care the poor remains of what was once most intimately a part of ourselves, and hope they will hold in hallowed remembrance the places where they lie.

But the appropriate burial of the dead is enforced by considerations of a different and most imperious character. All sentiment apart, it is a subject that must be cared for, in reference to the common weal. It is a public necessity that must be met. Our only choice is, whether the relics of the departed shall be " buried out of our sight " with decency and reverence, and with those appropriate rites and observances, which are equally due to the dead, and edifying and consolatory to the living, — or whether they shall be hurried away and disposed of anywise and anywhere, as the most obvious convenience may suggest as an offence and an annoyance. The busy industry of the great destoyer leaves us no other alternative. The earth is literally sown with the mortal remains of human beings. The details on this point must be somewhat startling to those foolish persons who say to themselves, " To-morrow shall be as this day." It has been computed, from a series of observations, by a competent inquirer, that the whole population of the earth, which is now supposed to be between nine and ten hundred millions of inhabitants, dies in thirty-three years, which gives fifty-five deaths for every successive minute, or nearly one for every second of time. If we apply a similar calculation to all past ages, since men have lived on. this earth, we shall at once see that, —

> " all who tread
> The globe, are but a handful to the tribes
> That slumber in its bosom."

In the vicinity of Alexandria, of Cairo, and indeed of all the principal cities of Egypt, catacombs containing the relics of the population of past ages, extend acres after acres, for many miles. It is supposed that the whole space between the borders of Lake Mœris and Gizeh was one vast cemetery. In the Necropolis, near ancient Thebes, it is computed, that eight or ten millions of the dead, lie in like manner inhumed. At Paris, when the churches and burial grounds were cleared, the relics of ten generations were piled up promiscuously in the quarries beneath that city. Indeed the necessity of making an appropriate provision for the sepulture of the departed is obvious in regard to great and crowded cities. As these ordinarily spring from small beginnings, this necessity is not at first felt. But it is one which continually increases with their growth, until it can be no longer withstood.

We are aware, indeed, that all our pious care even for the security of our places of sepulture may be unavailing. The most stupendous piles that human affection or human folly has reared have not sufficed to insure even so much as this. They have, on the contrary, often only served to tempt the cupidity of the invader, or afford a mark for the poor malice of foes. Those sepulchral urns, in which the ancients hoped to hold consecrate forever the ashes of their departed friends, are now found in no holier places than the museums of the curious, or in the cabinets of the antiquarian. Egyptian mummies, over which the pyramids have been piled, and which, as Sir Thomas Brown says, " Cambyses or time hath spared, avarice now consumeth. Mummy has become merchandise, Myzraim cures wounds, and Pharaoh is sold for balsams." The common fuel of the dwellers on the banks of the Nile is said to be the embalmed bodies of

their ancestors. The Arabs use the mummy cases for
firewood, and "an epicurean traveller may cook his
breakfast with the coffin of a king." A chamber of one
of the catacombs, near Alexandria, has actually been
used as a stable for one of the Pacha's regiments of
horse. The march of armies, and the violence of civil
commotions abroad, have held in small respect the dust
of the departed. The royal sepulchre of St. Denis, where
the French kings of nine centuries were entombed, and
whose wonders, according to Chateaubriand, "taught
strangers a profound veneration for France," was violated
and destroyed among the kindred atrocities of the French
Revolution.

Here in our own country, as is well known, the busy
hand of enterprise, that holds little as sacred that stands
in its way, recognize nothing absolutely inviolable in the
burial-places of the dead. A turnpike or a canal, or a
railroad, have found no insuperable barrier to their progress in the sacredness of the graveyard. But even
though the tomb were safely secured from external
violence, yet by the silent approaches of time, it is continually wasted away. If we visit almost any of our
older burial-places, we shall find in the sunken graves,
in the rank grass and unsightly weeds, in the dilapidated
tombs, in the prostrated, half-buried, moss-covered headstones, that time who "antiquates all antiquities," respects not the dead more than the living, and that at any
rate, the care that has been hitherto bestowed on this
subject has not rendered sacred and secure, for any long
period, the remains of departed friends. Still it is a duty
that natural feeling prompts, and decent respect requires,
that we render them as inviolable as we may. We
would, at any rate, have them remain undisturbed while
we ourselves live; and when it becomes our time to take

our places by their side, we cannot but desire, that our dust, like theirs, may be permitted to rest in peace.

But our interest for the remains of the departed is not confined to their security alone. We would also confer upon them some fitting honor, and we take a melancholy pleasure in rearing visible emblems of that worth, which can henceforth only be recognized in the remembrance of surviving friends. We would mark the spot where they lie by every appropriate memorial and adornment, as henceforth consecrate to tender recollections, to self-inquiry, to the suggestive lessons of the past, to good purposes for the future, to thoughtful views of the present life, and to those hopes and aspirations, which by the gracious efficacy of a Christian faith, are made to " blossom even in the dust." We know, indeed, that this care in perpetuating the memory of the departed, like that which we use to secure their remains, cannot be long availing. The enclosure by which we attempt to separate sacred from common dust, will soon be over-thrown. The trees long outlast the graves which they were placed to adorn. The remains of countless myriads rest beneath the earth, which has, long ages since, ceased to bear the slightest external mark of their existence. " Who can but pity," adds the affluent and racy old writer above quoted, " the founder of the pyramids." " In vain, too, we compute our felicities, by the advantage of our good names, since the bad have equal duration, and Thersites is as like to live as Agamemnon." " Twenty-seven names make up the first story before the flood." " Five languages secured not the epitaph of Gordianus." Indeed all biography is little more than a slightly varied obituary.

> " The annals of the human race,
> Their ruins since the world began,

> Of them afford no other trace
> Than this, — *there lived a man.*"

But still the thought of the short duration, at the
longest, of these memorials of our departed friends, de-
ducts nothing from the interest we feel in rearing them.
The absolute impossibility of all attempts to give a long
perpetuity to the memory of those we have lost, has no
relevancy to those emotions which leads us to hallow
the spot of their sepulture. We expect here no immu-
nity from that law of decay that is enstamped upon all
things earthly. But we seek in this to gratify a present
feeling, which we can neither worthily stifle nor disavow,
— to hold in peculiar sacredness the place, when all that
remains of those who were ineffably dear to us reposes,
and where what is mortal of ourselves is soon to lie down
in the dreamless slumber of the grave.

But there is another and a distinct class of considerations by which an appropriate burial of the dead is enforced, which are yet of a higher character. It should
not only be such as true and natural feeling for the departed suggests, but may and should be made tributary
to the improvement of survivors ; and we are wanting in
the common seriousness of human nature, if we have not
felt that the grave has lessons to teach us that we can
learn nowhere else.

In referring to these moral uses, that are suggested by
the sepulture of our departed friends, we speak, we think,
to the universal experience of men, when we say, that if
there be a spot on the broad earth, and beneath the all-
embracing sky, where the heart becomes unwontedly
serious ; where the interests of this life are seen in their
real character, and in their relative position ; where its
illusions vanish away ; where undue excitements are

abated ; and where its true aims and issues are revealed,
— it is the place of graves. Here — how obvious and
yet how homefelt is the suggestion ! — here repose those
who but as yesterday, were as active, as earnest, as en-
grossed in " things seen and temporal," as we are now.
Their emotions were as lively, their pursuits as ardent,
their passions as strong, their competitions as fierce as
ours. But these have all now ceased. The brief story
of life has been told. The follies, the pleasures, the
pursuits of this present state, are with them all over.
" The lust of the flesh, the lust of the eyes, and the pride
of life," are all passed away.

> " Shall we build to ambition ? — Ah no !
>   Affrighted, he shrinketh away ;
>   For see, they would pin him below
>   In a small, narrow cave, and begirt with cold clay,
>   To the meanest of reptiles a peer and a prey."

Envy has now ceased to carp at the desert it could not
rival ; anger no longer burns ; hatred forgets to plot ;
the " itching palm of avarice is cold ; simulation is weary
of feigning ; dissimulation is tired of concealing ; preten-
sion has strutted its little hour ; vanity has achieved all
its petty triumphs ; and the busy tongue of calumny is
still — at last." And does the night of death, we involuntarily ask, so soon settle down upon the short day of
human life ? And shall we plan long designs for a space
so brief ? Does not rather the simple thought of the
transientness of mere earthly cares and emotions, which
is thus pressed, as a cold weight upon the heart, at every
step we take among the graves of the departed, serve to
qualify and chasten betimes an overmastering interest
in any present object ?

But if the place of graves be peculiarly fitted to excite chastened views of the present life, and indeed of its essential nothingness, viewed as an entire and completed scheme ; it is not less friendly to those higher aspirations' which centre on what is truly worthy and enduring in character. While we linger with painful regret over the relics of what was once inexpressibly dear to us, we are yet assured that all that was truly theirs and them is not also dead, but lives on in an undying life. And if it be our privilege to connect with their memories much good they have intended and done, their pure affections and virtuous lives, — these we know are not buried in the dust, but are still cherished in our hearts, as valued treasures there, and are safer yet in the remembrance of God. In the solemn verse of Milton we find utterance to this thought : —

> " Thy works, and alms, and all thy good endeavor,
> Staid not behind, nor in the grave were trod,
> But as Faith pointed with her golden rod,
> Followed thee up to joy, and bliss forever."

And as it is the natural effect of elevated worth, in all cases, to inspire a kindling sentiment of emulation, so that " upon which death has set its seal " is peculiarly impressive. It is at once purer and more hallowed than any living example of kindred excellence. Those slight blemishes which nearness and familiarity are continually revealing in the brightest character here below, and which serve to dim, though they may not tarnish its lustre, all disappear, when it is viewed through the darkness of the grave and in the distance of eternity. It is henceforth regarded, moreover, now that the stress and strain of life are over, with something of that sacredness which belongs to things "not seen and eternal." It is an often quoted saying of Themistocles, that the monuments of departed heroes, in the grove of Academus, would not permit him to sleep. And to what a worthier emulation should we of this latter time, be stirred, by the memorials of those friends, who having done and suffered well in their earthly welfare, have entered 'on a reversion of glory, that never so much as dawned on the mind of the heathen warrior!

The grave, too, is not only a place hallowed to cherished and animated recollections, but it is there, after the first crushing force of bereavement is passed, we love to dwell on the immortality of pure and kind affections, and to strengthen those anticipations which look to a recognition and reunion with departed friends in a future state of existence. Thoughts like these are, perhaps, never fully realized but through the stern ministry of death, and are never so emphatically suggested, as by the near presence of the mortal remains of those we have loved.

There and then we fondly cherish the conviction, that when we buried these, we did not bury those sympathies and affections which united us in life; but that, as these flowed on together, in one united stream, through all the pathways of our earthly existence, so they will not lose themselves in the dark valley of the shadow of death, but still continue to flow on forever, when the portals of the grave are passed. We do not stop to balance arguments here; we feel that there must be an analogy between what has been and is to be; that we cannot lose our social sympathies, without losing our identity as conscious beings; and we cannot for an instant reconcile it with the goodness of God, to think that he would permit us, nay, oblige us, by the very constitution of our natures, to cherish hopes so pure, so strong and so abiding, merely as a prelude to a sad delusion; or that a love, which no

distance has separated, no absence chilled, no vicissitude
shaken, no adversity withered, no sickness weakened, and
no decay impaired, should be cut off and destroyed forever; and just at that moment too, when it had acquired
its highest strength, and had gained its closest hold upon
the heart. Thus we mourn the departed as " not lost,
but gone before," and linger over the memorials that
affection rears, as tokens of the living, rather than of the
dead, as types and symbols of an imperishable love.

Such are some of the high uses that burial-places,
properly arranged, are fitted to subserve. We believe
that they are real and important. It is their natural
effect to call forth and perpetuate feelings and sentiments
which refine and elevate the mind, and purify while they
soften the heart; to remove from spots, in themselves sad
and painful, all unnecessary gloom; and to gather around
them those associations, which at the same time, serve to
solemnize the soul, and render it tranquil, serene and
hopeful. We do not believe these influences are wholly
lost on any. We do not believe that even those, whose
minds are the most pre-occupied, the inveterate world-
ling, for example, or the slave of ambition, could visit a
well-ordered and beautiful cemetery, like our own Mount
Auburn, under circumstances propitious to the appropriate influences of the place, and not come away, for the
time at least, sadder it may be, but wiser and better
beings than they entered there.

We only add, on this part of the subject, that the
views of the burial of the dead, which we have thus been
led to take, are illustrated by the attention which has
always been given to this subject, among the people of
all climes. From the earliest historical records we learn
that this subject was recognized as one of primary con-
cern. The extraordinary attention which the ancient

Egyptians gave to this subject is well known. According to Diodorus Siculus, they called their houses "Inns," and bestowed upon them comparatively little attention, but denominated their tombs "Eternal Habitations." The august piles of their pyramids, though the whole mystery that rests upon them is not yet solved, had doubtless reference to the same object. An American traveller assures us that " while not a vestige of a habitation is to be seen, the tombs remain, monuments of splendor and magnificence, perhaps even more wonderful than the ruins of their temples." They not only excelled all other nations, in the grandeur and perpetuity of their structures, which were intended to guard the bodies of the dead, but also in preserving these bodies from decay. And even at this day, fallen, degraded, denationalized, as Egypt is, the attention yet paid there to the remains of the dead is striking and peculiar. The tomb of the Pacha is considered as the greatest structure of modern Egypt.

The Hebrews, also, were especially careful of the rites of interment. To be deprived of burial was deemed by them a marked dishonor and a great unhappiness. This last office was not denied even to enemies, and was only withheld from those who had forfeited all claims to respect. When God foretold to Abraham the disasters which were to befall his race, he added as a solace, " that he should be *buried* in a good old age." When Sarah, his wife died, he importuned the sons of Heth for a place, where " he might bury his dead out of his sight." His petition was granted, and for " four hundred shekels of silver, the field of Ephron, which was in Machpelah, which was before Mamre, and the cave that was therein, and all the trees that were in the field, that were in all the borders round about, were made sure unto him, for a possession "—of a burial-place. Abraham, together with Rebecca, Sarah, Isaac and Jacob, according to the promise, sanctioned by the usual oath of the period, extorted from his son, were buried there; and Joseph's bones were carried into Canaan, after they had been embalmed and kept four hundred years. David praises the men of Jabez Gilead for their pious care of the remains of their unworthy king Saul. The Jewish Scriptures threaten a denial of burial, as one of the greatest calamities. The prophet Jeremiah denounces, as a punishment of idolators, that their bones should be " thrown out of their graves," and be spread " before the sun and the moon and all the host of heaven, whom they have loved, and whom they have served, and after whom they have walked, and whom they have sought, and whom they have worshipped, and they shall not be gathered or buried."

Devout men, we are told, carried St. Stephen to his burial, making great lamentations over him, and our Saviour was pleased to admit the outpouring of Mary's ointment upon his head, because " she did it for his burial." Among the heathen nations of antiquity the same sentiment prevailed. Several Greek Dramas, which being addressed to a popular audience, were the best possible exponents of popular feeling, turn entirely upon contests, connected with the rites of burial. The Antigone of Sophocles is an instance in point. Ulysses, in the Hecuba of Euripides, is represented as saying, that he did not care how meanly he lived, provided he might find a noble tomb after death. These rites were not omitted in the fiercest wars. The earlier Athenian commanders were punished if they neglected them, and they were observed even towards enemies. The important place they occupy in the poems of Homer is well known.

The Elysian Fields, which those ancients supposed to be the residence of the blessed Manes after death, could only be entered by those, however worthy, on other accounts, whose bodies had been duly buried. Hence arose the practice of erecting Cenotaphs, or empty Mausoleums, to the memory of those whose bodies could not be obtained, which monuments, in such cases, were regarded as substitutes for burial. The Romans inherited from the Greeks, and rendered yet more elaborate, these funeral rites. The ancient Germans, as we learn from Tacitus, were punctilious in those peculiar to themselves; and in more modern times, both in Europe and in the East, a similar reverence for the dead prevailed. The ancient Christians, according to St. Ambrose, esteemed the proper burial of the dead so imperative a duty, that it was deemed lawful, if necessary, to melt down or sell the vases used in the sacred ceremonies of the church, in the fulfilment of it, thus placing it on a level with the obligation of redeeming captives and taking care of the poor.

The Chinese, at the present day, attend to nothing so carefully as to the tombs of their ancestors. It is almost the only thing that approaches to a religious sense among them. And the Bedouin Arabs, amidst all their wanderings, still hold cherished and sacred their peculiar burial-places in the desert, and deem it a great misfortune not to be buried there. Now it is obvious, from the very universality of these practices, among all people in all ages and of all climes, that they have their origin in the very soul of man; that they spring out of the natural fountains of sentiment in human bosoms, and that, therefore, if they be proofs of a weakness of mind, as some affect to say, it is a weakness that was benevolently imparted by him who created us.

LINES

WRITTEN IN WILFORD CHURCHYARD ON RECOVERY FROM SICKNESS.

BY HENRY KIRKE WHITE.

HERE would I wish to sleep. — This is the spot
Which I have long marked out to lay my bones in ;
Tired out and wearied with the riotous world,
Beneath this yew I would be sepulchred.
It is a lovely spot !   The sultry sun,
From his meridian height, endeavors vainly
To pierce the shadowy foliage, while the zephyr
Comes wafting gently o'er the rippling Trent,
And plays about my cheek.   It is a nook
Most pleasant.   Such a one, perchance, did Gray
Frequent, as with a vagrant muse he wantoned.
Come, I will sit me down and meditate.
For I am wearied with my summer's walk ;
And here I may repose in silent ease ;
And thus, perchance, when life's sad journey's o'er,
My harassed soul in this same spot, may find
The haven of its rest — beneath this sod,
Perchance may slumber sweetly, sound as death.

I would not have my corpse cemented down
With brick and stone, defrauding the poor worm
Of its predestined dues ; no, I would lie
Beneath a little hillock, grass-o'ergrown,
Swathed down with osiers, just as sleep the cotters.
Yet may not *undistinguished* be my grave ;
But there, at eve, may some congenial soul
Duly resort, and shed a pious tear,
The good man's benison — no more I ask.
And Oh ! (if heavenly beings may look down

From where, with cherubim, inspired they sit,
Upon this little dim-discovered spot
The earth,) then will I cast a glance below
On him who thus my ashes shall embalm ;
And I will weep too, and will bless the wanderer,
Wishing he may not long be doomed to pine
In this low-thoughted world of darkling woe, —
But that, ere long, he reach his kindred skies.

Yet 'twas a silly thought, as if the body,
Mouldering beneath the surface of the earth,
Could taste the sweets of summer scenery,
And feel the freshness of the balmy breeze !
Yet Nature speaks within the human bosom,
And, spite of reason, bids it look beyond
His narrow verge of being, and provide
A decent residence for its clayey shell,
Endeared to it by time.   And who would lay
His body in the city burial place,
To be thrown up again by some rude sexton,
And yield its narrow house another tenant,
Exposed to insult lewd, and wantonness ?
No!   I will lay me in the village ground ;
There are the dead respected.   The poor hind,
Unlettered as he is, would scorn to invade
The silent resting-place of death.   I've seen
The laborer returning from his toil,
Here stay his steps, and call his children round,
And slowly spell the rudely sculptured rhymes,
And in his rustic manner moralize.
I've marked with, what a silent awe he spake,
With head uncovered, his respectful manner,
And all the honors which he paid the grave,
And thought on cities, where even cemeteries,

Bestrewed with all the emblems of mortality,
Are not protected from the drunken insolence
Of wassailers profane and wanton havoc.
Grant Heaven, that here my pilgrimage may close !
Yet, if this be denied, where'er my bones
May lie, — or in the city's crowded bounds,
Or scattered wide o'er the huge sweep of waters,
Or left a prey, on some deserted shore,
To the rapacious cormorant, — yet still,
(For why should sober reason cast away
A thought that soothes the soul?) yet still my spirit
Shall wing its way to these my native regions,
And hover o'er this spot.   Oh then I'll think
Of times when I was seated 'neath this yew,
In solemn rumination ; and will smile
With joy that I have got my long'd release.

MODES OF BURIAL.

BY JOHN BRAZER, D. D.

SUCH being the uses of appropriate rites and modes of
burial, and such being the attention which the subject
has at all times excited ; it may not be uninteresting or
useless, to advert to the more prevailing methods, in
which this natural want of human bosoms has been met
and answered, in different ages and climes.

The modes of burial may be reduced to two, though
there are other and very curious methods of disposing of
the remains of the dead, that may demand a passing
notice.   These are *Inhumation*, or the placing these remains in the earth ; and *Cremation*, or the reducing of
them to ashes.

Inhumation, or interment in the earth, appears to have been the earliest, as it is certainly the most natural and appropriate method of burial. It probably dates back to the time when it was said to Adam, " dust thou art, and unto dust thou shalt return," though the first record that exists of the practice, is that of Sarah, the wife of Abraham, already referred to. Cicero says it prevailed in Athens from the time of Cecrops. Various structures have been employed, in reference to this mode of burial. *Entombment* is one of these. The most ancient tombs are supposed to be those tumuli, or immense mounds of earth, which are now found in almost all parts of the world. Dr. Clarke states that he " has seen those sepulchral heaps in Europe, in Asia, from the Icy Sea to Mount Caucasus, over all the south of Russia, Kuban Tartary, Asia Minor, Syria, Palestine, Egypt, and part of Africa." It is well known, too, that they exist in both North and South America. Unlike other receptacles of mortal remains, they are not diminished and destroyed by a silent, but inevitable progress of decay, but are continually renewed and increased by a superstitious but not unpleasing practice that prevails, of obliging every passer-by to cast a stone upon them. It is inferred that they are more ancient than the pyramids, both on account of the greater simplicity of their structure, and from their more ancient appearance, when both are subjected to the same atmospheric influences.

The *Pyramids* and *Labyrinths* of Egypt, which are among the most extraordinary works of that land of wonders, may be here referred to. Their builders, the time of their erection, and their precise use, are equally unknown, and no light has as yet been cast upon this subject by hieroglyphical researches. It is supposed, however, that they have been erected at a later period

than nine hundred years before the Christian era, since
Homer, who lived at that time, spoke of the hundred
gates of Thebes, but makes no allusion to them. And
there seems little reason to doubt, that their main design
was to cover the remains of those who projected and
built them, or those of the priests.

Catacombs have also been extensively employed for
purposes of sepulture. These are caverns, grottoes or
caves, which are found already existing in the bosom of
the earth, or have been originally excavated for the pro-
curing of building materials, or else have been made
expressly for tombs. They exist in Syria, Persia, and
among the most ancient provinces of the East. There
are extensive ones in the Tufa Mountains of Capo di
Monte, near Naples, which were originally quarries, as
were those in Paris. But the most remarkable are those
in Egypt. Five series of these have been described, —
those of Alexandria, Saccara, Silcillis, Gourna, and the
tombs of the kings of Thebes. They are placed out of
the reach of the overflow of the Nile, excluded as much
as possible from the air, and removed away from the
usual haunts of men. They are sometimes hewn out of
solid rock, and sometimes surmounted by pyramids.
They extend in some instances, as for example, in the
vicinity of Alexandria and Thebes, several miles. The
learned in such matters differ, whether these or the pyramids are the more ancient. Almost every city had its
Necropolis, or city of the dead, of this description.

Embalming, though not strictly a method of sepulture,
is too intimately connected with the subject to be wholly
passed by. This, as is well known, is a process of preserving the bodies of the dead from decay by means of
various medicaments. The ancient Egyptians surpassed
all other people in the practice of this art, though it was

not unknown to the Hebrews, Greeks, Romans, Scythians, Persians, Arabs, Ethiopians, and ancient Peruvians. It is, however, an art entirely unknown in Egypt, at the present day, and all our knowledge of it is to be drawn from ancient writers. Herodotus is the oldest and best authority; and those who desire details on this subject, may consult the second book of his history, of the " Euterpe." Diodorus Siculus, who lived four centuries and a half later, relates many additional particulars. The Guanches, or inhabitants of the Fortunate, or Canary Isles, embalmed their dead in a manner resembling . that of the ancient Egyptians. This practice has been sometimes resorted to in England, and with what success may be seen in Sir Henry Halford's account of the " Disinterment of several kings."

In certain parts of Peru, bodies are naturally embalmed and preserved for ages, by the saline nature of the earth, and by the dryness of the atmosphere, circumstances we may observe, in passing, which are much more efficacious in preserving bodies from decay, than any antiseptic applications that can be made.

Desiccation, or a process of drying, is another method of preserving corpses, intimately connected with the preceding. The most remarkable example of this is near Palermo, where is situated the Cemetery, or rather the Cadavery, of the convent of the Capuchins. It is a subterraneous hall, where all the bodies of the fraternity, together with those of several persons of distinction from the city, are found in an upright posture, and habited in their accustomed dress. Some have remained undecayed for two centuries and a half. The following account of this spectacle, we subjoin for the consideration of those who prefer to make provision, either by tombs, or vaults of any kind, for the remains of the dead, where they may

be visible or accessible, only remarking, that, in our
opinion, it varies from those in ordinary use, only in degree of hideousness. Smith says, that upon descending
into this Cadavery, " it is difficult to express the disgust
arising from seeing the human form so degradingly carica-
tured, in the ridiculous assemblage of distorted mummies,
that are here hung by the neck in hundreds, with aspects, features, and proportions, so strangely altered by
the operation of drying, as hardly to bear a resemblance
to human beings. From their curious attitudes, they are
rather calculated to excite derision, than the awful emotions arising from the sight of two thousand decayed
mortals." Well might Sonnini say, " that a preservation
like this is horrid."

Cremation, or the burning of the bodies of the dead,
and *Urn-Burial*, or the collecting of the ashes in funeral
vases, was, as we have intimated, the other practice that
very generally prevailed in antiquity. This dates back
to the early times of Greece, as all the readers of Homer
well know, and was especially used by the Athenians.
It was copied, as were many other practices relating to
burial, by the Romans; and prevailed also among the
northern tribes of Europe, as appears from the accounts
of Cæsar and Tacitus. Pliny denies the early prevalence
of Cremation. But in this he stands in opposition to
Plato, Cicero, Virgil and Ovid, all of whom recognize it
as a very ancient rite. What determined this question
in reference to the Romans is the law of the Twelve
Tables, which prohibited both the burying and the burning of dead bodies within the limits of the city. It was,
however, not used by the Egyptians and Persians, on
account of objections derived from their peculiar mythol-
ogy, the former regarding fire as a raging monster which
devoured everything with which it came into contact,

and died itself with what it last devoured ; and the latter considering fire as a god, who would be contaminated by the touch of a dead body. It is not known certainly when Cremation fell into disuse. It was not practised in the time of Theodosius the younger, since Marobius, who lived in his time, expressly says it was not. It was supposed to have fallen into desuetude, through the influence of the Christian Fathers, and to have ceased with the Antonini. " Perhaps," says Sir Thomas Brown, " Christianity fully established, gave the final extinction to these sepulchral bonfires." The practice is supposed to have had its origin in different causes. Some thought that the action of fire was necessary to purify the soul from its earthliness, so that it might return to its primal source. Others resorted to it, for the purpose of securing the remains of the dead from insult and outrage. " To be gnawed out of our graves," says the author just quoted, " to have our skulls made into drinking bowls, and our bones turned into pipes, to delight and sport our enemies, are magical abominations escaped in burning burials." Again, " he that hath the ashes of a friend, hath an everlasting treasure ; when fire taketh leave, corruption slowly enters.' There were some who were excluded from this rite. Thus the bodies of infants, as Pliny tells us, before the appearance of their first tooth, must be buried, not burned. The place was called *Suggrundarium*, in contradistinction to *Bustum*, or funeral pile, and to *Sepulchrum*, or grave ; there being no bones of consistency to be burned, and no perceptible bulk to be inhumed. Those stricken with lightning were in like manner prohibited from Cremation, but were buried if possible, where they fell.

We have stated that *Inhumation*, or burying the bodies of the dead in the earth, and *Cremation*, or burning those bodies, were the principal methods of disposing of them in ancient times. There have prevailed, however, other practices, to which in the hope of giving some completeness to this account of modes of burial, we shall briefly refer. The people who lived near the Riphean mountains, according to Pliny, buried the remains of their dead in water. The *Ichthyophagi*, or fish-eating people about Egypt, did the same. "And water certainly," according to Sir Thomas Brown, "has proved the smartest grave, which in forty days swallowed almost all mankind." Some tribes of people heap up stones on the corpses of the dead. The Persian Magi exposed them to dogs and wild beasts. The Ballarians crowded them into urns, without burying, and heaped wood upon them. The Scythians affixed them to trunks of trees, and kept them in snow and ice. Some of the Ethiopians, removing the fleshy integuments of the dead bodies, supplied their place with plaster, and laid on this a kind of fresco, which was made to imitate the natural body. This being kept in a glazed coffin, during the space of a year, was afterwards buried without the environs of the city.

The Colchians and Tartars exposed their dead to the air, tying the bodies to branches of trees, where they remained till they were dried, and then buried them. The Persians, Syrians, and ancient Arabians preserved the remains of the dead by a covering of asphaltum, wax and honey. According to Statius and others, the body of Alexander the Great was preserved in this way; and it is said by Strabo to be a custom common among the Babylonians. Certain people of Guinea disinter their dead, when they are supposed to have become skeletons, and then decorate these ghastly remains with feathers and ornaments, and hang them up in their houses. The Chinese often preserve the bodies of parents, carefully guarded from the air, for three or four years in their houses, or in small habitations, built for the purpose outside of the city, where one of the family, commonly the eldest son, presents offerings of rice, wine and tea, and takes especial care, that the sticks of incense are kept constantly burning. The Ethiopians, according to Herodotus, dry the bones of their dead, and then, to look as much like life as possible, by means of plaster and paint, enclose them within columns of glass or amber, or in a species of transparent fossil salt. But we need not dwell longer on these various methods of disposing of the relics of the dead. Among semi-barbarous people, they vary with almost every tribe; while nations of a higher culture have, almost without exception, confined themselves to Inhumation, or Interment, in some of its various forms, or to Cremation and Urn-Burial.

In connection with these modes of burial we refer, as briefly as possible, to some of the more remarkable rites and forms, in which these last offices have been performed. The earliest as well as fullest account, we have of these, is that of Homer. But they did not differ materially from that observed by the Romans, who, indeed, copied them from the former. We will omit them at present, to speak of the funeral rites of the Egyptians. These were very remarkable, and in some respects different from all others. Among them the following may be briefly referred to. When any one died, the females of the family, covering their heads and faces with mud, and leaving the body in the house, ran through the streets, striking themselves and uttering loud lamentations. Hired mourners were employed to increase these manifestations of grief. The body was then conveyed to the embalmers. The mourning family, during seventy-two days, continued their lamentations at home, singing the

funeral dirge, abstaining from all amusements, suffering
their hair and beard to grow, neglecting their personal
comfort and appearance, in token of their grief. The
body, having been embalmed, was restored to the family,
either already placed in the mummy case, or merely
wrapped in bandages. It was then " carried forth " and
deposited in the hearse, and drawn upon a sledge to the
sacred lake of the *Nome*, or department to which it belonged. Before the body could be finally buried, the
deceased must be adjudged worthy of the last funeral
rites by a tribunal, consisting of forty-two judges appointed for the purpose, who were placed in a semicircle,
near the bank of the sacred lake, and who examined the
details of his life and character. If, after due hearing,
the judges condemned him, his body was not permitted
to cross the sacred lake, and his memory was indelibly
disgraced. If, on the other hand, no charges were
brought against him, or being brought, were proved to
be groundless, his relatives took off the badges of mourning, and pronounced an eulogium on his virtues, but
without speaking of his birth or rank, as was done in
Greece, since the Egyptians thought that all their countrymen were equally noble. No one was exempted by
his rank from this ordeal. Kings, as well as subjects, the
high and the low, those whom while living none dared
to approach, and the humblest individual were, after
death, liable to be subjected to the most rigorous examination. The body was then taken across the lake, carried
to the catacombs, which were previously prepared, and
placed in its final resting-place.

Other circumstances are added to this account by
other writers. It is said there was a common burial
place called Acherusia ; that there was a pit called
Tartar, into which the bodies of the wicked were

thrown; that a small sum was paid to the ferrymen who carried the body across the lake in his boat; and that the cemetery on the further side, to which the remains of the good were consigned, was called Elisont, a word meaning a place of rest. The whole ceremony of interment is supposed to have consisted in simply depositing the prepared mummy in the appointed place, with the throwing upon it three handfuls of sand, and the utterance of three loud adieus. It is very obvious that in these circumstances, as well as in the whole arrangement of the Grecian Pantheon, which was probably derived from the Egyptians, we find the elements of the classical myths concerning Acheron, Tartarus, Charon, with his boat and ferriage money, and the fields of Elysium.

OUR LIFE.

By Miss L. L. A. Very.

Why should we live for time
When Life's horizon stretches far away,
And tokens on Thought's Sea from day to day
    Float from a kindlier clime?

There bright flowers float along,
Hope's amaranthine blooms from endless years;
And strains that move to extasy or tears
    From unknown warblers' song.

And still Thought's waves dash on,
Murmuring ever of the home they left,
And grieving like a weary child bereft
    Longing for joys to come.

Death spreads its shadows dark,
But cannot quite shut out th' Eternal Day!
Nor Crime extinguish, on its heavenly way,
   The spirit's rising spark!

Though wretched and defiled
The Father still his lineaments shall trace,
Shall wash away the stains that hide the face
   That once in beauty smiled;
And welcome to his own bright dwelling place
   His sin-repentant Child.

ROMAN OBSEQUIES.

BY JOHN BRAZER, D. D.

THE funeral rites of the Greeks and Romans were accurately and elaborately performed, in consequence of their prevalent belief that the manes or spirits of the dead could find no rest or peace while their bodies remained unburied. This fact is often referred to by their poets. Our remarks on this part of the subject will be confined to the Roman obsequies alone, both because the accounts relating to these are copious and accessible, and because they embrace, substantially, the ceremonies common to both nations.

Allusions to these rites are scattered over the whole range of Roman literature. Indeed the peculiar force of many passages, both in prose and poetry, is obscured or lost, unless these funeral rites be well understood. But they are nowhere, of set purpose, described by any classical author. The funeral rites of the Romans were arranged according to the age, wealth and dignity of those who were the subjects of them ; particular regard being had to their last expressed wishes. They were of two kinds — *Public*, to which the people were summoned by the voice of the public crier ; or *Private*, plebeian, common, which were not publicly announced, and were attended with no pomp, parade, or show of any kind. The former of these will only be referred to here. It consisted, properly, of four distinct parts : first, the rites before the funeral ; second, the *Elatio*, or carrying forth the body to the place where it was to be burned or buried, or both ; third, the *Sepultura*, or burial ; and fourth, the *subsequent ceremonies*.

The first and second of these we shall refer to in the briefest possible way, both because they do not strictly belong to the line of remark we are now pursuing, and because the facts are easily accessible. In regard to the *third* and *fourth* parts of a Roman funeral, we shall confine ourselves principally to those circumstances which bear especially on our present inquiry, and to those which, on any account, may appear to possess a peculiar interest.

A short summary of the rites before the funeral, is as follows. The last breath of the dying was inhaled by the nearest relatives, under the impression that the spirit or soul of the departing person thus and then left the body. Rings were taken from their fingers, their eyes and mouths closed, and the names of the deceased loudly and repeatedly called. The very singular custom prevailed of cutting off one or more of the fingers of the deceased. This was done, either for the purpose of ascertaining whether death was real, or only apparent ; or, which is the more probable supposition, for the purpose of securing some parts of the dead body, for the renewal of the funeral ceremonies, or parentation, as it was called in honor of the dead after burial. The body was then bathed, and anointed with various antiseptic and fragrant drugs; arrayed in the best robes which belonged to the deceased; adorned with crowns or public badges of distinction which they had worn, and then brought from the inmost apartments, and placed on a couch in the threshold of the house, with the feet towards the door. The house where the body was thus situated, was marked as in mourning, by placing on the door branches of the pine or cypress. This was especially intended as a signal to prevent the approach of those engaged in offering the public sacrifices, since it was supposed to be polluting to them to touch, or even to look upon, a corpse.

After these preparatory rites, next followed in order, the *Elatio*, or bearing forth of the corpse. Servius says this took place seven days after death. It seems probable, however, that there was no set time observed; but rather such a period as was rendered necessary for the elaborate preparations required, according to the peculiar circumstances of the case. The *Elatio* was prepared in the early times of the republic, in the night-time; but afterwards this practice was confined to private funerals, or those of a humble character, and the earlier hours of the day were preferred for this service in those which were public. Children, among the Athenians, were carried to the place of burial at dawn, since, as was thought, the sun should not be a spectator of such an untimely calamity. From the ancient custom, however, of funeral processions by night, the practice of bearing tapers and torches, which was always observed by day, in similar ceremonies, was borrowed. Hence the bearers were called, at first, Vesperones, and after, Vespillones. The bier was preceded by various persons; by musicians consisting of two kinds, the trumpeters and the flute players ; by Praeficæ, or females hired to sing, with loud and stridulous voices, the Naenia, which were rude and doleful, and sometimes idle and silly songs : by players and dancers ; by buffoons, one of whom imitated the appearance and bearing of the deceased ; and by freedmen, who sometimes bore on small couches, or on spears, the images, busts and insignia of the deceased or of his family. The body was carried forth by the nearest relations, or sometimes, by manumitted slaves, or by hired persons who bore different designations.

The bier was carried covered or uncovered. In the latter case, the body was richly clad and ornamented, and with the face painted. It was carried, in opposition to the Egyptian practice, *with the feet forward*, as indicating a final departure from the world. Relations, friends and all who wished to show affection and respect for the memory of the person who was the subject of the pageant, followed the bier, with tears, with hair cut off or dishevelled, with garments changed or torn, with all ornaments laid aside, with beating of the breast, complaints and reproaches of the gods, and with all external sign of grief. The surviving sons, who followed, were veiled, while the daughters were unveiled ; it being regarded, as is supposed, that a reversal of an ordinary custom is appropriate to mourning. The procession passed through the Forum, and the bier was placed before the *Rostra*, where a funeral oration was pronounced. It was then led to an appointed place, *without the city*, and the body was there burned or buried.

The sepulture, or burial, next followed. If the remains were to be burned and not buried, they were taken to a place called *Ustrina ;* but if they were to be both burned and buried, the place was called *Bustum*. They were laid upon a funeral pyre, or pile, which was simply a heap of wood prepared for the purpose. This was composed of those kinds of trees which are most easily ignited ; and they were in early times, unhewn and rough, according to a law of the Twelve Tables. The cypress, the myrtle, the cedar and the laurel were also added, on account of their fragrant odor. The pyre was built in the form of an altar, and was raised higher or lower, according to the dignity of the deceased, a fact frequently noted in the classical allusions to them. It could not be placed, according to a prohibition of the Twelve Tables, within sixty feet of any private dwelling ; and by a subsequent law, enacted in the time of Augustus, it was to be removed at least two miles from the city.

On a pile like this, the dead body, together with the bier on which it had been carried — for it was customary to burn both together — was placed ; and after kisses, and other tokens of endearment ; and after the eyes of the corpse, which had been closed at death, were reopened ; the fire was applied by the nearest relations, with eyes and head averted, as indicative that necessity and not choice, imposed the task ; and the winds were implored to excite and cherish the fire, that its office might be quickly done. After the fire was lighted, a solemn march, thrice repeated was, in some cases, made round the pile. This was in an inverted order, that is, from right to left, which in all cases was a token of grief, as that from left to right denoted joy and gratulation. This was done with all the insignia of office and distinction inverted, with weapons thrown aside, and sometimes with the music of wind instruments, in the case of illustrious persons.

But while the body was thus consumed, its remains were not buried alone. It was a singular and most re-

volting superstition of classical antiquity, that the souls
of the departed were thirsty for blood, without tasting
which, it was supposed, that they could not speak, or know
the living, though they were cognizant of events past and
to come. The spirits of Penelope's suitors, for example,
are said, while following the guidance of Mercury, to chirp
like birds. In consequence of this superstitious notion,
various animals, and particularly those which were supposed to be most dear to the deceased when living, were
sacrificed on the same funeral pile with them. Sometimes even human beings, such as captives, servants, and
women, were sacrificed on the pile. Gifts also of garments, perfumes, gems, and valuable pledges of affection,
were often added ; and in such profusion was this done,
at some periods, that they were restricted by a sumptuary
law of the Twelve Tables.

After the body had been sufficiently consumed, which
was indicated by the gradual settling of the white ashes
upon the live coals, the fire was extinguished, and wine
was sprinkled on the embers. Next followed the collecting of the remaining bones. This practice is playfully
alluded to by the festive poets of antiquity, intimating
that the wine, that was thus destined to quench their
burning bones after death, might be more seasonably
applied in moistening their living clay. This office fell to
the nearest friends ; their hands were carefully purified ;
their garments were black, unloosed or flowing ; and
their feet naked, in token of reverence. The remains
thus collected were bathed with wine, milk, odors, and
tears ; and being wrapped in a cloak of fine linen, were
exposed in some cases to the wind to be dried, in others
placed in the bosom of the mother, or some near female
friend.

The remains thus collected were placed in urns

These were made of gold, silver, brass, marble or clay.
Of this last kind were those " sad, sepulchral pitchers,
which have no joyful voices," that were dug up in Nor-
folk, England, in 1658, and to which we owe the remarkable essay, entitled " Hydriotaphia." In those urns were
frequently placed phials filled with tears, since called
Lachrymatories. They were finally placed in the earth,
and structures of various kinds, were placed over or beneath them. This office being performed, the Præfica
exclaimed ILICET, (*ire licet*), which indicated the close
of the ceremony. Those who remained at the funeral
pile were thrice purified with water, sprinkled by a
branch of olive or laurel, from the pollution which the
touch of a corpse was supposed to occasion. They then
shouted, in regular strains, their adieus — *Salve et Vale*
— and particularly the last, three times; and then followed the touching words, — " *Nos te ordine, quo natura
permiserit, cuncti sequemur ;* " — We must all follow thee,
according as the course of nature will permit us. The
prayers were then offered — " *Sit tibi terra levis* " — that
the earth might be light upon their remains. This part
of the service was then concluded by treading out the
remaining fire, their own bodies being previously sprinkled with water. They then returned home, and purified
the house where the dead had been, by burning sulphur
and laurel, and by sweeping it with a certain kind of
broom.

But the attention which the Romans bestowed on the
remains of the dead, did not terminate even with these
operose rites. They prepared their sepulchres with
great care, and considered this a very important part of
their obsequies. They were built by individuals for
themselves and families, or this office was expressly en-
joined upon their heirs, and the inscription sometimes re-

corded the names of those for whom, and for whom they were *not* intended. Kirchman cites one, in which a certain individual is forbid even to approach the spot where it was placed. These sepulchres were of various kinds. In the early period of Rome, they were nothing more than a ditch or furrow, rudely dug in the ground. But subsequently they were more elaborately constructed, and in some instances at a great expense. Some were made to resemble small dwellings or temples, and were overlaid by, or composed of flint, marble, iron, stone or shells, and were adorned by images, effigies, and representations of various kinds, such as fights, huntings, sacrifices, sporting scenes, satyrs, cupids, marine gods with tails of fishes and carrying nymphs, the rape of Proserpine, the four winds and the labors of Hercules. It was an ancient and wide-spread, as well as beautiful custom, to place in a common resting-place the remains of husbands and wives, lovers, twins, friends, and those who had lived together and loved each other in life. This practice was extended to urn-burials. " All urns contained not single ashes ; without confused burnings, they affectionately compounded their bones ; passionately endeavoring to continue their living unions. And when distance or death denied such conjunctions, unsatisfied affections conceived some satisfaction to be neighbors in the grave, to lie urn by urn, and touch but in their names."

The inscriptions on these monuments were in general very simple, and confined to literal facts, though sometimes they contained an eulogium on the deceased. They were begun ordinarily with the formal D. M. or D. M. S. (*Dis Manibus Sacrum*). This was followed by the name of the defunct, that of his parents, country, family, together frequently, with an account of the exact num-

ber of days and hours he had lived, the cause of his death,
and the amount of property he left to his heirs. If the
remains were those of a female, who had been married
only *once*, the fact was considered so creditable as to be
worthy of a distinct mention. And if the marriage had
been happy, this was deemed too great a boon not to be
inscribed on the monument. These sepulchres were held
sacred and inviolable. Their sacredness was guarded by
severe enactments, and was considered as violated, by the
demolition or injury of the monument; by improper
occupancy ; by removal of the remains ; by mutilation or
even touching of them; and by taking away anything
belonging to them.

Cenotaphs, or empty monuments, as already intimated,
were built in memory of those whose bodies were deposited in another place, or which, from any cause, remained
unburied. They had their origin in a superstition of the
Greeks, already mentioned, and which was afterwards
religiously adopted by the Romans, that the ghosts of
the departed would remain homeless and without a resting place, until a sepulchre, to which they were solemnly
invoked, was built for them. The story of Palinurus, in
the sixth book of the Æneid, may be taken as an expo-
nent of the common faith and feeling on this subject.
We only add to this sketch of Roman obsequies, that
they did not end with the final depositing of the remains
in the tomb or grave. Certain days were prescribed
when funeral rites were observed in memory of the dead.
The month of February, and in an especial manner the
nineteenth day thereof, were particularly set aside for
those of a public nature. It is considered by Kirchman
that the part of the corpse which was separated before
burial, as above mentioned, was thus used. Sacrifices,
or oblations, were offered to the infernal deities, or to the

ghosts of the departed. These consisted of water, wine, milk, blood, ointments, and perfumes. Feasts and games were in like manner observed. They decked also the sepulchres of friends with fillets, floral crowns of promiscuous flowers, and some, in an especial manner, which were appropriated to the purpose. Those of purple hue, lilies and especially roses were preferred. The Greeks, in similar services, used the amaranth, white pothos, parsley, and myrtle.

The time and observances of mourning for the departed were determined with much accuracy, though Seneca, and writers of the same school, affect to consider such practices as womanish. " A year," he says, " was the prescribed term of mourning for women ; not that they were obliged to mourn so long, but were not permitted to mourn longer. There is no legitimate period for a man to mourn for the dead, because there is no time in which it is becoming to do so." But the memorable words of Antoninus Pius are an answer to all such stoicisms. " Permit a friend in grief to be a man ; for it is no part of true philosophy to destroy the reign of the affections. " The time, within the space of a year, of legitimate mourning, had reference to the age and relationship of the departed. It was not permitted in the death of children under three years of age. From that period to the age of ten, it was lawful to mourn publicly, in the proportion of one month for every year of their life, in no case exceeding ten. These laws had reference to women particularly ; and it was held disreputable for them to be married in less time than a year after the death of a husband. As signs of grief, women cut off their hair, while men permitted theirs to grow ; ashes were scattered upon the head ; clothes of a black color worn ; all ornaments were laid aside ; an abstinence

from public amusements was observed; fire and lights in
the house were avoided as far as possible; doors were
kept closed; and cypress branches were placed upon the
houses of nobles, and pine upon those of the plebeians.

The places of sepulture, of every kind, whether of
graves, tumuli, monuments, or urns, among the Romans,
were, from their earliest history, *without the city*. Numa,
according to Livy, was buried on Janiculum; and this
was added to the city by Ancus Martius. The remains
of Servius Tullius were also carried outside of the city.
This practice was afterwards prescribed by a law of the
Twelve Tables. The same rule was observed by the
Athenians, Jews, and by all, or nearly all, the dwellers
on the borders of the Mediterranean Sea.

THE MEMORY OF THE DEAD.

By Mrs. Hemans.

FORGET them not! though now their name
   Be but a mournful sound,
Though by the hearth its utterance claim
   A stillness round.

Though for their sake this earth no more
   As it hath been, may be,
And shadows, never marked before,
   Brood o'er each tree.

And though their image dim the sky,
   Yet, yet forget them not;
Nor when their love and life went by,
   Forsake the spot!

They have a breathing influence there,
   A charm not elsewhere found;
Sad, — yet it sanctifies the air,
   The stream, the ground.

Then, though the wind an altered tone
   Through the young foliage bear,
Though every flower of something gone,
   A tinge may wear.

O fly it not! — no fruitless grief,
   Thus in their presence felt,
A record links to every leaf,
   There, where they dwelt.

Still trace the path that knew their tread,
   Still tend their garden bower,
Still commune with the holy dead,
   In each lone hour.

The holy dead! — Oh, blest we are,
   That we may call them so,
And to their image look afar,
   Through all our woe!

Blest, that the things they loved on earth,
   As relics we may hold,
That wake sweet thoughts of parted worth,
   By springs untold!

Blest, that a deep and chastening power
   Thus o'er our souls is given, .
If but to bird, or song, or flower,
   Yet all for Heaven.

EARLY CHRISTIAN OBSEQUIES.

By John Brazer, D. D.

After the introduction of Christianity, the forms of
burial were materially changed. Indeed the early
Fathers and Confessors of the Church seem to have
thought that everything regarding these, as well as other
ceremonies, was pro-Christian in the same degree that it
was anti-Pagan. The attention, moreover, which was
paid both to the dying and the dead, was not only marked
by those natural expressions of tenderness, which are
common to all nations, but by some peculiar tokens of
that Christian love which is the " fulfilling of the law,"
and of that hope which looks beyond the grave. The
final wishes, counsels, exhortations, and prayers of the
dying were religiously treasured up; their requests concerning the disposal of their property were carefully
observed; they were attended by the different orders of
their clergy who administered every possible solace and
support; prayers were offered for them in the churches;
the sign of the cross was administered to them; and
friends and relatives gathered round to give and receive
the last expressions of endearment.

It has already been mentioned, that the practice of
cremation, or burning, died out nearly at the time of the
two Antonines, and probably through the influence of the
Christian Fathers. It is certain it was always held in
abhorrence by the early Christians, " who retained " as
one of their apologists said, " the ancient custom of inhumation as more eligible and commodious." The practice, however, of embalming was, in the first ages of the
Church, by no means uncommon. This was probably
suggested by the usage of the Jews, and particularly by

what is said in the gospels of the burial of Christ, since it was hence esteemed a mark of honor. There was another obvious reason for it, and this was the fact, that they were often obliged to assemble for religious worship in their places of sepulture. It was observed also, in token of their faith in the future resurrection of the body, in its incorruptible state. They differed from the ancient heathens in respect to the time of burial, since they preferred, in all cases, when it was practicable, to perform this service by day, and not, as the latter did, by night. The use, however, of lighted tapers, or torches, was continued. The eucharist was frequently solemnized at their funerals. They observed the practice common to most nations, of closing the eyes of the dying, but did not open them again as the Romans did, since this, with them, was symbol of the peaceful slumber of the departed, until the last trump should wake them. They omitted the " conclamations " practiced by the Romans ; and instead of exposing the dead bodies at the porches of their houses, they placed them in the interior of their dwellings, or in the church. They appointed, in the true spirit of their faith, an order of men, who bore a semi-classical character, whose especial business it was to attend upon the sick poor, and give them a decent burial when dead. These were called " Parabolani," because they exposed their lives amidst contagious disease. In the time of Constantine, and through his influence, a class of persons was appointed called " Copiatæ," who performed certain important offices. The office of sexton was . held in high esteem. They substituted in the place of the doggrel Nænia of the Roman Præficæ, and of the pipers and trumpeters — anthems and sacred hymns, which were conceived in a tone of triumph, rather than of mourning. " What mean our hymns?" says Chrysostom. " Do we not glorify

God that hath crowned the departed, and set him free from all fear?" They used coffins, and in this respect observed the customs of the heathens, and departed from that of the Jews, who merely wrapped the body in graveclothes. They placed branches of laurel, ivy, and other evergreen plants, under the head of the corpse, when deposited in the sarcophagus, in token that death was not the end of life, and in contradistinction to the practice of the Greeks and Romans, who employed, for a similar purpose, the cypress, which, for the reason above stated, was an emblem of utter death.

The practice of these nations, of crowning the corpse with garlands, they rejected as idolatrous. Tertullian, with no great wisdom, urges this objection; and Minucius argued against it, with singular inaptness, when he said that " if the dead be happy, he needs no flowers, and if he be miserable, they cannot please him." They rejected, altogether, the repetition of the mourning ceremonies on the third, seventh, and ninth day, according to the Roman practice, as well as all offerings of milk, wine and flowers; and, in fine, substituted for all other offerings and ceremonies, solemn religious rites, prayers and alms-deeds. " Before the establishment of convents " (says Weever), " men and women, though of equal degree and equality, were borne in a different manner to their graves. Man was borne upon men's shoulders, to signify his dignity and superiority to his wife; and woman at the arm's end, to signify, that being inferior to man in her life-time, she should not be equalled with him at her death; which continued for a long time, until women, by renouncing the world, and living monastical, religious lives, got such an honorable esteem in the world, that they were thought no less worthy of honor in that kind, than men." Instead of the images, insignia and trophies, which were borne before the bier in heathen funerals, the early Christians carried a cross, and sometimes branches of palm. Church bells, which are said to have been first introduced by Paulinus, bishop of Nola (from which was derived the modern Latin term (Nola) for bell) were first tolled at funerals in the eighth century. The corpses were placed in the grave, in the posture of repose, and always facing the east. Professing, as the early Fathers of the Church did, to regard death as a release from toil and suffering, and as being, therefore, rather a joyful than a painful event, they discountenanced all excessive grief and mourning for the dead. Augustine severely censured the custom, derived from the Romans, of wearing black. It was, however, always employed as a sign of grief in the Greek Church, and its use afterwards became general. No particular period of mourning was prescribed. It was left to custom and to the feelings of survivors. Prayers for the dead were offered in the early ages of the Church ; and the practice of offering them lasted to the period of the Reformation. In other respects, the funeral rites were so similar to those which have since prevailed in Christendom, that we need not dwell longer upon them. We will now advert to the places which have been used by Christians of earlier and later times for the burial of the dead.

That the Christians in their very first origin, appropriated peculiar spots to this purpose, is evident, from the fact, that such places, in times of persecution, were used " in silence and in fear," for their public religious services. These were called by the beautiful appellation, *Dormitories*, or Places of Repose, because they regarded death as but a sleep, and the grave but as a quiet resting place, until the morning of the resurrection. They were called, also, *Arcæ Sepultorum*, and *Cryptæ*, and *Arena-ria*, because they were often subterranean crypts or vaults, dug out of the sand. These terms were used indiscriminately for burial places and places of public religious worship. These caves were commonly exca-vated at the foot of a hill, the entrance was carefully concealed, and they were rendered accessible by means of a ladder. They were sometimes of vast extent; and the depth so great, that two or three stories were placed one above another, and the whole aspect of them re-sembled a subterranean city. The early Christians were hence called by their contemporaries " a lighthating people." This habitual familiarity with the dead is supposed to be one cause of their well-known insensi-bility to death; and taken in connection with their vivid and realizing faith, led them to court, rather than to shun, the thorny crown of martyrdom. But it is a mistake to infer from this, as some have done, that it was the custom of the early Christians to bury their dead in churches. On the contrary, this was expressly forbid-den; and the truth is, that they did not bury in places of worship, but worshipped in places of burial.

When the Emperors and the laws became Christian, the prohibition against burying in cities remained in full force; and when an attempt was made in Constantinople to evade it by burying in churches, under pretence that this was not prohibited, it was reinforced by Theodosius, and all burying within churches was also prohibited, under heavy penalties, both of ashes and relics kept in urns above ground, and of bodies laid in coffins. They were all required to be carried and deposited without the city, and the same reasons relating to the public morals and the public health, assigned as stated already. In the fourth century, an especial honor was paid to the memory of the Martyrs, by erecting churches over the places where their remains had been burned, or by carrying these remains to the churches within the city. This seems to have first suggested the practice of burying in churches, but this distinction was for a long time confined to their relics.

Constantine had desired to be buried near the Apostles, to whose honor he had erected a church. This was literally complied with. He was buried, not within the church, as is commonly asserted, but " near " it, that is, in the atrium, or porch of the church. " His son," says St. Chrysostom, " thought he did his father great honor to bury him in the Fishermen's Porch. And what porters are to Emperors in their own palaces, the same are the Emperors to the Fisherman in their graves." From the death of Constantine, in the beginning of the fourth century, to the commencement of the sixth, the privilege first awarded to his remains, that of being buried in the porch of the church, was in like manner, in especial instances, granted to kings and emperors. In the beginning of the sixth century, the people, gennerally, seem to have been admitted to the same privilege of being buried in the atrium, or churchyard, but were still excluded from the church itself. Between the sixth and tenth centuries, this latter privilege was granted, by special laws, to certain kings, bishops, founders of churches, and other eminent persons.

From the last named period to the Decree of Pope Leo III., which is preserved by Gregory IX., in his Decretals, about the year A. D. 1230, the privilege, as it was considered, of being buried within the church itself, seems to have been left to be awarded, according to the discretion of the bishops and presbyters of the church. From the period of these Decretals, the ruin of the old

laws, according to Bingham, is to be dated, since "they
took away that little power that was left in the hands of
bishops, to let people bury in the church or not, as they
should judge proper in their discretion, and put the
right and possession of burying places into the hands of
private families. And those who had no such right,
being led by their ambition, or superstition, could easily
purchase a right to be buried in the church, which was
a thing which emperors themselves did not pretend to
ask in former ages." In confirmation of the above, we
quote a passage from Willis's Reports, to which we are
indebted for a sensible Essay, published in this country.
"When Popery," says the learned Justice Abney,
"grew to its height, and blind superstition had weakened
and enervated the laity, and emboldened the clergy to
pillage the laity, then, in the time of Pope Gregory the
First, and soon after, other canons were made, that
bishops, abbots, priests and faithful laymen, were permitted the honor of burial in the church itself, and
all other parishioners in the churchyard, on a pretence,
that their relations and friends, on a frequent view of
their sepulchres, would be moved to pray for the good of
their departed souls. And as the parish priest was, by
the common law, sole judge of the merits of the dead,
and the fitness of burial in the church, and alone could
determine who was a faithful layman, they only were
judged faithful, whose executor came up to the price of the
priest; and they only were allowed burial in he church,
and the poorer sort were buried in the churchyard."
Dr. Rees confirms the above, and adds, that to this superstition, and the profit arising from it, we may ascribe
the origin of churchyards.

We have thus endeavored to condense into as few
words as possible, what we suppose to be the true his-

tory of this subject. It appears that from the foundation
of the city of Rome, until the beginning of the fourth
century of the Christian era, a period of more than a
thousand years, no burials whatsoever were permitted
within the city, and still less within any temple or church.
That it was permitted to Constantine, about the year of
our Lord 300, to be buried " near " a church, that is,
in the atrium or porch ; and that in the subsequent part
of the fourth and during the course of the fifth century,
the privilege, so called, was granted sparingly to some
distinguished persons. That in the sixth century, the
practice began of admitting the people to burial in the
churchyard, but not in the church ; and also of allowing
some particularly eminent or favored persons to be
buried within the church. That from this period to the
thirteenth century, the subject of similar admissions was
left to the discretion of the clergy, who made of them a
profitable but most disgraceful use. And that from the
last mentioned period to the present, sepulture within
churches and churchyards, which had been granted as
above by the clergy to the laity, has been claimed as a
right.

But whatever may be the history of this practice, it is,
to the last degree, exceptionable. We respond entirely
to the sentiment of the learned Rivet, as quoted by
Bingham, in connection with this subject. " This custom," (says he,) " which covetousness and superstition
first brought in, I wish it were abolished, with other
relics of superstition among us; and that the ancient
custom was revived, to have public burying places *in the
free and open fields, without the gates of cities.*" This
practice, which has, of late, been happily renewed in
this country and in Europe, dates back at least to the
time of Abraham, who bought the " field of Ephron "

for this purpose. The body of Joseph was buried in a plat of ground in Shechem. Moses was buried in a valley of Moab; Eleazer on a "hill that pertained to Phinehas;" and Manasseh "in the garden of Uzza;" and the same practice continued down to the last period of the national existence of the Jews; since we find that the tomb of Joseph of Arimathea, which became the temporary sepulchre of our Saviour, was near Golgotha; those who are said to have arisen from the dead at the crucifixion, returned to the city; and the demoniac who broke his chains, is described as having *fled to the desert, and dwelt among tombs*. The Egyptians, as we have seen, placed their thronged "cities of the dead," without the borders of the cities of the living. While some of the Grecians permitted, at least occasionally, burials within cities, the Athenians disallowed the practice altogether.

The Ceramicus was a public cemetery, situated on the road to Thria, and it was here that all the distinguished Athenians were buried. Within the confines of this, the Academy of Plato was situated, with its garden and gymnasium, and the river Cephisus; and, according to Plato, the tomb of Ariadne was in the Arethusian Groves of Crete. The sepulchres and monuments of the Corinthians were among groves of cypresses. On the now deserted coast of Karamania, are still to be seen the remains of funeral monuments, which were placed in the environs of the once splendid cities of Asia Minor. The practice of the Romans, through the whole course of their history, was the same, and that also of the early Christians. The ancient Germans buried their dead in groves, consecrated by religious services. The Eastern nations, particularly the Turks, have always been distinguished for their reverential care of their places of interment. Viewing death with no terror or gloom, they endeavor to divest the grave of all sad and revolting associations, by surrounding it with every local charm, and by making it a place of common and delightful resort. It is made a part of their religion to plant at the head and foot of each grave, a cypress tree; and thus, in the course of time, their cemeteries are converted into dense and shady groves. The burial place of Scutari, is said to be the most delightful spot in the vicinity of Constantinople; " and probably," says Miss Pardoe, " the world cannot produce such another, as regards extent, or pictorial effect." The great Turkish burial ground, just outside of the wall of Jerusalem, near St. Stephen's Gate, is the favorite place of promenading for the whole Turkish population in that city. It is adorned with trees and flowers, in a high state of cultivation; and is regularly visited once a week, and, as a matter of religious observance, every holiday. The Afghans call their cemeteries the " cities of the silent," and hang garlands on the tombs of the departed, under the impression that their ghosts, each seated at the head of his own grave, enjoy their fragrance. The churchyards in the reductions of Paraguay were so many gardens.

The Moravian Brethren have long been in the habit of converting their burial places into haunts of rural loveliness; and they are beautifully designated by them as " Fields of Peace." The tombs of the Chinese are always erected out of their cities. In Denmark, Venice, Prague, Vienna, and many other places in continental Europe, the practice of interring the dead within cities is prohibited. Even the North American Indians remove them away from the abodes of the living. The same prohibition has, of late years, been adopted and enforced in France and England.

31*

In this country a strong and commendable interest in
regard to rural cemeteries has been awakened. The
successful establishment of that of Mount Auburn seems
to have been the proximate cause of this. A general
feeling, indeed, of the need of some appropriate resting
place for the remains of departed friends, has long prevailed with many intelligent persons in different parts of
the country; but it found no fitting expression, until it
found it here. The choice and general arrangement of
the grounds were, in the highest degree, felicitous. The
spot itself is singularly suggestive of those trains of
thought and feeling, that belong to the Place of Graves;
and when its native loveliness was revealed by the hand
of taste; when it was yet further illustrated, but not encumbered by the structures and ornaments that affection
reared; when, especially, it was hallowed by the relics
of the dead; it became a resort peculiarly sacred to
solemn musings and tender recollections. It was then
felt to be one, where a deep want of the soul, that had
long been experienced, was, for the first time, fully met
and supplied. It has been followed, in consequence, by
others in various parts of our broad land. We will only
add, that we regard the establishment of these rural
burying places as one of the happy signs of the times.
They are due to the dead. They are consolatory to the
living. They are fraught with moral and religious uses,
which no good man will willingly forego. They afford a
retreat from the conflicting interests, and false and frivolous shows of ordinary life, where our violent and wicked
strifes on religious and political subjects may, for a while,
be checked; when that all-absorbing lust of gain, which
is eating, canker-like, into the very heart of the people,
may find a temporary sedative; and where, in a word,
thoughtful persons may go, in silence and in peace, and

amidst propitious influences of earth and sky, and with all the suggestive tokens of the departed around them, to think of their highest aims, and their ultimate responsibilities; and to consider how solemn a thing it is to live in a world like this, to die out of it, and to enter ·on the unseen realities of an eternal state.

NOTE. — The preceding essays, by Dr. Brazer, are slightly abridged from two papers published in Vol. XXXI. of "The Christian Examiner," omitting the notes and references.

SORROW AND ITS RECOMPENSE.

THE benevolence of the Deity has converted all our generous instincts into sources of happiness; and in addition to this, has created sorrow to be the native source of compassion and the sanctifier of friendship. The sentiment of grief, with all the affliction that comes from its recent occurrence, was not given to man for pain; for those who are susceptible of it in the liveliest degree derive the most pleasure from the exercise of the affections. Imbued with this innate capacity for sorrow, one is transported with joy by everything that brings its alleviation. Hence our fondness for the contemplation of tombs, under circumstances that turn our thoughts upon the virtues of those who lie beneath them, and yield the expectation of some immortal reversion of their fate. We experience similar pleasure from those emblematic devices which, with true simplicity, afford one a vivid conception of the soul's immortality. It requires no elaborate effort to show that we are dependent on this sentiment for some of the most exalted of our mental pleasures.

The poets who have sung the pleasures of memory have done little more than to define the enjoyment that springs from looking, through a long vista of sorrow, upon painful as well as happy events. The memory of voices that greeted our childhood, and the general subjects of elegy and other pathetic compositions, are all sorrowful themes ; and we find pleasure in them, because there is a joy in sympathy that comes not in equal degree from thoughts of unmixed happiness. All the themes of sacred poetry are pathetic ; their sublimity is heightened by their pathos, and above all other lyric strains they serve to exalt the soul and to purify it by this exaltation. Those natural phenomena are the most poetical and the most deeply affecting, which are associated with melancholy, or with some incidents that awaken our sympathies. The blast that mingles with the tempest, the misty cloud that rises in the evening upon the lake, the whirling sound of leaves eddying to the winds of autumn, and the monotonous surges of waves upon the sea-shore, are the plaintive language of nature, and we listen to it as to the voice of one who is administering consolation.

The instinct of sorrow is the basis of the purest impulses of the soul, and is closely connected with benevolent deeds and religious aspirations. Its shadows are intimately blended with the light of our social affections, and through its veil we can look more steadfastly upon that true light which is the gift of heaven. It leads some to the contemplation of the Deity and his benevolence, through the works of nature ; others to the divine altar, that they may mingle their complaints with the great fountain of love, and find solace in prayers and ceremonials. It yields to man a sense of the dignity of his nature, by exalting the idols of his grief to the quality of angels, and by associating their human virtues with the attributes of heaven. It spreads a veil of affection over the cradle of infancy, and a halo of divinity above its grassy tomb. It mellows all things human with a celestial tint, and softens the harshness of material objects by its clouds and its shadows.

Sorrow is the alembic, in which our passions are divested of the dross of earthly corruption, and the faculties of the soul ennobled by the contemplation of heavenly themes. Poetry generally turns upon acts instigated by some exalted passion ; but there is none that affords such ever-new delight, as that which is drawn from the harp of sorrow, and borrows its inspiration from some theme of sadness. Hence the interest felt by all nations in the strains of elegy and other pathetic verse. Those flowers of the field that are supposed to emblemize grief, either by their colors, their solitary habits, or their drooping attitudes, are the favorites of all ; though not so often gathered in boquets, to decorate a scene of festivity, they are the chosen subjects of song, and affect us with the deepest emotions. The beauty of maidenhood is never so charming as when it wears the semblance of affliction, or the attitude of mercy. Christian nations have ever regarded the Holy Mother as the " fountain of love," and Jesus as the dispenser of mercy ; but even Jesus acquires new dignity in our eyes, when he is viewed not only as a comforter, but as a participator of human affliction, — as one " despised and rejected of men — a man sorrows and acquainted with grief." Thus does sorrow with its images ever exalt and sanctify what we have loved or revered, and weave the web of poetry over all the realities of human life.

We delight to witness the phenomena of nature under aspects that present her to our imaginations as a gentle

sympathizer, or a seeming partner in our afflictions.
Hence autumn is the favorite season of poets, because it
emblemizes sorrow, and fills the lap of nature with dead
leaves, which she strews over the graves of the flowers:
and we love to hear the low moaning of the winds at this
time, when they seem like dirges sung over the departed
things of summer. For the same reason we love the
evening twilight and Hesper's " melancholy star," because
they inspire tender sensations of melancholy, and raise
our souls at the same time to the contemplation of infinity. The pale light of the moon gives us intimations
of the sympathy of the serene goddess ; and while sitting
under her light, lovers and mourners, those who rejoice
and those who weep, feel the presence of a divinity and
an alleviation of those passions that agitate the soul.

The music that produces the most profound emotion is
of a plaintive kind ; and those sounds, — not of a musical
character, — which are nevertheless agreeable, have invariably a sorrowful cadence. The murmuring of winds
among the branches of trees, sounds from the dropping of
rain, and the voices of birds and insects, having a pathetic modulation, always enchain our attention, and
serve, while they gently excite, to sooth and alleviate the
sentiment of melancholy. The plaintiveness of the nightingale's song is the chief cause of its delightful character,
and the most interesting of the feathered songsters are
the chanters of plaintive strains. The pathetic pieces in
a minor key, so numerous in the old psalmodies, were
not, as it is often supposed, intended to afflict, but to inspire the soul ; and in the most sublime of musical compositions, there is an expression of sadness which is essential to their effects.

Sorrow, the gentle mother of musings, has thus ever
been the source of the most fervent and inspiring strains

of music and of poetry. From the earliest times she has been the ministrant of sweet sounds, — sitting ever at her harp, — ever through all ages, sweeping its strings with her mournful touch ; — now giving fire to the Epic Rhapsodists, when they sang of those who bled to deliver man from the first thraldom of barbarism ; also to the Hebrew Prophets, who, in their Psalms and Lamentations, predicted not more clearly the woes of their people, than the LIGHT that was to spring out of their present all-pervading darkness. She still pursues her heavenly themes — still inspires all music and all eloquence, gives human interest to the revelations of heaven, and softens with divine faith all human adversity.

Blessed be sorrow ! and blessed the branches of yew, and the wreaths of cypress and amaranth, with which she binds the brows of the dead, and fixes upon their tomb the symbols of the grave and of immortality ! Let us go to the resting-places of the dead, where the turfs lie in verduous heaps, and the flowers of the field scatter their incense over them and consecrate their repose. Here will the gentle mother receive us, and when we can no longer be comforted by reason or philosophy, she lulls us to rest by the assurances of religion, and drawing her lessons from the objects of the material world, she points to the gorgeous hues of twilight in the dark forms of the clouds — the light of a happy religious faith glowing serenely upon the formless masses that emblemize our sorrows.

THE END.